**These reviewers love *New York Times*
bestselling author**

Nora
Roberts

"You can't bottle wish fulfilment, but Nora Roberts
certainly knows how to put it on the page."
—*New York Times*

"Roberts' bestselling novels are some of the
best in the romance genre. They are
thoughtfully plotted, well-written stories
featuring fascinating characters."
—*USA TODAY*

"The publishing world might be hard-pressed to
find an author with a more diverse style or fertile
imagination than Roberts."
—*Publishers Weekly*

"The world's leading romance writer...she can make
romance seem fresh and hopeful every time."
—*TIME Magazine*

"Roberts is indeed a word artist, painting her story
and her characters with vitality and verve."
—*Los Angeles Daily News*

"Her stories have fuelled the dreams of
twenty-five million readers."
—*Entertainment Weekly*

"Everyt............................s to gold."

"Nora Ro...........................better."

Did you know that
New York Times **bestselling author**
NORA ROBERTS

- Started writing because she was snowbound by a blizzard and stranded at home with two small children

- Is the youngest of five children, and credits her Catholic schooling with giving her the discipline to write

- Sells on average **twenty-one** books a minute

- Has had over **one hundred and forty** *New York Times* bestsellers

- Was named by *Time* magazine as one of the most influential people of 2007?

Nora Roberts

The MacKades

Rafe & Jared

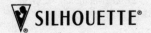

SILHOUETTE®

Silhouette and Colophon are registered trademarks of Harlequin Books S.A., used under licence.
Silhouette Books, Eton House, 18-24 Paradise Road, Richmond, Surrey TW9 1SR

First published in 2006 by Harlequin Mills & Boon Ltd. This edition published 2008.

THE MACKADE BROTHERS: RAFE AND JARED
© by Harlequin Books S.A. 2004

The publisher acknowledges the copyright holder of the individual works as follows:

The Return of Rafe MacKade © Nora Roberts 1995
The Pride of Jared MacKade © Nora Roberts 1995

ISBN: 978 0 263 86738 1

078-0708

Printed and bound in Spain by Litografia Rosés S.A., Barcelona

CONTENTS

The Return of
Rafe MacKade

To bad boys everywhere

Prologue

The MacKade brothers were looking for trouble. They usually were. In the small town of Antietam, Maryland, it wasn't always easy to find, but then, looking was half the fun.

When they piled into Jared's secondhand Chevy, they'd squabbled over who would take the wheel. It was Jared's car, and he was the eldest, but that didn't carry much weight with his three brothers.

Rafe had wanted to drive. He'd had a need for speed, a thirst to zip along those dark, winding roads, with his foot hard on the gas and his foul and reckless mood chasing behind him. He thought perhaps he could outdistance it, or perhaps meet it head-on. If he met it, bloodied it, conquered it, he knew he would just keep driving until he was somewhere else.

Anywhere else.

They had buried their mother two weeks ago.

Perhaps because his dangerous mood showed so clearly in Rafe's jade eyes and in the cold set of his mouth, he'd been outvoted. In the end, Devin had taken the wheel, with Jared riding shotgun. Rafe brooded in the back seat with his youngest brother, Shane, beside him.

They were a rough and dangerous group, the MacKade boys. All of them tall and rangy as wild stallions, with fists ready and often too eager to find a target. Their eyes, MacKade eyes, all varying shades of green, could carve a man into pieces at ten paces. When the dark mood was on them, a wise man stayed back eleven or more.

They settled on pool and beer, though Shane complained, as he was still shy of twenty-one and wouldn't be served in Duff's Tavern.

Still, the dim, smoke-choked bar suited them. The slam and crack of the balls had just enough of a violent edge, the gaze of the scrawny-shouldered Duff Dempsey was just uneasy enough. The wariness in the eyes of the other customers, gossiping over their beers, was just flattering enough.

Nobody doubted the MacKade boys were out for trouble. In the end, they found what they were looking for.

While a cigarette dangled from the corner of his mouth, Rafe squinted against the smoke and eyed his shot. He hadn't bothered to shave in a couple of days, and the rough stubble mirrored his mood. With a solid smack, a follow-through smooth as silk, he banked the cue ball, kissed it off the seven and made his pocket.

"Good thing you're lucky at something." At the bar, Joe Dolin tipped back his beer. He was, as usual after sundown, mostly drunk, and mean with it. He'd once been the star of the high school football team, had competed with the MacKades for the favors of pretty young girls. Now, at barely twenty-one, his face had begun to bloat and his body to sag.

The black eye he'd given his young wife before leaving the house hadn't really satisfied him.

Rafe chalked his cue and barely spared Joe a glance.

"Going to take more than hustling pool, MacKade, to keep that farm going, now that your mama's gone." Dangling his bottle from two fingers, Joe grinned. "Heard you're going to have to start selling off for back taxes."

"Heard wrong." Coolly Rafe circled the table to calculate his next shot.

"Oh, I heard right. You MacKades've always been fools, and liars."

Before Shane could leap forward, Rafe shot out his cue to block the way. "He's talking to me," he said quietly. He held his brother's gaze another moment before he turned. "Isn't that right, Joe? You're talking to me?"

"I'm talking to any of you." As he lifted his beer again, Joe's gaze skimmed over the four of them. At twenty, Shane was tough from farm work, but still more boy than man. Then Devin, whose cool, thoughtful gaze revealed little. Over Jared, who was leaning negligently against the jukebox, waiting for the next move.

He looked back at Rafe. There was temper, hot and ready. Recklessness worn like a second skin. "But you'll do. Always figured you for the biggest loser of the lot, Rafe."

"That so?" Rafe crushed out his cigarette, lifted his own beer. He drank as they completed the ritual before battle, and customers shifted in their chairs to watch. "How're things going at the factory, Joe?"

"Least I get a paycheck," Joe shot back. "I got money in my pocket. Ain't nobody going to take my house from over me."

"Not as long as your wife keeps putting in twelve-hour shifts working tables to pay the rent."

"Shut your mouth about my wife. I earn the money in my house. I don't need no woman paying my way, like your mama had to do for your old man. Went through her inheritance like it was water, then up and died on her."

"Yeah, he died on her." Anger and guilt and grief welled up inside him. "But he never laid a hand on her. She never had to come into town hiding behind scarves and dark glasses, and saying how she took a fall. Only thing your mother ever fell over, Joe, was your father's fist."

Joe slammed his beer onto the bar, shattering the glass. "That's a lie. I'm going to ram that lie down your throat."

"Try it."

"He's drunk, Rafe," Jared murmured.

Those lethal green eyes sliced toward his brother. "So?"

"So there isn't much point in breaking his face when he's drunk." Jared moved a shoulder. "He's not worth it."

But Rafe didn't need a point. He just needed action. He lifted his cue, studied it, then laid it across the table. "You want to take me on, Joe?"

"Don't you start in here." Though he knew it was already too late, Duff jerked a thumb toward the wall phone. "You make any trouble in here, I'm calling the sheriff, and the lot of you can cool off in jail."

"Keep your damn hand off the phone," Rafe warned him. His eyes were hard enough to have the bartender backing off. "Outside," he said simply.

"You and me." Curling his fists, Joe stared at the MacKades. "I ain't having your brothers jumping in on me while I whip your butt."

"I don't need any help with you." To prove it, the moment they cleared the door Rafe pivoted to avoid Joe's swing, rammed his fist into Joe's face and felt the first satisfying spill of blood.

He couldn't even have said why he was fighting. Joe meant less to him than the dust in the street. But it felt good. Even when Joe got past his guard and connected, it felt good. Fists and blood were the only clear solution. When he felt the satisfying crack of knuckles against bone, he could forget everything else.

Devin winced, then tucked his hands philosophically in his pockets when blood spurted from his brother's mouth. "I give it five minutes."

"Hell, Rafe'll take him down in three." Grinning, Shane watched the grunting opponents wrestle to the ground.

"Ten bucks."

"You're on. Come on, Rafe!" Shane shouted. "Whip his sorry butt!"

It took three minutes, plus thirty nasty seconds with Rafe straddling Joe and methodically pumping a fist into his face. Since Joe's eyes had rolled up white and his arms were limp at his sides, Jared stepped forward to drag his brother away.

"He's finished." To decide the matter, Jared rammed Rafe up against the brick wall of the bar. "He's finished," he repeated. "Let it go."

The vicious rage drained slowly, fading from Rafe's eyes, uncurling his fists. Emptying him. "Let go, Jare. I'm not going to hit him again."

Rafe looked to where Joe lay moaning, half-unconscious. Over his battered body, Devin counted out bills for Shane. "I should have factored in how drunk he was," Devin commented. "If he'd been sober, it would've taken Rafe the five."

"Rafe would never waste five full minutes on a punk like that."

Jared shook his head. The arm that was restraining Rafe slipped companionably around Rafe's shoulders. "Want another beer?"

"No." He glanced toward the window of the bar, where most of the patrons had gathered to watch. Absently he swiped blood from his face. "Somebody better pick him up and haul him home," he called out. "Let's get out of here."

When he settled in the car again, the aches and bruises began to make themselves known. With half an ear, he listened to Shane's enthusiastic play-by-play of the bout and used Devin's bandanna to mop more blood from his mouth.

He was going nowhere, he thought. Doing nothing. Being nothing. The only difference between him and Joe Dolin was that Joe was a drunk on top of it.

He hated the damn farm, the damn town, the damn trap he could feel himself sinking into with every day that passed.

Jared had his books and studies, Devin his odd and ponderous thoughts, Shane the land that seemed to delight him.

He had nothing.

On the edge of town, where the land began to climb and the trees to thicken, he saw a house. The old Barlow place. Dark, deserted and haunted, so it was said. It stood alone, unwanted, with a reputation that caused most of the townspeople to ignore it or eye it warily.

Just as they did Rafe MacKade.

"Pull over."

"Hell, Rafe, you going to be sick?" Not concerned so much as apprehensive, Shane gripped his own door handle.

"No. Pull over, damn it, Jared."

The minute the car stopped, Rafe was out and climbing the rocky slope. Brambles thick with thorns and summer growth tore at his jeans. He didn't need to look behind or hear the curses and mutters to know that his brothers were following him.

He stood, looking up at three stories of local stone. Mined, he supposed, from the quarry a few miles out of town. Some of the windows were broken and boarded, and the double porches sagged like an old woman's back. What had once been a lawn was overgrown with wild blackberries, thistles and witchgrass. A dead oak rose from it, gnarled and leafless.

But as the moon wheeled overhead and the breeze sang chants through the trees and tall grass, there was something compelling about the place. The way it stood two hundred years after its foundation had been laid. The way it continued to stand against time, weather and neglect. And most of all, he thought, the way it stood against the distrust and gossip of the town it overlooked.

"Going to look for ghosts, Rafe?" Shane stood beside him, eyes gleaming against the dark.

"Maybe."

"Remember when we spent the night there, on a dare?" Absently Devin plucked a blade of grass, rolled it between his fingers. "Ten years ago, I guess it was. Jared snuck upstairs and started creaking doors. Shane wet his pants."

"Hell I did."

"Hell you didn't."

This incited the predictable shoving match, which the older brothers ignored.

"When are you leaving?" Jared said quietly. He'd known it, saw it now in the way Rafe looked at the house, into it, beyond it.

"Tonight. I've got to get away from here, Jare. Do something away from here. If I don't, I'm going to be like Dolin. Maybe worse. Mom's gone. She doesn't need me anymore. Hell, she never needed anybody.''

''Got any idea where you're going?''

''No. South, maybe. To start.'' He couldn't take his eyes off the house. He would have sworn it was watching him, judging him. Waiting. ''I'll send money when I can.''

Though he felt as though someone were wrenching off one of his limbs, Jared merely shrugged. ''We'll get by.''

''You have to finish law school. Mom wanted that.'' Rafe glanced behind, to where the shoving match had progressed to wrestling in the weeds. ''They'll handle themselves okay once they figure out what they want.''

''Shane knows what he wants. The farm.''

''Yeah.'' With a thin smile, Rafe took out a cigarette. ''Go figure. Sell off some of the land, if you have to, but don't let them take it. We have to keep what's ours. Before it's over, this town's going to remember the MacKades meant something.''

Rafe's smile widened. For the first time in weeks, the gnawing ache inside him eased. His brothers were sitting on the ground, covered with dirt and scratches and laughing like loons.

He was going to remember them that way, he promised himself, just that way. The MacKades, holding together on rocky ground no one wanted.

Chapter 1

The bad boy was back. The town of Antietam was buzzing over it, passing fact, rumor and innuendo from one to another, the way the guests at a boardinghouse passed bowls of steaming stew.

It was a rich broth, spiced with scandal, sex and secrets. Rafe MacKade had come back after ten years.

Some said there would be trouble. Bound to be. Trouble hung around Rafe MacKade like a bell around a bull's neck. Wasn't it Rafe MacKade who'd decked the high school principal one spring morning and gotten himself expelled? Wasn't it Rafe MacKade who'd wrecked his dead daddy's Ford pickup before he was old enough to drive?

And surely it was Rafe MacKade who'd tossed a table—and that fool Manny Johnson—through the plate-glass window of Duff's Tavern one hot summer night.

Now he'd come back, a-riding into town in some fancy sports car and parking, bold as you please, right in front of the sheriff's office.

Of course, his brother Devin was sheriff now, had been for five years last November. But there'd been a time—and most remembered—when Rafe Mac-Kade spent more than a night or two in one of the two cells in the back.

Oh, he was as handsome as ever—so the women said. With those devil's good looks the MacKades were gifted—or cursed—with. If a female had breath in her body, she'd look twice, maybe even sigh over that long, wiry build, that loose-legged stride that seemed to dare anyone to get in the way.

Then there was that thick black hair, those eyes, as green and hard as the ones in that little Chinese statue in the window of the Past Times antique store. They did nothing to soften that tough, sharp-jawed face, with that little scar along the left eye. God knew where he'd gotten that.

But when he smiled, when he curved that beautiful mouth up and that little dimple winked at the corner, a woman's heart was bound to flutter. That sentiment came directly from Sharilyn Fenniman who'd taken that smile, and his twenty dollars for gas, at the Gas and Go, just outside of town.

Before Rafe had his car in gear again, Sharilyn had been burning up the phone wires to announce the return.

"So Sharilyn called her mama, and Mrs. Metz got right on her horse and told Mrs. Hawbaker down at the general store that Rafe maybe plans to stay."

As she spoke, Cassandra Dolin topped off Regan's coffee. The way snow was spitting out of the January sky and clogging streets and sidewalks, there was little business at Ed's Café that afternoon. Slowly Cassie straightened her back and tried to ignore the ache in her hip where it had struck the floor after Joe knocked her down.

"Why shouldn't he?" Smiling, Regan Bishop loitered over her mulligan stew and coffee. "He was born here, wasn't he?"

Even after three years as a resident and shopkeeper of Antietam, Regan still didn't understand the town's fascination with comings and goings. It appealed to and amused her, but she didn't understand it.

"Well, yeah, but he's been gone so long. Only came back for a day or so at a time, once or twice in ten whole years." Cassie looked out the window, where the snow fell thin and constant. And wondered where he had gone, what he had seen, what he had done. Oh, she wondered what there was out there.

"You look tired, Cassie," Regan murmured.

"Hmm? No, just daydreaming. This keeps up, they're going to call school early. I told the kids to come straight here if they did, but..."

"Then that's what they'll do. They're great kids."

"They are." When she smiled, some of the weariness lifted from her eyes.

"Why don't you get a cup? Have some coffee with

me?'' A scan of the café showed Regan there was a customer in a back booth, dozing over his coffee, a couple at the counter chatting over the stew special. ''You're not exactly overrun with business.'' Seeing Cassie hesitate, Regan pulled out her trump. ''You could fill me in on this Rafe character.''

''Well.'' Cassie nibbled on her lip. ''Ed, I'm going to take a break, okay?''

At the call, a bony woman with a frizzed ball of red hair stuck her head out of the kitchen. Sparkling-framed glasses rested on her scrawny chest, above her bib apron. ''You go ahead, honey.'' Her low voice rasped from two packs of cigarettes a day. Her face was carefully painted from red lips to red eyebrows, and glowed from the heat of the stove. ''Hey there, Regan. You're fifteen minutes over your lunch hour.''

''I closed at noon,'' Regan told her, well aware that her clocklike schedule amused Edwina Crump. ''People aren't looking for antiques in this kind of weather.''

''It's been a hard winter.'' Cassie brought a cup to the table and poured coffee for herself. ''We're not even through January, and the kids are already getting tired of sledding and making snowmen.'' She sighed, careful not to wince when the bruise on her hip ached when she sat. She was twenty-seven, a year younger than Regan. She felt ancient.

After three years of friendship, Regan recognized the signs. ''Are things bad, Cassie?'' Keeping her voice low, she laid a hand over Cassie's. ''Did he hurt you again?''

"I'm fine." But Cassie kept her eyes on her cup. Guilt, humiliation, fear, stung as much as a backhand slap. "I don't want to talk about Joe."

"Did you read the pamphlets I got you, about spousal abuse, the women's shelter in Hagerstown?"

"I looked at them. Regan, I have two children. I have to think of them first."

"But—"

"Please." Cassie lifted her gaze. "I don't want to talk about it."

"All right." Struggling to hold back the impatience, Regan squeezed her hand. "Tell me about bad boy MacKade."

"Rafe." Cassie's face cleared. "I always had a soft spot for him. All of them. There wasn't a girl in town who didn't moon a few nights over the MacKade brothers."

"I like Devin." Regan sipped at her coffee. "He seems solid, a little mysterious at times, but dependable."

"You can count on Devin," Cassie agreed. "Nobody thought any of them would turn out, but Devin makes a fine sheriff. He's fair. Jared has that fancy law practice in the city. And Shane, well, he's rough around the edges, but he works that farm like two mules. When they were younger and they came barreling into town, mothers locked up their daughters, and men kept their backs to the wall."

"Real upstanding citizens, huh?"

"They were young, and always seemed angry at something. Rafe most of all. The night he left town,

Rafe and Joe got into it over something. Rafe broke Joe's nose and knocked out a couple of his teeth.''

"Really?'' Regan decided she might like this Rafe after all.

"He was always looking for a fight, Rafe was. Their father died when they were kids. I'd have been about ten,'' she mused. "Then their mama passed on, right before Rafe left town. She'd been sick nearly a year. That's how things at the farm got so bad around then. Most people thought the MacKades would have to sell out, but they held on.''

"Well, three of them did.''

"Mmm...'' Cassie savored the coffee. It was so rare to have a moment just to sit. "They were barely more than boys. Jared would have been right about twenty-three, and Rafe's just ten months behind him. Devin's about four years older than me, and Shane's a year behind him.''

"Sounds like Mrs. MacKade was a busy woman.''

"She was wonderful. Strong. She held everything together, no matter how bad it got. I always admired her.''

"Sometimes you need to be strong to let things go,'' Regan murmured. She shook her head. She'd promised herself she wouldn't push. "So, what do you think he's come back for?''

"I don't know. They say he's rich now. Made a pile buying land and houses and selling them again. He's supposed to have a company and everything. MacKade. That's what he calls it. Just MacKade. My mother always said he'd end up dead or in jail, but…''

Her voice trailed off as she looked through the window. ''Oh, my,'' she murmured. ''Sharilyn was right.''

''Hmm?''

''He looks better than ever.''

Curious, Regan turned her head just as the door jingled open. As black sheep went, she was forced to admit, this one was a prime specimen.

He shook snow from thick hair the color of coal dust and shrugged off a black leather bomber jacket that wasn't meant for East Coast winters. Regan thought he had a warrior's face—the little scar, the unshaven chin, the slightly crooked nose that kept that mouth-watering face from being too pretty.

His body looked hard as granite, and his eyes, sharp green, were no softer.

In worn flannel, torn jeans and scarred boots, he didn't look rich and successful. But he sure looked dangerous.

It amused and pleased Rafe to see Ed's place was so much the same. Those could be the same stools at the counter that he'd warmed his seat on as a child, anticipating a sundae or a fountain drink. Surely those were the same smells—grease, frying onions, the haze from Ed's constant cigarettes, an undertone of pine cleaner.

He was sure Ed would be back in the kitchen, flipping burgers or stirring pots. And sure as hell that was old man Tidas snoring in the back booth while his coffee went cold. Just as he'd always done.

His eyes, cool, assessing, skimmed over the painfully white counter, with its clear-plastic-topped plates of pies and cakes, over the walls, with their black-and-white photos of Civil War battles, to a booth where two women sat over coffee.

He saw a stranger. An impressive one. Honey brown hair cut in a smooth chin-length swing that framed a face of soft curves and creamy skin. Long lashes over dark and coolly curious blue eyes. And a sassy little mole right at the corner of a full and unsmiling mouth.

Picture-perfect, he thought. Just like something cut out of a glossy magazine.

They studied each other, assessed each other as a man or woman might assess a particularly attractive trinket in a shop window. Then his gaze shifted to land on the fragile little blonde with the haunted eyes and the hesitant smile.

"Son of a bitch." His grin flashed and upped the temperature by twenty degree. "Little Cassie Connor."

"Rafe. I heard you were back." The sound of her giggle as Rafe plucked her from the booth had Regan's brow lifting. It was rare to hear Cassie laugh so freely.

"Pretty as ever," he said, and kissed her full on the lips. "Tell me you kicked that idiot out and left the path clear for me."

She eased back, always fearful of wagging tongues. "I've got two kids now."

"A boy and a girl. I heard." He tugged the strap of her bib apron, and thought with some concern that she'd lost too much weight. "You're still working here?"

"Yeah. Ed's in the back."

"I'll go see her in a minute." Resting a hand casually on Cassie's shoulder, he looked back at Regan. "Who's your pal?"

"Oh, sorry. This is Regan Bishop. She owns Past Times, an antique and decorating store a couple doors down. Regan, this is Rafe MacKade."

"Of the MacKade brothers." She offered a hand. "Word's already traveled."

"I'm sure it has." He took her hand, held it, as his eyes held hers. "Antiques? That's a coincidence. I'm in the market."

"Are you?" She'd risk her dignity if she tugged her hand from his. From the gleam in his eye, she was sure he knew it. "Any particular era?"

"Mid-to-late-1800s—everything from soup to nuts. I've got a three-story house, about twelve hundred square feet to furnish. Think you can handle it?"

It took a lot of willpower for her to keep her jaw from dropping. She did well enough with tourists and townspeople, but a commission like this would easily triple her usual income.

"I'm sure I can."

"You bought a house?" Cassie said interrupting them. "I thought you'd be staying out at the farm."

"For now. The house isn't for living in, not for me. After some remodeling, restoring, I'll be opening it up as a bed-and-breakfast. I bought the old Barlow place."

Stunned, Cassie bobbled the coffeepot she'd fetched. "The Barlow place? But it's—"

"Haunted?" A reckless light glinted in his eyes. "Damn right it is. How about a piece of that pie to go with the coffee, Cassie? I've worked up an appetite."

Regan had left but Rafe had loitered for an hour, entertained when Cassie's kids burst in out of the snow. He watched her fuss over them, scold the boy for forgetting to put on his gloves, listened to the big-eyed little girl solemnly relate the adventures of the day.

There was something sad, and somehow soothing, about watching the girl he remembered settling her two children at a booth with crayons and books.

A lot had stayed the same over a decade. But a lot had changed. He was well aware that news of his arrival was even now singing over telephone wires. It pleased him. He wanted the town to know he was back—and not with his tail between his legs, as many had predicted.

He had money in his pocket now, and plans for the future.

The Barlow place was the heart of his plans. He didn't subscribe to ghosts, under most circumstances, but the house had certainly haunted him. Now it belonged to him, every old stone and bramble—and whatever else it held. He was going to rebuild it, as he had rebuilt himself.

One day he would stand at the top window and look down on the town. He would prove to everyone—even to Rafe MacKade—that he was somebody.

He tucked a generous tip under his cup, careful to keep the amount just shy of one that would embarrass Cassie. She was too thin, he thought, and her eyes were too guarded. That weary fragility had been thrown into sharp relief when she sat with Regan.

Now there was a woman, he mused, who knew how to handle herself. Steady eyes, stubborn chin, soft hands. She hadn't so much as blinked when he offered her a shot at furnishing an entire inn. Oh, he imagined her insides had jolted, but she hadn't blinked.

As a man who'd earned his keep on the wheel and deal, he had to admire her for it. Time would tell if she'd hold up to the challenge.

And there was no time like the present.

"That antique place, two doors down?"

"That's right." Cassie kept one eye on her children as she brewed a fresh pot of coffee. "On the left. I don't think she's open, though."

Rafe shrugged into his jacket and grinned. "Oh, I bet she is."

He strolled out, hatless, jacket open, his footsteps muffled by the cushioning snow. As he'd expected, the lights were on inside Past Times. Instead of seeking shelter inside, he studied her window display and found it clever and effective.

A sweep of blue brocade like a pool of shimmering water flowed over varying levels. A bright-eyed porcelain doll sat on a child-size ladder-back rocker, an artful tumble of antique toys at her feet. A snarling jade dragon curled on a pedestal. A glossy mahogany jewelry box stood open, glittery baubles spilling out of its drawers as though a woman's hands had slid through them in search of just the right piece.

Perfume bottles were arranged in pretty sunbursts of color on an enameled shelf.

Put the sparkles up front, he thought with a nod, and rope the customers in.

Sleigh bells hung on the door tinkled musically when he opened it. The air inside was spiced with cinnamon and cloves and apples. And, he realized after a deep breath of it, of Regan Bishop. The subtle and sultry perfume he'd noted in the café just teased the air.

He took his time wandering. Furniture was meticulously arranged for traffic patterns. A settee here, an occasional table there. Lamps, bowls, vases, all doing double duty as display and decoration. A dining room table was gracefully set with china and glassware, candles and flowers, as if guests were expected any moment. An old Victrola stood open beside a cabinet filled with 78s.

There were three rooms, each as polished and organized as the last. Nowhere in her inventory did he notice a single speck of dust. He paused by a kitchen hutch filled with white stoneware dishes and blue-tinted mason jars.

"It's a nice piece," Regan said from behind him.

"We have one like this in the kitchen at the farm." He didn't turn. He'd known she was there. "My mother kept the everyday dishes in it. White ones, like these. And glasses. Thick ones that didn't break easy. She threw one at me once when I sassed her."

"Did she hit you?"

"No. Would have if she'd meant to." Now he turned and flashed that killer grin. "She had a hell of an arm. What are you doing in the middle of nowhere, Regan Bishop?"

"Selling my wares, Rafe MacKade."

"Your wares aren't half-bad. How much for the dragon in the window?"

"You have excellent taste. It's five-fifty."

"That's steep, Regan." Reaching out, he slipped open the single gold button of her navy blazer.

She found the little gesture oddly intimate, but refused to comment on it. "You get what you pay for."

"If you're smart, you can get more." He tucked his thumbs in the front pockets of his jeans and began to wander again. "How long have you been in town?"

"Three years last summer."

"From?" When she didn't answer, he glanced back, lifted one of those sexy black brows. "Just making conversation, darling. I like to get a handle on the people I'm doing business with."

"We haven't done any business, yet." She tucked her hair behind her ear and smiled. "Darling."

His laugh erupted, quick and charming. Little ripples of response skidded up her spine. He was, she was sure, the man every mother had ever warned her daughter about. As tempting as it was, business was business. And it always came first.

"I think I'm going to like you, Regan." He tilted his head. "You sure are a looker."

"Making conversation again?"

"An observation." With a smile hovering around his mouth, he glanced down at her hands. She wore rings, pretty, glittery stones and twists of gold. "Any of those mean anything that's going to get in my way?"

Her stomach fluttered. Her spine stiffened. "I'd say that depends on which way you're heading."

"Nope," he declared. "You're not married. You'd have tossed that in my face. So." Satisfied, he sat on a red velvet love seat, tossed his arm over the curved back. "Want to sit down?"

"No, thanks. Did you come in to do business, or to talk me into bed?"

"I never talk women into bed." He smiled at her.

No, she thought, he'd just have to flash that smile and crook his finger.

"Business, Regan." Relaxed, he crossed his booted feet. "For now, just business."

"All right. Then I'll offer you some hot cider."

"I'll take it."

She moved through a doorway, into the back.

Alone, Rafe brooded for a moment. He hadn't meant to be so obvious, hadn't realized he was quite so attracted. There had been something about the way she stood there, in her tailored blazer and tasteful jewelry, her eyes so cool and amused, her scent just short of hot.

If he'd ever seen a woman who announced a thorny road, it was Regan Bishop. Though he rarely chose the smooth path, he had too much on his plate to take the challenge.

Then she came back in on those long, glamorous legs, that pretty swing of hair half curtaining her face.

What the hell, he thought, he could always make room on his plate.

"Thanks." He took the steaming enameled mug she offered. "I figured on hiring a firm out of D.C. or Baltimore, maybe taking some time to hunt through some shops myself."

"I can acquire anything a firm in D.C. or Baltimore can, and offer a better price." She hoped.

"Maybe. The thing is, I like the idea of keeping the business close to home. We'll see what you can do." He sipped the cider, found it hot and pungent. "What do you know about the Barlow place?"

"It's falling apart. I think it's a crime that nothing's been done to preserve it. This part of the country is usually careful with its historic areas and buildings. But the town ignores that place. If I had the means, I'd have bought it myself."

"And you'd have gotten more than you bargained for. The house is solid as rock. If it wasn't so well built, it'd be rubble by now. But, it needs work..." he mused, and began to picture it all in his head. "Floors to be leveled and sanded and sealed, walls to be plastered or taken down, windows replaced. The roof's a mess."

He brought himself back, shrugged. "That's just time and money. When it's ready, I want to put it back the way it looked in 1862, when the Barlows lived there and watched the Battle of Antietam from their parlor window."

"Did they?" Regan asked with a smile. "I'd have thought they'd have been cowering in the root cellar."

"Not the way I imagine it. The rich and privileged watching the show, maybe annoyed when cannon fire cracked a window or the screams of the dead and dying woke the baby from its nap."

"You're a cynical one. Being rich wouldn't mean you wouldn't feel horror if you had to watch men dying on your front lawn."

"The heart of the battle didn't get quite that close. Anyway, that's what I want—the right colors, trim, wallpaper, furnishings, doodads. The works." He had an urge for a cigarette and banked it. "How do you feel about redoing a haunted house?"

"Interested." She eyed him over the rim of her mug. "Besides, I don't believe in ghosts."

"You will before it's done. I spent the night there once, as a kid, with my brothers."

"Creaking doors, rattling chains?"

"No." He didn't smile now. "Except the ones

Jared arranged to scare the guts out of the rest of us. There's a spot on the stairway that'll turn your skin to ice. You can smell smoke near the living room hearth. And you can feel something looking over your shoulder when you walk down the hallways. If it's quiet enough, and you're listening, you can hear sabers clash.''

Despite herself, she couldn't quite suppress a shudder. ''If you're trying to scare me off the commission, you won't.''

''Just laying out the blueprint. I'll want you to take a look at the place, go through the rooms with me. We'll see what kind of ideas you have. Tomorrow afternoon suit you? About two?''

''That'll be fine. I'll need to take measurements.''

''Good.'' He set his mug aside, rose. ''Nice doing business with you.''

Again she accepted his hand. ''Welcome home.''

''You're the first one who's said it.'' Enjoying the irony, he lifted her hand to his lips, watching her. ''Then again, you don't know any better. See you tomorrow. And, Regan,'' he added on his way to the door, ''take the dragon out of the window. I want it.''

On the way out of town, he pulled his car to the side of the road and stopped. Ignoring the snow and the icy fingers of the wind, he studied the house on the rise of the hill.

Its broken windows and sagging porches revealed nothing, just as Rafe's shadowed eyes revealed nothing. Ghosts, he mused, while snow drifted silently around him. Maybe. But he was beginning to realize that the only ghosts he was trying to put to rest were inside him.

Chapter 2

The beauty of owning your own shop, as far as Regan was concerned, was that you could buy and sell what you chose, your hours were your own to make, and the atmosphere was your own to create.

Still, being the sole proprietor and sole employee of Past Times didn't mean Regan Bishop tolerated any slack. As her own boss, she was tough, often intolerant, and expected the best from her staff. As that staff, she worked hard and rarely complained.

She had exactly what she'd always wanted—a home and business in a small rural town, away from the pressures and headaches of the city where she'd lived the first twenty-five years of her life.

Moving to Antietam and starting her own business had been part of her five-year plan after she graduated from American University. She had degrees in history and business management tucked under her belt, and by the time she donned cap and gown she'd already earned five years experience in antiques.

Working for someone else.

Now she was the boss. Every inch of the shop and the cozy apartment atop it was hers—and the bank's. The MacKade commission was going to go a long way toward making her share a great deal larger.

The minute Rafe left the afternoon before, Regan had locked up and dashed to the library. She'd checked out an armload of books to supplement her own research volumes.

By midnight, when her eyes had threatened to cross, she had read and taken notes on every detail of life as it applied to the Civil War era in Maryland.

She knew every aspect of the Battle of Antietam, from Lee's march to his retreat across the river, from McClellan's waffling to President Lincoln's visit to a farm outside Sharpsburg. She knew the number of dead and wounded, the bloody progress over hill and through cornfield.

It was sad and standard information, and she'd studied it before. Indeed, her fascination with the battle and the quiet area into which it had exploded had influenced her choice of a home.

But this time she'd been able to find bits and pieces on the Barlows—both fact and speculation. The family had lived in the house on the hill for almost a hundred years before that horrible day in September of 1862. Prosperous landowners and businessmen, they had lived like lords. Their balls and dinners had enticed guests from as far as Washington and Virginia.

She knew how they had dressed—the frock coats and lace and the hooped skirts. Silk hats and satin slippers. She knew how they had lived, with servants pouring wine into crystal goblets, their home decorated with hothouse flowers, their furniture glowing with bee's wax polish.

Now, negotiating snowy, windy roads under sparkling sunlight, she could see exactly the colors and fabrics, the furnishings and knickknacks that would have surrounded them.

Chiffoniers of rosewood, she mused. Wedgwood china and horsehair settees. The fine Chippendale chest-on-chest for the master, the graceful cherry-wood-and-beveled-glass secretaire for his lady. Brocade portieres and rich Colonial blue for the walls in the parlor.

Rafe MacKade was going to get his money's worth. And, oh, she hoped his pockets were deep.

The narrow, broken lane leading up to the house was deep in snow. No tire tracks or handy plow had marred its pretty, pristine—and very inconvenient—white blanket.

Annoyed that Rafe hadn't taken care of that detail, Regan eased her car onto the shoulder.

Armed with her briefcase, she began the long trudge up.

At least she'd thought to wear boots, she told herself as the snow crept past her ankles. She'd very nearly worn a suit and heels—before she remembered that impressing Rafe MacKade wasn't on her agenda. The gray trousers, tailored blazer and black turtleneck were acceptable business wear for an assignment such as this. And, as she doubted the place was heated, the red wool coat would come in handy, inside, as well as out.

It was a fabulous and intriguing place, she decided as she crested the hill. All those flecks of mica in the stone, glinting like glass in the sunlight, made up for the boarded windows. The porches sagged, but the building itself rose up tall and proud against the bitter blue sky.

She liked the way the east wing jutted off at a stern angle. The way the trio of chimneys speared from the roof as if waiting to belch smoke. She even liked the way the broken shutters hung drunkenly.

It needed tending, she thought, with an affection that surprised her. Someone to love it, and accept its character for what it was. Someone who would appreciate its strengths and understand its weaknesses.

She shook her head and laughed at herself. It sounded as though she were thinking of a man—one, perhaps, like Rafe MacKade—rather than a house.

She walked closer, through the deep, powdery drifts. Rocks and overgrown brush made uneven lumps in the snow, like children under blankets waiting to do mischief. Brambles were sneaky enough to grab at her trousers with sharp, wiry fingers. But once the lawn had been lush and green and vivid with flowers.

If Rafe had any vision, it would be again.

Reminding herself that the landscaping was his problem, she puffed her way to the broken front porch.

He was, she thought with a scowl, late.

Regan looked around, stomped her feet for warmth and glanced at her watch. The man could hardly expect her to stand out in the cold and the wind and wait. Ten minutes, tops, she told herself. Then she would leave him a note, a very firm note on the value of keeping appointments, and leave.

But it wouldn't hurt to take a peek in the window.

Maneuvering carefully, she inched her way up the steps, avoided broken planks. There should be wisteria or morning glories climbing up the side arbor, she mused, and for a moment she almost believed she could catch the faint, sweet scent of spring.

She caught herself moving to the door, closing her hand over the knob before she realized that had been her intention all along. Surely it was locked, she thought. Even small towns weren't immune to vandals. But even as she thought it, the knob turned freely in her hand.

It was only sensible to go in, out of the wind, begin to site the job. Yet she pulled her hand back with a jerk. Her breath was coming in gasps, shockingly loud on the silent air. Inside her neat leather gloves, her hands were icy and trembling.

Out of breath from the climb, she told herself. Shivering from the wind. That was all. But the fear was on her like a cat, hissing through her blood.

Embarrassed, she looked uneasily around. There

was no one to see her ridiculous reaction. Only snow and trees.

She took a deep breath, laughed at herself, and opened the door.

It creaked, of course. That was to be expected. The wide main hall gave her such a rush of pleasure, she forgot everything else. Closing the door, she leaned back against it and sighed.

There was dust and mold, damp patches on the walls, baseboards ruined by gnawing mice, spider-webs draped like filthy gauze. She saw rich, deep green paint, creamy ivory trim, the buff and shine of waxed pine floors under her feet, a runner blooming with cabbage roses.

And there, she thought a hunt table, with a Dresden bowl spilling more roses, flanked by silver candle-sticks. A little walnut hall chair with a pierced back, a hammered brass umbrella stand, a gilded mirror.

How it had been, and could be, spun through her mind, and she didn't feel the cold that sent her breath ahead of her in clouds as she wandered.

In the parlor, she marveled over the Adam fire-place. The marble was filthy, but undamaged. She had twin vases in the shop that would be perfect for the mantel. And a needlepoint footstool that was meant for weary feet in front of this very hearth.

Delighted, she pulled out her notebook and got to work.

Cobwebs dragged through her hair, dirt smudged her cheek, dust covered her boots, as she measured and plotted. She was in heaven. Her mood was so high that when she heard the footsteps, she turned with a smile instead of a complaint.

"It's wonderful. I can hardly—" She was talking to thin air.

Frowning, she walked out of the parlor and into the hall. She started to call out, then noted that there were no footprints in the dust but her own.

Imagining things, she told herself, and shuddered. Big, empty houses made all sorts of noises. Settling wood, wind against the windows...rodents, she thought with a grimace. She wasn't afraid of mice or spiders or creaking boards.

But when the floor groaned over her head, she couldn't muffle the shriek. Her heart flew straight to her throat and beat like a bird's. Before she'd managed to compose herself again, she heard the unmistakable sound of a door closing.

She was across the hall in a dash, fumbling for the knob when it hit her.

Rafe MacKade.

Oh, he thought he was clever, she thought furiously. Sneaking into the house ahead of her, creeping through the back, she imagined. He was up there right now, doubled over at the idea of her bolting from the house like some idiotic Gothic heroine with a heaving bosom.

Not on your life, she thought determinedly, and straightened her shoulders. She thrust her chin up and marched to the curving stairs.

"You're not funny, MacKade," she called out.

"Now, if you've finished your pathetic little joke, I'd like to get some work done."

When the cold spot hit her, she was too shocked to move. The hand she'd gripped on the rail went numb with it, her face froze with it. There, halfway up the graceful sweep of stairs, she swayed. It was her own whimper that broke her free. She was up to the first landing in four effortless strides.

A draft, she told herself, cursing her own sobbing breaths. Just a nasty draft.

"Rafe." Her voice broke, infuriating her. Biting her lip, she stared down the long hallway, at the closed and secretive doors that lined it. "Rafe," she said again, and struggled to put irritation in her voice, rather than nerves. "I have a schedule to keep, even if you don't, so can we get on with this?"

The sound of wood scraping wood, the violent slam of a door, and a woman's heartbroken weeping. Pride forgotten, Regan flew down the stairs. She'd nearly reached the bottom when she heard the shot.

Then the door she'd rushed to meet groaned slowly open.

The room whirled once, twice, then vanished.

"Come on, darling, snap out of it."

Regan turned her head, moaned, shivered.

"All the way out, pal. Open those big blue eyes for me."

The voice was so coaxing, she did. And found herself looking into Rafe's.

"It wasn't funny."

A bit dizzy with relief, he smiled and stroked her cheek. "What wasn't?"

"Hiding upstairs to scare me." She blinked to bring the world back into sharp focus and discovered she was cradled on his lap on the window seat in the parlor. "Let me up."

"I don't think so. You're still a little shaky on your pins. Just relax a minute." He shifted her expertly so that her head rested in the crook of his arm.

"I'm fine."

"You're white as a sheet. If I had a flask, I'd pour some brandy into you. Never saw a woman faint as gracefully, though. You sort of drifted down, gave me a chance to catch you before your head knocked against the floor."

"If you expect me to thank you, forget it." She shoved, found him unmovable. "It's your fault."

"Thanks. It's flattering to think the sight of me has a woman dropping at my feet. There." He traced a finger down her cheek again. "That brought some color back."

"If this is the way you do business, you can take your job and—" She ground her teeth. "Let me up."

"Let's try this." Lifting her, he plopped her down on the seat beside him. "Hands off," he added, lifting his. "Now why don't you tell me why you're ticked off at me?"

Pouting, she brushed at her smudged trousers. "You know very well."

"All I know is, I walked in the door and saw you doing a swan dive."

"I've never fainted in my life." And she was thoroughly mortified that she had done so now—in front of him. "If you want me to work on this house, scaring me into unconsciousness isn't the way to do it."

He studied her, reached into his pocket for the cigarettes he'd given up exactly eight days before. "How did I scare you?"

"By walking around upstairs, opening and closing doors, making those ridiculous noises."

"Maybe I should start off by telling you I got held up at the farm. I didn't leave until fifteen minutes ago."

"I don't believe you."

"I don't blame you." If he wasn't going to smoke, he had to move. Rising, he strolled over to the hearth. He thought he caught a whiff of smoke, as from a fire that had recently died. "Shane was there—and so was Cy Martin. He's mayor now."

"I know who Cy Martin is," she said testily.

"You should have known him in high school," Rafe mused. "He was a complete ass. Anyway, Cy dropped by to see if Shane could plow his lane. He was still there when I left. Fifteen minutes ago. I borrowed Shane's four-wheel to make the hill. Parked it and came to the door in time to see your eyes roll back in your head."

He walked back to her, stripped off his coat and tucked it over her legs. "By the way, how'd you get in?"

"I—" She stared at him, swallowed. "I opened the door."

"It was locked."

"No, it wasn't."

Lifting a brow, he jingled the keys in his pocket. "That's interesting."

"You're not lying," she said after a moment.

"Not this time. Why don't you tell me what you heard?"

"Footsteps. But there was no one there." To warm them, she tucked her hands under his coat. "Boards creaking upstairs. I started up. It was cold, bitterly cold, and it frightened me, so I went to the landing."

"You were scared, so you went up instead of out?"

"I thought you were up there. I was going to yell at you." Her smile was weak, but it was there. "I was furious that you'd managed to make me jump. Then I looked down the hallway. I guess I knew you weren't there. I heard wood scrape, and a door slam hard and someone crying. Then I bolted."

He sat beside her again, put his arm around her shoulders in a friendly squeeze. "Who wouldn't?"

"A shot," she remembered. "I was almost down the stairs when I heard a gunshot. It made my ears ring. Then the door opened, and lights-out."

"I shouldn't have been late." Unexpectedly, he leaned over and gave her a quick, casual kiss. "Sorry."

"That's hardly the point."

"The thing is, some people feel things in this place, some don't. You struck me as the cool, practical type."

She folded her arms over her chest. "Oh, really?"

"Single-minded," he added with a grin. "It seems you have more imagination than I expected. Feeling better now?"

"I'm fine."

"Sure you don't want to sit on my lap again?"

"Quite sure, thank you."

With his eyes on hers, he brushed a cobweb from her hair. "Want to get out of here?"

"Absolutely."

He picked up his coat. "I'd like to take you somewhere."

"That isn't necessary. I said I was..." She stood and, as he held his ground, bumped into his chest. "Fine," she managed.

"Business, darling." He tucked her hair behind her ear, flicked a finger over the square-cut aquamarine at the lobe. "For the moment. I think we can find someplace a little warmer and more hospitable to hash out the details."

That was reasonable, she decided. Perfectly sensible. "All right."

She picked up her briefcase and walked ahead of him to the door.

"Regan?"

"Yes?"

"Your face is dirty." He laughed at the smoldering look she shot at him, then scooped her up in his arms. Even as she stuttered a protest, he carried her over the broken porch. "Got to watch your step," he told her, setting her on her feet next to a Jeep.

"I make a habit of it."

"I bet you do," he murmured as he rounded the hood.

He maneuvered his way down the lane, circled around her car and kept going.

"I thought I'd follow you," she began.

"Since I don't think you mean to the ends of the earth, let's just take one car. I'll bring you back."

"From?"

"Home, sweet home, darling."

In the snow, with the sun glazing the white fields, the MacKade farm was Currier and Ives pretty. A stone house with covered porch, an arched roof on the red barn, weathered outbuildings and a pair of golden dogs, barking and yipping and kicking up snow completed the scene—one that appealed to Regan.

She'd driven past the MacKade place countless times—when the fields were brown and furrowed from the plow, when they were high with hay and corn. She'd even stopped once or twice when Shane was riding his tractor, and thought how completely suited he seemed to be to the land.

She couldn't picture Rafe MacKade in the same scene.

"You didn't come back to farm, I imagine."

"Hell, no. Shane loves it, Devin tolerates it. Jared looks on it as an ongoing enterprise."

She tilted her head as he parked the Jeep beside his car. "And you?"

"Hate it."

"No ties to the land?"

"I didn't say that. I said I hated farming." Rafe hopped out of the Jeep, clucking at the leaping golden retrievers. Before Regan could step down into the foot-deep snow, he'd plucked her up.

"I wish you'd stop that. I'm perfectly capable of walking through a little snow."

"City boots. Pretty enough, though," he commented as he carried her onto the porch. "You've got little feet. Stay out," he ordered the dogs. Smoothly he opened the door, elbowed it aside and carried her in.

"Hey, Rafe, what you got there?"

Grinning, Rafe shifted Regan in his arms and winked at Shane. "Got me a female."

"Good-looking one, too." Shane tossed the log he held onto the fire, straightened. His eyes, the color of fog over seawater, warmed in appreciation. "Hi there, Regan."

"Shane."

"Any coffee hot?" Rafe asked.

"Sure." Shane kicked the log into place with his boot. "Kitchen's never closed."

"Fine. Now get lost."

"Well, that was certainly rude." Regan blew her hair out of her eyes as Rafe carted her down the hall and into the kitchen.

"You're an only child, right?"

"Yes, but—"

"Figured." He dropped her into one of the cane

chairs at the kitchen table. "What do you take in your coffee?"

"Nothing—black."

"What a woman." He stripped off his coat, tossed it over a peg by the back door, where his brother's heavy work jacket already hung. From a glass-fronted cupboard, he chose two glossy white mugs. "Want anything to go with it? Some hopeful woman's always baking Shane cookies. It's that pretty, innocent face of his."

"Pretty, maybe. You're all pretty." She shrugged out of her coat with a murmur of appreciation for the warmth of the room. "And I'll pass on the cookies."

He set a steaming mug in front of her. Out of habit, he turned a chair around and straddled it. "So, are you going to pass on the house, too?"

Biding her time, she studied her coffee, sampled it, and found it superb. "I have a number of pieces in stock that I think you'll find more than suitable when you're ready to furnish. I also did some research on the traditional color schemes and fabrics from that era."

"Is that a yes or a no, Regan?"

"No, I'm not going to pass." She lifted her gaze to his. "And it's going to cost you."

"You're not worried?"

"I didn't say that, exactly. But now I know what to expect. I can guarantee I won't be fainting at your feet a second time."

"I'd just as soon you didn't. You scared the life out of me." He reached over to play with the fingers of the hand she'd laid on the table. He liked the delicacy of them, and the glint of stones and gold. "In your research, did you dig up anything on the two corporals?"

"The two corporals?"

"You should have asked old lady Metz. She loves telling the story. What kind of watch is this?" Curious, Rafe flicked a finger under the twin black elastic bands.

"Circa 1920. Elastic and marcasite. What about the corporals?"

"It seems these two soldiers got separated from their regiments during the battle. The cornfield east of here was thick with smoke, black powder exploding. Some of the troops were engaged in the trees, others just lost or dying there."

"Some of the battle took place here, on your fields?" she asked.

"Some of it. The park service has markers up. Anyway, these two, one Union, one Confederate, got separated. They were just boys, probably terrified. Bad luck brought them together in the woods that form the boundary between MacKade land and Barlow."

"Oh." Thoughtful, she dragged her hair back. "I'd forgotten the properties border each other."

"It's less than a half mile from this house to the Barlow place through the trees. Anyway, they came face-to-face. If either of them had had any sense, they'd have run for cover and counted their blessings. But they didn't." He lifted his mug again. "They managed to put holes in each other. Nobody can say who crawled off first. The Reb made it as far as the Barlow house. Odds are he was half-dead already, but he managed to crawl onto the porch. One of the servants saw him and, being a Southern sympathizer, pulled him inside. Or maybe she just saw a kid bleeding to death and did what she thought was right.''

''And he died in the house,'' Regan murmured, wishing she couldn't see it so clearly.

''Yeah. The servant ran off to get her mistress. That was Abigail O'Brian Barlow, of the Carolina O'Brians. Abigail had just given orders for the boy to be taken upstairs, where she could treat his wounds. Her husband came out. He shot the kid, right there on the stairway.''

Sadness jolted straight into horror. ''Oh, my God! Why?''

''No wife of his was going to lay her hands on a Reb. She herself died two years later, in her room. Story is that she never spoke a word to her husband again—not that they had much to say to each other before. It was supposed to be one of those arranged marriages. Rumor was he liked to knock her around.''

''In other words,'' Regan said tightly, ''he was a prince among men.''

''That's the story. She was delicate, and she was miserable.''

''And trapped,'' Regan murmured, thinking of Cassie.

''I don't suppose people talked much about abuse back then. Divorce...'' He shrugged. ''Probably not an option in her circumstances. Anyway, shooting that boy right in front of her must have been the straw, you know. The last cruelty she could take. But that's only half of it. The half the town knows.''

"There's more." She let out a sigh and rose. "I think I need more coffee.''

"The Yank stumbled off in the opposite direction,'' Rafe continued, murmuring a thank you when she poured him a second cup. "My great-grandfather found him passed out by the smokehouse. My great-grandfather lost his oldest son at Bull Run—he'd died wearing Confederate gray.''

Regan shut her eyes. "He killed the boy.''

"No. Maybe he thought about it, maybe he thought about just leaving him there to bleed to death. But he picked him up and brought him into the kitchen. He and his wife, their daughters, doctored him on the table. Not this one,'' Rafe added with a small smile.

"That's reassuring.''

"He came around a few times, tried to tell them something. But he was too weak. He lasted the rest of that day and most of the night, but he was dead by morning.''

"They'd done everything they could.''

"Yeah, but now they had a dead Union soldier in their kitchen, his blood on their floor. Everyone who knew them knew that they were staunch Southern sympathizers who'd already lost one son to the cause and had two more still fighting for it. They were afraid, so they hid the body. When it was dark, they buried him, with his uniform, his weapon, and a letter from his mother in his pocket.''

He looked at her then, his eyes cool and steady. ''That's why this house is haunted, too. I thought you'd be interested.''

She didn't speak for a moment, set her coffee aside. ''Your house is haunted?''

''The house, the woods, the fields. You get used to it, the little noises, the little feelings. We never talked about it much; it was just there. Maybe you'd get a sense of something in the woods at night, or in the fields, when the morning was misty and too quiet.'' He smiled a little at the curiosity in her eyes. ''Even cynics feel something when they're standing on a battlefield. After my mother died, even the house seemed…restless. Or maybe it was just me.''

''Is that why you left?''

''I had lots of reasons for leaving.''

''And for coming back?''

''One or two. I told you the first part of the story because I figured you should understand the Barlow place, since you're going to be involved with it. And I told you the rest…'' He reached over and loosened the duo of black buttons on her blazer. ''Because I'm going to be staying at the farm for a while. Now you can decide if you want me to bring you here, or if you'd rather I come to your place.''

''My inventory's at the shop, so—''

''I'm not talking about your inventory.'' He cupped her chin in his hand, kept his eyes open and on hers when he kissed her.

Softly at first, testing. Then with a murmur of satisfaction, deeper, so that her lips parted and warmed. He watched her lashes flutter, felt her breath sigh out and into his mouth, felt the pulse just under her jaw, just under his fingers, throb. The smoky scent of her skin was a seductive contrast to her cool-water taste.

Regan kept her hands gripped tight in her lap. It was shocking how much she wanted to use them on him. To drag them through his hair, to test the muscles under that faded flannel shirt. But she didn't. Her mind might have blurred for just an instant with astonished pleasure, even more astonishing greed, but she managed to hold on to her focus.

When he leaned back, she kept her hands where they were and gave herself time to level her voice. "We're business associates, not playmates."

"We have business," he agreed.

"Would you have pulled that maneuver if I'd been a man?"

He stared at her. The chuckle started low, bloomed into a full laugh while she squirmed at the ridiculous way she'd phrased the question.

"I can give you a definite no on that one. I figure in that case you probably wouldn't have kissed me back, either."

"Look, let's clear this up. I've heard all about the MacKade brothers and how they're irresistible to women."

"It's been a curse all our lives."

She would not smile—even if she had to clamp her teeth together. "The point is, I'm not interested in a quick roll, an affair, or a relationship—which should cover any and all possibilities.''

Damned if she wasn't even more alluring when she went prim. ''I'm going to enjoy changing your mind. Why don't we start with the quick roll and work our way up from there?''

She rose sharply and pulled her coat on. ''In your dreams.''

''You're right about that. Why don't I take you out to dinner?''

''Why don't you take me back to my car?''

''All right.'' Unoffended, he got up to pluck his coat from the peg. After he'd shrugged it on, he reached out and flipped her hair out from the collar of hers. ''Nights are long and cold this time of year.''

''Get a book,'' she suggested on her way down the hall. ''Sit by the fire.''

''Is that what you do?'' He shook his head. ''I'm going to have to add a little excitement to your life.''

''I like my life just fine, thanks. Don't pick me—'' The order ended with an oath as he scooped her up. ''MacKade,'' she said with a sigh as he carried her to the Jeep, ''I'm beginning to think you're as bad as everyone says.''

''Count on it.''

Chapter 3

It was a good sound. The thud of hammers, the buzz of saws, the whir of drills. Through it came the jingle of a radio set to country music, so that Wynonna wailed over the clomp of boots and male voices.

It was a noise, the music of labor, that Rafe had known all of his life. This was different from the clatter of the milking barn, the hum of a tractor in the field. He preferred it. He'd chosen it the day he left Antietam.

Construction work had probably saved him. He had no problem admitting he'd been looking to rumble when he roared out of Washington County a decade before on his secondhand Harley. But he'd needed to eat, so he'd needed to work.

He'd strapped on a tool belt and sweated out the worst of the frustration.

He still remembered when he'd stepped back and looked at the first house he'd had a part in building. It had come to him in a flash that he could make something that mattered. And that he could make something of himself.

So he'd saved, and he'd sweated, and he'd learned.

The first place he'd bought, in central Florida, was little more than a shack. He'd choked on drywall dust, hammered until his muscles wept with the strain. But he'd made a profit, and used that to buy again. To sell again.

In four years, the tiny shoestring company called MacKade had earned a reputation for reliable, quality work.

Still, he'd never stopped looking back. Now, standing in the parlor of the Barlow place, he understood he'd come full circle.

He was going to make something in the town he'd been so hell-bent to escape from. Whether he stayed or not after he was done was undecided. But he would, at least, have left his mark.

Hunkered down in front of the fireplace, Rafe studied the stone hearth. He'd already gone to work on the chimney, and was covered with soot and grime. She'd draw, he thought with satisfaction. The first thing he was going to do, when the new lining was installed to bring it up to code, was build a fire. He wanted to watch the flames and warm his hands on them.

He wanted just the right andirons, the right screen. He could depend on Regan for that.

With a little smile, he picked up his trowel to mix a bucket of mortar. He had a feeling Regan could be depended on for most anything.

With care, precision and enjoyment, he began to repoint the stone.

"I figured the boss would be sitting at a desk, running figures."

Rafe glanced back and lifted a brow. Jared stood in the center of the room, his gleaming black shoes resting on a spattered drop cloth. For some reason, his black Wayfarer shades didn't look out of place with his gray pin-striped three-piece suit.

"That stuff's for lawyers and bookkeepers."

Jared took off the sunglasses and tucked them into the pocket of his suit jacket. "And think what the world would be without them."

"Simpler." Rafe stuck his trowel in the mortar and gave his brother a once-over. "On your way to a funeral?"

"I had business in town, thought I'd drop by and see how things are going." He glanced around the room, then back toward the hall when something crashed, someone cursed. "So, how's it going?"

"Steady." Rafe sighed when Jared took out a slim cigar. "Blow some of that over here, will you? I quit ten really long days ago."

"Reforming yourself?" Obligingly, Jared walked over, crouched. He smoked lazily as he and Rafe frowned meaningfully at the stone. "Not too shabby."

Rafe knocked a fist against the rose-grained marble. "An Adam, pal."

Jared grunted, clamped the cigar between his teeth. "Need a hand around here?"

Blandly Rafe looked down. "You're wearing your lawyer shoes."

"I meant over the weekend."

"I can always use another back." Pleased with the offer, Rafe picked up the trowel again. "How's yours?"

"As good as yours."

"Still working out?" He gave Jared's biceps a testing punch. "I still say gyms are for sissies."

Jared blew out a stream of smoke. "Want to go a round, bro?"

"Sure, when you're not dressed so pretty." To torture himself, Rafe sucked in secondhand smoke. "I appreciate you handling the settlement on this place for me."

"You haven't got my bill, yet." Grinning, Jared straightened. "I thought you were crazy when you called and told me to go after it. Then I did a walkthrough." He turned, still grinning. "And I knew you were crazy. You practically stole the place, but I figure it's got to cost you two times the purchase price to make it livable."

"Three times," Rafe said mildly, "to make it the way I want it."

"How do you want it?"

"The way it was." Rafe scraped the edge of his trowel over stone, leveling his mortar.

"Picking up, thanks to your little brother. I have some estimates, figures, suggestions, paint and fabric samples," she said to Rafe. "I thought you'd like to look them over."

"You've been busy." He crouched again, flipped over the top of a small cooler. "Want a drink?"

"No, thanks."

"Jare?"

"One for the road. I've got another appointment." Jared caught the canned soft drink on the fly, then took his sunglasses out of his pocket. "I'll let you two get down to business. Nice to see you again, Regan."

"Saturday," Rafe called out as Jared left the room. "Seven-thirty. That's a.m., pal. And lose the suit."

"I didn't mean to chase him off," Regan began.

"You didn't. Want to sit down?"

"Where?"

He patted an overturned bucket.

"That's very gracious of you, but I can't stay. I'm on my lunch hour."

"The boss isn't going to dock you."

"She certainly will." Opening her briefcase, Regan took out two thick folders. "Everything's in here. Once you have a chance to look through it, let me know." For lack of anywhere better, she set the files across two sawhorses. She looked back over her shoulder, toward the hall. "You've certainly jumped right in."

"When you know what you want, there's no point in wasting time. So how about dinner?"

She looked back, narrowed her eyes. "Dinner?"

"Tonight. We can go over your files." He tapped a finger against them, left a smudge of soot. "Save time."

"Oh." Still frowning, she combed her fingers through her hair. "I suppose."

"How's seven? We'll go to the Lamplighter."

"The where?"

"The Lamplighter. The little place off of Main, at Church Street."

She tilted her head as she visualized the town. "There's a video store at Main and Church."

He jammed his hands in his pockets with an oath. "Used to be a restaurant. Your place used to be a hardware store."

"I guess even small towns have their changes."

"Yeah." He couldn't have said why it annoyed him. "Like Italian?"

"Yes. But the closest Italian place is across the river, into West Virginia. We can just meet at Ed's."

"No. Italian. I'll come by about six-thirty." Needing to gauge his time, he pulled a watch from his pocket. "Yeah, I can do six-thirty."

"That's a nice one." Without thinking, she crossed over, took his wrist gingerly in two fingers to get a better look at the pocket watch. "Hmm...American Watch Company, mid-1800s." Already appraising, she turned the watch over to study the case. "Sterling, good condition. I'll give you seventy-five for it."

"I paid ninety."

She laughed and shook back her hair. "Then you

got a hell of a bargain. It's worth a hundred and fifty.'' Her gaze danced up to his. ''You don't look like the pocket-watch type.''

''Wear one on your wrist on the job, they end up smashed.'' He wanted to touch her. She looked so neat and tidy that the idea of mussing her up was enormously appealing. ''Damn shame my hands are filthy.''

Alerted, she released his wrist, brushed one hand against the other. ''So's your face. But you're still pretty.'' After shifting her briefcase strap more comfortably on her shoulder, she stepped back. ''Six-thirty, then. Don't forget the files.''

She'd changed three times before she caught herself. A business dinner, Regan thought as she dropped down on the padded stool of her vanity, was a business dinner. Her appearance was certainly important, but it was secondary.

She bit her lip and wondered if she should have gone with the little black dress, after all.

No, no, no. Annoyed with herself, she snatched up her brush. Simplicity was best. The restaurant in West Virginia was casual, family-style. The purpose was professional. The blazer, slacks and silk blouse in forest green were right. There was no harm in jazzing it up with the moonstone lapel pin. But maybe the earrings were wrong. She could go with plain gold hoops instead of the more dramatic dangles.

The hell with it. She dropped her brush, then tugged on her suede ankle boots. She would not fall into the trap of thinking of this as a date. She didn't want to date Rafe MacKade. Just now, with her business showing real promise, she didn't want to date anyone.

A relationship, if indeed she decided to cultivate one, was three years down the road. Minimum. She would never make the mistake her mother had and depend on someone else for emotional and financial support. First, she would make certain she was solvent, solid and secure. And then, if and when she chose, she would think about sharing her life.

No one was going to tell her if she could work or not. She would never have to cajole an extra few dollars out of a man to buy a new dress. Maybe it suited her parents to live that way—and they'd certainly always seemed happy enough. But that wasn't the life Regan Bishop wanted.

It was just too damned bad that Rafe was so dangerously attractive. And, she noted when she heard the knock on the door, prompt.

Confident again after the quick pep talk, she walked out of the bedroom, through the small, cozily furnished living room, and opened the door.

And, oh, she thought one last time, it was really too bad.

He flashed that grin at her, and those wonderful green eyes swept down, then up. "Looking good." Before she could think to avoid it, his mouth brushed hers.

"I'll get my coat," she began, then stopped, the door still open to the wind. "What are those?"

"These?" He jostled the bags he carried. "These are dinner. Where's your kitchen?"

"I—" He was already in, kicking the door behind him. "I thought we were going out."

"No, I said we were having Italian." He took quick stock of the room. Lady chairs, gleaming tables, pretty little knickknacks and fresh flowers. All female, he mused. And the portrait of a gloomy-faced cow above the sofa added wit. "Nice place."

"Are you telling me you're cooking me dinner?"

"It's the quickest way, without physical contact, to get a woman into bed. The kitchen through there?"

When she'd managed to close her mouth, she followed him into the galley-style kitchen off the dining el. "Doesn't that depend on how well you cook?"

Appreciating her response, he smiled as he began pulling ingredients out of the bags. "You'll have to tell me. Got a skillet?"

"Yes, I have a skillet." She took a large cast-iron pan from its cupboard, then lips pursed, tapped it against her palm.

"You conk me with it, you'll miss out on my ziti with tomato and basil."

"Ziti?" After running her tongue around her teeth, she set the skillet on a burner. "I'll wait until after I eat." She got out a second pot for the pasta and handed it to him.

Once he'd added water and set it to boil, she watched him wash greens for a salad.

"Where'd you learn to cook?"

"We all cook. Chef's knife? My mother didn't believe there was women's work and men's work. Thanks,'' he added and began chopping with a quick, negligent flair that had Regan lifting her brows. ''There was just work,'' he continued.

''Ziti doesn't sound like farm food.''

''She had an Italian grandmother. Can you stand a little closer?''

''Hmm?''

''You smell good. I like to smell you.''

Ignoring that, and the little twist in her stomach, she picked up the wine he'd brought along. ''Why don't I open this?''

''Why don't you?''

After she'd set it on the counter to breathe, she scooted behind him to reach the cupboard to get a salad bowl. When he asked for music, she slipped back into the living room and put Count Basie on low. Why, she wondered, did a man look so sexy with his sleeves rolled up, grating carrots into a salad?

''Don't open that olive oil,'' she told him. ''I have some.''

''Extra virgin?''

''Of course.'' She tapped a long-spouted copper pitcher on the counter.

''Count Basie, your own olive oil.'' His eyes met hers, laughed. ''Want to get married?''

''Sure. I've got time on Saturday.'' Amused that he didn't have such a quick comeback for that, she reached overhead for wineglasses.

''I was planning on working Saturday.'' Watching her, he set the salad aside.

"That's what they all say."

Lord, she was one terrific piece of work. He moved closer as she poured the wine. "Tell me you like watching baseball on TV on hot summer nights, and we've got a deal."

"Sorry. I hate sports."

He moved closer still, and with a wineglass in either hand, she moved back. "It's a good thing I found this flaw now, before we had five or six kids and a dog."

"You're a lucky guy." Heart jittering, she backed up again.

"I like this," he murmured, and traced a finger over the little mole beside her mouth. Inching closer, he ran his finger down to flip open the buttons of her blazer.

"Why are you always doing that?"

"Doing what?"

"Fooling with my buttons."

"Just practicing." The grin was quick as lightning, and just as bold. "Besides, you always look so tidy, I can't resist loosening you up."

Her retreat ended with her back between the side of the refrigerator and the wall.

"Looks like you've backed yourself into a corner, darling."

He moved in slowly, slipping his hands around her waist, fitting his mouth to hers. He took his time sampling, his fingers spread over her rib cage, stopping just short of the curve of her breasts.

She couldn't stop her breath from quickening or

her lips from responding. His tongue flicked over them, between them, met hers. His taste was dark, and rabidly male, and streaked straight to her center like an arrow on target.

The small part of her mind that could still function warned her that he knew exactly how he affected women. All women. Any woman. But her body didn't seem to give a damn.

Her blood began to pound, her skin to vibrate, from the shock of dozens of tiny explosions. She was certain she could feel her own bones melt.

She was exciting to watch. His eyes were open as he changed the angle of the kiss, deepened it, degree by painfully slow degree. He found the flutter of her lashes arousing, the faint flush desire brought to her cheeks seductive. And that helpless hitch of breath, that quick shiver when his fingers skimmed lightly over the tips of her breasts, utterly thrilling.

With an effort, he stopped himself from taking more. "God. It gets better every time." Gently he nuzzled his way to her ear. "Let's try it again."

"No." It surprised her that what she said and what she wanted were entirely different. In defense, she pressed a wineglass against his chest.

He glanced down at the glass, then back at her face. His eyes weren't smiling now, weren't gently amused. There was an edge in them now, dark and potentially deadly. Despite all common sense, she found herself drawn to this man who would take, and damn all consequences.

"Your hand's shaking, Regan."

"I'm aware of that."

She spoke carefully, knowing that the wrong word, the wrong move, and what was in his eyes would leap out and devour her. And she would let it. She would love it.

That was something she definitely had to think over.

"Take the wine, Rafe. It's red. It'll leave a nasty stain on that shirt."

For one humming moment, he said nothing. A need he hadn't understood or counted on had him by the throat with rusty little claws. She was afraid of him, he noted, deciding she was smart to be afraid. A woman like her didn't have a clue what a man like him was really capable of.

Taking the glass, he tapped it against hers, making the crystal ring, then turned back to the stove.

She felt as though she'd barely avoided a tumble from a cliff. And realized she already regretted not taking the plunge. "I think I should say something. I, um…" She took a deep breath, then an even deeper gulp of wine. "I'm not going to pretend I'm not attracted to you, or that I didn't enjoy that, when obviously I am, and I did."

Trying to relax, he leaned back against the counter, studied her over the rim of his glass. "And?"

"And." She scooped back her hair. "And I think complications are…complicated," she said lamely. "I don't want—that is, I don't think…" She shut her eyes and drank again. "I'm stuttering."

"I noticed. It's a nice boost to the ego."

"Your ego doesn't need any boosting." She blew out a breath, cleared her throat. "You're very potent. I have no doubt sex would be memorable— Don't smile at me that way."

"Sorry." But the smile didn't dim. "It must have been your choice of words. *Memorable*'s good. I like it. Why don't we save time here? I get your point. You want to mull the idea over, make the next move when you're ready."

She considered, then nodded slowly. "That's close enough."

"Okay. Now here's my point." He turned on the burner under the skillet and added oil. "I really want you, Regan. It hit me right off, when I walked into Ed's and you were sitting there with little Cassie, looking so pressed and polished."

She fought to ignore the flutters in her stomach. "Is that why you offered me the job on the Barlow place?"

"You're too smart to ask a question like that. This is sex. Sex is personal."

"All right." She nodded again. "All right."

He picked up a plump roma tomato, examined it. "The problem here, as I see it, is that I don't much care for mulling over things like this. No matter how you fancy it up, sex is still the animal. Smell, touch, taste."

His eyes were dark again, reckless. He picked up the knife, tested its point. "Take," he added. "But that's just me, and there are two of us here. So you go on ahead with your mulling."

Baffled, she stared at him as he chose a clove of garlic. "I'm trying to decide if you expect me to thank you for that."

"Nope." Expertly he laid the flat of his knife over the garlic, gave one quick pound of his fist to crush it. "You're just supposed to understand it, like I'm understanding you."

"You're a real nineties man, MacKade."

"No, I'm not. And I'm going to make you stutter again. You can count on that."

Challenged, she picked up the wine, topped off their glasses. "Well, you count on this. If and when I decide to make my move, you'll do some stuttering of your own."

He scooped the minced garlic into the oil, where it sizzled. "I like your style, darling. I really like your style."

Chapter 4

Sunny skies and a southerly breeze brought in a welcome end-of-January thaw. Icicles dripped prettily from eaves and shone with rainbows. In front yards and fallow fields, snowmen began to lose weight. Regan spent a pleasant week earmarking stock for the Barlow place and hunting up additions to her supply at auction.

When business was slow, she revised and honed her room-by-room decorating scheme for what was going to be the MacKade Inn at Antietam.

Even now, as she described the attributes of a walnut credenza to a pair of very interested buyers, her mind was on the house. Though she hadn't realized it, yet, she was as haunted by it as Rafe had been.

The front bedroom, second floor, she mused, should have the four-poster with canopy, the rosebud wallpaper and the satinwood armoire. A romantic and traditional bridal suite, complete with little bowls of potpourri and vases of fresh flowers.

And what had been the gathering room, on the main level, had that wonderful southern exposure. Of course, Rafe had to pick the right windows, but it would be spectacular in sunny colors with a trio of ficus trees, hanging ferns in glazed pots, and pretty little conversation groups of boldly floral love seats and wingback chairs.

It was perfect for a conservatory, a place to gaze through the glass into the woods and gardens, with forced narcissi and hyacinths brightening midwinter gloom.

She couldn't wait to get her hands on the place, add those tiny, perfect details that would make it a home again.

An inn, she reminded herself. A business. Comfortable, charming, but temporary. And it wasn't hers. With an effort, she shook her head clear and concentrated on the sale at hand.

"You can see the marquetry is high-quality," she continued, keeping her sales pitch moderate and pleasant. "The bowfront cupboards on the side are the original glass."

The woman fingered the discreet tag longingly, and Regan's sharp eye caught the hopeful glance she sent her less enthusiastic husband.

"It really is lovely. But it's just a little more than we had in mind."

"I understand. But in this condition—"

She broke off when the door opened, furious with herself for the quick leap, then the quick disappointment when it wasn't Rafe who came in. Before she could smile a welcome at Cassie, she saw the livid bruises on the side of her friend's face.

"If you'd excuse me for just a moment, I'll give you time to talk it over."

An antique bangle jingling on her wrist, sensible shoes clacking, she moved swiftly through the shop. Saying nothing, she took Cassie's arm and led her into the back room.

"Sit down. Come on." Gently, she eased Cassie into a chair at the tiny iron table. "How bad are you hurt?"

"It's nothing. I just—"

"Shut up." Grinding back the spurt of temper, Regan slammed a kettle on the hot plate. "I'm sorry. I'm going to make some tea." She needed a moment, she realized, before she could deal with this rationally. "While the water's boiling, I'll go finish up with my customers. You sit here and relax for a minute."

Shame swimming in her eyes, Cassie stared down at her hands. "Thanks."

Ten minutes later, after ruthlessly hacking the price of the credenza to move the customers along, Regan hurried back. She told herself she'd gotten the anger under control. She promised herself she would be supportive, sympathetic.

One look at Cassie, slumped in the chair while the kettle belched steam, had her exploding.

"Why in the hell do you let him do this to you?

When are you going to get tired of being that sadistic bastard's punching bag? Does he have to put you in the hospital before you walk away?''

In utter defeat, Cassie folded her arms on the table, then dropped her head on them and wept.

Her own eyes stinging, Regan dropped to her knees beside the chair. In the tidy little office, with its ice-cream-parlor chairs and neat rolltop desk, she struggled to face the reality of battering.

"Cassie, I'm sorry. I'm so sorry, Cass. I shouldn't be yelling at you."

"I shouldn't have come here." Lifting her head, Cassie covered her face with her hand and fought to get her breath back. "I shouldn't have come. But I just needed somebody to talk to."

"Of course you should have come here. This is exactly where you should have come. Let me see," Regan murmured, easing Cassie's hand away. The bruises ran from temple to jaw, in ugly purple. One of Cassie's lovely smoke gray eyes was swollen nearly shut.

"Oh, Cassie, what happened? Can you tell me?"

"He...Joe...he hasn't been feeling well. This flu that's been going around." Cassie's voice hitched and jittered. "He missed a lot of work, being sick, and yesterday they laid him off."

Avoiding Regan's eyes, she fumbled in her bag for a tissue. "He was upset—he's worked there almost twelve years now, on and off. The bills. I just bought a new washing machine on credit, and Connor wanted these new tennis shoes. I knew they were too expensive, but—"

"Stop," Regan said quietly, and laid a hand over Cassie's. "Please stop blaming yourself. I can't bear it when you do."

"I know I'm making excuses." With a long, shuddering breath, Cassie shut her eyes. To Regan, at least, she could be honest. Because Regan, in the three years they had known each other, had always been there. "He hasn't had the flu. He's been drunk almost day and night for a week. They didn't lay him off, they fired him because he went to work drunk and mouthed off to his supervisor."

"And then he came home and took it out on you." Rising, Regan took the kettle off the hot plate and began to make the tea. "Where are the kids?"

"At my mother's. I went there last night, after. He hurt me pretty bad this time."

Unconsciously she touched her hand to her throat. Beneath the turtleneck there were more bruises, where Joe's hands had held and choked her until she accepted that he would kill her. Almost wished for it.

"I got the kids out, and I went to Mama, because I needed some place to stay."

"Okay, that's good." Ready to move step-by-step now, Regan brought two china cups to the table. "That's the best way to start."

"No." Very carefully, Cassie wrapped both hands around her cup. "She expects me to go back today. She won't let us stay another night."

"After you told her, after she saw you, what he'd done, she expects you to go back?"

"A woman belongs with her husband," Cassie said simply. "I married him for better or for worse."

Regan had never understood her own mother, the easy subservience, the catering. But, while it had infuriated her often, it had never appalled her like this.

"That's monstrous, Cassie."

"It's just Mama," Cassie murmured, wincing as the tea stung her puffy lip. "She believes a woman should make a marriage work. It's her duty to make it work."

"Do you believe that? That it's your responsibility to take this? Do you believe that means you are supposed to stay for better or worse, even if worse means being beaten whenever he has the whim?"

"I used to. I tried to. I took vows, Regan." She took a shuddering breath, because to her that had always been the bottom line. She had promised. "Maybe I was too young when I married Joe. Maybe I made a mistake, but I still took the vows. He didn't keep them. There were those other women, he didn't even care if I knew who they were. He was never faithful, never kind. But I took vows and I wanted to keep them."

She began to cry again, quietly now, because she had failed. "We've been married ten years. We have children together. I make so many mistakes—using my tip money to buy those shoes for Connor, and letting Emma play dress-up with my lipstick. And we couldn't afford that washing machine. I was never any good in bed, not like those other women he'd go to. I knew—''

She broke off when Regan only continued to watch her.

''Are you hearing yourself this time?'' Regan said quietly. ''Are you listening to yourself, Cassie?''

''I can't stay with him anymore.'' Her voice broke, shattering like thin, fragile glass. ''He's hitting me in front of the kids. He used to wait until they were in bed, and that was bad. But now he hits me in front of them, and he says terrible things. Things they shouldn't hear. It's not right. It makes them part of it, and it's not right.''

''No, Cass, it's not right. You need help now.''

''I thought about it all night.'' She hesitated, then slowly eased down the neck of her sweater.

At the sight of the raw marks scoring that pale, innocent flesh, Regan's face went white and cold. ''Oh, dear God—he tried to strangle you.''

''I don't think he meant to at first. I was crying, and he wanted me to stop. But then he did.'' Cassie lowered her hand again. ''I could see it in his eyes. It wasn't just the drinking, or the money, or the other women he seems to want. He hated me just for being there. He'll hurt me again if he gets the chance, and I have to think about the kids. I have to go to Devin and file charges.''

''Thank God.''

''I had to come here first, to get up my nerve.'' Knowing there was no more point in them, Cassie wiped at the tears. ''It's hard, being it's Devin. I've known him all my life. It's not like it's a secret. He's been out to the house I don't know how many times when the neighbors called in. But it's hard.'' She sighed. ''Being it's Devin.''

''I'll go with you.''

Cassie closed her eyes. That was why she had come here, to have someone stand with her. No, she admitted, ashamed all over again. To have someone hold her up.

''No, I need to do it myself. I haven't thought about after,'' she said, and soothed her raw throat with a sip of tea. ''I can't take the kids back to the house until I know what's going to happen.''

''The shelter—''

Stubbornly, Cassie shook her head. ''I know it's pride, Regan, but I can't go there. I can't take my kids there. Not yet, anyway.''

''All right, then you'll stay here. Here,'' Regan repeated as Cassie protested. ''I only have one extra bedroom, so you and the kids will have to rough it.''

''We can't pile in on you that way.''

''You were the first friend I made when I moved here. I want to help. So let me help.''

''I could never ask you that, Regan. I've saved some tip and overtime money. Enough for a motel for a couple of days.''

''You wouldn't want to hurt my feelings that way. You're going to stay at my place. For the kids,'' Regan murmured, knowing that nothing would tilt the scales as heavily.

''I'll go get them after I see Devin.'' She had no

pride when it came to her children. "I'm awfully grateful, Regan."

"So am I. Now."

"What's this? Tea party during business hours?" Because his eyes were on Regan, Rafe had stepped into the office and tossed his coat over the back of a chair before he saw Cassie's face.

Regan was stunned to watch charm metamorphize into pure violence in a split second. The quick, potent grin sharpened into a snarl. His eyes fired. Her first startled thought, as that lean body tensed to spring, was *wolf*.

When his hand shot out, Cassie flinched, and Regan leapt to her feet. Before Regan could step between them with some wild idea of protecting Cassie, Rafe's fingers stroked, gentle as a kiss, over the battered face.

"Joe?"

"It—it was an accident," Cassie stammered.

His opinion of that was one vicious word. He swung around, blood in his eye. Cassie was on her feet and racing after him.

"No, Rafe, please don't do anything." Desperate, she pulled at his arm, all but jumped on his back. "Please don't go after him."

He could have knocked her aside with a shrug. It was that knowledge that added bitter fuel to the fire. "You stay here. Stay with Regan."

"No, please." Cassie began to weep again, helplessly, as she pulled at him. "Please. Don't make me any more ashamed than I already am."

"The bastard's going to pay this time." He bit the words out, started to set her aside and looked down. The tears did what fists and threats could never have done. They stopped him cold. "Cassie." Undone, he wrapped his arms around her and cradled her against his chest. "Don't cry, baby. Come on now, it's going to be all right."

From the doorway of the office, Regan watched him. How could there be such tenderness, she wondered, side by side with such savagery? He was holding Cassie as though she were a child, his head close to hers as he murmured to her.

Regan's own throat burned, and her own cheeks were wet when he lifted his head and looked at her.

Yes, the violence was still there, alive and restless in his eyes. Vital and fierce enough to steal her breath from her throat and make her stomach muscles quiver. She swallowed hard before she spoke.

"Bring her back in here, Rafe. Please."

Every nerve inside him was tensed for battle. He craved the hunt, the fight, the blood. But the woman in his arms was trembling. And the one who watched him with shocked, frightened eyes was quietly pleading.

"Come on, baby." As if she were a fretful child, Rafe tucked Cassie under his arm. "Come on, let's go sit down."

"I'm sorry."

"Don't apologize to me." It took every ounce of control to lead her back into the office, to keep his

voice easy on the words. "Don't apologize to anyone."

"She's going to Devin." Because her hands were
shaking, Regan busied them with the tea and cups.
"She's going to file charges. That's the right way to
handle it."

"That's one way." He preferred his own, but he
eased Cassie into a chair, brushed her hair way from
her damp face. "Have you got a place to stay?"

Cassie nodded, took the tissues Regan handed her.
"We're going to stay with Regan for a little while.
Just until…"

"The kids okay?"

She nodded again. "I'm going to get them as soon
as I see Devin."

"You tell me what you need, and I'll go by the
house and pick it up for you."

"I…I don't know. I didn't take anything."

"You tell me later. Why don't I walk you down to
the sheriff's office?"

She shuddered out a breath, mopped her face. "No,
I need to do it by myself. I should go now."

"Here." Regan pulled open a drawer in her desk.
"Here's a key to the door upstairs. You and the kids
settle in." She put the key in Cassie's hand, closed
her fingers over it. "And lock it, Cassie."

"I will. I'll go now." It was the hardest thing she'd
ever done, just standing, walking to the door. "I always thought it would get better," she said, almost
to herself. "I always hoped it would." She left, with
her head bowed and her shoulders hunched.

"Do you know where he is?" Rafe murmured.

"No, I don't."

"Well, I'll find him." As he reached for his coat, Regan put her hand over his. His eyes lifted slowly to hers and burned. "Don't get in my way."

Instinct had her laying her other hand on his cheek, her mouth on his. The kiss was soft, soothing them both.

"What was that for?"

"A couple of things." She took a deep breath, then put both hands on his shoulders. "For wanting to kick the bastard's face in." She kissed him again. "For not doing it because Cassie asked you." And again. "And last, for showing her that most men, real men, are kind."

"Damn." Defeated, he laid his brow on hers. "That's a hell of a way to keep me from killing him."

"Part of me would like you to. I'm not proud of it." As the anger stirred again, she turned back to the hot plate. "Part of me would like to watch while you beat him senseless. Even worse, I'd like a shot at him myself."

Rafe stepped over, uncurled the hand she'd balled into a fist. Thoughtfully, he lifted it, pressed his lips to the palm. "Well, well... And I figured you for a cream puff."

"I said I'm not proud of it." But she smiled a little. "It's not what she needs now. Violence is just what she needs to get away from. Even if it's justified."

"I've known her since she was a kid." Rafe glanced down at the tea Regan poured him, shook his head at it. It smelled like a meadow at springtime, and would undoubtedly taste the same.

"She was always little, pretty and shy. All this sweetness." At Regan's curious look, he shook his head again. "No. I never made any moves in that direction. Sweet's never been my type."

"Thanks."

"Don't mention it." He stroked a hand over her hair, let his fingers drift into it, through it. "You're taking on a lot, letting her and the kids stay with you. I can take them out to the farm. We've got plenty of room."

"She needs a woman, Rafe, not a bunch of men—however well-intentioned. Devin will find him, won't he? And take care of it?"

"You can count on it."

Satisfied, she picked up her own tea. "Then I will, and so should you." Now that the step had been taken, she eyed him over her cup. "You must have come by for a reason."

"I wanted to look at you for a while." Her bland gaze had his lips curving. "And I figured to go over some of the wall treatments—and the parlor furniture. I want to complete that one room, give me a feel for the rest."

"That's a nice idea. I—" She broke off at the sound of movement and voices from the shop. "I've got customers. Everything's here—the paint samples and fabrics, itemized lists of furnishings."

"I picked up some samples of my own."

"Oh, well, then…" She crossed to the desk, booted

up her computer. "I have a room-by-room rundown here. Why don't you go over it? Several of the pieces I've suggested are here. You can take a look at them when you've finished here."

"All right."

Thirty minutes later, flush with three sales, Regan stepped back into the office. He looked so big, she thought, so...male, sitting at her lovely little Chippendale desk. She could smell him—wood dust, soot, oil.

His boots were scarred, his shirt was ripped at the shoulder. There were traces of plaster or drywall dust in his hair.

She thought he was the most magnificent animal she had ever seen. And she wanted him with a kind of primal, mindless lust.

Whoa! To steady herself, she pressed a hand to her jumpy stomach, took three deep breaths.

"Well, what do you think?"

"You're an efficient woman, Regan." Without turning, he flipped open a file with printouts of her lists. "It doesn't look like you've missed a trick."

Flattered, she walked over to look over his shoulder. "I'm sure we'll need to adjust, add a few details after we see one of the rooms completed."

"I've already made some adjustments."

She straightened again. "Oh, really?"

"This color's out." Briskly he tapped the paint chip, then located the page on-screen where her colors were listed. "I ditched this pea green here for—what's it called? Yeah. Loden."

"The original color is accurate."

"It's ugly."

Yes, it was, but— "It's accurate," she insisted. "I researched very carefully. The one you've chosen is entirely too modern for the 1800s."

"Maybe. But it won't spoil anyone's appetite. Don't get your panties in a twist, darling." When her breath hissed out at that, he chuckled and turned around in the chair. "Listen, you're doing a hell of a job here. I have to admit, I didn't expect this much detail, certainly not so fast. You've got a real feel for it."

She didn't care to be placated. "You hired me to help you reconstruct a particular era, and that's what I'm doing. It was your choice to make the house look the way it did in the past."

"And it's my choice to make adjustments. We've got to make some room here for aesthetics and modern taste. I've had a look at your place upstairs, Regan. It's a little too much on the female side for me—"

"Fortunately, that's hardly the issue here," she told him, stiffening all over again.

"And so neat a man'd be afraid to put his feet up," Rafe continued smoothly. "But you've got taste. I'm just asking you to use it, along with research and accuracy."

"It seems to me we're talking about your taste. If you're going to change the guidelines, at least make them clear."

"Are you always so rigid, or is it just with me?"

She refused to stoop to answering such an insulting question. "You asked for accuracy. I don't care to have rules changed in midstream."

Considering, Rafe picked up the paint chip that had started the ball rolling. "One question. Do you like this color?"

"That's not the point—"

"Simple question. Do you like it?"

Her breath whistled between her teeth. "Of course not. It's hideous."

"There you go. Guidelines are, if you don't like it, it doesn't fly."

"I can't take the responsibility."

"I'm paying you to take it." Since that settled the matter as far as he was concerned, he turned back to the screen, and scanned down the displays. "You got this what-do-you-call-it in stock, right? Isn't that what this I.S. stands for?"

"Yes. The double chairback settee." Her heart dropped to her feet. She'd bought it the week before at auction, with his parlor in mind. If he rejected it, her books were going straight into the red. "It's in the shop," she continued, keeping her voice coolly professional. "I've put a hold on it."

"So, let's take a look. I want to see this fire-screen and these tables."

"You're the boss," she muttered under her breath, and led the way.

Her nerves strained as she stopped by the settee. It was a gorgeous piece, and it had had a price to match. However much she coveted it, she would never have made the bid if she hadn't had a customer in the wings.

Now, she thought of that customer—the scarred boots, the ripped shirt, the potent aura of man. What had she been thinking of, she wondered frantically, imagining Rafe MacKade approving of an elegant, curvy, and decidedly feminine piece such as this?

"Ah, it's walnut..." she began, running a suddenly icy hand over the carved arm. "Around 1850. It's been reupholstered, of course, but the material is very much in keeping with the era. You can see the double-shaped backs are centered by a circular upholstered panel. The workmanship is first-rate, and the seat is surprisingly comfortable."

He grunted and crouched down to peer under the seat. "Pricey little thing."

"It's sixty-nine inches wide, and well worth the expense."

"Okay."

She blinked. "Okay?"

"Yeah. If I stay on schedule, I should have the parlor ready by the weekend. I could take delivery on this by Monday, unless I tell you different." He glanced up at her. "That suit you?"

"Yes." She realized she'd lost all feeling below the knees. "Of course."

"C.O.D. all right? I don't have my checkbook on me."

"That'll be fine."

"Let's see the Pembroke table."

"The Pembroke table." She looked dizzily around the shop. "Over here."

He straightened, holding back a grin. He wondered if she had any idea that, for a few minutes there, she'd been clear as glass. He doubted it.

"What's this?"

Distracted, she stopped. "Oh, that's a display table. Satinwood and mahogany."

"I like it."

"You like it," she repeated.

"It'd look good in the parlor, wouldn't it?"

"Yes, I had it down as a possibility."

"Send it over with the couch thing. Is this the Pembroke here?"

All she could do was nod weakly. When he left, an hour later, she was still nodding.

Rafe headed straight to the sheriff's office. He'd have to put in a couple of hours overtime on the job, but he wasn't leaving town until he knew Joe Dolin was in a cage.

When he stepped inside, he found Devin tilted back in his chair, his feet propped on his battered metal desk. Devin's uniform consisted of a cotton shirt, faded jeans and boots worn down at the heel. His only concession to his position was the star on his chest.

He was reading a dog-eared copy of *The Grapes of Wrath.*

"And you're responsible for law and order in this town."

In his slow, deliberate way, Devin marked his place

and set the book aside. "That's what they tell me. Always got a cell waiting for you."

"If you've got Dolin in one, I wouldn't mind you putting me in with him for five minutes or so."

"He's back there."

With a nod, Rafe walked to the coffeemaker. "Have any trouble with him?"

Devin's lips curved in a lazy and wicked smile. "Just enough to make it fun. I'll have a cup of that."

"How long can you keep him in there?"

"That's not up to me."

Devin reached out for the chipped mug Rafe offered. Since he insisted on making the coffee himself, it was the MacKade brew. Hot, strong and black as night.

"We'll transfer him to Hagerstown," Devin went on. "He'll get himself a public defender. If Cassie doesn't back down, he'll have his day in court."

Rafe sat on the corner of the cluttered desk. "You think she'll back down?"

Fighting frustration, Devin shrugged. "This is the closest she's ever come to doing anything about things. The son of a bitch has been pounding on her for years. Probably started on her on their wedding night. She can't weigh more than a hundred pounds. Got bones like a bird." His usually calm eyes went molten. "She's got bruises around her throat where he choked her."

"I didn't see that."

"I got pictures."

After rubbing a hand over his face, Devin dropped

his feet to the floor. Tussling with Joe, slapping cuffs on him, along with a few bruises—in the line of duty—hadn't taken the edge off.

"I had to take her statement, and pictures for evidence, and she sat there looking at me like she was getting beat up all over again. God knows how she'll handle it if she has to go to court and lay it all out."

Abruptly he pushed away from his desk, paced to the window, where he could look out on town. He'd given his word to serve the town, protect its citizens. Not to relieve his own bitter frustrations by pummeling one of them into the ground.

"I gave her the standard lines," he continued. "Therapy, counseling, shelters. And I put just enough pressure on when she started to waffle, so she'd sign the complaint. She just sat there crying, and I felt like scum."

Rafe studied his coffee, frowned. "You still have a thing for her, Dev?"

"That was high school," Devin snapped. With an effort, he uncurled his fist, turned back to his brother.

They might have been twins, with barely a year separating them. The same bold, dark looks, rangy build. Only Devin's eyes were cooler, more like moss than jade. And the scars he carried were on his heart.

"Sure I care about her," he said, calm again. "Hell, Rafe, we've known her all our lives. I've hated watching what he's been doing to her, not being able to stop it. Every time I got called out to their place, every time she had a fresh bruise, she'd just say it was an accident."

"Not this time."

"No, not this time. I sent my deputy with her to get the kids, whatever stuff she needs."

"You know she's going to stay with Regan Bishop."

"She told me." He drained his coffee, went back for more. "Well, she's taken the first step. It's probably the hardest."

Since there was nothing more he could do, Devin sat behind his desk again and put the matter in the corner of his mind. "Speaking of Regan Bishop, word is you've been sniffing around her."

"There a law against it?"

"If there is, it wouldn't be one you haven't broken before." Devin rose again, rooted through the side drawer of his deputy's desk. He confiscated two candy bars, tossed one to Rafe. "She's not your usual type."

"I'm upgrading my taste."

"'Bout time." Devin bit into chocolate. "Serious?"

"Getting a woman into bed's always serious, bro."

Mumbling an agreement over candy, Devin kicked back again. "So is that all there is?"

"I don't know. But I've got a feeling it'll be a hell of a start." He glanced over and grinned as Regan came through the door.

She stopped short, as any woman might when faced with two gorgeous men smiling at her. "I'm sorry. I'm interrupting."

"No, ma'am." All quiet country charm, Devin unfolded himself and stood. "It's always a pleasure to see you."

Angling his head, Rafe put a hand on Regan's shoulder. "Dibs," he said in a mild warning.

"Excuse me?" Regan stepped back and gaped. "I beg your pardon, but did you just say 'Dibs'?"

"Yeah." Rafe bit off candy, offered her the rest of the bar. When she smacked his hand away, he only shrugged and ate it himself.

"Of all the ridiculous, outrageous— You're a grown man, and you're standing there eating candy and saying 'Dibs' as if I were the last ice-cream bar in the freezer."

"The way I grew up, it was real important to stake your claim quick." To prove it, he cupped her elbows, lifted her to her toes and kissed her long and hard. "Gotta go," he said, releasing her just as arrogantly. "See you, Dev."

"Yeah." Too wise to let the laugh loose, Devin cleared his throat. Seconds passed, and Regan continued to stare at the door Rafe had slammed at his back. "You want me to go after him, haul him into the back room?"

"Have you got a rubber hose back there?"

"Afraid not. But I broke his finger once, when we were kids. I could probably do it again."

"Never mind." She shook herself. She'd deal with Rafe later, personally. "I came here to see if you'd arrested Joe Dolin."

"So did Rafe."

"I should have known he would."

"Want some coffee, Regan?"

"No, I can't stay. I just came to see if you had, and to ask, since Cassie and the children are going to be staying with me, if there are any precautions I should take."

Quietly he measured her. He'd known her casually for three years, admired her looks, enjoyed a few conversations with her at the café or on the street. Now he saw what had attracted his brother. Spine, good sense, compassion.

He wondered if Rafe understood the difference the combination could make in his life.

"Why don't you sit down," he told her. "We'll go over some things."

Chapter 5

On Monday morning, Regan was up early, a song on her lips. In a few hours, the first furnishings would be delivered to the house on the hill. With her payment deposited, she would dash to an auction in Pennsylvania scheduled for that afternoon.

It would be well worth closing the shop for the day.

She put the coffee on, popped bread into the toaster. Then turned and nearly jumped out of her slippers.

"Oh, Connor." Laughing, she pressed a hand to her speeding heart. "You scared me."

"I'm sorry." The boy was thin, pale, with big eyes the color of shadows. His mother's eyes, Regan thought as she smiled at him.

"It's okay. I didn't know anyone was up. It's early, even for a school day. Want some breakfast?"

"No, thank you."

She bit back a sigh. No eight-year-old boy should be so apologetically polite. She lifted a brow and took out a box of the cereal she'd learned was his favorite. With a wink, she gave it a shake.

"How about joining me for a bowl?"

He smiled then, so sweetly shy it broke her heart. "I guess if you're having some."

"Why don't you get the milk out, put it on the table?" Because it hurt to see how carefully, how deliberately, he performed the simple chore, she made her voice bright. "I heard on the radio we're in for some more snow. Maybe a big one."

She carried out bowls and spoons, set them down. When she lifted a hand to brush it over his tousled hair, he went very still. Cursing Joe Dolin, she kept the smile on her face. "I bet they close school tomorrow."

"I like school," he said then bit his lip.

"I always did, too." Brisk and determinedly cheerful, she breezed into the kitchen again for her coffee. "I never minded a day off now and again, but I really liked school. What's your favorite subject?"

"English class. I like to write things."

"Really? What kind of things?"

"Stories." He hunched his shoulders, looking down. "Just stupid stuff."

"I bet it's not." She could only hope she wasn't making a mistake, moving into territory best left to the experts. But her heart simply moved her hand. She cupped it under Connor's chin and lifted it gently as

she sat beside him. "You should be proud. I know
your mother's proud of you. She told me you won a
prize in your English class for a story you wrote."

"She did?" He was torn between wanting to smile
and wanting to let his head drop again. But Regan
had her hand on his face. It felt good there, warm.
The tears were in his eyes before he could stop them.
"She cries at night."

"I know, baby."

"He was always hitting her. I knew it. I could hear
them. But I never did anything to stop it. I never did
anything to help her."

"You're not to blame." Letting instinct rule, she
lifted him onto her lap, cuddling him close. "You're
not to blame, Connor. And there was nothing you
could have done. But now you and your mother and
your little sister are safe. You're all going to look
after each other."

"I hate him."

"Shh…" Jolted by how such fierceness could spurt
from someone so small, so young, Regan pressed her
lips to his hair and rocked.

In the hallway, Cassie stepped back. Torn in a
dozen different directions, she swayed there a moment, a hand over her mouth. Then she went back
into the little spare bedroom to wake her daughter for
school.

Regan arrived at the Barlow place just ahead of the
van and movers she'd hired. The cheerful noise of

construction blasted her the minute she opened the door. Nothing could have lifted her mood higher.

The hallway was draped with tarps and drop cloths. But the spiderwebs and the mustiness were gone. The dust that lay now was fresh, and somehow clean.

She supposed it was a kind of exorcism. Amused by the thought, she studied the stairway. As a kind of test, she walked toward it, started up.

The cold slapped her like a fist, sending her back two steps. She stood, one hand gripping the rail, the other pressed to her stomach as she struggled to get back the breath the icy air had stolen.

"You've got guts," Rafe murmured from behind her.

Though her eyes were still wide in shock, she looked down and met his levelly. "I wondered if it had just been my imagination. How do the laborers go up and down these steps without—?"

"Not everyone feels it. I'd say the ones who do grit their teeth and think about their paycheck." He walked up the steps to take her hand. "How about you?"

"I'd never have believed it if I hadn't experienced it." Without protest, she let him lead her down to the main level. "It should make for some interesting breakfast conversation among the guests, once you're open."

"Darling, I'm counting on it. Give me your coat. We've got the heat for this part of the house up and running." He slipped her coat off himself. "It's on low, but it takes the edge off."

"You're telling me." Pleased that it seemed warm enough to make shivering unnecessary, she flipped back her hair. "What's going on upstairs?"

"A little bit of everything. I'm putting in an extra bath. I want you to dig up one of those claw-foot tubs, a pedestal sink. Reproductions'll do, if you don't have any luck finding originals."

"Give me a few days. Well." She rubbed her hands together, not from cold, but nerves. "Are you going to show me, or do I have to beg?"

"I'm going to show you." He'd been itching to, looking out the window every five minutes to watch for her. But now that she was here, he was nervous. He'd slaved for more than a week, twelve- and four-teen-hour days, to make that one room, that one spot, that one step, perfect.

"I think the paint turned out." Rather than reach for her hand, he tucked his in his pockets and walked into the parlor ahead of her. "It's a nice contrast with the trim and the floor, I think. Had a little trouble with the windows, but I just had to diddle with the framing."

She didn't speak. For a moment, she merely stood in the doorway. Then, quietly, her boots clicking on the floor, she stepped inside.

It gleamed. The tall, elegant windows, with their graceful arches sent sun streaming over the newly polished floor of lovely old pine. The walls were a deep, warm blue against creamy carved trim in the most delicate of ivories.

He'd turned the window seat into a charming alcove, scrubbed the marble on the fireplace until it shone like glass. The molding along the ceiling bloomed with delicately carved florets that had been smothered and choked by the grime of decades.

"It needs furniture, drapes, and that mirror you picked out for over the mantel." He wished she would say something, anything. "I have to replace the pocket doors, yet." Scowling, he jammed his hands deeper into his pocket. "Well, what's the problem? Did I miss some vital, authentic detail?"

"It's absolutely wonderful." Enchanted, she ran a finger down the glossy trim of a window. "Absolutely perfect. I didn't realize you were this good." With a quick laugh, she glanced back at him. "That wasn't meant as an insult."

"It wasn't taken as one. I was pretty surprised myself, the first time I realized I had a talent for putting something together."

"It's more than that. It's bringing something to life. You must be proud."

He was, he realized, moved, and just a little embarrassed. "It's a job. Hammer and nails and a good eye."

She angled her head, and he watched the sun beam through the window and glow golden on her hair. His mouth watered, then went bone dry.

"You're the last man I'd expect to be modest about anything. You must have killed yourself to get so much accomplished in so little time."

"It was mostly cosmetic in here."

"You've done something," she murmured, and

looked around, turning a slow, graceful circle. "You've really done something."

Before he could comment, she was on her hands and knees, running her hands over the floor.

"It's like glass." She all but crooned over the golden planks. "Oh, look at the grain in this wood! What did you use? How many coats?" When he didn't answer, she tossed her head and sat back on her heels. The dazzled smile faded when he only stared at her. "What is it? What's wrong?"

"Stand up."

His voice was raw. As she rose to her feet, he kept his distance. He didn't dare touch her now. If he did, he'd simply never be able to stop.

"You look right in here. You should see yourself, how right you look. You're as polished and perfect as this room. I want you so much I can't see anything else but you."

Her heart did a long, unsteady cartwheel in her chest. "You're going to make me stutter again, Rafe." She had to make a conscious effort to pump air in and out of her lungs.

"How long are you going to make me wait?" he demanded. "We're not kids. We know what we feel and what we want."

"That's exactly the point. We're not kids, and we should be adult enough to be sensible."

"Sensible's for old lady's shoes. Sex may have to be responsible, but it sure as hell doesn't have to be sensible."

The thought of wicked, completely insensible sex with him numbed every nerve ending in her body. "I don't know how to handle you. I don't know how to handle the way you make me feel. I'm usually good at handling things. I guess we need to talk about this.''

"I guess you need to. I just said what I needed to say.'' Unbelievably frustrated, irrationally angry at his own helpless response to her, he turned to the window. "Your truck's here. I've got work upstairs. Put the stuff wherever the hell you want it.''

"Rafe—''

He stopped her, froze her before her hand could reach his arm. "You wouldn't want to touch me right now.'' His voice was quiet, very controlled. "It'd be a mistake. You don't like to make them.''

"That's not fair.''

"What the hell makes you think I'm fair?'' His eyes slashed her to ribbons. "Ask anybody who knows me. Your check's on the mantel.''

With her own temper sizzling, she stomped into the hall after him. "MacKade.''

He stopped on the steps, turned back. "Yeah?''

"I'm not interested in what anyone else thinks or says. If I were, you'd never have gotten within three feet of me.''

She glanced up as an interested laborer poked his head into the stairway. "Beat it,'' she snapped, and had Rafe's lips twitching reluctantly. "I make up my own mind, in my own time,'' she continued and turned on her heel to open the front door for the movers. "*You* ask anybody.''

When she looked back, he was gone, like one of his ghosts.

* * *

Nearly blew it, Rafe thought later. He wasn't entirely sure why he'd reacted that way. Anger and demands weren't his usual style with women. Maybe that, he mused as he troweled drywall compound on a seam, was the problem.

Women had always come easily.

He liked them, always had. The way they looked, thought, smelled, spoke. Soft, warm, fragrant, they were one of the more interesting aspects of life. Frowning, he slapped on more compound, smoothed it.

Women were important. He enjoyed cultivating them, the companionship they offered. And the sex, he acknowledged with a thin smile, he enjoyed that, too.

Hell, he was human.

Houses were important, he reflected, coating another seam of drywall. Repairing them was satisfying, using your own hands and sweat to turn them into something that lasted. And the money that came from the end result was satisfying, too.

A man had to eat.

But there'd never been a single house that was specifically important, as this one had come to be.

And there'd never been a single woman who was specifically important, as Regan had now become.

And he calculated that she would slice him into dog meat if she knew he was comparing her to stone and wood.

He doubted she would understand that it was the first time in his life he'd ever focused on something, and someone, so entirely.

The house had haunted him for a lifetime. He hadn't set eyes on her a month before. Yet they were both in his blood. He hadn't been exaggerating when he told her that he couldn't see anything but her. She was haunting him, just as the restless ghosts haunted these rooms and hallways.

Seeing her there that morning had turned him on his head, set his hormones raging, and he'd fumbled. He supposed he could make up ground. But this was the first time he could remember being tackled by emotion—emotion double-teamed with desire—and he wasn't at all sure of his moves.

Back off, MacKade, he told himself, and scooped more compound out of the bucket. She wants room, give her room. It wasn't as though he didn't have time—or as though she were some sort of life-altering encounter. Maybe she was unique, maybe she was more intriguing than he'd counted on. But she was still just a woman.

He heard the weeping, felt the stir of chilled air. With barely a hesitation, he leveled his seam.

"Yeah, yeah, I hear you," he muttered. "You might as well get used to company, 'cause I'm not going anywhere."

A door slammed. It amused him now, these endless little dramas. Footsteps and creaks, whispers and weeping. It was almost as though he were part of it all. A caretaker, he decided. Making the house livable for those who could never leave.

He thought it was too bad none of the permanent residents ever made an appearance. It would be quite an experience to see, as well as hear. An involuntary shudder worked up his back, as if fingers had trailed along his spine.

And feel, he thought.

Footsteps echoed down the hall outside as he moved to the next sheet of drywall. To his surprise and curiosity, they stopped just outside the door. He watched the knob turn, just as the work lamp behind him went out, plunging the room into darkness.

He'd have suffered torments from hell before admitting that his heart skipped several beats. To cover the lapse, he muttered oaths under his breath, rubbed his suddenly damp palms on his spattered jeans. From memory, he fumbled his way toward the door. It swung open fast and caught him full in the face.

He wasn't muttering oaths now, but spewing them. Stars were revolving in front of his eyes. And, with disgust, he felt blood trickle from his nose.

He heard the hoarse scream, saw the ghostly figure in the shadows of the hall, and didn't hesitate. Pain and fury had him shooting forward like a bullet. Ghost or not, anything that gave him a bloody nose was going to pay.

It took him several furious seconds to realize he had warm flesh wriggling in his arms, and little more to recognize the scent.

She was haunting him all right, he thought bitterly.

"What the hell are you doing?"

"Rafe?" Her voice squeaked out. In the dark, she threw up her arms, one flailing hand catching him sharply on the chin before she managed the whole-hearted embrace. "Oh, my God, you scared me to death. I thought— I don't know. I heard… I came up. Oh, it's you."

"What's left of me." Swearing, he set her firmly aside. There was enough light from the lamp hooked at the top of the stairs for him to see her pale face and huge eyes. "What are you doing here?"

"I picked up some things at auction and thought I'd put them— You're bleeding."

"No kidding." Scowling at her, he swiped a hand under his nose. "I don't think you broke it again. Quite."

"I—" She rubbed a hand over her heart to make sure it hadn't exploded from her chest. "Did I hit you with the door? I'm sorry. Here." She dug in the pocket of her jacket and found a tissue. "I'm really sorry," she repeated, and began to dab at the blood herself. "I was just…" Helpless, she tried to disguise a laugh as a hiccup. "I didn't realize." She gave up, wrapped her arms around her aching stomach, and slid to the floor.

"It's a real laugh riot."

"I'm sorry. I can't stop. I thought—I don't know what I thought. I heard them, or it, or whatever. I just had to come up and see, well, if I could see. Then you came barreling out."

"You're lucky I didn't punch you," he said, with relish.

"I know. I know."

His eyes narrowed as he watched her fold with mirth. "I still could."

"Oh, help me up." Still chuckling, she wiped at her eyes. "Let's get some ice on that nose."

"I can take care of it myself." But he took hold of her wrist and hauled her, none too gently, to her feet.

"Did I scare you?" She tried to keep her voice meek and apologetic as she followed him to the stairs.

"Get real."

"But you heard—you heard it, didn't you?" She braced, held her breath as they passed through the cold spot.

"Sure, I heard it. Goes on every night. A couple times during the day."

"And it doesn't…bother you?"

It boosted his ego to be able to flick a disdainful glance over his shoulder. "Why should it bother me? It's their house, too."

"I suppose." She looked around the kitchen. It was all but bare, and still grimy. There was a small, dented refrigerator, a stove that was down to two working burners, and an old door propped on sawhorses that served as a table. Rafe went directly to the pitted cast-iron sink and ran cold water. "Do you have a clean rag?"

In lieu of an answer, he bent over and scooped icy

water onto his face. Adopting a shamed pose, Regan folded her hands.

"I'm really terribly sorry, Rafe. Does it hurt?"

"Yes."

He snatched up a frayed towel and dried his face. Without another word, he strode to the refrigerator and pulled out a beer.

"It's stopped bleeding."

He twisted off the top, tossed it aside, then downed a third of the bottle. Regan decided that, under the circumstances, she could try again.

"I didn't see your car. That's why I didn't think anyone was here."

"Devin dropped me off." He decided that, under the circumstances, he could give her a break. "I've been putting in some extra time at night, camping out here. We're supposed to get hit with a snowstorm tonight, so it didn't make any sense to have the car. I can walk into town if I need to."

"Oh. Well. That explains it."

"Want a beer?"

"No thanks, I don't drink beer."

"Fresh out of champagne."

"Well, then, I really should be getting back. Actually, it's already starting to snow." Feeling awkward now, she pushed at her hair. "Ah, there were these candlesticks, and a really wonderful set of fire irons I bought today. I just wanted to bring them by, see how they looked."

He lifted the beer again, watching her. "So, how do they look?"

"I don't know. I set everything down in the hall when I came in and heard the, ah, evening performance."

"You decided to go ghost hunting instead of decorating."

"Looks that way. Well, why don't I set them up now, before I take off?"

Taking the beer along, he went with her. "I guess you've cooled off since this morning."

"Not exactly." She spared him a brief look as she headed to the main hall. "Though giving you a bloody nose, even inadvertently, was satisfying. You acted like a jerk."

His eyes narrowed as she picked up the box she'd left in the hall and sailed into the parlor. "I was giving it to you straight. Some women appreciate honesty."

"Some women like jerks." She set the box on a drum table she'd had the movers place at the window. "I don't. I like simplicity, manners, tact. Which, of course, you're completely without." Then she turned, and smiled. "But I think, under the circumstances, a truce is in order. Who broke your nose before?"

"Jared, when we were kids and fighting in the hayloft. He got lucky."

"Hmm..." She supposed she would never understand why brotherly affection meant bloody noses to the MacKades. "So this is where you're camping out." She gestured toward the sleeping bag tossed in front of the fire.

"It's the warmest room in the house right now. And the cleanest. What circumstances equal a truce?"

"Don't set that bottle down without a coaster." Heaving a sigh, she walked over, took one from the silver-plated basket and offered it. "You can't treat antiques like..."

"Furniture?" he finished, but he used the coaster. "What circumstances, Regan?"

"Our ongoing business relationship, for one." Because her fingers were tense again, she busied them by unbuttoning her coat as she walked back to the window. "We're both trying to accomplish the same thing with this house, so it doesn't make sense to be at odds. These are nice, aren't they?" She took the fire irons from the box, stroked a finger over the curved handle of the coal shovel. "They could use some polish."

"It ought to work better than the crowbar I've been using." Tucking his thumbs in his pockets, he watched her carry the irons to the fire, set them carefully and individually in their stand on the stone hearth.

"Whatever you used, it's a nice fire." Torn between courage and doubt, she stared at the flames. "I'm still looking for the right screen. This one doesn't really suit. It would be better in one of the rooms upstairs. I imagine you'll have them all working. The fireplaces."

"Eventually."

He'd only known her for a few weeks, he realized. How could he be so sure she was arguing with herself? With the firelight flickering over her, her back so straight, that sweep of hair curtaining half her face, she looked relaxed, confident, perfectly at ease. Maybe it was the way she had her fingers linked together, or the way she wasn't looking at him. But he was certain some small inner war was being waged.

"Why are you here, Regan?"

"I told you." Dragging her fingers apart, she went back to the box. "I have some other stuff from the auction in my car, but you're not ready for it. But these..." With care, she unwrapped heavy crystal candlesticks. "I could see them in here, right on this table. You'll want flowers for this vase. Even in the winter."

She fussed with the arrangement, placing the candlesticks just so on one side of the Doulton vase she'd already sold him.

"Tulips would be lovely, when you can get them," she continued, carefully unwrapping the two white tapers she'd brought along. "But mums would do, and roses, of course." She put a smile on her face again and turned. "There, what do you think?"

Saying nothing, he took a box of wooden matches from the mantel and walked over to light the tapers. And watched her over the delicate twin flames. "They work."

"I meant the whole effect, the room." It was a good excuse to move away from him, wandering the space, running a finger along the curved back of the settee.

"It's perfect. I didn't expect any less from you."

"I'm not perfect." The words burst out of her, unexpected on both sides. "You make me nervous when you say so. I was always expected to be perfect, and I'm just not. I'm not carefully arranged, like this room, with every piece in place, no matter how much I want to be. I'm a mess." She dragged nervous fingers through her hair. "And I wasn't, before. I wasn't. No, stay over there." She backed up quickly when he stepped forward. "Just stay over there."

Frustrated, she waved her hands to ward him off, then paced. "You scared me this morning. You made me angry, but more, you scared me."

It wasn't easy for Rafe to keep his hands to himself. "How?"

"Because no one's ever wanted me the way you do. I know you do." She stopped, rubbing her hands over her arms. "You look at me as though you already know how it's going to be with us. And I have no control over it."

"I figured I was giving you control, laying it out for you."

"No. No," she repeated, flinging up her arms. "I don't have any control over the way I'm feeling. You have to know that. You know exactly the way you affect people."

"We're not talking about people."

"You know exactly the way you affect *me*." She almost shouted it before she fisted her hands and fought for composure. "You know I want you. Why wouldn't I? It's just as you said, we're adults who know what we want. And the more I backpedal, the more stupid I feel.''

His eyes were shadowed in the shifting light. ''You're going to stand there and say these things to me and expect me to do nothing about it?''

''I expect to be able to make a sane and rational decision. I don't expect my glands to overwhelm my brain.'' She blew out a breath. ''Then I look at you and I want to rip your clothes off.''

He had to laugh. It was the safest way to defuse the bomb ticking inside of him. ''Don't expect me to stop you.'' When he stepped forward, she jumped back like a spring. ''Just the beer,'' he muttered, lifting the bottle. ''I need it.'' He took a long, deep gulp, but it didn't do much to put out the fire. ''So, what have we got here, Regan? Two unattached, healthy adults who want pretty much the same thing from each other.''

''Who barely know each other,'' she added. ''Who've barely scratched the surface of any sort of relationship. Who should have more sense than to jump into sex as if it was a swimming pool.''

''I never bother testing the water.''

''I do. An inch at a time.'' Ordering herself to be calm, she linked her hands again. ''It's important to me to know exactly what I'm getting into, exactly where I'm going.''

''No detours?''

''No. When I plan something, I stick to it. That works for me.'' She was calmer now, she told herself. Rational now. ''I had a lot of time to think, driving to Pennsylvania and back. We need to slow down, take a look at the whole picture.''

If she was calm, why couldn't she stop fiddling with her blazer, twisting her rings?

"It's like this house," she continued quickly. "You've finished one room, and it's beautiful, it's wonderful. But you didn't start this project without a complete plan in mind for the rest of it. I think intimacy should certainly be as carefully thought out as the renovation of a house."

"Makes sense."

"Good." She drew in a breath, released it. "So, we'll take a few steps back, get a clearer view of things." Her hand was still unsteady when she reached for her coat. "That's the sensible, the responsible route to take."

"Yeah." He set down his beer. "Regan?"

She gripped her coat like a lifeline. "Yes."

"Stay."

Her fingers went numb. Her breath came out in a long, shuddering sigh. "I thought you'd never ask."

With a jittery laugh, she threw herself into his arms.

Chapter 6

"This is crazy." Already breathless, she curled her fingers into his hair to drag his mouth to hers. Everything in her strained into the kiss, the heat of it, the danger, the promise. "I wasn't going to do this."

"That's okay." He dragged his lips from hers to race over her face. "I'll do it."

"I'd thought it all through." When her knees trembled, she gave a quick, helpless laugh. "I had. Everything I just said made perfect sense. This is just chemistry. It's just superficial attraction."

"Yeah." In one fluid movement, he yanked her blazer down her shoulders, locking her arms, trapping her body to his. Her gasp of alarm stirred his blood. The huge, wary eyes tightened his loins. "Stop thinking."

A smile curved his lips as he tugged the bunched

material, pressing her against him. He watched her eyes glaze, heard the ragged moan when his mouth fed on hers. Then his lips rushed down over the line of her throat. It was as smooth, as scented, as he'd imagined it. So he feasted.

Her hands clutched at his hips, her head falling back to offer him whatever he chose to take. All the while the heat coursed through her painfully, forcing her breath out in harsh, ragged moans.

With a jerk, he freed her arms. Before she could reach out, his hands, his wide, clever hands, streaked under her sweater to mold, to possess.

Flesh and lace, curves and shudders. He found everything he wanted, and wanted more. His mouth continued its relentless assault, while his fingers tortured her skin, and her skin tortured him.

With a flick of his wrist, he unsnapped her trousers, then skimmed the tips of his fingers along her quivering belly, under the edge of more lace. She moved against him, pressed urgently against him, her teeth scraping along his neck in greedy bites.

He could take her now, fast and hot, where they stood. The speed would release this terrible pressure that burned inside him.

But he wanted more.

He dragged the sweater over her head, tossed it aside and filled his palms with her breasts. The lace covering was smooth, delicate, and the flesh beneath already flushed and warm with desire. Ruthlessly controlling the pounding need to rush, Rafe watched her face, the flicker of light and shadow over it, while he rubbed his work-roughened thumbs over the points of her breasts.

"I've imagined you like this."

"I know."

His lips curved again, and his eyes were focused keenly on hers when he nudged a slim strap down her shoulder. "I don't think you've imagined what I've thought of doing to you. I don't think you could. So I'm going to show you."

His eyes stayed on hers, watching, measuring, as he skimmed a finger along the valley between her breasts, up over the curve, then back to flick open the center clasp.

So he saw that lovely sky blue gaze darken with the storm he set off inside her. And he felt it quake, in both of them.

Her breath caught in her throat when he jerked her off her feet and set his hungry mouth to work. Shocked, she arched back, her hands fumbling in his hair, over his shoulders, tugging desperately at his shirt. His teeth nipped into her, just short of savage, just short of pain. His tongue tormented, and aroused needs too violent to bear.

Wild, frantic, she clawed at him. Even as she felt herself falling, she tore and ripped at his shirt. She was on her back, on the thin cushion of the sleeping bag, and bucking desperately beneath him.

Finally she tugged his shirt away, cursing when she found yet another layer separating them. She wanted flesh, craved it with a mindless hunger. The moment he'd dragged the thin undershirt aside, she sank her teeth into his shoulder.

"Touch me." Her words were raw and urgent. "I want your hands on me."

They were, everywhere at once. Her world became primitive, dangerously exciting, pumped full to bursting with unspeakable sensations. Each rough, impatient caress sent fresh shocks erupting, until her body was nothing but sweaty flesh over sparking nerves.

Beside her, the fire shot hissing embers against the screen. Inside her, flames leapt and burned.

She could see him through the haze that blurred her vision. The dark hair, the fierce eyes, the muscles that glistened with sweat in the dance of light. Her moan of protest when his mouth left hers turned to one of giddy pleasure as his lips streaked down over throat, over breasts and torso.

He levered back and, blind with need, she reared up, her arms circling possessively, her lips searching for each new taste.

His oath was brief and vicious. "Boots," he managed, fighting to pry hers off while his blood screamed. She was draped around him, that wonderful body sliding over his, her hands... Those incredible elegant hands.

Boots thudded where he heaved them aside, then, quick as a snake, turned to take her.

She was tangled around him, all long, silky limbs. He wanted her naked and writhing beneath him. He wanted to hear her scream his name and watch the jolts and shocks of pleasure glaze her eyes. Breath ragged, he dragged the slacks down her hips. In one reckless swipe, he tore the lace to shreds. Even as her gasp echoed off the walls, he shoved her back. And used his mouth.

The climax slammed into her, a bare-knuckled punch that knocked her senseless. Reeling from it, she sobbed out his name. And, shuddering, shuddering, hungered for more.

He gave her more. And took more. Each time she thought he would end it, must end it, he found some new way to batter her senses. There was only him, the taste, the feel, the smell of him. They rolled over the floor in a wild, glorious combat, her nails digging ruthlessly into his back, his mouth searing hers.

Nearly blinded by need, he gripped her hands, fingers vised. He thought his own breathing must tear his lungs apart. Her face was all he could see as he drove himself into her. Twin groans mixed. A log shattered thunderously in the grate.

They trembled, watching each other as they savored that timeless instant of mating.

Muscles straining, he lowered his head, covered her mouth. When the kiss was at its deepest, when her flavor filled him as intimately as he was filling her, they began to move together.

It was the cold that finally roused Regan. Though it seemed impossible, she thought she must have fallen asleep. As she struggled to orient herself, she discovered her back was against the cold, hard wood of the floor, pressed firmly against it by the weight of Rafe's body.

She looked around dazedly. Somehow or other, they'd gotten themselves several feet from the fire.

"You awake now?" Rafe's voice was thick, a little sleepy.

"I guess." She tried a deep breath, was relieved to find she could accomplish it. "I can't really tell."

He shifted his head, skimmed his lips over the curve of her breast. Her exhausted body quivered in response.

"I guess I can tell after all," she said.

"You're cold." He shifted, hauled her up and put her back on the sleeping bag. Wished, for her, that it was a feather bed. "Better?"

"Yeah." Not quite sure of her moves, she tugged a corner of the bag up to her chin. She'd never been so exposed, so completely naked, body and soul, before anyone. "I must have dozed off."

"Just a couple minutes." He grinned at her. He felt as though he'd climbed a mountain. And could climb ten more. "I'll put another log on."

Naked and easy, he rose to go to the woodbox. The scratches scoring his shoulders had Regan's mouth falling open. She'd done that. She'd actually... Good God. "I, ah, should go. Cassie'll be worried."

Rafe set the screen back in place. Without a word, he reached into the duffel bag beside the woodbox and took out a cell phone. "Call her."

"I...didn't realize you had a phone."

"It's a tool on a job like this." He handed it to

her, then sat down beside her. "Call her," he repeated. "And stay."

She was sure there were reasons why she should go. But she dialed her own number, watching Rafe as the phone rang.

"Cassie, it's Regan. Yes, everything's fine. Snow?" Baffled for a moment, she pushed her hair away from her face. "Oh, yes, it's really coming down. That's why I'm calling. I got, um, involved, and I think…"

She trailed off as Rafe tugged the corner of the bag out of her hand, as his fingers trailed down the curve of her breast.

"What?" She swallowed, then bit back a moan. His mouth had replaced his fingers. She slid bonelessly to her back. "Pennsylvania?" she murmured. "No, I'm not in Pennsylvania."

Rafe took the phone from her limp fingers. "She's with me. She's staying with me. No kidding? She'll call you tomorrow. Right."

He clicked the phone off, set it aside. "Cassie says we've got over a foot out there, the streets are a mess, and you should stay put."

"Oh." She closed her eyes, lifted her arms. "That's very sensible."

The candles had guttered out and the fire had burned to embers when she awoke. The house was so still, so quiet, she could hear her own heartbeat. The room was filled with shadows and darkness, but it was oddly peaceful. Perhaps the ghosts slept, she mused.

Or perhaps she felt at ease with them because Rafe slept beside her.

She turned her head and studied his face in the dying firelight. Asleep or not, she mused, there was no innocent-little-boy look about him. All that power, and the potential for violence, were still there, carved into his face.

She knew he could be gentle, caring. She'd seen that in the way he was with Cassie. But as a lover, he was demanding, relentless and rough.

And, for the first time in her life, she'd been the same.

Now, with the quiet like a blanket over her, she found it hard to believe she had done what she'd done, had allowed him—wanted him—to do what he had done.

Her body ached from bruises, and she wondered if in the full light of day she would wince at the memory of how she'd come by them. Of how she'd ached and trembled and hungered under those big, hard hands.

Even more, of how she'd used her own.

Of how, she realized with a jolt, she wanted to use them now.

Taking a shallow breath, she eased out from under Rafe's possessive arm. She moved as quietly as she could, settled on slipping on his flannel shirt for covering. Buttoning it as she went, she padded toward the kitchen.

A cold drink of water, she told herself. A few moments to evaluate the situation.

At the sink, she filled a glass. As her eyes adjusted,

she watched the drift of snow falling outside the window.

She didn't regret. That, she mused, would be foolish. Fate had placed an extraordinary lover in her path. The kind of man few women ever knew. She could, and would, be content with the physical thrill of it. She could, and would, prevent it, and him, from complicating her life.

They were both adults, as he had said. They both knew what they wanted. When the house was finished, he would probably grow restless and move on. Meanwhile they would enjoy each other. And when it was over, it would end with mutual understanding, and, she hoped, affection.

It would probably be wise to discuss those expectations, or the lack of them, before things went any further. But she found herself torn at the very idea of voicing them.

From the doorway, Rafe studied her, the way she stood, leaning a little on the counter, her eyes on the window. Her face reflected in it. His shirt skimmed her thighs, worn flannel against creamy skin.

It struck him, hard, that he'd never in his life seen anything more beautiful. He had the words to tell her; he was good with them. But he found there were none this time, none good enough to show how much she mattered.

So he chose easy ones, casual ones, and ignored the ache just looking at her had spreading around his heart.

"I like your dress, darling."

She jolted, nearly bobbled the glass before she turned. He'd tugged on jeans, but hadn't bothered to fasten them. Grinning, he leaned against the unframed doorway.

"It was handy," she said, matching his tone.

"That old shirt's never had it so good. Restless?"

"I was thirsty." But she set the glass down without taking so much as a sip. "I guess the quiet woke me. It's odd, don't you think, how quiet it is?"

"The snow always makes it quiet."

"No, I mean the house. It seems different. Settled."

"Even dead soldiers and unhappy women have to sleep sometime." He crossed the room to pick up the glass and drink himself. "It's almost dawn," he murmured. "My brothers and I spent the night here once when we were kids. I guess I told you that already."

"Jared rattling chains. And all of you telling ghost stories and smoking stolen cigarettes."

"You got it. I came into this room then, too. It was just about this time of day, but it was late summer. Everything was so green, and the woods were so dense and thick they made you wonder what was in them. There was a mist over the ground like a river. It was beautiful, and I thought—" He broke off, shrugged.

"No." She laid a hand on his arm. "Tell me."

"I thought I could hear the drums, slowly, the sounds of camps breaking to prepare for battle. I could smell the fear, the excitement, the dread. I thought I could hear the house waking around me, the whispers and creaks. I was petrified, paralyzed. If I could have moved, I'd have hauled my butt out of here. The guys would've rubbed my nose in it for years, but I'd have run like a rabbit if my legs had moved.''

''You were just a boy.''

''You've never been a boy, so you don't know that made it ten times worse. I'd gotten through the night, even gotten a kick out of it. And here it was morning, dawn breaking, and I stood here with my teeth chattering. When it passed, I just stood looking out this window. And I thought, no damn house is going to get the better of me. Nothing's going to get the better of me. I'll own this house before I'm finished.''

He smiled then, set the glass down. ''I don't know how many times I came back here, alone, after that. Waiting for something to happen, wishing it would, just so I could stand up to it. I crept through every room of this place at one time or another. I heard things, saw things, felt things. The night I left town, I promised myself I'd come back.''

''Now you have it,'' she said quietly.

''Yeah.'' Faintly embarrassed, he looked down at her. ''I never told anyone that.''

''Then neither will I.'' She lifted a hand, touched his cheek. ''Whatever your reasons, you're doing something important. This house has been neglected too long.''

''Were you frightened, staying here through the night?''

''No. Not of the house.''

His brow lifted. "Of me?"

"Yes. I'm frightened of you."

The humor faded from his eyes. "I was rough with you," he said carefully.

"I don't mean that." She turned away. Out of habit, she set a kettle on the stove, flicked on the burner. "I've never been the way I was last night, with anyone. So out of control. So…needy. I'm a little surprised when I think back and… Well." She let out a shaky breath, searched out a filter for the drip cone.

"Surprised? Or sorry?"

"Not sorry, Rafe." Making the effort, she turned back and met his eyes. "No, not sorry at all. Uneasy, because I know now exactly what you can do to me. I knew making love with you would be exciting. I didn't know it would be so shattering. Nothing about you is tidy or predictable. The way I like things to be."

"I want you now. That should be predictable."

"My heart jumps," she managed. "Literally, when you say things like that. But I do need things to be tidy." Opening the can of coffee, she deliberately measured out scoops. "I imagine your men will be coming along in an hour or so. This probably isn't the best time to talk this out."

"Nobody's coming today. There's better than two feet of snow out there, on top of what we already had."

"Oh." Her hand faltered, spilling ground coffee on the stove.

"We're snowbound for a while, darling. You can talk all you want."

"Well." After clearing her throat, she faced him again. "I just think it's best if we both understood things."

"What things?"

"Things." She bit the word off, furious at herself for hesitating. "Things that we didn't quite finish outlining last night. That what we're having is a mutual satisfying and physical affair, no strings, no entanglements, no..."

"Complications?"

"Yes." Relieved, she nodded. "Exactly."

Surprised to find himself annoyed with her coolheaded description—one that should have mirrored his own wishes—he scratched his head. "That's tidy enough. But if that means you're planning on seeing somebody else, it'll get messy when I break him in half."

"Oh, of all the ridiculous—"

"And cut off his—"

"Stop that." She blew out a heated breath. "I have no intention of seeing someone else while we're involved, but if I—"

"Smarter to stop there," he said quietly. "Let's just say we have a mutually satisfying and exclusive physical relationship. That suit you?"

Calmer, she turned back to pour boiling water through the filter. "Yes, I can agree to that."

"You're a piece of work, Regan. You want the contract in triplicate?"

"I only want to make sure we expect the same things." She concentrated hard on covering the grounds with water, on being sure not to pour too much water, or too little. "We haven't taken time to really get to know each other. Now we're lovers. I don't want you to think I'm looking for any more than that."

"And if I'm looking for more?"

Her fingers whitened on the handle of the kettle. "Are you?"

He looked away from her, toward the window and the softly falling snow. "No."

She closed her eyes, telling herself it was relief she felt at his answer. Only relief. "Well, then there's no problem."

"No, everything's dandy." His voice was as cool and detached as hers. "You don't want romance, saves me the trouble. You don't want promises, I don't have to lie. We want each other in bed." He reached for two mugs. "That keeps it simple."

"I want you in bed." Pleased with her casual tone, she took the mugs from him. "But if I didn't like who you are, we wouldn't have gotten there. I've wanted other men."

In a deceptively calm gesture, he flicked her hair behind her ear. "Now you're trying to make me mad."

The fact that he couldn't see how difficult it was for her to be so open, to keep things simple, made it easier. Oddly enough, this kind of openness seemed completely natural with him. "I'm trying to give you a compliment. I wouldn't have come here last night, hoping you'd be here, if I hadn't cared about you.''

"You came to drop off candlesticks.''

"You're an idiot.'' Amused at both of them, she poured coffee. She hadn't realized sexual frankness could be fun. "You didn't really buy that, did you?''

Intrigued, he took the mug she offered. "Yeah, I did.''

She sipped, smiled. "Sucker.''

"Maybe I don't like sneaky, aggressive women.''

"Yes, you do. In fact, you're hoping I'll seduce you right now.''

"Think so?''

"I know so. But I want my coffee first.''

He watched her take another delicate sip. "Maybe I want my shirt back. You didn't ask if you could borrow it.''

"Fine.'' With one hand, she undid the buttons. "Take it.''

He nipped the coffee from her hand, set both mugs aside. Her smug smile had him scooping her off her feet. She was laughing and assaulting his ear as he carried her back down the hall. The front door swung open, letting in cold and blowing snow and a figure crusted with white.

Shane dragged off his cap and shook himself like a dog. "Hey.'' Casually he kicked the door closed. "Your car's buried to the wheel wells, Regan.''

"Oh.'' With a fumbling hand, she clutched the shirt together and tried to mirror his easy tone. "We got a lot of snow.''

"Over two feet." Unabashed, he grinned at his brother. "Figured you'd need someone to plow you out."

"Does it look like I want you to rescue me?" Disgusted, Rafe strode into the parlor and dumped Regan on the settee. "Stay right there."

"Rafe!" Futilely she tried to tug the hem of the shirt down over her legs. "For heaven's sake!"

"Right there," he repeated, and headed back into the hall.

"That coffee I smell?" Shane asked conversationally. "I could use some."

"Give me one reason why I shouldn't break your neck."

Shane took off his gloves, blew on his chilled fingers. "'Cause I rode over here in a blizzard to save yours." He leaned forward, but couldn't quite see into the parlor. "She's sure got legs."

"Where do you want to die?"

"Just an observation." His grin only widened, the MacKade dimple flashing. "Hey, who knew? I figured you were stuck here, without transportation. Alone. Then, when I saw her car, I thought maybe she needed a lift into town." Again he inched forward, hopeful. "Maybe I should ask her."

"One more step and they won't find your body till spring."

"If I win, can I keep her?" When Rafe snarled, Shane erupted with laughter. "Don't hit me, I'm frozen. I'll break."

Muttering threats, Rafe grabbed Shane by the collar

and dragged him down the hall. "Eyes front, MacKade." In the kitchen, he found a thermos, filled it with coffee. "Now beat it."

"I'm going." But Shane drank straight from the thermos. "The wind's a bitch." Grateful for the heat, he drank again. "Look, I didn't mean to horn in on your little love nest," he began, then stopped, lowered the thermos when he read quick fury in Rafe's eyes. "Hey, are you serious about her?"

"Mind your own damn business."

Shane whistled out a breath, screwed the top on the thermos. "You've always been my business. Regan's a real lady. I mean that."

"So?"

"So nothing." Embarrassed now, Shane shifted position. "I like her, always have. I thought about…" Realizing he'd taken a wrong turn, he pulled out his gloves again and whistled a cheerful tune.

"Thought about what?"

Cautious, Shane ran his tongue around his teeth. He really wanted to keep all of them. "Just what you think I thought. Hell, look at her. A man's bound to think." Agile, he evaded Rafe's lunging arm. "Think is all I did. I'm not going to fight you over thinking." In a gesture of peace, he threw up his hands. "What I'm saying is, it's great. You hit the jackpot."

Temper vanished. Rafe reached for the pot again. "We're sleeping together. That's all."

"You gotta start somewhere."

"She's different, Shane." He hadn't been able to admit it to himself, but it came easily brother to brother. "I haven't sorted it out, but she's different. She matters a lot."

"Everybody's got to take the big fall sometime." Shane slapped a hand on Rafe's bare shoulder. "Even you."

"I didn't say anything about falling," Rafe muttered. He knew the implications of that. Falling in love. Being in love.

"You didn't have to. Look, I'll plow the lane, just in case. You got any food around here?"

"Yeah, there's enough."

"I'll take off, then. It's supposed to let up by midmorning. I have animals to tend to, so if you need something, try Devin first. I might be out."

"Thanks. Shane?" He turned, eyeing his brother. "If you so much as glance in that parlor on your way out, I'll have to kill you."

"I already got a good look at her legs." Whistling cheerfully, Shane ambled down the hall. "See you, Regan." It cost him, but he kept his eyes averted on his way to the door.

The minute she heard it slam, Regan pressed her face on her updrawn knees. Stepping into the parlor, Rafe winced at her defensive posture, her trembling shoulders.

"Look, darling, I'm sorry. I should have locked the damn door." Gently he patted her shoulder and sat down beside her. "Shane doesn't mean to be an idiot. He was born that way. He doesn't mean any harm. Don't be upset."

She made a strangled sound, and when she lifted

her face, it was wet with tears. Her laughter bubbled out like wine. "Can you imagine what we looked like, the three of us, in that hall?" She pressed her hand over her mouth and rocked. "The two of us half-naked, Shane looking like the abominable snowman."

"You think that's funny?"

"No, I think it's hysterical." Weak with laughter, she collapsed against him. "The MacKade brothers. Oh, God, what have I gotten myself into?"

Delighted with her, he hauled her into his lap. "Give me back my shirt, darling, and I'll show you."

Chapter 7

Cozy in the sleeping bag, Regan dozed by the fire. It sizzled, logs crackling, and brushed heat over her face and her outflung arm. She sighed, cruising with the dream, shifting toward her lover.

Her dreams were nearly as erotic as the reality of the past hours, vivid enough to have her stirring, and yearning. When she reached out and found herself alone, she sighed again, in disappointment.

The fire was lively, so she knew Rafe had built it up once more before he left her. The room was quiet enough that she could hear the ticking of the mantel clock marking time. Evidence of the night's activities was all around her, in the hastily strewn clothes littering the floor, the torn bits of lace and the jumbled boots. And the evidence was within her as she stretched, feeling the warm glow of desire.

She wished he was there, so that he could stoke it as he had stoked the fire.

Still, it was a wonderful shock to realize she could lay claim to such a bottomless well of passion.

It had never been so before, she reflected, sitting up to exercise her stiff and sore muscles. Physical relationships had always been far down on her list of priorities. She wondered if, after her recent behavior, Rafe would be surprised to know that before him, she had considered herself hesitant, even a little shy, when it came to intimacy.

With a yawn, she reached for her sweater and pulled it over her head.

Knowing him, she decided, he'd just be smug.

It was a pity she couldn't blame her celibacy of the past few years for her wildfire response to him. It felt as though her libido had been nothing more than dry timber set to the torch the moment he put his hands on her. But using abstinence as the major reason for her response would be far from honest.

Whatever her life had been before, he'd changed it just by stepping into her path. It was certain she would never look at cozy nights by a fire in the same way again. It was doubtful she would look at anything in quite the same way again, she mused, now that she knew what she was capable of with the right...mate.

Just how, she wondered, did a woman go back to a quiet, settled life once she'd had a taste of Rafe MacKade? That was something she was going to have to deal with, one cautious day at a time.

At the moment, the only thing she wanted was to find him.

In her stocking feet, she began to wander the house. He could be anywhere, and the challenge of hunting him down, finding him busy with some chore—one she was determined to distract him from—amused her.

The chill of the bare floors seeped through and had her rubbing her hands together for a little warmth. But curiosity far overweighed a little discomfort.

She'd been through the first-floor rooms only twice before. First on her initial viewing to take notes and measurements. The second time to recheck them. But there were no workmen now, no sounds of voices or hammering.

She slipped into the room beyond the parlor, dreaming a bit.

This would be the library—glossy shelves filled with books, deep-cushioned chairs inviting a guest to curl up to read. A library table would stand there, she mused, a Sheraton if she could find one, with a decanter of brandy, a vase of seasonal flowers, an old pewter inkwell.

Library steps, of course, she continued visualizing, seeing it all perfectly, almost to the grain of wood. And the wide-backed chairs near the crackling fire would need cozy footstools.

She wanted a reading stand in the far corner, one with a cabriole base. She'd set a big, old Bible with gilt-edged pages open on it.

there. Figured out I was better at swinging a hammer than running a plow.'' Out of habit, he reached into his shirt pocket, found it empty. Swore. ''Quit smoking,'' he muttered.

''Good for you.''

''It's driving me nuts.'' To keep himself busy, he walked over to check a seam he'd finished the night before.

''You went to Florida,'' she said prompting him.

''Yeah, that's where I ended up. Lots of construction work in Florida. I started buying houses—dumps—fixing them up, turning them over. Did pretty well. So I came back.'' He turned to her. ''That's about it.''

''I wasn't prying,'' she began.

''I didn't say you were. There just isn't much to it, Regan. I had a rep when I left here. Spent my last night in town in a bar fight. With Joe Dolin.''

''I wondered if there was history there,'' she murmured.

''Not much of one.'' He slipped off the bandanna he'd twisted at his forehead to keep the hair out of his eyes, stuffed it in his pocket. ''We just hated each other's guts.''

''I'd say your taste in enemies is excellent.''

Restless again, he moved his shoulders. ''If it hadn't been him, it would have been somebody else. I was in the mood that night.'' His grin flashed, but there wasn't much humor in it. ''Hell, I was usually in the mood to cause trouble. Nobody ever figured I'd amount to anything, not even me.''

He snatched her hand. "What kind of bet?"

She laughed, tugged him into the hall. "Rafe, I'm joking. Give me a tour."

"Just hold on. MacKades never back down from a dare."

"I'm daring you to quote Shelley?" She sighed, shook her head. "Okay, I dare you."

"No, that's not how it works." Considering, he lifted her hand, nibbled on her fingers. The flicker of arousal in her eyes inspired him. "I say I can have you so crazy about me within a month that you'll wiggle into a leather miniskirt. A red one. Walk into the tavern for beer and nine-ball."

Arousal turned quickly into amusement. "What odd fantasies you have, MacKade. Can you actually see me in some tarty little skirt, playing pool?"

The smile turned wicked. "Oh, yeah. I can see that just fine. Make sure you wear those really high heels, too. The skinny ones."

"I never wear leather without stilettos. Anything less would be tacky."

"And no bra."

Her laughed puffed out. "Really into this, aren't you?"

"I'm getting there. You'll do it, too." He cupped a hand on her hip to nudge her closer. "Because you'll be crazy about me."

"It's obvious one of us has already lost his mind. Okay." Not one to refuse a challenge, she put a hand on his chest, pushed him back. "I say within that same period of time, I'll have you on your knees, clutching a bouquet of…ah…lilacs—''

"Lilacs?''

"Yes, I'm very fond of lilacs. You'll quote Shelley like a champ.''

"What's the winner get?''

"Satisfaction.''

He had to smile. ''That ought to be enough. Deal.'' They shook hands on it. ''Am I going to get that tour now?''

"Sure.'' He draped an arm around her shoulders and entertained himself with the vision of those very fine legs beneath a tight red skirt. ''We went with your idea of a kind of bridal suite.'' He led the way down the hall, opened a six-paneled door. ''Just about ready for trim work in here.''

"Rafe.'' Delighted, she stepped inside.

The delicate floral wallpaper was nearly all hung. The coffered ceiling gleamed with fresh paint. French doors were in place, and would one day open onto the wide porch, overlook gardens in riotous bloom. The floor was covered with drop cloths, but she could imagine it glossy and accented with a lovely faded tapestry rug.

She stepped around buckets and ladders, already arranging furniture in her head. ''It's going to be beautiful,'' she murmured.

"It's coming along.'' He lifted a tarp from the fireplace. ''The mantel was shot. I couldn't fix it. Found a good piece of yellow pine, though. The wood-worker's using the original as a guide.''

"That rose-colored trim is going to be wonderful in here." She looked through an adjoining doorway. "And this is the bath."

"Mmm…" He studied the room over her shoulder. It was good-sized, and the plumbers had roughed it in. "Used to be a dressing room."

She reached for his hand, gripped it. "Can you smell it?"

"Roses." Absently he rubbed his cheek over her hair. "It always smells like roses in here. One of the paper hangers accused his partner of wearing perfume."

"This was her room, wasn't it? Abigail's. She died in here."

"Probably. Hey." He tipped up her face, watched uncomfortably as a tear trailed down her cheek. "Don't."

"It's so sad. She must have been terribly unhappy. Knowing the man she'd married, the father of her children, was capable of such cold-blooded cruelty. How did he treat her, Rafe? Did he love her, or did he only own her?"

"There's no way to know. Don't cry." Awkward, he brushed the tear away. "It makes me feel like I have six thumbs. I mean it." For lack of something better to do, he patted her head. "There's no use crying over something that happened more than a hundred years ago."

"But she's still here." Wrapping her arms around him, Regan snuggled into his chest. "I feel so sorry for her, for all of them."

"You're not going to do yourself, or me, any good if you get tangled up every time you come in here."

"I know." She sighed, comforted by the way his heart beat strong and steady against her. "It's odd how you get used to it, a little bit at a time. Rafe, when I was downstairs alone…"

"What?" Uneasy, he tilted her face toward his again.

"It's nothing."

"What?" he repeated, giving her chin a little shake.

"Well, I walked into the library. What was the library," she went on, torn between the need to tell him and embarrassment. "What will be the library. And I— Rafe, I could see it."

His eyes were sharp, narrowed, totally concentrated. "See what?"

"The room. Not the stained floors and the new wiring you've put in. The room. Books on the wall, flowers on the table, drapes at the windows. I could really see it," she repeated, her own brow creasing. "Not the way I do in my head when I'm planning things out. Not exactly like that. I was thinking to myself, sort of projecting, I suppose. I imagined this, well, I thought I was imagining a Bible stand, with an old family Bible opened on it. And I could read the page, almost touch it. Marriage and births and death."

She took time to catch her breath. "You're not saying anything."

"Because I'm listening to you."

"I know it sounds crazy."

"Not in this house, it doesn't."

"It was so real, so sad. The way the scent of roses in this room is real, and sad. Then it was so cold, bitter, like a window had been flung open to the weather."

She moved her shoulders, laid her head on his chest again. "That's all."

"That's a lot for one day." Wanting to soothe, he stroked his hand over her hair. "I can give Devin a call, have him come get you."

"No, I don't want to leave. It shook me for a moment, but it's just as I said before. You get to accept it. I can handle it."

"I shouldn't have left you alone."

"Don't be silly. I don't need to be guarded against grieving ghosts."

But he wanted to guard her. He wished she had called for him. It surprised him just how much he wished she had needed him enough to call out for him.

"Next time you want to go in the library, let me know. I'll go with you."

"The house is already changing," she said quietly. "You've done that by caring for it. I like feeling I've had a part in that, too."

"You have." He pressed his lips to her hair.

"When people live in it, make love in it, laugh in it, it'll change again. The house needs people."

She shifted, lifted her mouth to his. "Make love with me."

He cupped her face in his hands, deepened the kiss.

When he picked her up, carried her from the room, the scent of roses followed. She looped her arms around him, pressed her lips to his throat. Already her blood was heating, already her pulse was pounding.

"It's like a drug," she murmured.

"I know." He stopped at the top of the stairs, found her mouth again.

"I've never been like this before." Swamped with emotions, she turned her face into his shoulder.

Neither had he, he thought.

As he carried her down, neither noticed that the air had remained warm and calm.

He laid her in front of the fire. Levering himself up on his elbow, he traced the shape of her face with a fingertip. Something kindled inside her, simmered with desire and flamed around her heart.

"Rafe."

"Ssh…"

To quiet her, he brushed his lips over her brow. She didn't know what she would have said, was grateful he'd stopped her. The wanting was more than enough. She could be relieved that neither of them needed words.

She should have been relieved.

Her mouth was ready for his, and it warmed beautifully under the pressure of lips and tongue. Though desire remained, poised and trembling, everything in her seemed to soften.

Here was tenderness, so sweet, so unexpected. Her sigh whispered out like a secret.

He felt the change, in her, in himself. Marveled at

it. Why had they always been in such a hurry? he wondered. Why had he hesitated to savor, and be savored, when there was so much here?

He loved the flavor of her, that quietly seductive taste that clung to her skin. The feel of her, soft curves, long lines. The smell of her hair, her clothes, her shoulders.

So he savored it now, all of it, with long, slow kisses that clouded his mind and made him forget there was anything beyond this room for either of them.

His hands were careful this time as he drew her sweater off, slipped the trousers down her hips. Rather than touch, rather than take, he kissed her again, drawing out the simple meeting of lips until her body went limp.

"Let me." With a dreamy murmur, she shifted until they were both kneeling. Already clouded, her eyes stayed on his while she unbuttoned his shirt. Trapped in the silky mood, she slipped it away and, with her hands resting lightly on his shoulders, swayed to him.

They held each other, moving only for quiet, sipping tastes, soft, gentle caresses. She smiled when his lips brushed her shoulder, sighed when hers tasted his throat.

When they were naked, he drew her down so that she lay over him, so that her hair fell to curtain them both.

She could have floated on this whisper-thin cloud of sensations endlessly, with the winter sun slanting cold light through the windows, the fire crackling, his body strong and hard beneath hers.

The feel of his hands on her, stroking, soothing even as they aroused, was like a gift. She felt the wonder of it in every pore, in every nerve, with every pulse.

There was no clash and fury now, no desperation, no vicious drive to mate. Now she was aware of everything—the dust motes spinning in the sunbeam that rayed over the floor, the sedate hiss of flame on wood, the scent of roses and man.

She could count his heartbeats, quicker, stronger, as her lips trailed over his chest. The bunching and quivering of a muscle beneath her hand, the sound of her own thickening breath.

With a sigh that caught in her throat, she wrapped around him as he rolled her to her back.

Time spun out, stretched, quivered. The clock on the mantel ticked the seconds away, and the minutes. But that was another world. Here there were only needs lazily satisfied, and hearts quietly lost.

For pleasure—his as well as hers—he eased her gently to the edge and over. His name was only a murmur on her lips as she arched, tensed, softened to silk. She opened for him, drawing him close with a velvety moan as he slipped into her.

Overwhelmed by her, by the simplicity of it, he burrowed his face in her hair. The tenderness shattered them both.

* * *

They didn't speak of it. When they parted in the morning, both of them were determinedly casual. But they thought of it. And they worried.

Rafe watched her drive off as the sun struggled over the mountains to the east. When she was gone, when there was no one to see, he rubbed the heel of his hand over his heart.

There was an ache there that he couldn't quite will away. He had a very bad feeling that she was the cause of it, and that somehow, in a matter of hours, he'd gotten in over his head.

God, he missed her already.

He swore at himself for that, then swore again for reaching like a trained dog for the cigarettes that weren't there. Both were just habits, he assured himself. If he wanted, he could just go buy a pack of cigarettes and smoke his brains out. Just as he could snatch her back anytime.

Sex was a powerful bond. It wasn't surprising it had caught him, as well.

It didn't have to be any more than that. They'd tidied that up, hadn't they? A man was entitled to be a little shaky after thirty-odd hours of sex and solitude with a gorgeous woman.

He didn't want anything more. Neither did she.

It was a relief and a pleasure to find a lover who wanted no more and no less than he did himself. A woman who didn't expect him to play games, make promises neither expected to be kept, say words that were only words, after all.

Scowling, he grabbed a shovel and began to deal with the snow that piled the walk. The sun was strengthening, and he worked fast, so that even with the bite of the northern wind he sweated satisfactorily under his coat.

She'd probably head straight for the shower, he mused, tossing heavy snow off the path. Wash that pretty doe-colored hair of hers.

He wondered what it looked like wet.

She'd dig some of those neat, classy clothes out of her closet. Nope, he thought, correcting himself. Regan would never dig. She'd select. Quiet colors, simple lines. One of those professional-woman's jackets, with a pin on the lapel.

She'd fix her face, nothing too obvious. Just hints of blush along the cheekbones, a touch of color above those ridiculously long lashes. Then lipstick—not red, not pink, a kind of rose that accented those full lips and that sassy little mole beside them.

Halfway down the walk, he stopped, leaned against the shovel and wondered if he was losing his mind. He was actually thinking about her makeup.

What the hell did he care what paint she slapped on before she went down to open the shop?

She'd put on the kettle for tea, or have cider simmering so that the place smelled of apples and spices. Then she'd go through the day without giving him a thought.

Snow flew as he attacked it. Well, he had plenty to do himself, and no time to brood about her.

He'd reached the end of the walk, and the end of his patience, when Devin rattled up the lane in the sheriff's cruiser.

"What the hell do you want?" Rafe shouted. "Haven't you got somebody to arrest?"

"Funny how a little blizzard quiets things down." Leaning on the open car door, Devin watched his brother with amusement. "Saw Regan's car was gone, figured it was safe to drop by."

"I've got men due any minute. I don't have time to chat."

"In that case, I'll take my doughnuts and go."

Rafe swiped a hand over his chilled face. "What kind?"

"Apple and brown sugar."

Some things were sacred, and an apple doughnut on a cold morning topped the list.

"Well, are you going to stand there all morning with that idiot grin on your face? Give me a damn doughnut."

Obligingly, Devin took the bag out of the car and sauntered over. "Had three fender benders in town yesterday from people not smart enough to stay put."

"Antietam's a wild town, all right. Have to shoot anybody?"

"Not lately." Devin took out a doughnut for himself before passing the bag to Rafe. "Broke up a fistfight, though."

"Down at the tavern?"

"Nope, at the market. Millie Yeader and Mrs. Metz were going at it over the last pack of toilet paper."

Rafe's lips twitched. "People get a little nervous over necessities when a big snow hits."

"Tell me about it. Miz Metz conked Millie with a

bunch of bananas. Took a lot of diplomacy to keep Millie from filing charges.''

''Assault with tropical fruit. Could've done hard time for that.'' Calm again, Rafe licked apple from his thumb. ''Did you come by to give me the latest trials and tribulations of Antietam?''

''That's just a bonus.'' Devin polished off his doughnut, reached for a cigarette. His grin was wide and unsympathetic when Rafe groaned. He lit it, inhaled lavishly. ''I hear food tastes better when you quit.''

''Nothing's better,'' Rafe shot back. ''But some of us have real willpower. Blow it over here, you bastard.''

''Secondhand smoke's the real killer,'' Devin told him, and blew a stream in Rafe's direction. ''You look a little out of sorts, Rafe. Trouble in paradise?''

Rafe gave some thought to beating his brother to death with the snow shovel and stealing all his cigarettes. Reminding himself it was all a matter of self-control, he leaned on the shovel, instead.

''How long did it take Shane to open his big mouth?''

''Let's see.'' Considering, Devin smoked and studied the landscape. ''The way the roads were yesterday, I'd say it took him, oh, about seven minutes to get from here to my office.'' He flicked ash aside. ''Let's say seven minutes and ten seconds.''

''Now you're here to offer your sage advice?''

''Hey, it was pretty sage to talk those two snarling women into splitting the six-pack of pink toilet paper.

But no.'' With a self-deprecating smile, he took a last drag, then flicked the cigarette away.

Rafe watched it wistfully as it hissed in the snow.

''I'm not exactly the expert on romance in the MacKade family.'' Devin's grin was crooked, and didn't last long. ''I thought you might like the latest on Joe Dolin.''

''He's locked up.''

''For now. I got word he's copping to second-degree assault. If he listens to his lawyer, he'll agree to alcohol counseling. He'll get a fine, suspended sentence with probation, and a stern warning not to hit his wife again.''

''What the hell kind of deal is that?''

''Prisons are crowded. Domestic disputes don't usually equal tough sentencing. He says 'Yeah, I did it, I'm sorry. I lost my temper, I was drunk, I lost my job. My self-esteem is really low.' The judge says 'Get yourself into counseling, my boy, and sin no more.'''

Rafe studied his brother's face. Beneath the calm, he caught the twitches of fury and frustration. ''You're just going to let it go at that?''

''I don't sentence.'' Devin struggled to bite back on his sense of anger and impotence. ''There's nothing I can do except talk Cassie into letting me issue a restraining order, and make sure he doesn't get near her or the kids.''

''Meanwhile, they're bunked down at Regan's. That puts her in the middle.''

"I don't like it any better than you do. I've got the law to work around."

"I don't."

Devin's gaze was cool and level. "No, you don't. But you start something with Dolin, and it's going to come down in his favor. He'll make a mistake, Rafe. All it takes is one, and I'll have him caged again. Until I do... I don't know where things stand between you and Regan, but if you were staying there, it'd hold a lot more weight with me than some useless restraining order."

"You want me to ask Regan to let me move in with her?"

"And Cassie, and the kids."

The idea was surprisingly appealing. Waking up beside her, sharing that first cup of coffee. "You going to deputize me, Dev?"

"Not on your life."

"Too bad. Well, I'll run it by Regan and let you know."

Chapter 8

"Absolutely not." Regan planted her feet, folded her arms over her chest. "You are not sleeping in my bed with two little children in the next room."

"This isn't about sex," Rafe said patiently. "That's just a bonus. I'm telling you, this is an official request from the sheriff."

"Who just happens to be your brother. No." She turned away to set glassware back on the shelf she'd been dusting. "It would make Cassie uncomfortable and set a poor example for the children."

And if they weren't there? He found the question leaping to the tip of his tongue like a frog. He was barely in time to prevent himself from letting it jump out.

"It's Cassie and the kids who are the issue," he insisted. "You think Dolin's just going to leave them alone because Cassie signs some paper telling him to?''

''I have no idea what he'll do, but he'll have to get past me first.''

The thought of it, just the thought of it, had his blood icing over. ''Now you listen...''

She jerked his hand from her shoulder and whirled back. ''No, *you* listen. The man is a bully and a drunk. I'm not afraid of drunken bullies. I offered Cassie my home, and she's welcome to stay there as long as she wants. I have a good solid lock on the door, which I'll use. I know the number for the sheriff's office, which I'll use, as well, if it's necessary.''

''There's no lock on that door.'' Rafe jerked a thumb toward the front of the shop. ''What's to stop him from walking in here during business hours and harassing you? Or worse.''

''I am.''

''Right.'' He wondered if shaking her would rattle her brains back into place. ''Putting Dolin on the receiving end of that stubborn chin of yours isn't going to stop him. In case you haven't figured it out, he likes hurting women.''

''I'll take a moment to remind you that for the past three years I've been here and you haven't. I've seen exactly what he's done to Cassie.''

''And you figure because you're not married to him, you're safe?'' He did shake her. ''You can't be that stupid.''

''I'm not stupid,'' she shot back. ''I'm competent. I don't need or want you for a bodyguard.''

His eyes changed, going from full heat to slow burn. On her shoulders, his hands tensed, then lifted away.

"I guess that's the bottom line, isn't it? You don't need or want my help."

Ego, she thought with a muffled sigh. There was no monster so fierce or so vulnerable as a man's ego. "The sheriff's office is five minutes away, if I need to call out troops." Hoping to calm them both, Regan put her hands on his shoulders. "Rafe, I appreciate your concern, really I do. But I can take care of myself, and Cassie, too, if it comes to that."

"I bet you can."

"I worked a shop in D.C. for years. One memorable evening, I was robbed at gunpoint. I know how to be sensible, how not to take chances and how to defend myself. I appreciate the fact that you're worried, but I'm not Cassie. He can't frighten or intimidate me."

"Regan—"

"Wait, let me finish. Cassie is so fragile right now, and the children are too quiet. I'm not sure how they would handle having a man around. The kids don't know you."

He jammed his hands in his pockets. "I'm not going to kick them around."

"They don't know that. Little Emma sits at Cassie's feet with her doll and barely says a word. And the boy— God, Rafe, he breaks my heart. They need time to feel safe again. You're too big, you're too strong, you're too...male."

Stubbornly he ignored the fact that she'd hurt him—that he could be hurt—and concentrated on the situation at hand. "You're being pigheaded."

"I'm doing what seems right to me. That's the only way I know how to handle things. Believe me, I've thought this through, weighed the options. Having you move in just isn't one of them."

"Invite me to dinner," he said abruptly.

"You want to come to dinner?"

"Ask me to dinner, so I can get to know the kids, so they'll get used to me being around."

"Now who's pigheaded?" But she sighed. It was a reasonable compromise. "All right, seven-thirty, and you're out by ten."

"Can we neck on the couch after the kids go to bed?"

"Maybe. Now go away."

"Aren't you going to kiss me goodbye?"

She huffed out a breath, then kissed him primly on the cheek. "Business hours," she said, then laughed when he grabbed her. "Rafe, we're right in front of the window. I—"

The rest was lost as he crushed his mouth to hers. "Might as well give them something to talk about." And give her something to think about, he told himself. She was damn well going to do a lot of thinking about Rafe MacKade.

He nipped her lip, let her go, then sauntered out the door.

A block away, Cassie sat in Devin's office, twisting her hands together. She knew it should be easier because it was Devin, someone she'd known all her life. But it only made the shame worse.

"I'm sorry, we got busy, and I couldn't take my break until now."

"That's all right, Cassie." It had become habit to keep his voice quiet when he spoke to her, as a man might speak to a wounded bird. "I've got the paperwork filled out for you. You just have to sign it."

"He's not going to go to jail."

A fist squeezed his heart at the emptiness in her tone. "No."

"Is it because I let him hit me?"

"No." He wished he could reach out to soothe those nervous hands. But the desk was between them, an official barrier. "He admitted that he hurt you, but the court took other things into consideration. His drinking problem, his loss of a longtime job. He'll have to go into counseling, report to his probation officer. Stay out of trouble."

"It could be good for him." She looked up, then, just as quickly, down again. "The counseling. If he stops drinking, maybe everything would be all right."

"Yeah." And he could run a Popsicle stand in hell, Devin thought. "In the meantime, you need to protect yourself. That's what the restraining order's for."

She lifted her gaze again, and this time her eyes held his. "That paper is going to keep him from coming back?"

Devin grabbed a cigarette out of his pack, then tossed it down. When he spoke, his voice was cool and official. "This bars him from coming near you. He can't come into the diner when you're working there. He can't approach you on the street, or come to Regan's house as long as you're staying there. If he breaks any one of the regulations set down here, he'll void his parole and serve the eighteen months."

"He knows about this?"

"He's been notified."

She moistened her lips. He couldn't come near her. The idea whirled around in her head. If he couldn't come near her, he couldn't hit her.

"I only have to sign it."

"Yes, you only have to sign it." Devin rose then, came around the desk to offer her a pen. When she made no move to take it, he bit back an oath. "Cassie, what do you want? Can you just tell me what you want?"

She shook her head, took the pen. She signed her name quickly, as though it hurt. "I know I've put you through a lot of trouble, Devin."

"It's my job," he said shortly.

"You're a good sheriff." When he glanced back, obviously surprised, she tried to smile. "You are, quiet and competent and good with people. Everyone knows they can count on you. My mother always said you and your brothers would end up behind bars." She flushed and stared down at the floor. "I'm sorry. That was stupid."

"No, it wasn't. I used to think the same myself." He smiled then, because just for a moment she'd sounded like the girl he remembered. "You know,

Cass, that's about the longest little speech I've heard out of you in close to ten years.''

"I'm always putting my foot in my mouth."

"Don't do that." He'd taken her chin to lift her head before he realized he meant to—before she flinched like a startled doe. Moving with care, he dropped his hand, eased a hip on the corner of the desk. "How are the kids?"

"They're all right. Better."

"Getting along all right at Regan's?"

"She's wonderful. I forget I'm imposing, because she makes everything so normal. She and Rafe—" She broke off, her color rising again. "You've got better things to do than listen to me gossip."

"No, I don't." He'd have done anything to keep her talking. To keep her there. "What do you think about them? Regan and Rafe?"

"I— She looked happy when she came home this morning."

"He looked miserable when I dropped by the house this morning."

Her smile was slow and shy. "That's a good sign. Rafe always needed a woman who could make him unhappy. It was always too easy for him. For all of you."

"Was it?" Thoughtful, he picked up his cigarette again, ran it through his fingers. "I remember you turned me down."

"Oh." Fumbling, she rose. "That was a hundred years ago."

"Not quite twelve. You were sweet sixteen."

"I was going with Joe." As she tugged on her coat, she wondered if she'd really ever been sixteen. "I can't even remember who we were then, or what we were looking for. Thanks, Devin, for taking care of this."

"That's what I'm here for, to take care of things."

At the door, she paused, but didn't look back. It was easier to speak if she didn't have to look into those cool, pitying eyes. "You asked me what I wanted, Devin. I just want to feel safe." She said it so quietly, he barely heard. "That's really all."

In a coat that was too thin to fight off the biting wind, she walked back to the café.

Rafe arrived ten minutes early for dinner and squirmed on Regan's doorstep like a nervous suitor. He had a bottle of wine in one hand and a bakery box of cookies designed to win the kids over in the other.

He wished he'd remembered before his brainstorm that he knew nothing about people under the age of sixteen.

As a test, he turned the knob. It was somewhat satisfying to find it locked tight. He knocked sharply, stepped back. It was Regan who opened it, as far as the thick security chain allowed.

"Okay, so far you're passing. But you should have asked who it was first."

"I looked out the window." She shut the door in his face, then, after a rattle of chain, opened it. "I had the feeling there'd be a quiz.'' Smiling, she studied the offerings. ''No lilacs?''

''No chance.'' He would have kissed her if he hadn't noticed the solemn gray eyes watching him from the cushions of the sofa. ''Looks like you've got a mouse in the house.''

Regan jerked, then smiled when she saw Emma. ''She's quiet as one, but prettier. Emma, this is Mr. MacKade. You met him at Ed's, remember?'' Regan held out a hand. Eyeing him warily, Emma slipped from the couch.

She was five, Rafe knew, and tiny as a fairy princess, with her mother's pale hair and smoky eyes.

''I knew your mama when she was your age,'' he told her.

Emma darted behind Regan's legs and peered up at him.

Knowing it was a shameless bribe, he shook the bakery box. ''Want a cookie, honey?''

That earned him the faintest of smiles, but Regan took the box out of his hands. ''Not before dinner.''

''Spoilsport. But dinner smells good.''

''Cassie's chicken and dumplings. I had to practically tie her down to keep her from taking the kids and eating at the diner. We compromised and had her cook dinner. Come on, Emma, we'll take the cookies in the kitchen.''

With one hand clutching Regan's slacks, Emma darted looks over her shoulder.

She thought he was big, but his eyes weren't mean. She'd already learned how to read eyes. And he looked a lot like the sheriff, who sometimes picked her up and gave her lemon drops.

But Emma watched her mother carefully to gauge her reaction to the man.

Cassie looked up from the stove and smiled. "Hi, Rafe."

He moved to her, lightly kissed her bruised cheek. "How's it going?"

"Fine, everything's fine." She laid a hand on the shoulder of the boy beside her. "Connor, you remember Mr. MacKade."

"Nice to see you again, Connor." Rafe offered a hand. The little boy with the pale hair and the dusky blue eyes shook hands hesitantly. "You'd be, what, in third, fourth grade?"

"Third, yes, sir."

Rafe lifted a brow and passed the bottle of wine to Regan. That would make him about eight, Rafe figured, and the kid spoke as quietly as an old priest. "Miz Witt still teaching there?"

"Yes, sir."

"We used to call her Miz Dimwit." When the boy's eyes widened, Rafe plucked a carrot from beside the salad bowl. "Bet you still do."

"Yes, sir," Connor mumbled, slanting a look at his mother. "Sometimes." Screwing up the courage he'd worked on building ever since he'd been told Rafe MacKade was coming, Connor drew in his breath. "You bought the Barlow Place."

"That's right."

"It's haunted."

Rafe bit off some carrot and grinned. "You bet."

"I know all about the battle and everything," Connor said in one quick burst. "It was the bloodiest day of the Civil War, and nobody really won, because—" He broke off, embarrassed. This, he thought miserably, was why some of the kids called him nerdhead in school.

"Because nobody went for the final push," Rafe finished for him. "Maybe you'd like to come by the house sometime, take a look. I could use somebody who knows all about the battle."

"I've got a book. With pictures."

"Yeah?" Rafe took the wine Regan offered him. "Let's see."

It was simple enough to draw the boy out, as long as they were discussing McClellan's flawed strategy or the Battle of Burnside Bridge. Rafe saw a bright, needy boy, too bookish to fit neatly with his contemporaries, too shy to showcase his own brain.

The girl, a miniature of her mother, never strayed far from Cassie or Regan, ate her dinner in small, neat bites. And watched him like a baby hawk.

"Ed would be better off having you in the kitchen than waiting tables," Rafe commented after he'd polished off a second helping. "Her business would double in a month."

Off guard, Cassie blinked at him. No one had complimented her cooking in too many years to count. "I'm glad you liked it. I could put some of the leftovers in a dish for you. You'd just have to heat them up."

"I'll take them."

When Cassie rose and began to clear, Regan held up a hand. "No, you don't. You cooked, I clear."

"But—"

"That was the deal. And since Rafe ate enough for two growing boys, he can help."

The Dolins looked on, awed, as Rafe cheerfully stacked plates. The men they knew would have belched, loosened their belts and plopped down in front of the TV with a six-pack.

"Daddy says girls and sissies do dishes," Emma announced, in a surprisingly clear voice.

"Emma!" Paling, Cassie stared at Rafe and waited for the retribution.

He considered making a comment about her father's brains but decided against it. "My mama always said a meal has to be earned." He said it lightly and winked at her. "And if I do the dishes with Regan, I'll probably be able to kiss her."

"Why?"

"Because she tastes almost as good as your mama's chicken and dumplings."

Satisfied with that, Emma nibbled solemnly on her cookie.

"I'll just give Emma her bath, then." Flustered, Cassie shooed her children along. "I have to turn in early. I have the breakfast shift in the morning."

"Thanks for dinner, Cassie."

"You handled that very well," Regan murmured. "That's probably the first time in years they've sat at the dinner table with a man and had a civilized conversation.''

"Dolin's not only a swine, he's a fool." Rafe set stacked plates on the kitchen counter. "Sweet woman like that, beautiful kids. Any man would be lucky to have them."

A home of your own, Rafe mused. A woman who loved you. Kids racing out to meet you at the end of the day. Family meals around a table. Noise in the kitchen.

Funny, he'd never thought that was something he'd wanted, or needed.

"You made an impression," Regan went on as she filled the sink with hot, soapy water. "A good one. I can't think of anything better for all of them than seeing a strong, intelligent man behaving in a strong, intelligent way."

She glanced back, and her smile faltered at the look in his eye. She was used to the way he stared at her, or she nearly was. But this was different, deeper.

"What is it?"

"Hmm?" He caught himself, realized he felt like a man who had nearly skidded hard and landed on very thin ice. "Nothing. It's nothing." Good God, he'd actually been thinking about marriage and kids and picket fences. "The boy, Connor. He's awfully bright, isn't he?"

"Straight *A*s," Regan said, as proudly as if he were her own. "He's bright, sensitive and sweet—which made him a perfect target for Joe. The man bullied the poor kid mercilessly."

"He hit him?" The question was mild, but the fire was already burning.

"No, I don't think so. Cassie's fiercely protective of her children. But emotional abuse doesn't leave bruises." She shrugged. "Well, they're out of it now." She handed him a plate to dry. "Did your father do dishes?"

"Only on Thanksgiving." Rafe polished off the plate, set it aside. "Buck MacKade was a man's man."

"Buck?" Impressed, Regan pursed her lips. "Sounds formidable."

"He was tough. Had eyes that could drill holes in you if you messed up. Devin got his eyes. I got his hands." Bemused, Rafe stared down at his palms, flexed his fingers. "It was a hell of a surprise to me when I looked down one day and saw my father's hands on the end of my arms."

She couldn't have said why it touched her so to see him smiling down at his hands, a dishcloth tossed over his shoulder. "You were close to him?"

"Not close enough. Not for long enough."

"When did you lose him?"

"I was fifteen. Tractor rolled on him. It took him a week to die."

She plunged her hands into the water again, struggled with tears. "Is that why you hate the farm?"

"Yeah, I guess it is." Odd, he'd never realized it was that simple, that direct. The farm had taken his father, so he had to hate the farm. "He loved it, every rocky acre. The way Shane does."

"What did Jared get from him?"

"The mouth—Jared can horse-trade just like the old man, and make you think you got the best end of the deal."

"Then I'm relieved he's my lawyer." She offered another plate. "My father never did a dish in his life. I'm sure my mother would be horrified if he tried. The kitchen is a woman's domain," she said dryly. "They agree on that completely. She brings him his first cup of coffee every morning before he goes to the hospital. He's a surgeon."

"Hard feelings?"

"I used to have them," she admitted. "She made herself into exactly the woman he wanted her to be. If she was ever anything else, wanted to be anything else, anything more, it doesn't show. She's Dr. Bishop's wife, and that's all."

He began to see just why she was so set on marking her own boundaries, taking her own stands. "Maybe that's all she wants to be."

"Apparently. It just infuriated me to see the way she catered to him, the way he patted her on the head. He actually gives her an allowance and calls her 'the little woman.'"

It still made her grit her teeth. "She loved living in D.C., but a few years ago when he decided that he wanted to relocate to Arizona, she packed up without a murmur." Regan sighed. "But they're blissfully happy. I baffle them as much as they baffle me."

"Because you don't have a rich husband, a big house and a membership at the country club."

"Exactly." Surprised and amused, she glanced at him. "Have you met them?"

"I think I just did." And, in doing so, caught a fresh new glimpse of her. "So, darling, why don't you have a rich husband, a big house and a membership at the country club?"

"Because I like independence, my own space and my golf game is dreadful." She shook back her hair. "Actually, my mother had high hopes for me when she met Jared."

The bowl he was drying clattered when he set it down. "Run through that again."

"They came to visit right after settlement. He took us out to dinner."

"Jared," Rafe said carefully, "took you out to dinner."

"Mmm-hmm… A couple of times. My mother really liked the idea that I was seeing a lawyer. Next-best thing to a doctor, in her mind."

"Seeing. As in dating. You dated Jared?"

"We went out a few times. It was right after his divorce." She held out another bowl, lifting a brow when he made no move to take it. "Is there a problem?"

"You dated my brother?"

"I believe we just established that." She decided it was a better idea to bite the inside of her lip than to let it curve. "Didn't he mention it?"

"No. I think I'd like your definition of *date.*"

"You mean, did I sleep with him?" Struggling to keep her face composed, she tilted her head. "Are you going to go beat him up, big guy? Can I come watch?''

Obviously she didn't know how close she was to having her pretty face dumped in dishwater. ''It's a simple question.''

''You've got a muscle twitching in your jaw, Rafe. It looks good on you. No,'' she said, and then she did laugh. ''Of course I didn't sleep with him.'' Enjoying herself, she shoved the bowl into his hands. ''I did kiss him good-night. A couple of times. I'm now in the position to state, unequivocally, that at least fifty percent of the MacKade brothers are champion kissers.''

''Think twice before you try for a hundred percent—or even seventy-five.'' He set the bowl aside, picked up his wine. ''Why didn't you sleep with him?''

''Really, Rafe.'' She rolled her eyes. ''In the first place, he didn't ask me. And in the second, I didn't ask him. We were more comfortable being friends. Satisfied?''

''Maybe I'll beat him up anyway. On principle.''

After setting his wine aside, he took her by the shoulders, turned her to face him. Even as she grinned at him, he pressed her back into the sink.

Hard, possessive, his mouth covered hers. The little purr that sounded in her throat enticed him to draw the kiss out, soften it, until all points of pleasure narrowed and centered just there.

When her head fell back in surrender, her hands slid limply down his arms, he eased back.

"That's so you remember which MacKade you're with now."

She had to remind herself to breathe. "What was your name again?"

He grinned, then closed his teeth over her sensitized bottom lip. "Tell you what. Why don't we skip necking on the couch and go try out the back seat of my car?"

"That's quite an offer." It was fascinating to feel her own head spin. "I think I'll take you up on it."

Rafe let himself into the Barlow house at midnight. He'd recognized the car at the top of the lane, and he wasn't surprised to find Jared in the parlor, brooding over a beer.

"Foreclosing already, Lawyer MacKade?"

Instead of rising to the bait, Jared stared down at his beer. "I put my house on the market today. Didn't feel like staying there."

Rafe grunted, sat down on his sleeping bag to pull off his boots. He knew the dark moods, often had them himself. Either he'd manage to shake Jared out of it, or they'd both ride through it.

"Never liked that house, no personality. Just like your ex-wife."

It was so cold, and so true, Jared had to laugh. "Decent investment, though. I'll make a profit."

Rafe shook his head at the beer Jared held out. "They don't taste the same without a smoke. Besides, I gotta be up in six and a half hours. I was going to come look for you," he added.

"Oh? Why?"

"To beat the hell out of you." With a yawn, Rafe lay back. "It'll have to wait till tomorrow. I'm too relaxed."

"Okay. Any particular reason?"

"You kissed my woman." Rafe figured he had just about enough energy to strip off his pants.

"I did?" Jared tossed his legs up over the settee. A slow smile curved his lips. "Oh, yeah. Oh, *yeah...*" he said again, with more feeling. "It's all coming back to me. When'd she get to be your woman?"

Rafe heaved his jeans aside, started on his shirt. "That's what comes from living in the city. You're out of the loop, bro. She's mine now."

"Does she know that?"

"*I* know." With his eyes closed, he dragged the sleeping bag over him. "I'm thinking about keeping her."

Jared choked on his beer. "You mean like a wife?"

"I mean like keeping her," Rafe repeated. No way was he going to try to get his tongue around a word like *wife*. "Keeping things the way they are now."

This was interesting, Jared mused. And even more fun than brooding. "And how are things now?"

"Things are good." Rafe could smell her on the quilted material of the sleeping bag. "I'm still going to have to break your face. It's the principle."

"Understood." Jared stretched out, settled back. "Then again, I never did pay you back for talking

Sharilyn Bester, now Fenniman, into riding out to the quarry with you to skinny-dip.''

"I was just easing her broken heart after you'd dumped her.''

"Yeah. But it's the principle.''

Considering, Rafe scratched his face. "You got a point. But Sharilyn, pretty as she is, is no Regan Bishop.''

"I never got to see Regan naked.''

"That's why you're still breathing.'' Rafe shifted, folded his arms under his head. "Maybe we'll call it even.''

"I can sleep easy now.''

Rafe's lips twitched at the dry tone. "I'm sorry about your house, Jared, if you are.''

"I'm not sorry about it, really. It just brought a lot of things back. I screwed up as much as Barbara did, Rafe. It would have been easier if we'd yelled at each other, threw things.'' He took a last swig and set the empty bottle on the floor. "There's nothing more demoralizing than a civilized divorce between two people who couldn't care less about each other.''

"It's got to be better than getting your heart broken.''

"I don't know. I kind of wish I'd had the chance.''

They were both silent as the sound of weeping drifted down the stairs.

"Ask her,'' Rafe suggested. "I'd bet she'd tell you you're better off.''

"Maybe you should start thinking exorcism,'' Jake

said, smiling at the idea as his eyes drooped and he settled himself for sleep.

"No. I like having them around. I've had plenty of time to be alone."

Chapter 9

It was rare for Rafe to dream. He preferred his fantasies during waking hours, so that his consciousness could appreciate them.

But he dreamed that night, as the fire burned low and the moon rose over drifts of snow, if you could call it a dream...

He was running, terror and smoke at his heels. His eyes were burning from fatigue, and from the horror he'd already seen.

Men blown apart before they could scream from the shock and agony. The ground exploding, hacked by mortar fire, drenched with blood. The smell of death was in his nostrils, and he knew he'd never be free of it.

Oh, and he longed for the scent of magnolias and roses, for the lush green hills and rich brown fields of his home. If he had had tears left, he would have wept them for the quiet gurgling of the river that wound through his family's plantation, the bright laughter of his sisters, the crooning songs of the field hands.

He was afraid, mortally afraid, that everything he'd known and treasured was already gone. His most desperate wish was to get back, to see it again.

He wanted to see his father again, to tell him his son had tried to be a man.

The battle raged everywhere. In the fields, through the corn, in his heart. So many of his comrades lay dead on these godforsaken rocky hills of Maryland.

He'd lost his way. He hadn't been able to see through the choking smoke, or hear through the thunder of guns and the horrible shrieks of men. Suddenly he was running, running as a coward runs for any hole to crawl in.

Mixed with the horror now was a shame just as terrible. He'd forgotten his duty, and lost his honor. Now, somehow, he must find them both again.

The woods were thick, carpeted with the dying leaves that fell, brilliant in golds and russets, from the trees. He had never been so far north, seen such color, or smelled the poignant decay of autumn.

He was only seventeen.

A movement ahead had him fumbling his rifle onto his shoulder. The blue uniform was all he could see, and he fired too quickly, and poorly. The answering shot had fire singeing his arm. Driven by pain and terror, he gave a wild Rebel yell and charged.

He wished he hadn't seen the eyes, the eyes of the enemy, as wide and terror-glazed and young as his own. Their bayonets crashed, point to point. He smelled the blood, and the stinking scent of fear.

He felt the steel of his blade slice into flesh, and his stomach roiled. He felt the rip of his own, and cried out in agony. He fought, blindly, bitterly, recklessly, until there was nothing inside him but the battle. And when they both lay in their own blood, he wondered why.

He was crawling, delirious with pain. He needed to get home for supper, he thought. Had to get home. There was the house, he could see it now. He dragged himself over rocks and dying summer flowers, leaving his blood staining the grass.

Hands were lifting him. Soft voices. He saw her standing over him, an angel. Her hair like a halo, her eyes warm, her voice filled with the music of the South he yearned for.

Her face was so beautiful, so gentle, so sad.

She stroked his head, held his hand, walking beside him as others carried him up curving steps.

I'm going home, he told her. *I have to go home.*

You'll be all right, she promised. *You'll go home as soon as you're well again.*

She looked away from him, up, and her lovely face went pale as a ghost's.

No. He's hurt. He's just a boy. Charles, you can't.

He saw the man, saw the gun, heard the words.

I'll have no Confederate scum in my house. No wife of mine will put her hands on a Rebel.

Rafe jolted awake with the sound of a gunshot ringing in his ears. He sat where he was while it echoed away, until all that was left was his brother's quiet breathing.

Chilled, he rose, added logs to the fire. Then he sat, watching the flames and waiting for dawn.

Regan slept like a baby. With the kids off to school and Cassie taking the early shift at the diner, she indulged herself with a second cup of coffee. She still prized her privacy, but she'd discovered she liked having the company.

It was nice having the children pad around the house in the morning, having Emma offer one of her solemn kisses or Connor one of his rare smiles.

She liked beating Cassie to the kitchen so that she could fix breakfast and smooth down pale, sleep-tousled hair.

Motherhood had never been one of her ambitions, but she was beginning to wonder if she wouldn't be good at it.

She picked up a crayon Emma had left on the table. She smelled it, and smiled. It was funny, she thought, how quickly a house could smell like children. Crayons and white paste, hot chocolate and soggy cereal.

And it was funny how quickly she'd come to look forward to finding them there after work.

Absently she tucked the crayon in her pocket. Work was exactly where she had to go.

Out of habit, she rinsed her coffee cup in the sink, set it on the drain. After a last glance around, she opened the door in the kitchen and headed down the stairs to open the shop for the day.

She'd barely turned the Open sign around, unlocked the door and moved behind the counter to unlock the till when Joe Dolin walked in.

The quick spurt of alarm came first. Then she soothed it by reminding herself that he was here, and Cassie wasn't.

He'd put on weight even in the three years she'd known him. There was muscle there still, but it was cushioned by too many six-packs. She imagined he'd been an attractive man once, before his square face had bloated and his moody brown eyes had sunken behind bags.

He had a chipped front tooth she didn't know was courtesy of a younger Rafe's fist, and a nose that had been broken by Rafe, and several others.

With disgust, she remembered that he had tried, once or twice, to touch her. Had watched her, more than once or twice, with greedy eyes and a knowing smile.

Regan hadn't even told Cassie that. And never would.

She braced herself for the altercation, but he shut the door quietly, took off his billed cap and held it humbly in his hands, like a peasant before the queen.

"Regan. I'm sorry to bother you."

The penitent sound of his voice and bowed head almost softened her. But she remembered the bruises on Cassie's neck. "What do you want, Joe?"

"I heard Cassie's staying with you."

Just Cassie, she noted. Nothing about his children. "That's right."

"I guess you know about the trouble."

"Yes, I know. You beat her, and you were arrested."

"I was awful drunk."

"The court may find that an excuse. I don't."

His eyes narrowed and flashed, but he kept his head down. "I feel terrible about it. Done nothing but worry about her for days. Now they've fixed it so I can't even go near her to tell her so. I come to ask you a favor."

He lifted his head then, and his eyes were moist. "Cassie sets a lot of store by you."

"I set a lot of store by her," Regan said evenly. She would not let the sight of a man's tears blur her judgment.

"Yeah, well. I was hoping you'd talk to her for me. See that she gives me another chance. I can't ask her myself, long as there's that damn restraining order. But she'll listen to you."

"You're giving me credit for influence over Cassie I don't have, Joe."

"No, she'll listen to you," he insisted. "She's always running off at the mouth about how smart you are. You tell her to come on home, and she'll do it."

Very slowly, Regan placed her palms on the countertop. "If she'd listened to me, she would have left you years ago."

His unshaven jaw tightened. "Now, you look. A man's got a right—"

"To beat his wife?" she snapped. "Not in my book, he doesn't, and not in the law's. No, I won't tell her to come back to you, Joe. And if that's all you came in for, you'll have to leave."

His lips peeled back, showing clenched teeth, his eyes hardened like marbles. "Still all high-and-mighty. You think you're better than me."

"No, I don't. I *know* I'm better than you. Get out of my shop or I'll have Sheriff MacKade throw you in jail for harassment."

"A woman belongs to her husband." He crashed his fist on the counter, hard enough to have a crack splitting through the glass. "You tell her to get her skinny butt home, if she knows what's good for her. And what's good for you."

Fear trembled in Regan's throat, and was swallowed, hard. As if it were a talisman, she closed a hand around the crayon in her pocket. "Is that a threat?" she asked coolly. "I don't believe your parole officer would approve. Shall I call him and ask?"

"Bitch. You're nothing but a frigid, dried-up bitch who can't get herself a real man." He wanted to hit her, to feel his fist pound into that ice-queen face. "You get between me and my wife and both of you'll find out what it's like. When I finish with her, I'll come after you. We'll see if you're so high and mighty when I'm finished."

He jammed his hat back on his head, spun to the door. "You tell her what I said. You tell her I'm waiting. She'd better have that bastard MacKade tear up those papers and be home by suppertime."

The instant the door slammed behind him, Regan slumped against the counter. Her hands were shaking, and she hated it, hated being afraid, hated being vulnerable. She grabbed the phone, had nearly followed through on her first instinct to call Rafe when she stopped herself.

That was wrong, she thought, carefully replacing the receiver. For so many reasons it was wrong. Wouldn't his first reaction be to hunt Joe down, to fight? He'd probably get hurt and certainly more fighting wasn't going to solve anything.

She straightened and drew a few calming breaths. Where was her pride, her sense of control? She had always handled herself and any situation that came her way. Her feelings for Rafe shouldn't—couldn't change that intrinsic part of her. She wouldn't allow it. So, she would do what was right, what was practical, and what was necessary. Regan picked up the phone and dialed the sheriff's office.

"He was almost pitiful at first." The tea sloshed in her cup. With a grimace, Regan set it down again. "I guess he spooked me more than I'd thought."

"Shake all you want," Devin told her, and frowned at the crack in her counter. It could have been worse, he thought grimly. A lot worse. "I have to say, I didn't think he was fool enough to pull a stunt like this."

"I don't think he'd been drinking." Regan cleared her throat. "At least he wasn't drunk. He got steadily more angry, steadily more abusive." She reached for her tea again. "I don't have any witnesses. It was just him and me."

"You file charges, I'll go after him."

Her lips trembled upward. "It sounds like you're looking forward to it."

"You don't know the half of it."

"I'll file charges. Cassie?"

"I had one of my deputies go to the diner as soon as you called. He'll hang out there and get paid for drinking coffee and flirting with Ed. I've got another one driving by the school."

"The kids." Her blood ran cold. "You don't think he'd go after the kids?"

"No, I don't think he gives two damns about them."

"You're right." She tried to feel relieved. "He never said a word about them. Only Cassie. It was as if his children didn't exist. Well, I'll lock up and go with you now, if that's all right."

"The sooner the better. Odds are he's at home, knocking back a bottle and waiting for her."

Once the complaint was official, Regan detoured to the market. She had a feeling both she and Cassie were going to need a lift that evening. Comfort food was in order. Spaghetti and meatballs, she decided, and double-fudge brownies.

While she waited for her purchases to be bagged, she tried not to chuckle at the darting looks and whispers. The gossip brigade, she thought, was in full march.

Mrs. Metz, all two hundred and twenty pounds of her, waddled over. "Why, Regan Bishop, I thought that was you."

"Hello, Mrs. Metz." Here, Regan thought, was the brigade's head scout. "Do you think we're going to get hit with snow again?"

"Ice storm," she said with a shake of her head. "Heard on the radio. Into February now, and don't look like this winter's ever going to end. Surprised to see you in here this time of day."

"Business is slow." Regan counted out bills for the groceries. "Everybody's hibernating."

"Know what you mean. Still, you got yourself some business over at the old Barlow place, don't you?"

"Yes, indeed." Willing to play, Regan set the bag on her hip. "It's really coming along, too. It'll be a showplace when it's finished."

"Never thought to see the day anybody'd bother fixing her up. Never thought to see Rafe MacKade come riding back into town, neither." Her curious eyes brightened. "Guess he did pretty well for himself down South."

"Apparently."

"You can't tell about those MacKade boys. They fool you every time. You know that Rafe crashed his daddy's Ford pickup on Marble Quarry Road before he so much as had a license. That was right after Buck died, as I recall. He was wild as wild can be, that Rafe. Chasing girls, picking fights, flying around on the back roads on that noisy motorcycle of his. Time was, when you found trouble, there was always a MacKade boy in the middle of it.''

''Times change, I suppose.''

''Not that much, they don't.'' Her chins wagged as she chuckled. ''I seen him around town. He's still got that look in his eye. Little bird told me he had that eye on you.''

''Well, your little bird's right. And I've got mine right back on him.''

Mrs. Metz laughed so hard she had to put down her box of Ho-Hos to hold her belly. ''With a boy like that, you'd better keep it there. He'd be harder to keep down than spit on a hot griddle. He was a bad one, Regan. Bad boys turn into dangerous men.''

''I know.'' Regan winked. ''That's why I like him. You come in and browse real soon, Mrs. Metz.''

''I'll do that.'' Chuckling to herself, she emptied her cart. ''Stop gawking, boy,'' she snapped at the skinny clerk, who was still watching Regan's retreat, ''and ring me up here. You ain't never going to be dangerous enough to reel in that kind of woman.''

Amused by the encounter, Regan strolled down the sidewalk. It was a good town, she thought, lifting a hand in response to a greeting from across the street. The sidewalks were uneven, heaved up by tree roots and frost, the library was only open three days a week, and the post office was closed for a full hour every afternoon.

But despite that, or perhaps because of it, it was a good town. She didn't think Rafe realized he'd been welcomed home.

No fatted calf, she mused, crossing at the corner and turning down Main. That wasn't their style. The prodigal son just slipped back into the town's rhythm with neither a hitch nor fanfare.

When he left again, his departure would be just as unheralded. A few comments over the counter at the post office, some speculation at the diner. Then the town would move along, as easy as ever.

She hoped she would.

Shifting her bag, she circled around the side of the shop. Enjoy the moment, she reminded herself. Don't project into the future. Those were the rules; she'd stated them herself. All she had to do was follow them.

And if she found an excuse to slip by his house later, steal an hour with him, so much the better.

Bolstered by the idea, she took her keys from her pocket. She jingled them as she climbed the stairs with her groceries.

If she'd been paying attention, if she hadn't been thinking about Rafe, perhaps she would have noticed sooner. But her hand was already reaching for the door when she saw that it wasn't on its hinges, but was propped there.

Her mind stayed blank for an instant too long.

Even as she spun around to run, Joe hauled the door aside. The crash dragged a shriek from her. It was choked off to a gurgle when his arm jerked around her neck.

"Wondered which one of you'd come first. This is good." His breath panted out, sour with whiskey and excitement. ''Been wanting to get my hands on you for a long time.''

He pressed his mouth to her ear, excited by the way she tried to curl away from him. ''I'm going to show you what a real man's all about. Going to get you out of those prim and proper clothes and show you real good.''

He panted as his free hand came around to squeeze hard on her breast. Her skin crawled, and for one hideous moment the fear was so bright it blinded her eyes, and her reason.

''I'm going to get me some of what I hear that bastard Rafe MacKade's been getting. Then I'm going to fix your face so nobody thinks it's so pretty anymore.''

As he started to drag her over the broken door and inside, the horror of what he would do flashed through her. She swung back. Groceries flew, smashing into the little alley below. Her heels skidded back over the door.

''Cassie gets here, I'm going to give her the same. But first I'm going to enjoy taking you down a few pegs.'' With his free hand, he yanked her hair, darkly pleased when she whimpered.

Then she remembered the keys that were still gripped in her frozen fist. With prayers screaming in her head, she flung her hand back, hacking with the point she'd pushed between her clenched fingers.

He howled like a wild dog, and the vicious grip released. Dragging in air, she flew down the steps, certain he would be on her again in an instant. At the bottom, she stumbled, went down hard on her hands and knees. Prepared to scream, she looked back.

And saw him crumpled on the landing, holding a hand to his face, while blood dripped through his fingers. Like a woman in a trance, she rose to her feet, put one foot slowly in front of the other until she reached the diner. The buzzing in her ears warned her to take deep, careful breaths.

She stepped inside, closed the door behind her, unaware that her coat was hanging by one sleeve and the knees of her slacks were torn and bloody.

Cassie dropped the tray she was holding, shattering dishes. "Regan! My God!"

"I think you should call Devin," Regan said, testing each word as she spoke it. "Joe's on the landing of my apartment. I think I hurt him." When the room revolved, she braced a hand on the back of a booth. "I have to sit down now."

"Go call Devin," Ed snapped, and rushed over to ease Regan into a booth. "Head down." In a quick movement, she had Regan's head between her knees. "Long, deep breaths, that's a girl." Eyes sharp, she scanned the room, where a half a dozen customers sat staring. "Well, what are you waiting for? One of you big strong men get on over there and hold that son of a bitch for the sheriff. You, Horace, get up off your lard butt and get this girl a glass of water."

Ed's rasped orders had everyone moving at once. Satisfied, she eased Regan up again. "Got a little color back," she declared, and sat back on her haunches. She took a cigarette from the pack in her apron pocket, lit it with a wooden match. After one long drag, she smiled. "Hope to hell you hurt him bad, honey. Real bad."

Sitting in Devin's office, with the coffee Shane had poured for her warming her hands, Regan was sure she was over the worst of it. Everything had happened too fast for anything but pure emotion. But the rabbity fear had passed now, and she could think.

Beside her, Cassie sat saying nothing. Shane paced, like a boxer revving up for a match. At his desk, Devin coolly filled out a report.

"I'm sorry to ask you to go through it again, Regan," he began. "The clearer your statement, the easier it'll be to close it all up."

"That's all right. I'm fine now, really." Absently she picked at her torn slacks. The knees beneath still burned. As much, she thought, from Ed's liberal application of antiseptic as from their abrupt meeting with asphalt. "I'd like to get it over with. I can—"

She broke off when the door burst open. For an instant, she saw nothing but Rafe's face—pale, hard as rock, lit with eyes green enough, sharp enough, to murder in one vicious slice.

The rabbit pulse pounded in her throat. Before she could get to her feet, he was on her, dragging her up, crushing her in an embrace that bruised ribs.

"You're all right? Are you hurt?" His voice was raw, brittle as broken glass. He couldn't think. There'd been nothing inside him but bright terror from the moment he got word of the attack. His body was ice, enveloping hers as he buried his face in her hair.

Perhaps that was why she began to tremble helplessly. "I'm okay. Really, I'm—" But her voice shuddered off. If she could have burrowed inside him, she would have.

"Did he hurt you?" With a hand he was fighting to steady, he stroked her hair, eased her face back so that he could see for himself. "Did he touch you?"

She could only shake her head and press her face against his shoulder.

With his arms tight, as possessive as they were protective, he stared at Devin over Regan's head. His eyes fired like torches. "Where is he?"

"He's in custody."

Rafe's gaze whipped toward the cells in the back.

"He's not here, Rafe." Though his voice was calm, Devin was braced for the attack. "You're not going to be able to get to him."

"You think you can stop me?"

From behind, where he'd stood since he'd followed Rafe in, Jared laid a hand on his brother's shoulder. "Why don't you sit down?"

With a snarl humming in his throat, Rafe jerked the restraining hand aside. "Back off."

"This is the law's problem now," Devin told him, rising slowly.

"The hell with the law, and you with it. I want to know where he is."

"You find him, Rafe, I'll hold your coat." Primed

for action, Shane smiled thinly. "If you had a coat. Always hated the son of a bitch."

"Shut up," Jared muttered, glancing down at the silent Cassie.

"You can stick your lawyer talk," Shane told him, fists already bunched. "I'm with Rafe on this."

"I don't need you or anybody else with me. Don't get in my way, Devin."

"I'm already in your way. Now sit down, or I'll throw your ass in a cell."

He moved so fast, Regan had time only to squeak while Rafe lunged over the desk and had Devin by the shirtfront. She'd never considered herself sheltered, but the things they shouted at each other, the echo of the sentiments from the two MacKades behind her, had her already shocked system shuddering.

There was no doubt in her mind that blood would flow any moment.

"Stop it," she said, but the order was shaky and weak under the vicious words hurling through the room. "I said stop it," she repeated, hugging herself. Something crashed behind her, and shot her pulse to critical. "Stop it this minute!" she bellowed.

The surprising power in her voice halted Rafe's fist and put a stop to the shoving match behind her. Four hard-eyed men stared at her, like statues frozen in battle.

"You're acting like children. *Worse* than children. What good is it going to do anyone for the four of you to punch each other out? It's just typical," she said, more disgusted now than frightened. "Just the sort of typical behavior I'd expect from a bunch of boneheaded baboons. Real heroes.'' With a sniff, she grabbed her coat. ''Well, I'm certainly not going to stand here and watch the four of you beat one another to a pulp.''

''Sit down, Regan.'' When she continued toward the door, Rafe swore and went after her. ''Sit down,'' he repeated, holding back his rage and turning her gently. ''God, look at your hands.''

Shaken all over again, he gathered them carefully in his, pressed his lips to the abraded palms. It was a gesture that had the remaining MacKades shifting in embarrassment.

''What do you expect me to do?'' The rest of the anger drained and left him helpless. ''What do you expect me to feel?''

''I don't know.'' She no longer knew exactly what she was feeling herself, not with those eyes so concentrated on her face. ''I just want to get this over with, Rafe. Please, let me tell Devin what he needs to know, so I can get this over with.''

''Fine.'' He let her go, stepped back. ''Do what you have to do.''

She walked back to her chair, accepted the fresh mug Jared offered. Devin questioned, she answered. Rafe listened. Then he left, without a word.

She tried not to be hurt by it, tried to understand it. ''Devin, can you tell me what to expect now?''

''My deputy will call in once they're finished with Joe at the hospital. He'll be transferred. He broke parole, and the restraining order, so he'll serve his full time on the earlier charges.''

It was a small satisfaction, Devin thought with a quick look at Cassie. She hadn't moved or spoken in thirty minutes.

''Now he'll face additional charges,'' Devin went on. ''Breaking and entering, assault, attempted rape. We'll toss in the property damage. There may be a trial, and you'd have to testify.''

''I'm prepared for that.''

''Under the circumstances, his lawyer may advise him to deal and plead guilty.''

At Devin's questioning glance, Jared nodded. ''That's what I'd do.''

''Yeah, well.'' It was hard not to hate the system, Devin mused, when it got personal. ''Either way, he's going away for a good while. I figure three to five. He won't be bothering you again. Either of you.''

''Well, then.'' Regan drew in a deep breath. ''It's done. Cassie and I can go home now?''

''Sure. I'll be in touch.''

''I can't go home with you.'' For the first time since she'd come into the office, Cassie tried her voice. It was small and rusty.

''Of course you can.''

''How can I?'' She stared at the lovely smoke gray slacks Regan wore, at the nasty tears in the soft material. ''How could you even want me after what he's done to you?''

''What *he's* done,'' Regan said quietly. ''Not you, Cassie. You're not responsible.''

"Of course I am." It cost Cassie to lift her head, to look into Regan's eyes. "I know what he might have done to you if you hadn't been strong enough to stop him. Done to you to get to me, Regan. You're the best friend I've ever had."

"Then let me keep being your friend."

"I want that, and I know you've already forgiven me."

"Cassie, there's nothing to forgive. Don't take this on," Regan murmured, covering Cassie's hands with hers.

"I have to, because I have to start figuring out how to forgive myself now. I'm going to start by taking my kids home and finding a way to make the kind of life for them they deserve. I need to start taking care of myself and them. I need to do that."

"In a few more days," Regan protested.

"No, now." She closed her eyes, steadied herself, then opened them and looked at Jared. "Can you help me, Jared?"

"Of course I can. Whatever you need, honey. There are plenty of programs—"

"No." She pressed her lips together hard. It was time, she told herself, long past time, that she took a stand. "I want to file for divorce. Today. I need you to tell me what to do."

"All right." He took her hand to help her up, then slipped an arm gently around her shoulders. "Why don't you come with me now? We'll take care of everything."

"'Bout time," Shane muttered, the minute the door

closed behind them. He shrugged at the blazing look Devin aimed at him. "Hey, we all know she should have ditched that bastard years ago."

"You won't get any argument there." Regan rose, surprised she wasn't as steady as she'd believed. "But that was hard for her. It's going to be hard for her to follow through."

"She wouldn't have done it if he hadn't hurt somebody else," Devin mumbled. "That's the kind of thing it would take for her."

"Then I'm glad he did. And I'm glad I hurt him right back." Regan took a deep breath, then asked the question that had been hovering in a corner of her mind. "His eye, Devin?"

"I can let you know when I find out. If you want me to."

"I think I have to know." She held out a hand for his, not to shake, but to hold. "You've been wonderful. I know Rafe was upset, but he was wrong in the things he said to you. You did everything you could. You did everything right."

"If I'd done everything right, it wouldn't have happened."

"You know better than that." She squeezed, then winced as her hand throbbed. "I'm going home, take a bottle of aspirin, and crawl into bed for a few hours. Please call when you hear anything."

"I will. Shane?"

"Ahead of you, like always." He already had Regan's coat, and he helped her into it. "I'll drive you home and fix that door for you."

"Thanks." With a smile, she kissed his cheek. "Baboons or not, the MacKade brothers aren't half-bad."

"Baby—" he put an arm around her waist to lead her out "—we're all bad. Later, Dev." When he'd helped her into his truck, he paused. "Rafe'll come around. He just needs to go punch something."

"That's the answer?"

"Hey, it works." He slammed her door, then circled the truck to climb behind the wheel.

"You'd have gone with him. After Joe."

"We'd have all gone with him." Shane glanced in the rearview, then whipped the truck into a quick and illegal U-turn. "Dev and Jared would have spouted off for a while about law and order. We'd have shoved each other around. Then we'd have gone with him." With some regret, he shook his head. "It would've been fun."

"Fun." She could almost laugh as she let her head sink back on the seat.

"Nobody messes with a MacKade woman."

"Oh, really? And is that my status at this point?"

He caught the tone, and then, with a wary glance, the martial look in her eyes. "I just meant...seeing as you and Rafe... That is, the way he's..." Even a MacKade knew the value of retreat. "I ain't touching this one."

He pulled up at the base of her stairs and looked up to study the door. "Looks like somebody beat me to it."

"What?" She was still simmering.

"I'll check it, but it looks from here like it's already been fixed." He got out of the truck, climbed the stairs. "Yep. Few nicks and scratches, but it's back on its hinges." As a precaution, he tried the lock, gave it a good shove. "Solid. Rafe probably took care of it."

"I see." It did nothing to appease her. "I'll have to be sure to thank him, won't I?"

"Yeah." Shane retreated again, backing down the stairs. "Are you going to be all right? Want me to get you anything, or hang around?"

"No, no, I'm fine. Just fine." It wasn't pleasant to take out her keys, but she did it, turned the lock. "I appreciate the ride."

"No problem." As he hurried back to his truck, Shane decided Rafe had a problem. A big one. It gave him a reason to smile all the way through town.

Chapter 10

It felt good to beat on something. Even if it was only a nail. To prevent himself beating on something, or someone else, Rafe had closed himself inside the east-wing bedroom. The look in his eye had warned any and all of his men to keep their distance—if they wanted to keep their teeth.

The sounds of construction bumped against the walls, a sound just violent enough to suit his black mood. Rafe ignored the nail gun at his disposal and beat in nails with hammer and muscle. Every new stud that he secured with nails and a swing of his arm was Joe Dolin's face.

When the door opened behind him, Rafe bared his teeth without looking around. "Get the hell out. Stay out or you're fired."

"Go ahead and fire me." Regan slammed the door

at her back. "Then I can say what I have to say to you without damaging our professional relationship."

He looked over his shoulder now, briefly. She'd changed, he noted. Not just the slacks, but everything—shirt, blazer, jewelry. From her hair to her shoes, she was neat as a pin.

But he remembered exactly how she'd looked, frazzled, pale, with blood on her clothes.

"You don't want to be here right now." He set another nail, shot it home.

"You couldn't be more accurate on that, MacKade, but I'm here."

She'd had to shower first, had to scrub herself everywhere and throw out every stitch she'd been wearing when Joe touched her. But she was steady again, and ready to deal with Rafe MacKade.

"I want to know what the hell is wrong with you."

If he told her, she was liable to laugh in his face. And that, he was dead sure, would push him over that final edge.

"I'm busy, Regan. Weather's cost me a full day."

"Don't hand me that. Look at me when I'm talking to you, damn it." When he didn't, just kept battering nails into wood, she fisted her hands on her hips. "Why did you leave Devin's office that way? Just leave?"

"I had things to do."

To illustrate her opinion of that, she kicked at a toolbox. "I suppose I'm to thank you now for fixing my door."

"I'll bill you."

"Why are you mad at me?" she demanded. "I didn't do anything to—"

Her breath sucked in as the hammer sailed across the room and crashed into a newly framed wall.

"No, you didn't do a damn thing. You just got yourself tossed around, bruised, bloodied up and damn near raped. Why the hell should that bother me?"

Someone had to be calm, she told herself. Obviously, the way his eyes were glowing, it was going to have to be her. "I know you're upset about what happened."

"Yeah, I'm upset." He picked up the toolbox, heaved it, because it made more sense than throwing her around. Metal and steel crashed and scattered like small bombs. "I'm just a little upset. Now get out."

"I won't." Instead she angled her chin. "Go ahead, big guy, throw something else. When you've got it out of your system, we'll have a civilized conversation."

"You'd better get it through that thick head that there's nothing civilized about me."

"Oh, that's coming through loud and clear," she tossed back. "What's next? You want to take a shot at me? That should prove you're a bigger man than Joe Dolin."

His eyes went black. For an instant, a heartbeat, she thought she saw hurt mixed with the rage. And it shamed her. "I'm sorry." Fumbling, she lifted her hands. "You didn't deserve that. I didn't mean that."

Now there was only rage, viciously controlled.

"You usually say what you mean." He held up a hand before she could speak again. "You want to have a conversation, fine. We'll have a damn conversation."

He strode to the door, simmering when she flinched. Yanking it open, he bellowed to every corner of the rambling house. "Out! Everybody out, now!"

He slammed the door again, satisfied by the scramble of feet and the clatter of tools.

"There's no need for the work to stop," she began. "I'm sure this will only take a few minutes."

"Sometimes it just can't be your way."

"I don't know what you mean."

"No, I don't guess you do." Disgusted, he hauled open the door again. "Somebody give me a damn cigarette," he shouted. But as there was no one brave enough to approach, he ended up slamming the door again.

Regan watched, quietly fascinated, while he paced and swore. His shirt was shoved up to the elbows, a tool belt was slung at his hips like a holster. He'd wrapped a bandanna around his forehead to catch the sweat. He looked, she thought, like a bandit who would just as soon kill as steal.

And it was certainly ridiculous to be aroused.

"I could make coffee," she began, then let out a breath at the razor-edged look he shot her. "Maybe not. Rafe—"

"Just shut up."

Her back jammed straight as a poker. "I don't care to be spoken to that way."

"Get used to it. I've held back long enough with you."

"Held back?" Her eyes went wide. If he hadn't looked like a maniac, she might have laughed. "You've been holding back? I'd like to see what you consider cutting loose."

"You're about to." He gnawed off the words like stringy meat from a bone. "You're ticked off that I left? Well, now you're going to be treated to what would have happened if I'd stayed."

"Don't you touch me." Her arms shot up, hands fisted like those of a boxer ready to spar. "Don't you dare."

Eyes simmering, he closed a hand over her fist and used his leverage to push her back to the door. "Same goes, darling. I gave you a chance to walk, you didn't take it."

"Don't call me darling in that tone of voice."

The way his lips peeled back, she wouldn't have been surprised to see fangs. "God, you're a piece of work." He tossed her hand down and walked away, because it was safer for both of them. "You want to know why I left. That's the big, burning question, isn't it? That's what had you coming over here? Coming to me?"

"Yes."

"But you didn't come to me this morning when he threatened you. You didn't come to me when he hurt you." And that, Rafe thought, however it devastated him, was that.

"I had to tell Devin," she began.

"Yeah. You had to tell Devin." Bitterly calm now, he turned back. "You know what I heard in that nice and detailed statement you made, Regan? Dolin came into your place this morning, just like I thought he would."

"And I handled it," she countered. "Just like I told you I would."

"Sure, you're great at handling things. He threatened you. He scared you."

"Yes, all right, he scared me." And she was scared now, too, she realized, of where this was leading. "That's why I called Devin."

"But not me. You went down to Devin's office, filed your charges."

"Yes, of course. I wanted Joe arrested."

"Nice and tidy. Then you went *grocery* shopping."

"I..." She linked her hands together, pulled them apart. "I thought—I knew Cassie was going to be upset, and I wanted... I just thought if I fixed a meal it would make us both feel better."

"And in all that time, going to Devin's, to the market, walking there and back, you never stopped to call me. It never even occurred to you, did it?"

"I was—" She opened her mouth, closed it again. "All right, yes. It was my first reaction, but I calmed down and decided against it."

"You calmed down?"

"Yes, I realized it was my problem, and my responsibility to handle it."

Her simple honesty sliced through him like a blade. He could almost see himself split in half, one part rage, one part misery. "And after he had you, after he had his hands on you, and hurt you, tried to—"

He couldn't say it. If he did, he'd fall to pieces.

"You didn't think to call me then, either. I only heard it from Shane because he was in with Devin when the call came through, and he figured I'd be interested."

Somehow, she realized, she *had* hurt him. She'd never meant to. Hadn't known he could be hurt. "Rafe, I wasn't thinking at all." She started forward, stopped, knowing it would do no good to go farther. "I was numb. By the time I could really think again, I was in Devin's office. It all happened so fast," she said hurriedly, desperate now to make him see. To understand. "And part of the time it seemed as if I wasn't really there at all."

"You were handling it."

"I had to. It wouldn't have done any good to fall apart."

"You're real good at keeping yourself together." He walked over, picked up the hammer. "All by yourself."

"I have to be. I expect myself to be, because—"

"You don't want to be like your mother," he finished for her.

It sounded so callous, and so foolish. "All right, yes, that's partially true. It's important for me to be a certain way, but that really doesn't apply to this. If I didn't call you, it was only because..."

"You didn't need me." His eyes were level, and no longer hot. He had very little heat left inside him. "You don't need me."

A new kind of panic was twisting through her. "That's not true."

"Oh, the sex is great." He smiled then, coolly, humorlessly. "That's a need we handle together real well. It's my problem that I let it get personal. I won't make the mistake again."

"It's not about sex."

"Sure it is." He plucked a nail out of his pouch, set it in place. "It's been about sex right from the get-go. That's all we've got. It's plenty." He rammed the nail home. "You know where to find me when you've got the itch."

The blood drained from her cheeks and froze around her heart. "That's a horrible thing to say."

"Your rules, darling. Why complicate a good thing, right?"

"I don't want things to be this way between us, Rafe."

"Well, now I do. Take it or leave it." He rammed another nail into wood. She wasn't going to get the chance to hurt him again, he told himself. No woman hurt him like this.

She opened her mouth, primed to tell him she'd leave it. Leave him. And couldn't. Tears burned in her eyes, in her throat. Could there have been a worse possible time, she wondered, for her to realize she was in love with him?

"Is that the way you really feel?"

"I try to say what I mean, too."

Unwilling to humiliate herself, she swallowed the tears. "And all this is because you're angry about what happened. About how I dealt with it."

"Let's just say it made everything clear. You don't want to clutter up your life, right?"

"No, I—"

"Hell, neither do I. Call it ego— I've got one. I didn't like you running to my brother instead of me. Like you said, I've got it out of my system. We can just go back to the way things were. The way things are."

She hadn't realized how much she could prefer that lethal temper over this calculated disinterest. "I'm not sure that's possible. I can't give you an answer right at the moment."

"You mull it over, Regan. You do that real well, too."

"Would you rather—" She pressed a hand to her lips, waited until she could steady her voice. "If you'd rather suspend our business relationship, I can give you the names of some other dealers in the area."

"No reason for that. I'm already behind." When he turned to her, all he saw was that her eyes were dry, her face was composed. "I can take shipment on this room in about a week, if you've got a problem with storage."

"That'll be fine. I'll make the arrangements." She turned and reached blindly for the doorknob. Terrified she'd crumble, she walked away quickly. She didn't start to run until she was outside, with the wind slapping her wet cheeks.

When he heard the door close below, Rafe sat down on the floor. At the sound of weeping shimmering in the air, he rubbed his hands hard over his face.

"I know just how you feel," he muttered.

It was the first time in his checkered career that anyone had managed to break his heart. His only solace was that he'd make damn sure it was the last.

The predicted ice storm raged through, glazing the snow, turning the streets to glass. It was days before the temperature inched up enough to soften it. Each night the thermometer would plunge again, hardening and slickening every coated surface.

It didn't mean a damn thing to Rafe. The lousy weather gave him an excuse to stay just where he was, work twenty out of every twenty-four hours. With every nail he hammered, every wall he sanded, the house became more his.

When he couldn't sleep, even after exhausting himself, he wandered the house with the other ghosts.

He was too busy to think about Regan. Or so he tried to convince himself.

Whenever he did, whenever she snuck through his well-fortified defenses, he just worked harder, longer.

"You look a little ragged, pal." Devin lit a cigarette and watched Rafe hammer freshly painted base-board into place. "Remember that book—*Dorian Gray?* The way it's starting to look, you're the picture in the closet, and this house is old Dorian."

"Pick up a hammer, or beat it."

Instead, Devin crouched, ran a fingertip over the wide, carved trim. "Sure is pretty as a picture. What'd you call this color?"

"Rose dust." He framed the words like a dare.

"Yep, sure is pretty." Devin used an empty coffee can as an ashtray. "If you're into pink."

Rafe spared him a look. "You trying to start some-thing?"

"Nope, just making conversation. They transferred Joe from the hospital today."

Rafe's eyes iced over before he turned away. "None of my business."

"He didn't lose his eye," Devin went on easily. "Be wearing a patch for a while though. They can't tell yet if there'll be permanent damage."

"She should have aimed between his legs."

"Yeah, too bad about that. Well, I thought you'd want to know, he pleaded guilty to the B and E, the assault, on advice of counsel. They dumped the at-tempted rape charges to get the guilty plea and avoid trial, but he's not going to pass Go."

Rafe didn't want to care. "How long?"

"My guess is three, solid. Before you say it's not enough, I'm going to the sentencing tomorrow my-self, and adding weight. When he's up for parole, in a year or so, I'll go back and add more."

"I said it's none of my business." Rafe toed in the last piece of baseboard. "How's Cassie holding up?"

"Okay, I guess. Jared's pushing through the divorce. With the spousal abuse and adultery, it won't take the usual year. Joe's not in much of a position to contest it. The quicker it's done, the quicker she and the kids can get on with things."

Thoughtfully he tapped his cigarette out in the can. "Aren't you going to ask how Regan's holding up?"

"No."

"Well, I'll tell you." Ignoring Rafe's snarl, Devin folded his legs and sat. "She doesn't look like she's been getting a lot of sleep, if you ask me."

"I didn't."

"Ed says she hasn't been coming in for lunch, so I guess her appetite's off, too. I could figure that experience with Joe shook her up enough to interfere with her sleeping and eating. But I got a hunch it's something else."

"She'll handle it. She's good at taking care of herself."

"Good thing, too. Odds are, if Joe had managed to drag her inside that day, somebody would've seen the door quick enough, heard the ruckus. Still, he could've done a lot of damage in a short time."

"Don't you think I know that?" Rafe shot out. "Do you think I don't know what he could have done to her?"

"Yeah, I think you know it. I think it's eating at you, and I'm sorry. Are you ready to listen to me?"

"No."

But there wasn't any heat behind the denial, so Devin prepared to say his piece. "Witnesses in the diner said they thought she was drunk at first when she came in, the way she was walking. She'd have passed out if Ed hadn't gotten her down first."

"I don't need to hear this."

"Yeah," Devin murmured, watching Rafe's knuckles whiten on the hilt of the hammer, "you do. When I got to her, Rafe, she was in shock. Are you getting this? Her pupils were as narrow as the point of one of those nails. I was set to have her taken into Emergency, but she pulled herself together. I watched her do it. It was impressive."

"So she's tough." The image projecting into his mind scraped him raw. "Tell me something I don't know."

"Okay. I don't figure you were in any shape to see the way she looked at you when you walked into my office. She'd pulled herself together because she had to, because that's the way she's made, I guess. Then you walked in. A man could go his whole life without having a woman look at him the way she looked at you."

"She doesn't need me."

"That's bull. You may be stupid, but you should know that."

"I know I was stupid enough to let her matter. To let what she thought of me, what she wanted from me, matter. I'm not doing it again." He rose, hooked his hammer in his tool belt. "I don't need her, either."

With a sigh, Devin unfolded himself and stood. "You're cross-eyed in love with her."

"No, I'm not. I got soft on her for a while, then I got over it."

Devin pursed his lips. There was one quick, potentially painful way to handle this. "You're sure?"

"I just said so, didn't I?"

"Good." Devin smiled. "That clears the way. When I thought you had a thing for her, I didn't want to muscle in. Since you don't, I'll go see if I can...stimulate her appetite."

He was expecting the punch, and took the fist on the jaw philosophically. It was always satisfying to make a point. He lifted a hand, wiggled his jaw, mildly relieved it wasn't broken.

"Yeah, I can see how you got over it."

"I ought to hit you again," Rafe said between his teeth. It was infuriating, humiliating, to know how neatly he'd been conned.

"I wouldn't. That one was free." Cautious, Devin moved his jaw again. "Damn, Rafe, you've still got a nice right jab."

Almost amused, Rafe flexed his aching fingers. "You've still got a face like a rock. You son of a bitch."

"I love you, too." Cheered, Devin draped an arm over his brother's shoulders. "Feel better now?"

"No." Then he paused. "Maybe."

"You want to go find her and straighten this mess out?"

"I'm not crawling after some woman," Rafe mumbled.

You will, Devin thought. Sooner or later. "Well then, I got the night off. Want to get drunk and disorderly?"

"Yeah." They walked into the hall, started down the steps. "Why don't I meet you at the tavern? Ten o'clock."

"Suits me. I'll see if I can round up Shane and Jared."

"Just like old times. When Duff sees us coming, it'll scare the—" Rafe broke off, felt his heart skip. Regan stood straight-backed and cool-eyed at the base of the stairs.

"I've got your delivery." She'd worked very hard on being able to speak without inflection. "Your message said you'd be ready for it by three."

"Just." His stomach quivered, infuriating him. "You can have it hauled up."

"All right. Hello, Devin."

"Hello, Regan. I'm just on my way out. See you tonight, Rafe."

"Yeah." Rafe kept his eyes on Regan's as he came down the last few steps. "Have any trouble on the roads?"

"No. They're mostly clear now." She wondered that he couldn't see her heart bleeding. "I was able to get that feather mattress you wanted for the four-poster. I'll be happy to set it up so you can be sure you want to go with it."

"Appreciate it. I'll get out of your way. I've

got—'' Nothing, he realized. He had nothing. ''Work,'' he said finally. ''Give a yell when you're ready. I'll have your check.''

She wanted to say something, anything, but he was already walking away. Squaring her shoulders, she went back to the door to instruct the movers.

It was nearly five when she finished arranging things exactly as she wanted them. She hadn't noticed the quiet that drifted in to replace the steady bang and buzz of labor. But as the light changed, she switched on the rose-patterned globe lamp by the button-backed chair she'd angled toward the fireplace.

There was no mantel there yet, no flames crackling. Faintly the scent of paint stirred in the air. But she thought the room was waiting to be lived in.

And the scent of roses hung like tears in the air.

A wedding-ring quilt, she mused, running her hand over one of the posts of the bed. A few pillows edged with lace to match the canopy that would drape overhead. A cedar chest, a hope chest, at the foot of the bed, filled with sweet-smelling linens and net bags of lavender sachet.

Yes, she thought, those would be just the right touches to finish it off. Perhaps some Irish lace at the windows, a silver-backed brush for the vanity.

It would be beautiful. It would be perfect.

She wished to God she'd never seen the room, the house, or Rafe MacKade.

He stood in the doorway, saying nothing, watching her move through the room, as graceful as any ghost.

Then her back stiffened. She turned and faced him. Seconds passed, though it could have been eons for both of them.

"I was just finishing up," she managed to say.

"So I see." He stayed where he was, tore his gaze from hers and scanned the room. "It looks terrific."

"I have some tintypes and antique silver frames. I think they'd add a nice touch to the mantel when it's in place."

"Great."

The strain of manners was tearing at her stomach. "I noticed you've made a lot of progress on the next bedroom."

"It's coming along. I've got a couple more ready for drywall."

"You work fast."

"Yeah, that's what they always say." He pulled a check out of his pocket, stepped forward. "Payment on delivery."

"Thank you." Very deliberately, she opened the purse she'd set on a table, slipped the check inside. And damned him to hell. "I'll be going, then," she said briskly. She turned back and bumped solidly into him. "Excuse me." She took a step around. He shifted, blocked her. Made her heart pound like a drum. "You're in my way."

"That's right." And since he was, he took a good long look. "You look lousy."

"Thank you so much."

"You've got shadows under your eyes."

So much for cosmetics, she thought in disgust. "It's been a long day. I'm tired."

"How come you haven't been eating over at Ed's?"

She wondered why she'd ever thought she liked small towns. "Despite what you and the Antietam grapevine might think, what I do on my lunch hour is my business."

"Dolin's locked up. He's not going to bother you again."

"I'm not afraid of Joe Dolin." She tossed back her hair, proud of her own bravado. "I'm thinking about buying a gun."

"Think again."

She hadn't really thought of it the first time, but it grated to have him dictate to her. "That's right, you're the only one who can defend himself, or anyone else. Back off, MacKade. I'm finished here."

When he grabbed her arm, she swung out without thinking. Her hand cracked against his cheek before she could stop it. Appalled, she stumbled back.

"Now look what you've made me do." Enraged and close to tears, she tossed down her purse. "I can't believe you goaded me into that. I've never struck anyone in my life."

"You did a pretty good job on your debut." Watching her, he ran his tongue over the inside of his stinging cheek. "You want to put your shoulder into it next time. Not much of a crack if you swing from the wrist."

"There won't be a next time. Unlike you, I don't

have to hit people to make a point.'' She took a steadying breath. "I apologize."

"If you head for the door again, I'm going to get in your way again, and we're going to start this all over."

"All right." She left her purse where it lay. "Obviously there's something you want to say."

"If you keep aiming that chin at me, you're going to make me mad. I'm being civilized, asking how you are. Civilized is how you like it, isn't it?"

"I'm fine." She bit the words off. "And how are you?"

"Good enough. You want some coffee, a beer?"

"No, thank you so much." Who the hell was this man, she thought, making uselessly polite conversation while her insides tangled into dozens of frayed knots? "I don't want coffee or beer."

"What do you want, Regan?"

Now she recognized him. It took only that sharp, impatient tone to bring him back. And to make her yearn. "I want you to leave me alone."

He said nothing at all, just stepped out of her way.

Once more she picked up her purse. Once more she set it down again. "That's not true." The hell with her pride, with sense, even with her heart. It couldn't be any more battered than it already was.

"You'd never have made it to the door," he said quietly. "You probably knew that."

"I don't know anything except I'm tired of fighting with you."

"I'm not fighting. I'm waiting."

She nodded, sure she understood. If it was all he was willing to give her now, she would accept that. And she would make it enough. She stepped out of her shoes, unbuttoned her blazer.

"What are you doing?"

"Answering your ultimatum of last week." She tossed the blazer on the chair and unbuttoned her blouse. "You said take it or leave it. I'm taking it."

Chapter 11

It was a curve he hadn't been expecting. By the time he could speak, she was wearing nothing but two scraps of black silk. And all the blood had drained out of his head.

"Just like that?"

"It was always just like that, wasn't it, Rafe? Chemistry, pure and simple?"

He'd want her, she promised herself. By God, when she was done with him, he'd never stop wanting her. Keeping her eyes locked on his, she walked slowly toward him.

"Take it or leave it, MacKade." She put her hands on his shirt and stunned them both by ripping it open and sending buttons flying. "Because I'm about to take you."

Her mouth was fire on his, burning, flashing, shooting dozens of wild blazes into him. Rocked to the core, he gripped her hips, fingers digging through silk to flesh.

''Put your hands on me.'' She sank her teeth into his shoulder. ''I want your hands on me.'' Hers were dragging at his jeans, closing around him.

''Wait.'' But the bombs erupting inside him drowned out everything but pulsing, grappling need. With only his wounded heart as a pitiful weapon, he was defenseless against the spear thrust of desire. Against her.

He kicked himself free of clothes, lifted her off the floor.

He was deep inside her before they fell onto the bed.

It was all sweat and speed and blind sex. The hard slap of flesh against flesh, the raspy gasps of labored breathing. Teeth and nails and tangled tongues drove them both over the sumptuous mattress, rolling and riding.

It was a battle both had already surrendered to. Hot and hard and hurried, fast and frenzied and frantic, they pounded together. Wanting more, accepting less. The scent of roses choked the air with strong, sad perfume.

She straddled him, bowed back as his hands streaked over her. She wanted him to take her to that tenuous edge between pleasure and pain. There she would be alive, as she hadn't been since he'd turned from her.

She had to know that here, at least here, he was as

helpless as she, as unable to resist, as pathetically needy. She could feel that need riot through him, taste it each time he dragged her mouth back to his with a ravenous hunger.

While her heart screamed at him to love her, just a little, her quivering body greedily devoured, fueling itself with whatever scraps he would give.

No room for pride, no time for tenderness.

When she sank toward him, limp as water, he rolled her ruthlessly onto her back and drove her on.

He couldn't breathe, didn't think, just battered himself into her. He had to fill her, to empty her, to claim her in the only way he knew she would accept. With a jerk of his head, he tossed the hair out of his eyes. It was vital that he see her, every flicker of shock and pleasure on her face, every tremble of her lips.

Love for her swamped him. All but destroyed him.

"Look at me." He grated the words out. "You look at me."

Her eyes opened, but remained blind with passion. He felt her body quake under his, saw those eyes glaze as her head fell back.

He was powerless to stop himself from following her recklessly over the edge. But he cursed her, then himself, as he fell.

It didn't seem possible to have been so completely aroused, and to feel so utterly empty. He'd never understood how vitally entwined the heart and the body were, until now. And now, staring at the ceiling, with

Regan silent beside him, he understood it would never be possible to separate his again.

Not with her.

And he wanted only her.

She'd taken something from him that he'd struggled for years to build. His self-respect. How odd that he hadn't realized that, either, until this moment.

He wasn't sure he could forgive either of them for it.

She desperately wanted him to reach out to her, to fold her to him as he had in the past. It was miserable to be left like this, so cold, so alone, even as she was still quivering from him.

Yet how could she reach out for him, when she was the one who had taken the step, made the stand, and agreed to take him on his own terms? His own terms, she thought, closing her eyes against the lovely rosy glow of the lamp. Bad Rafe MacKade had returned, she thought bitterly, and taken it all.

"Well, we managed to have sex in a bed for a change." She sat up, kept her back to him. She could control her voice, but was certain her face would show him that she was shattered. "It's always firsts with us, isn't it, MacKade?"

"Yeah." He wanted to stroke that back, but it was so stiff and straight. "We'll have to try it with sheets sometime."

"Why not?" Her hands trembled as she slid off the bed, reached down for her underwear. "We could even throw in a couple of pillows, and a pretense of affection. Just for a change of pace."

His eyes sharpened, narrowed, as she snapped her bra into place. Hurt and fury bubbled together in a messy stew. Rising, he snatched his jeans, jammed his legs in them.

"I don't like pretenses much."

"Oh, that's right." She grabbed her shirt. Silk whipped through the air and onto her back. "Everything's up-front with you. No frills, no spills."

"What the hell's wrong with you? You got what you wanted."

"You don't know diddly about what I want." Terrified she might weep, she jerked on her slacks. "Apparently neither do I."

"You're the one who took off your clothes, darling." His voice was entirely too smooth. "You're the one putting them right back on so you can move right along."

"And you're the one who rolled off me the minute you were done, as if your twenty bucks was up." Rushing now, she jammed her feet into her shoes.

She might have had a chance if she'd been looking at him. A slim one. But he moved fast, and she was six inches off the ground, his hands like a vise on her, his eyes drilling holes in hers before she drew a second breath.

"Don't say that. I've never treated you that way. I've never thought that way."

"You're right." Oddly enough, it was the lash of his temper that calmed her. Stopped her, she hoped, from being a perfect fool. "I'm sorry, Rafe. That was unfair and untrue."

Very slowly, he set her back on her feet. He realized his fingers were digging hard enough into her flesh to meet bone, and dropped his hands. "Maybe I moved too fast, but you caught me off guard."

"No." Yes, she felt very calm, she thought as she turned to pick up her blazer. Very calm, and very, very fragile. If he touched her again, she would crack like flawed glass. "I initiated things, and I agreed to your terms."

"My terms—"

"Are clear," she said, finishing for him. "And acceptable. I suppose the problem is that we're both volatile personalities under the right circumstances. Any circumstances, as far as you're concerned. And as for me, the past few days have been difficult. That doesn't mean I should take it out on you."

"Do you have to be reasonable, Regan?"

"No, but I'm going to be." Though her lips curved brightly, she couldn't move the smile into her eyes. "I don't know what we're fighting about, when we've found the perfect solution. A simple, physical relationship. It's perfect, because the rest of our common ground is narrow to nonexistent. So, I'll apologize again for picking a fight. I'm just a little tired and out of sorts."

She made herself rise on her toes and kiss him lightly. "If you'd like to come by tomorrow after work, I'll make it up to you."

"Yeah, maybe." Why the hell couldn't he read her eyes? He could always read her eyes if he looked hard enough. "I'll take you home."

"No, really." She had to will herself not to run to the door and escape. Instead, she picked up her purse. "I've got my car," she added. "And I really am tired. I could use an early night."

He just wanted to hold her, to fold her into his arms and keep her there. "Whatever you say. I'm supposed to meet my brothers at the tavern in a few hours, anyway."

"Good, then we'll try for tomorrow." She made it to the door without stumbling. He didn't offer a good-bye, and neither did she. Her coat was a bright red slash over the newel post, or she might have walked outside without it. She put in on, buttoned it carefully.

Outside, she got into her car, turned the key in the ignition. She concentrated on backing down the lane as if her life depended on it. She took the turn toward town, drove a half mile.

Then she pulled over to the side of the road, carefully put the car in gear, turned the engine off. And cried like a baby.

Twenty minutes later, exhausted, she let her head fall back against the seat. It was freezing, but she didn't have the energy to turn the car on again and pump up the heater.

She was a competent woman, Regan thought. Everyone said so. She was bright, well-organized, moderately successful, and levelheaded.

So why, if she was indeed all of those fine, admirable things, had she managed to mess up her life so miserably?

Rafe MacKade was responsible, of course. She

hadn't had a full day's easy running since he'd swaggered back into town. He was messy, arrogant, angry. Oh, so angry. And charming, she thought with a sigh, with all those unexpected sweet spots mixed with the rough.

She should never have fallen for him. She certainly shouldn't have deluded herself that she could have an affair with him and stay objective.

He hadn't been completely objective, either, she remembered. He'd had feelings tangling him up, too. Before she'd ruined it. If she had been just a little more of what he needed, if she hadn't been so dead set on doing it all her way, he might have stayed tangled. Until he'd fallen in love.

Oh, that was wrong, she thought, and banged her fist against the steering wheel. That was her mother's kind of thinking. Make everything pretty, everything perfect for the man. Stroke his ego, cater to his whims. Play the game and win the prize.

Well, she wouldn't. She was appalled she'd even considered it. She would not squash her own needs, her own personality, her own ego, to lure a man into love.

But hadn't she just done that? She shuddered, but not from the cold. Hadn't she just done that, up in that bedroom?

At a loss, she braced her elbows on the wheel, her head in her hands. She wasn't sure of anything any longer. Except that she loved him. She loved him, and in her stubborn stance against luring him into love with her, she had blocked, perhaps even rejected his feelings. And humiliated herself in the bargain.

That, Regan concluded, made her an idiot.

So what if she had to make some changes in herself? Hadn't he, in his way, done the same?

He'd been hurt, she remembered. She had hurt him, infuriated him. Yet he had gone off to pound nails, instead of picking a fight. It was she who was the coward, who had been unwilling to trust, refusing to bend. He'd never tried to run her life, or her thoughts, or tried to change her. No, he'd given her room, he'd given her affection, and he'd given her the kind of passion a woman dreamed of.

But she'd held back anyway, foolishly, in a knee-jerk response rooted in her upbringing.

Why hadn't she thought of his needs, his pride? Wasn't it time she did so? She could be flexible, couldn't she? Compromise wasn't capitulation. It couldn't be too late to show him she was willing. She wouldn't let it be too late to...

The thought that came into her mind was so simple, and so ridiculous, she knew it had to be right. Without giving herself a moment to think it through, she revved up the car and hit the gas. In minutes, she was on Cassie's doorstep, banging.

"Regan." With Emma on her hip, Cassie dragged a hand through her tousled hair. "I was just—you've been crying." Alarm sprinted through her. "Joe—"

"No, no. I'm sorry. I didn't mean to scare you. I need help."

"What is it?" In a flash, Cassie had closed the door and locked it. "What's wrong?"

"What's nine-ball?"

"What—?" Baffled, Cassie set Emma down, gave her a little pat on the bottom to send her along. "What's nine-ball?"

"Yes. And where am I going to find a red leather miniskirt at this hour?"

Cassie thought for a moment, brushing a hand over the wet spot on her sweater that was courtesy of Emma's bath. "If that's what you want, we'll have to call Ed."

"Suck it in, sweetie."

"I am." Valiantly Regan gritted her teeth and held her breath as Ed tugged at the zipper of a skirt the size of a place mat.

"Trouble is, you've got a figure. I've got bones." Mouth clamped tight in determination, Ed hauled, and tugged. Then, with a wheeze of triumph, sat back on Cassie's bed. "She's on, but I wouldn't make any sudden moves."

"I don't think I can make *any* moves." Testing, Regan took a step. The skirt, already dangerously high, snuck up another fraction.

"You got a little height on me, too," Ed announced, and pulled out a cigarette. Her eyes sparkled with amusement as she let her rhinestone glasses fall to her chest. "If it was much shorter on you, Devin would have to arrest you."

"I can't see." Though she rose on her toes and

turned carefully, Cassie's mirror offered nothing but a view from the waist up.

"You don't have to, honey. Take my word, he will."

"I got the kids settled," Cassie said as she walked in. She stopped short, her mouth forming a shocked circle. "Oh, my…"

"It's a hot little number," Ed agreed. When she'd worn it last time, at the Legion dance, eyes had popped loose. The way Regan was filling it out, Ed imagined they'd not only pop, but go flying across the room.

"Try those shoes with it now," she ordered. "I stuffed some tissue in the toes to bring 'em down to size."

Regan braced a hand on Cassie's dresser, stepped gingerly into the four-inch spikes. "I'll get a nosebleed in these."

"Honey, you'll cause nosebleeds." Ed gave a raspy laugh. "Now let's try some war paint." Happily she upended her enormous purse onto the bed.

"I'm not sure I can go through with this. It's a crazy idea."

"Don't go chicken on me now." Ed riffled her hand through a department-store array of cosmetics. "You want that man, don't you?"

"Yes, but—"

"Then sit down here on the bed and let me buff you up. This here red's a killer," she murmured fondly as she unscrewed a lipstick.

"I can't sit," Regan stated after a single attempt. "I'd damage an internal organ."

"Then stand." After making her choices, Ed rose and went to work. "Now, you said nine-ball, right?"

"Yeah."

In her forty-two years—forty-five, if God was listening—she'd never seen a woman less likely to chalk a stick than Regan Bishop. "Ever play pool, honey?"

"Billiards." Regan uttered a silent prayer as Ed advanced with eyeliner. "With my father. Several times."

"Hell, honey, billiards ain't nothing. Why, nine-ball's the second-best thing you can do on a pool table." She cackled when Cassie flushed scarlet. "Now listen up while I explain how it works."

Balls smacked and clattered when Rafe shot his cue. The five ball thumped satisfactorily into the corner pocket.

"Luck," Jared said, and lazily chalked his cue.

Rafe only snorted. "Six off the nine and in the side." He made his shot, lined up the next.

"Never could beat Rafe at nine-ball." More interested in the little redhead at the bar than the game, Shane leaned on the juke. She was all alone, and looked as cuddly as a new down pillow. "Seen her around before, Dev?"

Devin glanced up, over. "Holloway's niece, from up on Mountain View. She's got a boyfriend the size of a semi who'll break you in half if you breathe on her."

It was all the challenge Shane needed. He sauntered over, leaned on the bar and turned on the charm.

Devin gave a resigned smile. If the boyfriend came in, Devin would have to use his badge. And that would blow his night.

"My game." Rafe held out his hand for the ten dollars Jared owed him. "You're up, Dev."

"I need a beer."

"Jared's buying." Rafe grinned at his older brother. "Right, bro?"

"I bought last round."

"You lost the last game."

"So be a gracious winner. His tab," Jared told the bartender, and held up three fingers.

"Hey, what about me?"

Jared flicked a glance at Shane. The redhead was clutching his arm like a fast-growing vine. "You're driving, kid."

"Flip for it."

Obligingly, Jared took a coin from his pocket. "Call it."

"Heads."

He flipped the coin, caught it neatly. "Tails. You're driving."

With a philosophical shrug, Shane turned back to the redhead.

"Does he have to hit on everything in a skirt?" Rafe muttered while Devin racked the balls.

"Yep. Somebody had to take up where you left off." Devin stepped back, chose his cue. "And since you're spoken for..."

"Nobody said I was spoken for." Rafe gave the curvy redhead a long look, felt nothing more than a low-level tug of basic appreciation. And thought of Regan, just thought of her and his heart shattered. "We've got an understanding." He bit the words off, but still tasted bitterness. "Nothing serious."

"He's hooked." Jared grinned and lifted his beer. "And his heart looks so pretty, right there on his sleeve."

No way he was going to take the bait, Rafe thought. It was bad enough having your heart broken without having your family watch you fumble with the pieces. "You want to eat this cue?" Rafe executed his break, smugly pleased when two balls rolled into pockets.

"She came into the house today," Devin said conversationally, "and that hook in his mouth dragged him right down the stairs like a trout on a fly. I think there were stars in his eyes, too." Devin met Rafe's steely look equably. "Yep, I'm sure of it."

"Pretty soon he's going to start shaving regular and wearing clean shirts." Jared shook his head, as if in mourning. "Then we'll know we've lost him."

"Then it'll be antique shows and ballets." Devin heaved a heavy sigh. "Poetry readings."

Because that hit entirely too close to home, Rafe jerked the cue and missed his shot. He wasn't going to think of her. Damn it, he wasn't going to give Regan or the hole in his gut a single thought. "Keep it up and I'll take both of you on."

"Well, I'm shaking." After lining up his shot, Devin leaned over the table. He made his ball cleanly.

As he circled the table, he sniffed at Rafe. "That cologne, lover-boy?"

"I'm not wearing any damn—" Rafe hissed out a breath. "You're just jealous 'cause you're sleeping alone on some cot outside a cell every night."

"You got me there."

Enjoying himself, Jared plugged coins into the jukebox. "What time do you have to be home, Rafe? We wouldn't want you getting conked with a rolling pin for missing curfew."

"How long have you been a practicing ass?" It was some small satisfaction to note that Duff was shooting them uneasy glances. A man didn't like to lose his touch. "What's the fine for breaking up a couple of chairs?"

Nostalgia swam sweetly along with the beer in Devin's bloodstream. Unless he counted breaking his brothers up, and you could hardly count that, he hadn't been in a decent fight in years.

"Can't let you do it," he said, with mildly drunk regret. "I carry a badge."

"Take it off." Rafe grinned. "And let's beat hell out of Shane. For old times' sake."

Jared tapped his fingers on the juke in time to the music. He eyed their youngest brother, who was definitely making progress with the redhead. That alone was reason enough to punch him a few times.

"I've got enough on me to post bond," Jared told them. "And a little extra to bribe the sheriff, if we have to."

Devin sighed, straightened from the table. With

brotherly affection, he studied the unsuspecting Shane. "Hell, he's going to get his butt whipped before the night's over, anyway, if he keeps playing with that girl. We might as well do it first."

"We'll be more humane," Jared agreed.

The bartender watched them move together, recognized, with despair, the look in each eye. "Not in here. Come on now, Devin, you're the law."

"Just doing my brotherly duty."

"What's the idea?" Scenting trouble, Shane danced back from the bar. He scanned his brothers, shifted as they moved to flank him. "Three against one?" His mouth curved in a wide, reckless grin as other customers moved to safety. "Come on, then."

He crouched, braced, then made the mistake of glancing over as the door opened. His mouth had already fallen open in surprise when Rafe caught him low and sent them both crashing into a table.

"You make it too easy." Laughing, Rafe turned and caught him in a cheerful headlock. Then he went numb, right down to his toes.

The skirt barely made it past the legal limit. It wasn't tight. It went beyond tight as it squeezed possessively over curvy hips in an eye-popping fire-engine red. The legs went on. And on. Rafe's dazzled gape followed them down to the razor-sharp skyscraper heels in that same bold color.

When he managed to lift his gaze, he saw that the skinny black top was as snug as the skirt, and dipped down low over firm, unfettered breasts. It took him a full ten seconds to get to her face.

Her mouth was red and wet and curved. Beside it, the little mole was a bold exclamation of sex. Her hair was tousled, and her eyes were shadowed and heavy. She looked like a woman who'd just climbed out of bed, and was willing to climb right back in.

"Holy hell." It was Shane's strained muttering that jolted him out of shock. "Is that Regan in there? She is *hot*."

Rafe didn't have the strength to put much behind the punch. When he gained his feet and moved to the door, his head was still buzzing, as if he'd been the one to take the blow.

"What are you doing?"

She moved a shoulder, causing the excuse for a blouse to follow her stretch. "I thought I'd play a little nine-ball."

There was something stuck in his throat. "Nine-ball?"

"Yeah." She sauntered over to the bar, leaned an elbow on it. "Going to buy me a beer, MacKade?"

Chapter 12

If he kept staring at her, she was going to lose it, Regan thought. She was already so nervous that if her clothes hadn't been girdled on, she'd have jumped out of them.

Because she'd wanted to make an entrance, she'd left her coat in the car. Only the heat of possible humiliation kept her teeth from chattering.

Her feet were killing her.

When Rafe didn't answer, she scanned the room and tried not to swallow audibly at the stares. Gathering courage, she flashed a smile at the bartender. Even the weary-eyed Duff was goggling at her.

"I'll have what he's having." When she had the beer in her hand, she turned back. No one had moved a muscle. It was either run or play it out, Regan told herself, taking a quick swallow of beer.

She hated beer.

"Are you going to rack them, MacKade, or am I?"

"I'll rack them," Jared interjected helpfully. His hands were still a little sweaty, but he'd gotten over the worst of the shock. Rafe's face was almost as much of a pleasure to watch as the sway of Regan's hips, as she sauntered over to study the arsenal of cues.

Rafe heard the clatter of balls, and blinked. "You said you wanted an early night."

"Changed my mind." Her voice was breathy from necessity, rather than design. The leather and Spandex™ were cutting off her air supply. "I had all this...energy all of a sudden." She walked slowly to the table, resisting the urge to tug at the hem of the skirt. "Who wants to play?"

Half a dozen men moved with scraping chairs and clattering boots. Rafe's snarl was the low, vicious sound of a wild dog guarding his bone. Half a dozen men decided they weren't in the mood for pool after all.

"This is a joke, right?"

Regan took the cue Devin offered, smiled and stroked her fingertips from the tip down the shaft. Someone moaned. "I felt like some action, that's all."

With her confidence building, she passed the bottle of beer to Jared. This, at least, she thought, she knew how to do. Planting her feet, bending one knee for balance, she leaned over the table. Leather strained.

Rafe's elbow plowed into Shane's gut. "Keep

looking where you're looking, and you'll be blind for a week.''

"Jeez, Rafe.'' Shane tucked his hands in his pockets and prepared to watch the show. "Where's a guy supposed to look?''

She broke cleanly, even managed to sink a ball. With the rules of the game Ed had drilled into her flipping through her head, she circled the table. She had to stop, smile, as Devin was still rooted in her path.

"You're blocking the table, Sheriff.''

"Oh. Yeah, right. Sorry.'' When she draped herself over the felt this time, his eyes met Jared's. They grinned at each other like two kids over a shiny new bike.

She managed to sink one more. That made her cocky enough to try a complicated shot that required a little English. Her hips wiggled as she set her position. From behind her, Jared stuck a hand under his shirt and mimed a thumping heart.

"You think what you're thinking again, and I'll rip your lungs out,'' Rafe muttered.

As the ball missed the pocket by a good six inches, Regan pouted with that red-slicked mouth. "Oops.'' She straightened, batted thickly mascaraed eyes at Rafe. "Your turn.'' She put her weight on one foot and ran a hand down his shirtfront. "Want me to…chalk your cue?''

The room exploded with whoops and whistles. Some brave soul made a suggestion that had Rafe's lips peeling back in a growl. "That does it.''

He grabbed her cue, tossed it at Devin, then clamped a hand over hers to drag her toward the door.

"But we haven't finished the game," she protested, forced to scramble on the skinny heels to keep up with him.

He yanked his jacket from the hook by the door and bundled it around her. "Put this on before I have to kill somebody." She was still struggling with it when he shoved her through the door.

Devin let out a long, appreciative sigh. "He's a dead man."

"Yeah." Shane rubbed a hand over his stomach. "Did you ever notice her—"

In Rafe's stead, Jared rapped him with a cue.

"I have my car," Regan began, while Rafe towed her along.

He dragged open the door of his own. "Get in. Now."

"I could follow you."

"Now."

"All right." It wasn't a simple operation to get into his car. Snug red leather rode higher as she tried for graceful and dignified as she lowered herself into the seat. Rafe ground his teeth audibly. "Where are we going?"

"I'm taking you home." He slammed her door, stormed around the hood, then slammed his own hard enough to rock the car. "And if you're smart, you won't talk to me."

She was smart. When his brakes squealed at the base of her steps, she stayed where she was. There was no possible way she could maneuver herself out of the tiny sports car without help.

He gave it to her, though no one would have called the hard yank a gentlemanly gesture. "Keys," he snapped, then snatched them out of her hand and unlocked the door himself.

Miffed, she strode in ahead of him. "I assume you're coming in, so—"

She was rapped back against the door, his mouth hotly devouring hers. The heels put them head-to-head, heat to heat, with a pressure that fried his already overheated brain. Both his mouth and his hands were hard, possessive. He could only think of branding her his.

His breath was ragged when he jerked back. He'd be damned if she'd work him this way again, make him a victim of his own needs.

He tugged his jacket off her shoulders, tossed it aside. "Get out of those clothes."

Something in her sank. With her lashes lowered, she reached around for the zipper of the skirt.

"No, I didn't mean— God." If she peeled herself out of that leather in front of him, he was lost. It was the confusion in her eyes that had him leveling his voice. "I meant I'd appreciate it if you changed into something else. Please."

"I thought you—"

"I know what you thought." He was dying here. "Just change, so I can talk to you."

"All right."

He knew it was a mistake to watch her walk toward the bedroom. But he was only human.

Inside, Regan stepped out of the ankle-breaking shoes, stripped off the red leather. It was good to breathe again. She wanted to be amused, at both of them, but she felt so incredibly stupid. She'd made a spectacle of herself, thrown aside every scrap of dignity. For nothing.

No, she thought as she fastened on pleated trousers. For him. She'd done it for him, and he didn't even have the sense to appreciate it.

When she came back in, face washed, her hair brushed back into place, an ivory sweater tucked neatly into the waistband of black slacks, he was pacing.

"I want to know what you were thinking of," he said without preamble. "Just what you were thinking of, walking into a bar dressed like that?"

"It was your idea," she tossed back, but he was too busy clenching his jaw and muttering to himself to listen.

"Five more minutes in there, and we'd have had a riot. I'd have started it myself. I've seen you naked, and I'm not sure I knew you were built like that. Now everybody in town's going to know."

"You said you wanted—"

"I don't give a damn what they say about me, but nobody's going to talk behind their hands about you. Where the hell did you get that skirt?" he exploded. "Tarts R Us?"

"Well, really…"

"Yeah, really. And leaning over the pool table that way, so everyone was looking at your—"

Her eyes narrowed to slits. "Watch it, MacKade."

"Now I'm going to have to go bash all of my brothers' brains in for what they were thinking."

"You like bashing their brains in," she retorted.

"That's beside the point."

"I'll give you a point."

She picked up her favorite Milton vase and tossed it to the floor. Rather than smashing satisfactorily, it bounced and rolled on the dainty floral rug. But the gesture shut him up.

"I humiliated myself for you. It nearly took a crowbar to get me into that ridiculous skirt, and I think I bruised my intestines. I'll probably never get all this makeup out of my pores, my arches are screaming, and I have not an ounce of dignity left. I hope you're satisfied."

"I—"

"Shut up. This time you just *shut up*. You wanted me to be that way, so I tried. I was willing to be what you wanted, and now all you can do is stand there and criticize and worry about gossip. Well, go to hell!"

She plopped down in a chair, because her feet were cramping painfully.

He waited until he was sure she'd run down, watched her sniffle and rub her bare feet. "You did that for me?"

"No, I did it because I like teetering on four-inch heels and going around half-naked in the middle of winter. I live for it," she said nastily.

"You did it to get to me."

The bout of temper had drained her. She sat back, closed her eyes. "I did it because I'm crazy about you. Just like you said I'd be. Now go away and leave me alone. You'll have to wait till tomorrow to beat your chest and drag me off by the hair. I'm too tired.''

He studied her a moment, then walked to the door and shut it quietly behind him.

She didn't bother to get up, or even to move. She didn't feel like crying. If she'd been ridiculous, she would weather it. She'd given him everything now, and there was no taking it back. Why should she bother? She'd never stop loving him.

She heard the door open again, and kept her eyes closed. ''I really am tired, Rafe. Can't you gloat tomorrow?''

Something fell into her lap. Regan blinked her eyes open and stared at the bouquet of lilacs.

''They're not real,'' he told her. ''You can't get them in February. I've had them in the trunk of my car for a few days, so they're cold.''

''They're lovely.'' Slowly she ran her fingers over the chilly silk blooms. ''A few days,'' she murmured, and looked up again.

''Yeah, so?'' He scowled, jammed his hands in his pockets, shifted. ''Man.'' He thought facing a noose would be easier than what he was about to do. It certainly couldn't burn his throat any less.

He got down on his knees.

''What are you doing?''

''Just keep quiet,'' he warned her. ''And if you laugh, you pay.'' Mortified, he swore under his breath, dragged a hand through his hair. And bit the bullet.

"'When I arose and saw the dawn, I sighed for thee.'"

"Rafe…"

"Don't interrupt me." Miserably embarrassed, he glared at her. "Now I have to start over."

"But you don't have to—"

"Regan."

She drew in a breath, wondered if there was another woman in the world who had ever had Shelley quoted to her with eyes that threatened murder. "Sorry. You were saying?"

He shifted his weight. "Okay. 'When I arose and saw the dawn, I sighed for thee; When the light rode high, and the dew was gone, and…' Oh, hell." He raked his fingers through his hair and tried to concentrate. "I got it. 'And noon lay heavy on flower and tree, And the weary Day turned to her rest, lingering like an unloved guest, I sighed for thee.'"

His breath came out on a huff of tremendous relief. "That's all I've got. It took me more than a week to memorize it. If you mention this to anyone—"

"I wouldn't dream of it." Incredibly moved, she laid a hand on his cheek. "That was very sweet of you."

"It kind of fits the way I feel about you." And now that it was over—thank God—it hadn't been as bad as he'd feared. "I think about you, Regan, all day. Every day. So if you want poetry—"

"No." With a quick shake of her head, she reached out and laid her cheek on his shoulder. "No, I don't need poetry, Rafe."

"I haven't bothered to give you much romance."

And he knew now, by the way her eyes had gone soft and dreamy, that he should have. "Now it's fake flowers and somebody else's words."

She had to cry now, but they were lovely tears, soothing ones. "I love the flowers, and I loved the words. But I don't need them. I don't want you to change for me, Rafe. There's nothing about you I'd want to change. I said I'd take you as you are and I mean it."

"I like you the way you are, Regan, all neat and tidy. Not that I didn't appreciate the way you filled out that leather."

"I'm sure I could borrow it from Ed again."

"Ed?" He rolled his eyes and chuckled weakly. "No wonder it fit you like skin." Then he felt the warm drops on his neck. "Oh, don't do that, baby. Please don't."

"I'm not really crying. I'm just touched that you'd memorize Shelley for me. That you'd care enough." She gave him a hard squeeze before leaning back. "I guess we both won the bet, or lost it, depending on your viewpoint." She dried off her cheeks with the back of her hand. "Of course, you didn't lose yours in public."

"If you think you can talk me into giving that little recital down at the tavern, you really are crazy. I'd never get out alive."

She drew in a deep breath. "I think we should both stick with who and what we are. I do like who and what you are, Rafe. And I need you more than you think. I needed you when Joe came into the shop and frightened me. I just didn't want you to know it. I was afraid to let you know how much I count on you.''

He picked up her hand, kissed it, and felt dozens of wounds heal. ''You didn't have to be.''

''I figured that out for myself. I like figuring things out for myself.''

''Tell me about it.'' He smiled and no longer felt foolish being on his knees. ''I like the way you figure things out for yourself. The way you handle yourself, Regan. Even when it ticks me off, I like your style.''

''I like yours, too.'' She leaned forward and kissed him lightly. ''I'm going to get something to put these in.''

He reached behind him and picked up the vase she'd thrown. ''How about this?''

''That'll be fine.'' She took it from him and rose to arrange the silk bouquet on the table. ''I can't believe I actually threw it.''

''It's been an eventful evening. So far.''

She glanced back, smiled. ''It certainly has. Would you like to stay, and see what happens next?''

''There we are, on the same wavelength again. You know, Regan, I think we've got more common ground than either one of us realized. You shoot decent pool, I like antiques.'' He stood, moving restlessly, picked up a china cat in suddenly nerveless fingers, then set it down again. ''So, you want to get married?''

She tucked a sprig of lilacs into place. ''Hmm... You asked me that before, as I remember. And never took me up on it, because I won't watch baseball.''

''I mean it.''

She twirled to face him, and her limp hand knocked against the table. "Excuse me?"

"Look, we haven't known each other very long." He stepped toward her, stopped cold. She was staring at him as though he'd lost his mind. He was certain he had. "But we've got something going here. I know we said it was just going to be sex, and we've just finished deciding we really like each other."

"Rafe, I can't—"

"If you'd just let me fumble through this." His tone went from quiet to testy in an instant. "I know how you are with having to weigh your options and think things through. But the least you can do is look at this from my perspective for one damn minute. It's not just sex for me, and it never was. I'm in love with you."

She stared into those sharp, angry eyes, heard the treasured phrase delivered in a furious snarl. And felt her heart swell like a rose blooming in her chest. "You're in love with me," she repeated.

It had always been easy to say the words when it didn't count—when they were just words, and not these tiny, razor-edged little pellets in his throat. "I'm in love with you," he said again. "It probably happened five minutes after I met you, maybe five minutes before. I don't know. It's never happened to me before."

"Me, either," she murmured.

He didn't hear her, didn't hear anything but the roaring in his head. "No one's ever needed me. I've never wanted anyone to need me. It gets in the way. But I want that from you. I have to ask that from you.'' He paused, fought to steady himself. ''I don't like asking.''

''I know. You don't have to.'' She walked to him, framed his face in her hands. ''Rafe, you don't have to ask.''

''If you'd give me a chance—'' he gripped her wrists ''—I could make it work. We could make it work. Come on, Regan, take a risk. Live dangerously.''

''Yes.''

His grip on her wrists went lax. ''Yes, what?''

''Why do we have such a hard time hearing each other?'' she asked. ''Listen up,'' she ordered, and kissed him firmly. ''Yes, I'll marry you.''

''Just like that? You're not going to think about it?''

''Nope.''

''Good. Great.'' A little dazed, he stepped back. ''We could, ah, t-take care of…it. Take care of it tomorrow. The license. Whatever. You want a ring…or something?''

''Yes, I do. Rafe, you're stuttering.''

''No, I'm not.'' He stepped back when she stepped forward. ''I just didn't expect you to take the jump so quick.''

''If you're trying to change your mind, forget it. Was it the skirt?''

His eyes went blank and baffled. ''What skirt?''

No answer could have pleased her more. ''I think you should tell me you love me again.'' Before he could evade her, she wrapped her arms around his neck, linked her fingers. "I think you should get used to saying it."

"I do love you."

"And you were in love with me that first night, when we were alone, in the house on the hill?"

"I guess I was."

"I didn't know, didn't have a clue. I wonder if the house did. I remember how quiet it got that night—how settled it all seemed. Would you like to go back there, tonight?"

"Yes." He rested his brow on hers. "I would."

"There's something I should tell you first, Rafe. Something I think we should clear up between us."

"Regan, if you're going to slap down more rules and parameters—"

"I think I should tell you," she said interrupting him, "that as attracted as I was to you, as aroused as I was by you, I could have slept with you without loving you."

"I know." He refused to be hurt by it. "It's okay."

"I could have done that because you're the most incredibly attractive man I've ever met, all the way through. But there's no way I would have squeezed myself into that ridiculous outfit tonight unless I'd been wildly, stupidly and completely in love with you." Her eyes shimmered and smiled. "Is that okay?"

"Say it again." He took her face in his hands. "Look at me straight-on and say it again."

"I love you. I'm so very much in love with you, Rafe. There's nothing I want more than to go on loving you, and needing you for the rest of my life."

The thrill of it sprinted through him, then settled, warm and easy. "You could get used to saying it, too."

"I'm a very quick study. I love you," she murmured against his mouth, then poured the words into the kiss.

"It's going to get complicated." He gathered her close and held her. Just held her. "Life's going to be messy."

"I hope so." Eyes closed, she pressed her cheek against his. "Oh, I hope so. Why was I so scared?" she whispered. "Why was I so afraid to let you know?"

"Probably for the same reason I was." He tilted her head back. "It happened so fast, and it matters so much. And it always will."

"It always will," she agreed.

Later, when they were curled together in the deep feather bed, she laid her hand on his heart and smiled.

"I'm awfully glad you came back to town, MacKade. Welcome home."

The house was quiet around them, and slept as they slept.

* * * * *

*The Pride of
Jared MacKade*

For women with a past

Prologue

The woods echoed with war whoops and running feet. Troops were fully engaged in the battle, peppering the fields beyond the trees with sporadic shelling. The day rang with the crash of weapons and the cries of the wounded.

Already dozens of lives had been lost, and the survivors were out for blood.

Leaves, still lush and green from the dying summer, formed a canopy overhead, allowing only thin, dusty beams of sunlight to trickle through. The air was thick and humid and carried the rich scent of earth and animal in its blistering heat.

There was no place Jared MacKade was happier than in the haunted woods.

He was a Union officer, a captain. He got to be captain because, at twelve, he was the oldest, and it was his right. His troops consisted of his brother Devin, who, being ten, had to be content with the rank of corporal.

Their mission was clear. Annihilate the Rebels.

Because war was a serious business, Jared had plotted out his strategy. He'd chosen Devin for his troops because Devin could follow orders. Devin was also a good thinker.

And Devin was a vicious take-no-prisoners hand-to-hand fighter.

Rafe and Shane, the other MacKade brothers, were ferocious fighters too, but they were, Jared knew, impulsive. Even now, they were racing through the woods, whooping and hollering, while Jared waited patiently in ambush.

"They're going to separate, you watch," Jared muttered as he and Devin hunkered down in the brush. "Rafe figures on drawing us out and clobbering us." Jared spit, because he was twelve and spitting was cool. "He doesn't have a military mind."

"Shane doesn't have a mind at all," Devin put in, with the expected disdain of brother for brother.

They grinned over that, two young boys with disheveled black hair and handsome faces that were grimy with dirt and sweat. Jared's eyes, a cool grassy green, scanned the woods. He knew every rock, every stump, every beaten path. Often he came here alone, to wander or just to sit. And to listen. To the wind in the trees, the rustle of squirrels and rabbits. To the murmur of ghosts.

He knew others had fought here, died here. And it

fascinated him. He'd grown up on the Civil War battlefield of Antietam, Maryland, and he knew, as any
young boy would, the maneuvers and mistakes, the tri-
umphs and tragedies of that fateful day in September
1862.

A battle that had earned its place in history as the
bloodiest day of the Civil War was bound to tug at the
imagination of a young boy. He had combed every foot
of the battlefield with his brothers, played dead in
Bloody Lane, raced through his own cornfields, where
black powder had scorched the drying stalks so long
ago.

He had brooded many a night over the concept of
brother against brother—for real—and wondered what
part he might have played if he had been born in time
for those terrible and heroic days.

Yet what fascinated him most was that men had
given their lives for an idea. Often, when he sat quietly
with the woods around him, he dreamed over the fighting for something as precious as an idea, and dying
proudly.

His mother often told him that a man needed goals,
and strong beliefs and pride in the seeking of them.
Then she would laugh that deep laugh of hers, tousle
his hair and tell him that having pride would never be
his problem. He already had too much of it.

He wanted to be the best, the fastest, the strongest,
the smartest. It wasn't an easy target, not with three
equally determined brothers. So he pushed himself.
Studied longer, fought more fiercely, worked harder.

Losing just wasn't an option for Jared MacKade.

"They're coming," Jared whispered.

Devin nodded. He'd been listening to the crackle of twigs, the rustle of brush. Biding his time. "Rafe's that way. Shane circled behind."

Jared didn't question Devin's assessment. His brother had instincts like a cat. "I'll take Rafe. You stay here until we're engaged. Shane'll come running. Then you can take him out."

Anticipation brightened Jared's eyes. The two brothers' hands clutched in a brief salute. "Victory or death."

Jared caught his first sight of the faded blue shirt, a blur of movement as the enemy dashed from tree to tree. With the patience of a snake, he waited, waited. Then, with a blood curdling cry, leaped.

He brought Rafe down in a flying tackle that had them both skittering over the rough dirt into the prickle of wild blackberries.

It was a good surprise attack, but Jared wasn't foolish enough to think that would be the end of it. Rafe was a vicious opponent—as any kid at Antietam Elementary could attest. He fought with a kind of fiendish enjoyment that Jared understood perfectly.

There really was nothing better than pounding someone on a hot summer day when the threat of school was creeping closer and all the morning chores were behind you.

Thorns tore at clothes and scratched flesh. The two boys wrestled back to the path, fists and elbows ramming, sneakers digging in at the heels for purchase. Nearby, a second battle was under way, with curses and grunts and the satisfying crunch of bodies over aged dried leaves.

The MacKade brothers were in heaven.

"You're dead, Rebel scum!" Jared shouted when he managed to grab Rafe in a slippery headlock.

"I'm taking you to hell with me, bluebelly!" Rafe shouted right back.

In the end, they were simply too well matched, and they rolled away from each other, filthy, breathless, and laughing.

Wiping the blood from a split lip, Jared turned his head to watch his troops engage the enemy. It looked to him as though Devin were going to have a black eye, and Shane had a rip in his jeans that was going to get them all in trouble.

He let out a long, contented sigh and watched the sunlight play through the leaves.

"Going to break it up?" Rafe asked, without much interest.

"Nah." Casually, Jared wiped blood from his chin. "They're almost finished."

"I'm going to go into town." Energy still high, Rafe bounded up and brushed off his pants. "Gonna get me a soda down at Ed's."

Devin stopped wrestling Shane and looked over. "Got any money?"

With a wolfish grin, Rafe jingled the change in his pocket. "Maybe." Challenge issued, he tossed the hair out of his eyes, then took off at a dead run.

The delightful prospect of shaking quarters from Rafe's pockets was all the impetus Devin and Shane needed. Suddenly united, they scrambled off each other and chased after him.

"Come on, Jare," Shane called over his shoulder. "We're going to Ed's."

"Go on. I'll catch up."

But he lay there on his back, staring at the sunlight flickering through the awning of leaves. As his brothers' pounding footsteps faded away, he thought he could hear the sounds of the old battle. The boom and crash of mortars, the screams of the dead and dying.

Then, closer, the ragged breathing of the lost and the frightened.

He closed his eyes, too familiar with the ghosts of these woods to be unnerved by their company. He wished he'd known them, could have asked them what it was like to put your life, your soul, at risk. To love a thing, an ideal, a way of life, so much you would give everything you were to defend it.

He thought he would for his family, for his parents, his brothers. But that was different. That was...family.

One day, he promised himself, he would make his mark. People would look at him and know that there was Jared MacKade, a man who stood for something. A man who did what had to be done, and never turned his back on a fight.

Chapter 1

Jared wanted a cold beer. He could already taste it, that first long sip that would start to wash away the dregs of a lousy day in court, an idiot judge and a client who was driving him slowly insane.

He didn't mind that she was guilty as sin, had certainly been an accessory before and after the fact in the spate of petty burglaries in the west end of Hagerstown. He could swallow defending the guilty. That was his job. But he was getting damn sick and tired of having his client hit on him.

The woman had a very skewed view of lawyer-client relations. He could only hope he'd made it clear that if she grabbed his butt again, she was out on hers and on her own.

Under different circumstances, he might have found it only mildly insulting, even fairly amusing. But he had too much on his mind, and on his calendar, to play games.

With an irritated jerk of the wrist, he jammed a classical CD into his car stereo system and let Mozart join him on the winding route toward home.

Just one stop, he told himself. One quick stop, and then a cold beer.

And he wouldn't even have had that one stop, if this Savannah Morningstar had bothered to return his calls.

He rolled his shoulders to ease the tension and punched the gas pedal on a curve to please himself with a bit of illegal speed. He drove along the familiar country road quickly, barely noticing the first tender buds of spring on the trees or the faint haze of wild dogwood ready to bloom.

He braked for a darting rabbit, passed a pickup heading toward Antietam. He hoped Shane had supper started, then remembered with an oath that it was his turn to cook.

The scowl suited his face, with its sculptured lines, the slight imperfection of a nose that had been broken twice, the hard edge of chin. Behind shaded glasses, under arching black brows, his eyes were cool and sharply green. Though his lips were set in a line of irritation, that didn't detract from the appeal of them.

Women often looked at that mouth, and wondered... When it smiled, and the dimple beside it winked, they sighed and asked themselves how that wife of his had ever let him get away.

He made a commanding presence in a courtroom. The broad shoulders, narrow hips and tough, rangy build always looked polished in a tailored suit, but the elegant cover never quite masked the power beneath.

His black hair had just enough wave to curl appealingly at the collar of one of his starched white shirts.

In the courtroom he wasn't Jared MacKade, one of the MacKade brothers who had run roughshod over the south of the county from the day they were born. He was Jared MacKade, counselor-at-law.

He glanced up at the house on the hill just outside of town. It was the old Barlow place that his brother Rafe had come back to town to buy. He saw Rafe's car at the top of the steep lane, and hesitated.

He was tempted to pull in, to forget about this last little detail of the day and share that beer he wanted with Rafe. But he knew that if Rafe wasn't working, hammering or sawing, or painting some part of the house that would be a bed and breakfast by fall, he would be waiting for his new wife to come home.

It still amazed Jared that the baddest of the bad MacKades was a married man.

So he drove past, took the left fork in the road that would wind him around toward the MacKade farm and the small plot of land that bordered it.

According to his information, Savannah Morningstar had bought the little house on the edge of the woods only two months before. She lived there with her son and, as the gossip mill was mostly dry where she was concerned, obviously kept to herself.

Jared figured the woman was either stupid or rude. In his experience, when people received a message from a lawyer, they answered it. Though the voice on her answering machine had been low, throaty, and stunningly sexy, he wasn't looking forward to meeting that voice face-to-face. This mission was a favor for a colleague—and a nuisance.

He caught a glimpse of the little house through the trees. More of a cabin, really, he mused, though a second floor had been added several years ago. He turned onto the narrow lane by the Morningstar mailbox, cutting his speed dramatically to negotiate the dips and holes, and studied the house as he approached.

It was log, built originally, as he recalled, as some city doctor's vacation spot. That hadn't lasted long. People from the city often thought they wanted rustic until they had it.

The quiet setting, the trees, the peaceful bubbling of a creek topped off from yesterday's rain, enhanced the ambience of the house, with its simple lines, untreated wood and uncluttered front porch.

The steep bank in front of it was rocky and rough, and in the summer, he knew, tended to be covered with high, tangled weeds. Someone had been at work here, he mused, and almost came to a stop. The earth had been dug and turned, worked to a deep brown. There were still rocks, but they were being used as a natural decorative landscaping. Someone had planted clumps of flowers among them, behind them.

No, he realized, someone *was* planting clumps of flowers. He saw the figure, the movement, as he rounded the crest and brought his car to a halt at the end of the lane, beside an aging compact.

Jared lifted his briefcase, climbed out of the car and

started over the freshly mowed swatch of grass. He was very grateful for his dark glasses when Savannah Morningstar rose.

She'd been kneeling amid the dirt and garden tools and flats of flowers. When she moved, she moved slowly, inch by very impressive inch. She was tall—a curvy five-ten, he estimated—filling out a drab yellow T-shirt and ripped jeans to the absolute limit of the law. Her legs were endless.

Her feet were bare and her hands grimed with soil.

The sun glinted on hair as thick and black as his. She wore it down her back in one loose braid. Her eyes were concealed, as his were, behind sunglasses. But what he could see of her face was fascinating.

If a man could get past that truly amazing body, he could spend a lot of time on that face, Jared mused.

Carved cheekbones rose high and taut against skin the color of gold dust. Her mouth was full and unsmiling, her nose straight and sharp, her chin slightly pointed.

"Savannah Morningstar?"

"Yes, that's right."

He recognized the voice from the answering machine. He'd never known a voice and a body that suited each other more perfectly. "I'm Jared MacKade."

She angled her head, and the sun glanced off the amber tint of her glasses. "Well, you look like a lawyer. I haven't done anything—lately—that I need representation for."

"I'm not going door-to-door soliciting clients. I've left several messages on your machine."

"I know." She knelt again to finish planting a hunk of purple phlox. "The handy thing about machines is that you don't have to talk to people you don't want to talk to." Carefully she patted dirt around the shallow roots. "Obviously, I didn't want to talk to you, Lawyer MacKade."

"Not stupid," he declared. "Just rude."

Amused, she tipped her face up to his. "That's right. I am. But since you're here, you might as well tell me what you're so fired up to tell me."

"A colleague of mine in Oklahoma contacted me after he tracked you down."

The quick clutching in Savannah's gut came and went. Deliberately she picked up another clump of phlox. Taking her time, she shifted and hacked at the dirt with her hand spade. "I haven't been in Oklahoma for nearly ten years. I don't remember breaking any laws before I left."

"Your father hired my colleague to locate you."

"I'm not interested." Her flower-planting mood was gone. Because she didn't want to infect the innocent blooms with the poison stirring inside her, she rose again and rubbed her hands on her jeans. "You can tell your colleague to tell my father I'm not interested."

"Your father's dead."

He'd had no intention of telling her that way. He hadn't mentioned her father or his death on the phone, because he didn't have the heart to break such news over a machine. Jared still remembered the swift, searing pain of his own father's death. And his mother's.

She didn't gasp or sway or sob. Standing straight,

Savannah absorbed the shock and refused the grief. Once there had been love. Once there had been need. And now, she thought, now there was nothing.

"When?"

"Seven months ago. It took awhile to find you. I'm sorry—"

She interrupted him. "How?"

"A fall. According to my information, he'd been working the rodeo circuit. He took a bad fall, hit his head. He wasn't unconscious long, and refused to go to the hospital for X rays. But he contacted my colleague and gave him instructions. A week later, your father collapsed. An embolism."

She listened without a word, without movement. In her mind Savannah could see the man she'd once known and loved, clinging to the back of a bucking mustang, one hand reaching for the sky.

She could see him laughing, she could see him drunk. She could see him murmuring endearments to an aging mare, and she could see him burning with rage and shame as he turned his own daughter, his only child, away.

But she couldn't see him dead.

"Well, you've told me." With that, she turned toward the house.

"Ms. Morningstar." If he had heard grief in her voice, he would have given her privacy. But there'd been nothing at all in her voice.

"I'm thirsty." She headed up the walkway that cut through the grass, then climbed onto the porch and let the screen door slam behind her.

Yeah? Jared thought, fuming. Well, so was he. And he was damn well going to finish up this business and get a cold one himself. He walked into the house without bothering to knock.

The small living room held furniture built for comfort, chairs with deep, sagging cushions, sturdy tables that would bear the weight of resting feet. The walls were a shade of umber that melded nicely with the pine of the floor. There were vivid splashes of color to offset and challenge the mellow tones—paintings, pillows, a scatter of toys over bright rugs that reminded him she had a child.

He stepped through into a kitchen with brilliantly white counters and the same gleaming pine floor, where she stood in front of the sink, scrubbing garden earth from her hands. She didn't bother to speak, but dried them off before she took a pitcher of lemonade from the refrigerator.

"I'd like to get this over with as much as you," he told her.

She let out a breath, took her sunglasses off and tossed them on the counter. Wasn't his fault, she reminded herself. Not completely, anyway. When you came down to it, and added all the pieces together, there was no one to blame.

"You look hot." She poured lemonade into a tall glass, handed it to him. After giving him one quick glimpse of almond-shaped eyes the color of melted chocolate, she turned away to get another glass.

"Thanks."

"Are you going to tell me he had debts that I'm

obliged to settle? If you are, I'm going to tell you I have no intention of doing so.'' The jittering in her stomach had nearly calmed, so she leaned back against the counter and crossed her bare feet at the ankles. ''I've made what I've got, and I intend to keep it.''

''Your father left you seven thousand, eight hundred and twenty-five dollars. And some change.''

He watched the glass stop, hesitate, then continue to journey to her lips. She drank slowly, thoughtfully. ''Where did he get seven thousand dollars?''

''I have no idea. But the money is currently in a passbook savings account in Tulsa.'' Jared set his brief-case down on the small butcher-block table, opened it. ''You have only to show me proof of identity and sign these papers, and your inheritance will be transferred to you.''

''I don't want it.'' Her first sign of emotion was the crack of glass against counter. ''I don't want his money.''

Jared set the papers on the table. ''It's your money.''

''I said I don't want it.''

Patiently Jared slipped off his own glasses and hooked them in his top pocket. ''I understand you were estranged from your father.''

''You don't understand anything,'' she shot back. ''All you need to know is that I don't want the damn money. So put your papers back in your fancy briefcase and get out.''

Well used to arguments, Jared kept his eyes—and his temper—level. ''Your father's instructions were that if you were unwilling or unable to claim the inheritance, it was to go to your child.''

Her eyes went molten. ''Leave my son out of this.''

''The legalities—''

''Hang your legalities. He's my son. Mine. And it's my choice. We don't want or need the money.''

''Ms. Morningstar, you can refuse the terms of your father's will, which means the courts will get involved and complicate what should be a very simple, straightforward matter. Hell, do yourself a favor. Take it, blow it on a weekend in Reno, give it to charity, bury it in a tin can in the yard.''

She forced herself to calm down, not an easy matter when her emotions were up. ''It is very simple and straightforward. I'm not taking his money.'' Her head jerked around at the sound of the front door slamming. ''My son,'' she said, and shot Jared a lethal look. ''Don't you say anything to him about this.''

''Hey, Mom! Connor and me—'' He skidded to a halt, a tall, skinny boy with his mother's eyes and messy black hair crushed under a backward fielder's cap. He studied Jared with a mix of distrust and curiosity. ''Who's he?''

Manners ran in the family, Jared decided. Lousy ones. ''I'm Jared MacKade, a neighbor.''

''You're Shane's brother.'' The boy walked over, picked up his mother's lemonade and drank it down in several noisy gulps. ''He's cool. That's where we were, me and Connor,'' he told his mother. ''Over at the MacKade farm. This big orange cat had kittens.''

''Again?'' Jared muttered. ''This time I'm taking her

to the vet personally and having her spayed. You were with Connor," Jared added. "Connor Dolin."

"Yeah." Suspicious, the boy watched him over the rim of his glass.

"His mother's a friend of mine," Jared said simply.

Savannah's hand rested briefly, comfortably, on her son's shoulder. "Bryan, go upstairs and scrape some of the dirt off. I'm going to start dinner."

"Okay."

"Nice to have met you, Bryan."

The boy looked surprised, then flashed a quick grin. "Yeah, cool. See you."

"He looks like you," Jared commented.

"Yes, he does." Her mouth softened slightly at the sound of feet clumping up the stairs. "I'm thinking about putting in soundproofing."

"I'm trying to get a picture of him palling around with Connor."

The amusement in her eyes fired into temper so quickly it fascinated him. "And you have a problem with that?"

"I'm trying to get a picture," Jared repeated, "of the live wire that just headed upstairs and the quiet, painfully shy Connor Dolin. Kids as confident as your son don't usually choose boys like Connor for friends."

Temper smoothed out. "They just clicked. Bryan hasn't had a lot of opportunity to keep friends. We've moved around a great deal. That's changing."

"What brought you here?"

"I was—" She broke off, and her lips curved.

"Now you're trying to be neighborly so that I'll soften up and take this little problem off your hands. Forget it." She turned to take a package of chicken breasts out of the refrigerator.

"Seven thousand dollars is a lot of money. If you put it in a college fund now, it would give your son a good start when he's ready for it."

"When and if Bryan's ready for college, I'll put him through myself."

"I understand about pride, Ms. Morningstar. That's why it's easy for me to see when it's misplaced."

She turned again and flipped her braid behind her shoulder. "You must be the patient, by-the-book, polite type, Mr. MacKade."

The grin that beamed out at her nearly made her blink. She was sure there were states where that kind of weapon was illegal.

"Don't get to town much, do you?" Jared murmured. "You'd hear different. Ask Connor's mama about the MacKades sometime, Ms. Morningstar. I'll leave the papers." He slipped his sunglasses on again. "You think it over and get back to me. I'm in the book."

She stayed where she was, a frown on her face and a cold package of raw chicken in her hands. She was still there when his car's engine roared to life and her son came darting back down the stairs.

Quickly she snatched up the papers and pushed them into the closest drawer.

"What was he here for?" Bryan wanted to know. "How come he was wearing a suit?"

"A lot of men wear suits." She would evade, but she wouldn't lie, not to Bryan. "And stay out of the refrigerator. I'm starting dinner."

With his hand on the door of the fridge, Bryan rolled his eyes. "I'm starving. I can't wait for dinner."

Savannah plucked an apple from a bowl and tossed it over her shoulder, smiling to herself when she heard the solid smack of Bryan's catch.

"Shane said it was okay if we went by after school tomorrow and looked at the kittens some more. The farm's really cool, Mom. You should see."

"I've seen farms before."

"Yeah, but this one's neat. He's got two dogs. Fred and Ethel."

"Fred and—" She broke off into laughter. "Maybe I will have to see that."

"And from the hayloft you can see clear into town. Connor says part of the battle was fought right there on the fields. Probably dead guys everywhere."

"Now that sounds really enticing."

"And I was thinking—" Bryan crunched into his apple, tried to sound casual "—you'd maybe want to come over and look at the kittens."

"Oh, would I?"

"Well, yeah. Connor said maybe Shane would give some away when they were weaned. You might want one."

She set a lid on the chicken she was sautéing. "I would?"

"Sure, yeah, for, like, company when I'm in

school.'' He smiled winningly. "So you wouldn't get lonely."

Savannah shifted her weight onto her hip and studied him owlishly. "That's a good one, Bry. Really smooth."

That was what he'd been counting on. "So can I?"

She would have given him the world, not just one small kitten. "Sure." Her laughter rolled free when he launched himself into her arms.

With the meal over, the dishes done, the homework that terrified her finished and the child who was her life tucked into bed with his ball cap, Savannah sat on the front-porch swing and watched the woods.

She enjoyed the way night always deepened there first, as if it had a primary claim. Later there might be the hoot of an owl, or the rumbling low of Shane MacKade's cattle. Sometimes, if it was very quiet, or there'd been rain, she could hear the bubble of creek over rocks.

It was too early in the spring yet for the flash and shimmer of fireflies. She looked forward to them, and hoped Bryan wasn't yet beyond the stage where he would chase them. She wanted to watch him run in his own yard in the starlight on a warm summer night when the flowers were blooming, the air was thick with their perfume, and the woods were a dense curtain closing them off from everyone and everything.

She wanted him to have a kitten to play with, friends to call his own, a childhood filled with moments that lasted forever.

A childhood that would be everything hers had never been.

Setting the swing into motion, she leaned back and drank in the absolute quiet of a country night.

It had taken her ten long, hard years to get here, on this swing, on this porch, in this house. There wasn't a moment of it she regretted. Not the sacrifice, the pain, the worry, the risk. Because to regret one was to regret all. To regret one was to regret Bryan. And that was impossible.

She had exactly what she had strived for now, and she had earned it herself, despite odds brutally stacked against her.

She was exactly where she wanted to be, who she wanted to be, and no ghost from the past would spoil it for her.

How dare he offer her money, when all she'd ever wanted was his love?

So Jim Morningstar was dead. The hard-drinking, hard-living, hardheaded son of a bitch had ridden his last bronco, roped his last bull. Now she was supposed to grieve. Now she was supposed to be grateful that, at the end, he'd thought of her. He'd thought of the grandchild he'd never wanted, never even seen.

He'd chosen his pride over his daughter, and the tiny flicker of life that had been inside her. Now, after all this time, he'd thought to make up for that with just under eight thousand dollars.

The hell with him, Savannah thought wearily, and closed her eyes. Eight million couldn't make her forget, and it sure as hell couldn't buy her forgiveness. And no lawyer in a fancy suit with killer eyes and a silver tongue was going to change her mind.

Jared MacKade could go to hell right along with Jim Morningstar.

He'd had no business coming onto her land as if he belonged there, standing in her kitchen sipping lemonade, talking about college funds, smiling so sweetly at her boy. He'd had no right to aim that smile at her— not so outrageously—and stir up all those juices that she'd deliberately let go flat and dry.

Well, she wasn't dead, after all, she thought with a heartfelt sigh. Some men seemed to have been created to stir a woman's juices.

She didn't want to sit here on this beautiful spring night and think about how long it had been since she'd held a man, or been held. She really didn't want to think at all, but he'd walked across her lawn and shaken her laboriously constructed world in less time than it took to blink.

Her father was dead, and she was very much alive. Lawyer MacKade had made those two facts perfectly clear in one short visit.

However much she wanted to avoid it, she was going to have to deal with both those facts. Eventually she would have to face Jared again. If she didn't seek him out, she was certain, he'd be back. He had that bull dog look about him, pretty suit and tie or not.

So, she would have to decide what to do. And she would have to tell Bryan. He had a right to know his grandfather was dead. He had a right to know about the legacy.

But just for tonight, she wouldn't think, she wouldn't worry, she wouldn't wonder.

She wasn't aware for a long time that her cheeks were wet, her shoulders were shaking, the sobs were tearing at her throat. Curling into a ball, she buried her face against her knees.

"Oh, Daddy..."

Chapter 2

Jared wasn't opposed to farm work. He wouldn't care to make it a living, as Shane did, but he wasn't opposed to putting in a few hours now and again. Since he'd put his house in town on the market and moved back home, he pitched in whenever he had the time. It was the kind of work you never forgot, the rhythms easy to fall back into—ones your muscles soon remembered. The milking, the feeding, the plowing, the sowing.

Stripped down to a sweaty T-shirt and old jeans, he hauled out hay bales for the dairy stock. The black-and-white cows lumbered for the trough, wide, sturdy bodies bumping, tails swishing. The scent of them was a reminder of youth, of his father most of all.

Buck MacKade had tended his cows well, and had taught his boys to see them as a responsibility, as well as a way of making a living. For him, the farm had been very simply a way of life—and Jared knew the same was true of Shane. He wondered now, as he fell back into the routine of tending, what his father would have thought of his oldest son, the lawyer.

He probably would have been a little baffled by the choice of suit and tie, of paper drafted and filed, of appearances and appointments. But Jared hoped he would have been proud. He needed to believe his father would have been proud.

But this wasn't such a bad way to spend a Saturday, he mused, after a week of courtrooms and paperwork.

Nearby, Shane whistled a mindless tune and herded the cows in to feed. And looked, Jared realized, very much as their father would have—dusty jeans, dusty shirt loose on a tough, disciplined body, worn cap over hair that needed a barber's touch.

"What do you think of the new neighbor?" Jared called out.

"Huh?"

"The new neighbor," Jared repeated, and jerked a thumb in the direction of Morningstar land.

"Oh, you mean the goddess." Shane stepped away from the trough, eyes dreamy. "I need a moment of silence," he murmured, and crossed his hands over his heart.

Amused, Jared swiped a hand through his hair. "She is impressive."

"She's built like… I don't have words." Shane gave one of the cows an affectionate slap on the rump. "I've only seen her once. Ran into her and her kid going into

the market. Talked to her for about two minutes,
drooled for the next hour.''

"How did she strike you?''

"Like a bolt of lightning, bro.''

"Think you can keep your head out of your shorts
for a minute?''

"I can try.'' Shane bent to help break up bales.
"Like a woman who can handle herself and isn't look-
ing for company,'' he decided. "Good with the kid.
You can tell just by the way they stand together.''

"Yeah, I noticed that.''

Shane's interest was piqued. "When?''

"I was over there a couple of days ago. Had a little
legal business.''

"Oh.'' Shane wiggled his eyebrows. "Privileged
communication?''

"That's right.'' Jared hauled over another bale and
nipped the twine. "What's the word on her?''

"There isn't much of anything. From what I get, she
was in the Frederick area, saw the ad for the cabin in
the paper down there. Then she blew into town,
snapped up the property, put her kid in school and
closed herself off on her little hill. It's driving Mrs.
Metz crazy.''

"I bet. If Mrs. Metz, queen of the grapevine, can't
get any gossip on her, nobody can.''

"If you're handling some legal deal for her, you
ought to be able to shake something loose.''

"She's not a client,'' Jared said, and left it at that.
"The boy comes around here?''

"Now and again. He and Connor.''

"An odd pairing."

"It's nice seeing them together. Bry's a pistol, let me tell you. He's got a million questions, opinions, arguments." Shane lifted a brow. "Reminds me of somebody."

"That so?"

"Dad always said if there were two opinions on one subject, you'd have both of them. The kid's like that. And he makes Connor laugh. It's good to hear."

"The boy hasn't had enough to laugh about, not with a father like Joe Dolin."

Shane grunted, gathering up discarded twine. "Well, Dolin's behind bars and out of the picture." Shane stepped back, checking over his herd and the land beyond. "He's not going to be beating up on Cassie anymore, or terrorizing those kids. The divorce going to be final soon?"

"We should have a final decree within sixty days."

"Can't be soon enough. I have to see to the hogs. You want to get another bale out of the barn?"

"Sure."

Shane headed over to the pen, prepared to mix feed. At the sight of him, the fat pigs began to stir and snort. "Yeah, Daddy's here, boys and girls."

"He talks to them all the time," Bryan announced from behind them.

"They talk right back." With a grin, Shane turned, and saw that the boy wasn't alone.

Savannah stood with one hand on her son's shoulder and an easy smile. Her hair was loose, falling like black rain over the shoulders of a battered denim jacket.

Shane decided the pigs could wait, and leaned on the fence.

"Good morning."

"Good morning." She stepped forward, looked into the pen. "They look hungry."

"They're always hungry. That's why we call them pigs."

She laughed and propped a foot on the bottom rung of the fence. She was a woman used to the sight, sound and smell of animals. "That one there certainly looks well fed."

He shifted closer so he could enjoy the scent of her hair. "She's full of piglets. I'll have to separate her soon."

"Spring on the farm," she murmured. "So, who's the daddy?"

"That smug-looking hog over there."

"Ah, the one who's ignoring her. Typical." Still smiling, she tossed back her hair. "We're here on a mission, Mr. MacKade."

"Shane."

"Shane. Rumor is, you've got kittens."

Shane grinned down at Bryan. "Talked her into it, huh?"

All innocence, Bryan shrugged, but his quick, triumphant grin betrayed him. "She needs company when I'm at school."

"That's a good one. They're in the barn. I'll show you."

"No." To stop him, Savannah put a hand on his arm. There was a glint in her eyes that told him she knew exactly where his thoughts were heading. "We won't interrupt your work. Your pigs are waiting, and I'm sure Bryan knows exactly where to find the kittens."

"Sure I do. Come on, Mom." He had her by the hand, tugging. "They're really cool. Shane's got all kinds of neat animals," Bryan told her.

"Mm-hmm…" With a last amused glance, she let herself be hauled away. "Magnificent animals." And, she thought as she watched Jared stride out of the barn with a bale over his shoulder, here was another one now.

His eyes met hers, held, as he stopped, tossed the bale down. The suit had been deceiving, she realized. Though he hadn't looked soft in it, he'd looked elegant. There was nothing elegant about the man now.

He was all muscle.

If she'd been a lesser woman, her mouth might have watered.

Instead, she inclined her head and spoke coolly. "Mr. MacKade."

"Ms. Morningstar." His tone was just as cool. But it took a focused effort to unknot the tension in his stomach. "Hi, Bryan."

"I didn't know you worked here," Bryan began. "I've never seen you working here."

"Now and again."

"How come you were wearing a suit?" he asked. "Shane never wears a suit."

"Not unless you knock him unconscious first." When the boy grinned, Jared noticed a gap in his teeth that hadn't been there the day before. "Lose something?"

Proudly Bryan pressed his tongue in the gap. "It came out this morning. It's good for spitting."

"I used to hold the record around here. Nine feet, three inches. Without the wind."

Impressed, and challenged, Bryan worked up saliva in his mouth, concentrated and let it fly. Jared pursed his lips, nodded. "Not bad."

"I can do better than that."

"You're one of the tops in your division, Bry," Savannah said dryly. "But Mr. MacKade has work to do, and we're supposed to be looking at kittens."

"Yeah, they're right in here." He took off into the barn at a run. Savannah followed more slowly.

"Nine feet?" she murmured, with a glance over her shoulder.

"And three inches."

"You surprise me, Mr. MacKade."

She had a way of sauntering on those long legs, he thought, that gave a man's eyes a mind of their own. After a quick internal debate, he gave up and went in after her.

"Aren't they great?" Bryan plopped right down in the hay beside the litter of sleeping kittens and their very bored-looking mama. "They have to stay with her for weeks and weeks." Very gently, he stroked a fingertip over the downy head of a smoke-gray kitten. "But then we can take one."

She couldn't help it. Savannah went soft all over. "Oh, they're so tiny." Crouching down, she gave in to the need and lifted one carefully into her hand. "Look, Bry, it fits right in my palm. Oh, aren't you sweet?" Murmuring, she nuzzled her face against the fur. "Aren't you pretty?"

"I like this one best." Bryan continued to stroke the tiny gray bundle. "I'm going to call him Cal. Like for Cal Ripkin."

"Oh." The soft orange ball in her hand stirred and mewed thinly. Her heart was lost. "All right. The gray one."

"You could take two." Jared stepped into the stall. Her face, he thought, was an open book. "It's nice for them to have company."

"Two?" The idea burst like a thousand watts in Bryan's brain. "Yeah, Mom, we'll take two. One would be lonely!"

"Bry—"

"And it wouldn't be any more trouble. We've got lots of room now. Cal's going to want somebody to play with, to hang around with."

"Thanks, MacKade."

"My pleasure."

"And anyway," Bryan went on, because he'd come out of his own excitement long enough to see the way his mother was cuddling the orange kitten, "this way we could each pick one. That's the fair way, right?"

Smiling, Bryan reached out to brush his finger over the orange kitten. "He likes you. See, he's trying to lick your hand."

"He's hungry," Savannah told him, but she knew there was no possible way she was going to be able to resist the little bundle rooting in her hand. "I suppose they would be company for each other."

"All right, Mom!" Bryan sprang up, kissed her without any of the embarrassment many nine-year-old boys might feel. "I'm going to tell Shane which ones are ours."

With a clatter of feet, Bryan dashed out of the barn.

"You know you wanted it," Jared said.

"I'm old enough to know I can't have everything I want." But she sighed and set the kitten down so that it could join its siblings in a morning snack. "But two cats can't be that much more trouble than one."

She started to rise, flicking a glance upward when Jared put a hand under her arm and helped her up. "Thanks." She stepped around him and headed for the light. "So, are you a farm boy moonlighting as a lawyer, or a lawyer moonlighting as a farm boy?"

"It feels like both these days. I spent the last few years living in Hagerstown." He matched his pace to her long, lazy one. "When I moved back a couple of months ago, I had a lot of things to deal with in the city, so I haven't been able to give Shane and Devin much of a hand."

"Devin?" She paused outside, where the sun was strong and warming quickly. "Oh, the sheriff. Yes, Bryan's mentioned him. He lives here, too."

"He sleeps here now and again," Jared said. "He lives in the sheriff's office."

"Fighting crime, in a town with two stoplights?"

"Devin takes things seriously." He looked over to where Bryan was dancing around Shane as Shane herded the cows back to pasture. "Have you given any more thought to your father's estate?"

"*Estate*. Now, that's a very serious word. Yes, I've thought about it. I have to talk to Bryan." At Jared's cocked brow, she spoke quietly. "We're a team, Mr. MacKade. He gets a vote in this. We have a Little League game this afternoon, and I don't want to distract him from that. I'll have an answer for you by Monday."

"Fine." Jared's eyes shifted from hers again, narrowed. The warning glint in them had Savannah's lips curving.

"Let me guess. Your brother's looking at my butt again."

Intrigued, Jared looked back at her. "You can tell?"

Her laugh was quick and rich. "Honey, women can always tell. Sometimes we let you get away with it, that's all." She cast a lightning grin over her shoulder, winked at Shane. "Come on, Bryan. You've got chores to finish up before the game."

She walked back through the woods with Bryan, listening to him chatter endlessly about the kittens, the ball game, the animals at the MacKade farm.

He was happy, was all she could think. He was safe. She'd done a good job. On her own. She caught herself before she could sigh and alert her son to the troubles in her mind. It was often so hard to know what was right.

"Why don't you run ahead, Bry? Get those chores done and change into your uniform. I think I'll sit here awhile."

He stopped, kicked at a pebble. "How come you sit here so much?"

"Because I like it here."

He studied her face, looked for signs. "We're really going to stay in this place?"

Her heart broke a little as she bent down and kissed him. "Yes, we're really going to stay."

His grin was quick and bright. "Cool."

He raced off, leaving her standing alone in the path. She sat on a fallen log, closed her eyes and emptied her mind.

So much tried to intrude—memories, mistakes, doubts. She willed them away, concentrating on the quiet and that place in her own head that was safe from worry.

It was a trick she'd learned as a child, when the confusion of life had been too overwhelming to face. There had been long rides in a rattling pickup, endless hours in smelly paddocks, loud voices, the gnaw of real hunger, the cries of fretful babies, the chill of under-heated rooms. They could all be faced, again and again, if she could just escape into herself for a few minutes.

Decisions became clearer, confidence could be rebuilt.

As fascinated as if he'd come across some mythical creature in the woods, Jared watched her. That exotic face was utterly peaceful, her body utterly still. He wouldn't have been surprised to see a butterfly or a bright bird land on her shoulder.

These woods had always been his. His personal place. His intimate place. Yet seeing her here didn't feel like an intrusion. It seemed expected, as if in some part of his mind he'd known he'd find her here if he just knew when to look.

He realized he was afraid to blink, as if in that fraction of a second she might vanish, never to be found again.

She opened her eyes slowly and looked directly into his.

For a moment, neither of them could speak. Savannah felt the breath rush into her throat and stick there. She was used to men staring at her. They had done so even when she was a child. It annoyed, amused or interested her by turns. But it had never left her speechless, as this one long, unblinking stare out of eyes the color of summer grass did.

He moved first, stepping closer. And the world started again.

"I hate stating the obvious." Because he wanted to—and because his knees were just a little weak—he sat on the log beside her. "But you are staggering."

Steadier now, she inclined her head. "Aren't you supposed to be plowing a field or something?"

"Shane's gotten proprietary about his tractor over the years. Aren't you supposed to be going to a ball game?"

"It's not for a couple hours." Savannah took a deep breath, relieved that it went smoothly in and out. "So, who's trespassing, you or me?"

"Technically, both of us." Jared took out a slim cigar and found a match. "This is my brother's property."

"I assumed the farm belonged to all of you."

"It does." He took a drag, watched the smoke drift into the sunlight. "This strip here is Rafe's land."

"Rafe?" Her brows shot up. "Don't tell me there are more of you."

"Four altogether." He tried to smother his surprise when she plucked the cigar out of his fingers and helped herself to a casual drag.

"Four MacKades," she mused. "It's a wonder the town survived. And none of the women managed to rope you in?"

"Rafe's married. I was."

"Oh." She handed him back the cigar. "And now you're back on the farm."

"That right. Actually, if I hadn't waffled, I'd be living in your cabin."

"Is that so?"

"Yep. My place in town's on the market and I'm looking for something around here. But you already had a contract on your place by the time I started looking." He picked up a stick and drew in the dirt. "The farm," he said, sketching lines. "Rafe's. The cabin."

Savannah pursed her lips at the triangle. "Hmm... And the MacKades would have owned a nice chunk of the mountain. You missed your shot, Lawyer Mac-Kade."

"So it seems, Ms. Morningstar."

"I suppose you can call me Savannah, since we're neighbors." Taking the stick from him, she tapped the point of the triangle. "This place. It's the stone house you can see on the hill from the road into town?"

"That's right. The old Barlow place."

"It's haunted."

"You've heard the stories?"

"No." Interested, she looked over at him. "Are there stories?"

It only took him a moment to see she wasn't playing games. "Why did you say it was haunted?"

"You can feel it," she said simply. "Just like these woods. They're restless." When he continued to stare at her, she smiled. "Indian blood. I'm part Apache. My father liked to claim he was full-blooded, but..." She let words trail off, looked away.

"But?"

"There's Italian, Mexican, even a little French mixed in."

"Your mother?"

"Anglo and Mex. She was a barrel racer. Rodeo champion. She was in a car accident when I was five. I don't remember her very clearly."

"Both of mine are gone, too." Companionably he offered her the cigar. "It's tough."

She drew in smoke. "This one shouldn't have been, for me. I lost my father ten years ago, when he booted me out. I was sixteen, and pregnant with Bryan."

"I'm sorry, Savannah."

"Hey, I got by." She passed back the cigar. She didn't know why she'd told him, except that it was quiet here, and he listened well. "The thing is, Jared, I've been thinking more about my father in the last day or so than I have in years. You can't imagine what eight thousand dollars would have meant to me ten years ago. Five.'' With a shrug, she pushed back her hair. ''Hell, there was a time eight dollars would have made the difference between— Well, it doesn't matter.''

Without thinking, he laid a hand over hers. ''Sure it does.''

She frowned down at their hands, then slowly, casually, slipped hers away and stood. ''The thing is, I have Bryan to think of. So I'll talk this over with him.''

''Let me state the obvious again. You've done a terrific job raising your son.''

She smiled. ''We've raised each other. But thanks. I'll be in touch.''

''Savannah.'' He rose, faced her on the path. ''This is a good town, mostly a kind one. No one has to be alone here unless they want to.''

''That's something else I have to think about. I'll see you around, Lawyer MacKade.''

Jared hadn't been to a Little League game in years. When he pulled up at the park just outside of town and absorbed the scents and sounds, he wondered why. The single swatch of wooden stands was crowded and noisy. And kids who weren't on the field were running and racing behind the low chain-link fence or wrestling under the shade of the stands.

The concession stand drew others, with the smell of steaming hot dogs and sloppy joes.

He pulled his car behind the long line of others along the bumpy shoulder of the narrow road and walked across the uneven grass. He had an eye peeled for Savannah, but it was little Connor Dolin who caught his gaze.

The pale-haired boy was waiting quietly in line for food, staring at his feet as a couple of burly older kids harassed him.

"Hey, it's nerd brain Dolin. How's your old man like his cell?"

Connor stood stoically as they bumped and shoved him. The woman ahead of him in line turned and clucked her tongue at them, which had no effect at all.

"Why don't you bake him a cake with a file in it, butthead? Bet a wussy like you bakes a real good cake."

"Hey, Connor." Jared stepped up, aimed one look that had the two bullies scrambling away. "How's it going?"

"Okay." Humiliation had stained his cheeks, fear of abuse had dampened his palms around the money he clutched. "I'm supposed to get hot dogs and stuff."

"Mm-hmm." In the way of males, Jared knew better than to mention what he'd just seen. "How come you're not playing ball?"

"I'm not any good." It was said matter-of-factly. He was much too used to being told he wasn't any good to question it. "But Bryan's playing. Bryan Morningstar. He's the best on the team."

"Is he?" Touched by the sudden light in those shy gray eyes, Jared reached out to flip up the visor of Connor's ball cap. The boy jerked instinctively, went still, and reminded Jared that life had not been all ball games and hot dogs for this nine-year-old. "I'm looking forward to watching him," Jared continued, as if the moment had never happened. "What position does he play?"

Ashamed of his own cowardice, Connor studied the ground again. "Shortstop."

"Yeah? I used to play short."

"You did?" Astonished by the idea, Connor just stared.

"That's right. Devin played third, and—"

"Sheriff MacKade played baseball?" Now the astonishment was mixed with a pure case of hero worship. "I bet he was real good."

"He was okay." It pricked the pride, just a little, to remember he'd never been able to outhit, or outfield Devin. "How many dogs you want, Connor?"

"I've got money. Mom gave me money. And Ms. Morningstar." He fumbled with the bills. "I'm supposed to get one for her, too. With mustard."

"It's my treat." Jared held up three fingers at the vendor as Bryan worried his lip and stared at his money. "This way I get to hang out with you and Ms. Morningstar."

Jared handed the boy the first hot dog, watched him carefully, deliberately squeeze on a line of bright yellow mustard. "Are your mother and sister here?"

"No, sir. Mom's working, and Emma's with her down at the diner. She said it was okay for me to come down and watch, though."

Jared added drinks to the order, and packed the whole business up in a flimsy cardboard box. "Can you handle this?"

"Yes, sir. Sure." Pleased to have been given the job, Connor walked toward the stands, holding the box as if the hot dogs were explosives and the soft drinks a lit match. "We're way up at the top, 'cause Ms. Morningstar says you can see everything better from up high."

And he could see her, Jared mused, as they approached the stands. She sat with her elbows on her knees, her chin cupped in her hands. And her eyes—though he had to imagine, as they were shielded with dark glasses—focused on the field.

He was wrong about that. She was watching him, walking beside the boy, flashing that killer smile or giving a quick salute whenever someone hailed him. And noticing several women—of varying ages—who put their shoulders back or patted at their hair as he passed.

That was what a man who looked like that did to a woman, Savannah supposed. Made her instinctively aware of herself on a purely physical level. It was like pheromones, she decided. The scent of sex.

Those long legs of his carried him up the stands behind the small boy. Now and again his hand touched a shoulder or shook a hand. Savannah picked up the jacket she'd set in Connor's place and squeezed over toward the rail.

"Nice day for a ball game," Jared said as he sat beside her. He took the box from Connor and, to make room for the boy, shifted closer to the woman. "Crowded."

"It is now. Thanks, Con."

"Mr. MacKade bought them," Connor told her, and solemnly handed her back her money.

She started to tell him to keep it, but she understood pride. "Thanks, Mr. MacKade."

"What's the score?"

"We're down one, bottom of the third." She took a healthy bite of her hot dog. "But the top of our batting order's coming up."

"Bryan bats third." Connor chewed and swallowed politely before he spoke. "He has the most RBIs."

Jared watched the first boy come out in the bright orange uniform of the team sponsored by Ed's Café. "Have you met Edwina Crump?" Jared murmured near Savannah's ear.

"Not yet. She owns the diner where Cassandra works, doesn't she?"

"Yeah. Be grateful your boy's not wearing lipstick pink."

Savannah started to comment, then let out an encouraging shout when the bat cracked. The crowd hollered with her when the batter raced to first.

"Tying run's on, right, Con?"

"Yes'm. That's J. D. Bristol. He's a good runner."

She devoured her hot dog, fueling her nerves, while the second batter struck out, swinging. Someone shouted abuse at the ump, and several hot debates erupted in the stands.

"Apparently these games are taken as seriously as ever," Jared commented.

"Baseball's a serious business," Savannah muttered.

Her stomach did a fast boogie as Bryan stepped toward the plate.

Now the crowd murmured.

"That's the Morningstar kid," someone announced. "Got a hot bat."

"Way that pitcher's hurling, he's going to need a torch. Nobody's getting a good piece of that ball today."

Savannah lifted her chin, and bumped the man in front of her with her knee. "You just watch," she told him when he glanced around. "He'll get all of it."

Jared grinned and leaned back on the iron rail. "Yeah, a serious business."

She winced when Bryan took a hard swing and met air. "I've got a buck says he knocks the tying run in."

"I don't like to bet against your boy, or the home team," Jared mused. "But MacKades are betting men. A buck it is."

Savannah held her breath as Bryan went through his little batter's routine. Out of the box, kicking at dirt with his left foot, then his right, adjusting his helmet, taking two practice swings.

"Eye on the ball, Bry," she murmured when he stepped to the plate. "Keep your eye on the ball."

He did—as it sailed past him and into the catcher's mitt.

"Strike two."

"What the hell kind of call is that?" she demanded. "That was low and outside. Anybody could see that was low and outside."

The man in front of her turned around, nodded seriously. "It surely was. Bo Perkins's got eyes like my grandma, and she needs glasses to see her own opinion."

"Well, somebody ought to give Bo Perkins a kick in the…" She let the words trail off, remembering Connor who was watching her with huge eyes. "Strike zone," she decided.

"Good save," Jared said under his breath, and watched Bryan step to the plate again.

The pitcher wound up, delivered. And Bryan gave a mighty swing that caught the ball on the meat of the bat. It flew above the leaping gloves of the infield, and rose beautifully over the outfield grass.

"It's gone!" Savannah shouted, leaping to her feet with the rest of the crowd. "That's the way, Bry!" Her victory dance wiggled her hips in a way that distracted Jared from watching the running of the bases. She kept shouting, her hands cupped to carry the sound, while Bryan rounded the bases and stomped on home plate.

For the hell of it, she grabbed her new friend in front of her and kissed him full on his mouth. "He got a piece of it, didn't he?"

The man, thirty years her senior, blushed like a schoolboy. "Yes, ma'am, he sure did."

"Not exactly the shy, retiring type, are you?" Jared said when she dropped back onto her seat.

"Pay up." She stuck out her hand, palm up.

Jared took out a bill, held it out. "It was worth it."

"You ain't seen nothing yet, Lawyer MacKade."

Jared thought about the promise of those agile, curvy hips and sincerely hoped not.

Chapter 3

It was probably a mistake, Savannah thought, to be sitting across a booth at Ed's from Jared MacKade, eating ice cream. But he'd been very persuasive. And Bryan and Connor had been so excited when he offered to treat them to a victory sundae after the Antietam Cannons batted their way to a win.

And it did give her a chance to see him with Cassandra Dolin.

Connor's mother was a frail little thing, Savannah mused. Blonde and pretty as a china doll, with eyes so haunted they could break your heart. Jared was very gentle with her, very sweet, coaxing smiles from her.

Evidently the shy, vulnerable type was right up his alley.

"Come on, Cassie, have some ice cream with us."

"I can't." Cassie paused by their table long enough

to brush a hand over her daughter's hair as little Emma ate her hot fudge with tiny, serious bites. "We're swamped. But I appreciate you treating the kids, Jared."

She was thin enough to blow away in a spring breeze, Jared thought, and held up a spoonful of sundae. "Have a bite, anyway."

She flushed, but opened her mouth as obediently as a child when he held the spoon to her lips. "It's wonderful."

"Hey, Cass, burgers up."

"Right there." Cassie hurried off to pick up the orders from the counter where Edwina Crump reigned supreme.

The owner of the diner sent Jared a lusty wink. The fact that she was twenty years his senior didn't stop her from appreciating a fine-looking man. "Hey, big fellow, don't see you in here often enough." She patted her frizzed red bowling ball of a hairdo. "When you taking me dancing?"

"Whenever you say, Ed."

She gave a chicken-cackle laugh, wiggled her bony body. "Got a hot band over at the Legion tonight. I'm ready and waiting," she told him before she swung back into the kitchen.

Amused, Savannah propped her elbows on the table. "The Legion, huh? I bet it gets pretty wild."

"You'd be surprised." He cocked a brow. "Wanna go?"

"I'll pass, thanks. Bry, do you think you can shovel any more into your mouth at one time?"

He scooped up a dripping spoon of ice cream, butterscotch and sprinkles. "It's great," he said around it. "What's yours taste like, Con?" To see for himself, Bryan reached over the table to dip his spoon into Connor's. "Strawberry's okay," he decided, "but butterscotch is the best."

Willing to be wrong, he eyed Emma's hot fudge avariciously.

"No," Savannah said mildly, and watched with approval as the five-year-old Emma curled a hand protectively around her bowl. She might be a quiet one, Savannah mused, but the kid knew what was hers. "Pack it away, honey," Savannah told her. "I bet you can eat these boys under the table."

"I like ice cream," Emma said, with one of her rare smiles.

"Me too." With a grin, Savannah scooped up some of her own. "And hot fudge is the best, right?"

"Uh-huh, and the whipped cream. Miss Ed gives you lots of it." She put her spoon down carefully beside her empty bowl and announced, "I can go to Regan's now. My mama said."

"What's Regan's?" Bryan wanted to know.

"She's friends with my mom," Connor told him. "She has a shop just down the street. It has lots of neat things to look at."

"Let's go see."

Before he could dart from the booth, Savannah laid a hand on his arm. "Bryan."

It took him a minute. "Oh, yeah, thanks. Mr. MacKade. The ice cream was great. Come on, Con."

"Thanks, Mr. MacKade." Since Emma already had his hand and was tugging on it, Connor slid from the booth. He looked down at his sister, wrinkled his brow.

"Thank you," she said, keeping an iron grip on her brother's hand.

"You're welcome. Say hi to Regan."

"We will. Mama," Connor called out, "we're going down to Regan's."

"Don't touch anything," Cassie told them, balancing two plates on one arm and serving another. "And come right back if she's busy."

"Yes'm."

Bryan was already out of the door, and Connor followed, hampered by his sister's sedate pace.

"I'd say you hit a home run," Savannah commented, leaning back to drape an arm over the back of the booth.

"You hit one yourself. That's one of the longest conversations I've ever heard out of Emma."

"It must be hard, being shy. She looks like an angel. Like her mother."

Angels who'd already been through hell, Jared thought. "Cassie's doing a terrific job with them, on her own. You'd appreciate that."

"Yes, I would." Savannah glanced over to where Cassie was busy wiping down a booth. "You're... close?"

"I've known her most of my life, but no, not the way you mean. She's a friend." Pleased she was interested enough to ask, he took out a cigar. "And a client. Anything beyond friendship wouldn't be ethical, when I'm representing her.''

"And you'd be a very ethical man, wouldn't you, Lawyer MacKade?''

"That's right. You know, you've never mentioned what you do.''

"About what?''

"About making a living.''

"I've done all sorts of things.'' With a sizzling look, she took the cigar from him.

"I'll just bet you have,'' he murmured.

"Right now I'm an illustrator. Kids' books, mostly.'' Laughing, she passed the cigar back to him. "Doesn't quite fit the image, does it?''

"I don't know. I'd have to see some of your illustrations.'' He glanced up, and his lips curved. "Hey, Dev.''

Savannah shifted to see the man who had just come in. He had the same dark, go-to-hell looks as Jared, a body that was tall and tough and rangy. The eyes were green, as well, but they were different.

She recognized the way they swept the room, checked for details, looked for trouble. Instinctively her muscles tightened, her face went blank. She didn't need the badge on his chest to tell her this was the sheriff. She could spot a cop at half a mile on a speeding horse. She could smell one at twenty paces.

"Saw your car.'' After one quick scan of the room, one quick smile for Cassie, Devin dropped into the booth beside his brother.

"Savannah Morningstar, Devin MacKade.''

"Nice to meet you." An eyeful was Devin's first impression. Then he caught the chill, and wondered about it. "You bought the cabin? The doctor's place."

"That's right. It's my place now."

Not just a chill, he mused. Ice was forming. "That must be your kid I've run into out at the farm. Bryan, right?"

"Yes, Bryan's my son. He's well fed, he's in school, and he's had his shots. Excuse me, I'd better go see what the kids are up to."

And straight into frostbite, Devin mused as she slid from the booth. He winced as the door swung to behind her. "Ouch. What the hell was that about?"

"I don't know," Jared murmured. "But I'm going to find out." He pulled bills out of his pocket.

"You want a guess?" Devin made way so that Jared could climb out of the booth. "The lady's had trouble with the law."

Damn, damn, damn. On the sidewalk, Savannah struggled to regain her composure. That had been stupid, she berated herself. That had been foolish. The trouble with letting yourself relax, she reminded herself, was that all sorts of nasty things could sneak up and bite you in the back.

Now that she was outside, her fists jammed into the snug pockets of her jeans, she realized that she didn't know what this Regan's shop was, much less where it was. All she wanted was to get her son and take him home.

"You want to tell me what just happened?" Jared stepped up behind her, touched a hand to her shoulder.

Savannah made herself take a careful breath before turning. "I finished my ice cream."

"Then maybe you should walk it off." He twined his fingers around her arm and had them quickly and fiercely shaken off.

"Don't take hold of me unless I ask you."

He felt the MacKade temper stir and clamped down on it. "Fine. Why don't you tell me why you were rude?"

"I'm often rude," she shot back. "Especially to cops. I don't like cops. They're one step down from lawyers. I'm not interested in socializing with either one. Which way are the kids?"

"It seems to me we were just socializing up a storm."

"Now we're not. Go back and talk law and order with your brother." The old fury, the old fears, wouldn't quite let go. "You can tell him to go ahead and run a make on me. I'm clean. I have valid employment, and money in the bank."

"Good for you," Jared said equably. "Why should Devin run a make on you?"

"Because cops and lawyers love to stick their noses in other people's business. That's what you've been doing with me ever since you drove up my lane. The way I live and the way I raise my son are my concern and nobody else's. So back off."

It was fascinating. Even through his own bubbling temper, it was fascinating to watch her simmer and spew. "I haven't gotten in your way yet, Savannah.

You'll know when I do. Believe me, you'll know. Right now, I'm just asking for an explanation.''

She didn't know how he did it. How he could look searing daggers at her and still speak in that controlled, reasonable voice. She hated people who could manage that.

"You've just got the only one I'm giving. Now where's my son?''

Jared kept his eyes on hers. "Past Times—two doors behind you." But when she started to whirl away, he took her arm again.

"I told you not to—''

"You listen to me. You're not going to charge in there like some fire-breathing Amazon.''

The heat in her eyes could have boiled the skin off a man. "You'd better take your hand off me before I damage that pretty face of yours.''

He only tightened his grip. Under different circumstances, he might have enjoyed seeing her try. "There are two abused kids in that shop,'' he began, and watched her face change. Fury to surprise, surprise to painful sympathy.

"Connor and Emma. I should have seen it.'' Her gaze darted to the wide glass window of Ed's. "Cassandra.''

"Those kids watched their mother get beaten by their father, and that's more violence in those two short lives than anyone deserves. You go storming in there, you'll—''

"I don't make a habit of frightening children,'' Savannah snapped back. "Whatever you by-the-book types think, I'm a good mother. Bryan's never done without. He's had the best I could give him, and—''

She shut her eyes and fought back the rage. Jared thought it was like watching a volcano capping itself.

"Let go of my arm," she said, calmly now. "I'm going to take my son home."

Jared studied her face another moment, saw the licks of temper just behind the molten brown of her eyes. He released her, watched her walk to Regan's shop, take one more calming breath before pulling open the door and going inside.

Devin strolled out. He stopped beside Jared and scratched his head. "That was quite an interesting show."

"I have a feeling it was just the overture." Intrigued, Jared tucked his hands in his pockets, rocked back on his heels. "There's a lot going on in there."

"A woman like that could make a man forget his own name." With a faint smile, Devin looked over at his brother. "You remember yours?"

"Yeah, just barely. I think you were right about her having problems with the law."

Devin's eyes narrowed. The law, the town and everyone in it were his responsibility. "I could run a make on her."

"No, don't do that. It's just what she expects." Thoughtfully Jared turned toward his car. "I've got an urge to give the lady the unexpected. We'll see what happens."

"Your call," Devin murmured as Jared climbed behind the wheel. Your call, he thought again. As long as the lady stays out of trouble.

Bryan stared out the car window, his face averted coolly from his mother's. He didn't see why Connor couldn't spend the night. It was still Saturday, and there were hours and hours left until the dumb bell rang for school on lousy Monday.

What was a guy supposed to do with all those hours without his best bud? Chores, he thought, rolling his dark brown eyes. Homework. Might as well be in jail.

"Might as well be in jail," he said aloud, turning his face now in challenge.

"Yeah, they play a lot of baseball, eat a lot of butterscotch sundaes, in the joint."

"But I've got nothing to do at home," he said—the desperate lament of every nine-year-old.

"I'll give you something to do," Savannah shot back—the typical response of every frustrated parent. And when she heard that come out of her mouth she nearly groaned. "I'm sorry, Bry, I've got a lot on my mind, and it's just not a good night for a sleep-over."

"I could've stayed at Con's. *His* mother wouldn't care."

Direct hit, she thought grimly as she turned up the lane. "Well, yours does, Ace, and you're stuck with me. You can start by taking out the trash you didn't take out this morning, cleaning that black hole that passes as your room, then studying your math so you don't end up in summer school."

"Great." The minute she stopped the car, he

slammed out. He muttered another comment about it being worse than jail that had smoke coming out of her ears.

"Bryan Morningstar." His name lashed out. When he pivoted back, they stood glaring at each other, angry color riding high on each set of cheekbones, eyes almost black with passionate temper. "Why the hell are you so much like me?" she demanded. She threw her face up to the sun. "I could have had a nice, quiet, well-mannered little girl if I'd tried really hard. Why did I think I'd like having some snotty, bad-tempered boy with big feet?"

It made his lips twitch. "Because then you'd have to take out the trash yourself. A girl would whine and say it was too messy."

"I could take the trash out," she said consideringly. "In fact, I think I will, after I put you in it." She made a grab, but he danced back, laughing at her.

"You're too old to catch me."

"Oh, yeah?" She streaked forward, pounded up the bank after him. He stood hooting at her, taunting. Which was his mistake. She snagged him, making the catch more from her advantage of reach and experience than from speed, and tumbled with him to the grass.

"Who's old, smart mouth?"

"You are." He shrieked with laughter as her fingers dug mercilessly into his ribs. "You're almost thirty."

"I am not. Take it back." She whipped him into a headlock, rubbed her knuckles over his hair. "Take it back, and do the math, Einstein. What's twenty-six from thirty?"

"Nothing," he shouted. "Zero." Then, fearing he might wet his pants if she kept tickling, he surrendered. "It's four, okay? It's four."

"Remember that. And remember who can still take you down." She pulled him back against her, hugged him so suddenly, so fiercely, he blinked. "I love you, Bryan. I love you so much."

"Jeez, Mom." He wriggled in mortification. "I know."

"I'm sorry I snapped at you."

He rolled his eyes, but trickles of remorse found their way through the embarrassment. "I guess I'm sorry, too."

"You and Connor can have a sleep-over next weekend. I promise."

"Okay, that's cool." When she didn't release him, he frowned. But it wasn't so bad, letting her hold him—since none of the guys were around to see. She smelled nice, and her arms were soft. There were flickers of memory of being rocked and soothed.

He was simply too young to do anything but take them for granted. She'd always been there. She always would. He let his head rest on her shoulder, and didn't feel like squirming when she stroked his hair.

"Could we maybe cook out on the grill later?"

"Sure. Want superburgers?"

"Yeah, and french fries."

"What's a superburger without fries?" she murmured, then sighed. "Bryan, has Con said anything to you about his father?"

She felt her son go still, and pressed a light kiss to his hair. "Is it a secret?"

"Sort of."

"I don't want you to betray a confidence. I found out today that Connor's father used to hit his mother. I thought if Con had talked to you about it, you might want to talk to me."

He'd wanted to, ever since Connor had told him. But Connor had cried some—even though Bryan had pretended not to notice. And a guy just didn't tell his mother things like that.

"Con's said he's in jail for hitting her. Con said he used to hurt her real bad, and he drank a lot and gave her bruises and everything. They're getting divorced."

"I see." She'd seen plenty of men who were Joe Dolin's type in her life, but that didn't stop her from despising them. "Did he hit Con, too? And Emma?"

"Not Emma." Here was another dicey part, but Bryan heard himself blurting it out before he could stop. "But he hit Con. Not when his mom was around and could see. He'd call him names and shove him. He said Con was a sissy 'cause he liked to read books and write stories. Con's no sissy."

"Of course he's not."

"He's just real smart. He doesn't hardly have to study to get the answers right. But he doesn't raise his hand in class very much. The teacher calls on him anyway." As he stared off into the woods, Bryan's face darkened with rage. "Some of the kids give him a hard time about things. About his father, and how he's teacher's pet and how he can't throw a baseball very far. But they back off when I'm around.''

Savannah closed her eyes, laid one cheek on Bryan's head. ''You're quite a guy.''

''Hell—heck.'' He corrected himself quickly. ''Bullies are just wimps underneath, right?''

''Right. Con's not the only one who's smart.'' She let out a sigh. ''Bryan, I need to talk to you. Do you remember the other day, when you came home and Mr. MacKade was here?''

''Sure.''

''He's a lawyer, and he came here on business.''

''Are we in trouble?''

''No.'' She turned him so that they were face-to-face. ''We're not in trouble. We're fine. He came about... My father died, Bryan.''

''Oh.'' He felt nothing but mild surprise himself. He'd never met his grandfather, knew of him only because his mother had explained that Jim Morningstar was a rodeo rider who moved around a lot. ''I guess he was pretty old.''

''Yeah.'' Fifty? she wondered. Sixty? She didn't have a clue. ''I never really explained things to you, exactly. Your grandfather and I had a fight a long time ago, and I left home.''

How could she tell this child, her beautiful child, that he'd been the cause of it? No, that she wouldn't do. That she would never do.

''Anyway, I left, and we sort of lost touch.''

''How did Mr. MacKade know he was dead? Did he know him?''

"No, it's a lawyer thing. Your grandfather got hurt, and it started him thinking, I guess. He hired this lawyer out in Oklahoma to find us, and the lawyer called Mr. MacKade. It all took a while, then Mr. MacKade came out to tell me. And to let me know that your grandfather left some money."

"Wow, really?"

"It's about seven thousand—"

"Dollars?" Bryan finished for her, eyes popping. It was all the money in the world. Enough for a new bike, a new mitt, the Cal Ripkin rookie baseball card he lusted for. "We get to keep it? Just like that?"

"I have to sign some papers."

The dollar signs faded from his eyes long enough for Bryan to read his mother's face. "How come you don't want it?"

"I... Oh, Bryan." Defeated, she curled up her legs and rested her brow on them. "I don't know how to explain it to you. I've been so mad at him all these years. Now I'm mad at him for waiting until he was dead."

Bryan patted her head and thought it over. "Is it like him saying he's sorry? And if you take it you'd be saying you were sorry, too?"

She let out a half laugh at the simplicity of it. "Why couldn't I have thought of that?" Wearily she lifted her head, studied his face. "You think we should take it."

"I guess we don't need to." He watched Cal Ripkin fly gracefully away. "I mean, you've got your job, and we've got a house now."

"No," she murmured. "We don't need to." She felt the weight slip from her shoulders. They didn't need to, and that was exactly why they could. "I'll go see Mr. MacKade on Monday and tell him to put the money through."

"Cool." Bryan leaped to his feet. "I'm going to call Con and tell him we're rich."

"No."

He skidded to a halt. "But, Mom..."

"No. Bragging about money is very uncool. And I might as well break it to you now, Ace. It doesn't make us rich, and I'm dumping it into a college fund."

His mouth dropped open, nearly scraping his shoes. "College? That's a hundred years away. Maybe I won't even go."

"That'll be up to you, but the money'll be there."

"Oh, man." At nine, Bryan was experiencing the pain of a fortune won and lost. "All of it?"

"All—" his shattered face changed her mind in midstep "—except some." You can have one thing. It'll be like a present from your grandfather."

Hope bloomed. "One anything?"

"One any reasonable thing. A gold-plated Corvette slides over to the unreasonable side."

He let out a whoop, leaped over to hug her. "I've gotta go look up something in my baseball-card price guide."

She watched him go, full steam, catapulting onto the porch, streaking into the house with the screen door slamming like a gunshot behind him.

* * *

Later, while she grilled burgers on the porch with Bryan curled up with his price guide and dreams of glory, Jared sat on the other side of the haunted woods and thought of her.

He was tempted, very tempted, to stride through those woods and finish the altercation she had started that afternoon out on the sidewalk in front of Ed's.

Prickly women weren't his style, Jared reminded himself and set the chair rocking. Prickly women with lightning tempers and murky pasts were even less so. Not that she wasn't interesting, and not that he didn't like fitting puzzle pieces together.

But his life was cruising along at a very comfortable pace at the moment. He would have enjoyed her companionship—on a purely superficial level, of course. A few dates, leading to physical contact. After all, a dead man would fantasize about rolling around with a woman who looked like that.

And Jared MacKade wasn't dead.

He also wasn't stupid. The woman who'd blasted him that afternoon was nothing but trouble. The last thing one hot temper needed was to crash up against another. That was why he preferred his women cool, composed and reasonable.

Like his ex-wife, he thought with a grimace. She'd been so cool there were times he wanted to hold a mirror in front of her mouth to see if she was still breathing.

But that was another story.

First thing Monday morning, he was going to draft a nice formal letter advising Savannah Morningstar of

her inheritance and the steps she was required to take
to accept or decline it.

He didn't mind getting his hands dirty for a client,
sweating for one, even losing sleep for one. But she
wasn't his damn client, and he'd taken professional
courtesy to his colleague out west as far as he intended
to.

He was out of it.

Hell, the woman had a kid. A very appealing kid,
but that was beside the point. If he pursued a personal
relationship with her, it would involve the kid, as well.
There was no way around that one and, Jared admitted,
there shouldn't be one.

Then there was that fact that, beneath that scorching
beauty, the woman was tough as shoe leather. There
was no doubt that she'd been around, knew the ropes
and had probably climbed plenty of them. A woman
didn't get eyes that aware by spending all her time
baking biscuits.

He imagined she could chew a man up, spit him out,
and have him come crawling back for more.

Well, not this man.

He could handle her, of course. If he wanted to.

That exotic, unbelievable face zipped straight to the
center of his mind and taunted him.

God, he wanted to.

In disgust, Jared sprang up and headed into the
woods. He needed to walk, he decided. And he preferred the company of ghosts to his own thoughts.

Chapter 4

"Good afternoon, MacKade law offices." Sissy Bleaker, Jared's secretary, answered the phone on the fly. It was quarter to five, she had a hot date in exactly one hour, and the boss had been like a bear with a sore tooth all day. "Oh, yes, hello, Mr. Brill. No, Mr. MacKade is in conference."

Sissy could have spit nails when the front door opened. How the devil was she supposed to look irresistibly sexy in an hour if she couldn't get out of here?

"I'll be happy to take a message." As she picked up a pad, she glanced up. And decided she could have a week at her disposal and not pull off the kind of in-your-face sexy that had just walked into Jared Mac-Kade's outer office.

Savannah hated being here. She hated that she'd felt obliged to change out of jeans into pleated trousers and a jacket. Something about visiting official places compelled her to put on a front.

And this place certainly looked official. The pretty plants and bland pastel paintings on matte-white walls didn't hide the fact that law was the order here. The carpet was a muted gray, the deeper-toned chairs in the waiting area were likely just the wrong side of comfortable.

We wouldn't want people to be at their ease now, would we? she thought bitterly.

She'd never known a den of authority—social services, a principal's office, an unemployment line—to offer comfort. Still, she'd thought the man had more style than to choose such a cold, formal setting for his work.

The secretary behind the polished reception-area desk was young, bright-eyed and, Savannah was sure, fiercely efficient. The quick greeting smile she sent in Savannah's direction was carefully empty of curiosity and perfectly balanced between warm and cool.

Savannah had no idea Sissy was curdling with envy inside.

"Yes, Mr. Brill, I'll see that he gets your message. You're welcome. Goodbye." Wondering just where the mystery visitor had come across that terrific jacket, all sweeping lines and bold colors, Sissy hung up the phone and aimed her most professional smile.

"Good afternoon. May I help you?"

"I'd like to see Mr. MacKade."

"Do you have an appointment?" Sissy knew very

well she did not. Jared's schedule was filed in her brain right alongside her own.

"No, I was..." Damn, she hated this. "I was in town, and I thought I'd take a chance he'd be free for a minute."

"I'm afraid he's in conference, Ms...."

"Morningstar." Of course he was in conference, Savannah thought nastily. Where else was a lawyer when he wasn't on the putting green but in conference? "Then I'd like to leave a message."

The name Morningstar rang all sorts of bells in Sissy's brain. It had been said through gritted teeth that morning, when Jared dictated a briskly formal letter with all kinds of interesting hums between the lines.

"Certainly. If it's personal, you could write it down and I'll... Oh." Sissy beamed at her phone. "Mr. MacKade's just finished his conference call, I see. Why don't I buzz him, see if he can squeeze you in?"

"Fine, great." Restless, Savannah turned away to pace.

Sissy decided that if she grew six inches in height, filled out several more in the right places, she might just look that impressive on the move.

"Mr. MacKade, there's a Ms. Morningstar to see you, if you have a moment. Yes, sir, she's in the office now. Yes, sir." Careful to keep her lips from sliding into a smile, Sissy hung up the phone. "He'll see you, Ms. Morningstar. It's right up those stairs and to the left. First door."

"Thanks." Savannah turned toward the short curve

of stairs, put one hand on the pristine white rail and climbed.

Must have been a town house at one time, she decided. Or a duplex. Though she wouldn't have called the place homey, Savannah admitted it had class—if you went in for snooty and nondescript.

There was a short hallway at the top of the steps, a print of a spray of white orchids in a white vase that was so soulless and ordinary it offended her artist's eye, and two doors facing each other.

She strode to the one on the left, rapped once and opened it.

Of course he'd look terrific in charcoal gray, she thought. A lot better than the office did, with its dull grays and punishing whites. Someone should tell him work was more pleasant in an environment with a little color and life.

But it wouldn't be her.

He rose, elegant in his three-piece suit and carefully knotted tie. A tie he'd just jerked back into place. She thought, with an inner sense of rebellion, that he looked like more of a lawyer than ever.

"Ms. Morningstar." He inclined his head. He thought that her stepping into the room was like having some brilliant bolt of lightning strike a placid pond. "Have a seat."

"It won't take long." She remained standing, stubbornly. "I appreciate you taking the time to see me."

"I had the time." To illustrate the point, he moved a file from the center of his desk to the side, and sat. "What can I do for you?"

In answer, she pulled papers out of her purse, tossed them on his desk. "I signed them, in triplicate, and had them notarized." Her driver's license landed with a plop on top of the papers. "That's my ID." She threw in her social security card for good measure. "I don't have a birth certificate."

"Mm-hmm..." Taking his time, Jared pulled brown horn-rims out of his jacket pocket and slipped them on to study the papers.

Savannah stared at him, swallowed hard. It didn't seem to matter that she told herself it was ridiculous. Her heart *had* skipped a beat. He looked gorgeous, intellectually sexy, in those damn glasses. And made her feel like a fumbling fool.

"It's all in order," she began.

"Afraid not." Thoughtfully, He picked up her driver's license, perused it. "This is invalid."

"The hell it is. I just had it renewed a couple of months ago."

"That may be," he continued, studying her now. "But as the picture actually looks like you, and is, in fact, flattering, this driver's license is obviously a fraud, and therefore, invalid."

She closed her mouth, jammed her hands in her pockets. "Are you making a joke? Is that allowed in hallowed halls?"

"Sit down, Savannah. Please."

With a bad-tempered shrug, she sat. "Did you ever hear of color?" she demanded. "This place is dull as a textbook, and your art is pathetically ordinary."

"It is, isn't it?" he agreed easily. "My ex-wife decorated the place. She was a tax accountant, had the office across the hall.'' He leaned back and scanned the room. ''I've gotten used to not seeing the place, but you're right. It could use something.''

''It could use an obituary.'' Annoyed with herself, she pushed a hand through her hair. ''I hate being here.''

''I can see that.'' He picked up the papers again, skimmed through them. ''You understand that you're agreeing to accept a payment, by cashier's check, that equals the total cash balance of your father's estate?''

''Yes.''

''And his effects?''

''I thought...I thought that meant the money. What else is there?''

''Apparently there are a few personal effects. I can get you an itemized list if you like, so that you can decide if you want them sent or discarded. The shipping would be deducted from the estate.''

Discarded, she thought. As she had been. ''No, just have them sent.''

''All right.'' Methodically he made notes on a yellow legal pad. ''I'll have my secretary draft a letter tomorrow confirming the status and apprising you that you'll receive full disbursement of the estate within forty-five days.''

''Why do you need a letter when you've just told me?''

He glanced up from the papers, the eyes behind the lenses amused. ''The law likes to cover its butt with as much paperwork as humanly possible.''

He signed the papers himself as proxy for his colleague, then handed Savannah back her license and social security card.

"That's it, then?"

"That's it."

"Well." Feeling awkward, and relieved, she rose. "It wasn't as painful as I expected. I suppose if I'm ever in the market for a lawyer, I'll give you a call."

"I wouldn't have you as a client, Savannah."

Her eyes fired as he took off his glasses and stood to come around the desk. "That's very neighborly of you."

"I wouldn't have you as a client," he repeated, standing behind her, "because then this would be unethical."

He caught her off guard. She'd had no idea any man could still catch her off guard. But she was in Jared's arms and being thoroughly kissed before she had a chance to evade.

If she'd wanted to evade.

There was heat, of course. She expected that, enjoyed that. But it was the lushness of it that surprised her—the silky, sumptuous spread of it that bloomed in that meeting of lips, flowering through her body.

He held her close, in a smooth, confident embrace, no fumbling, no grappling. He gave her room to resist, and as that clever, wide-palmed hand skimmed lightly up her spine, she thought only a fool would step away from that caress, that mouth, that heat.

So she stepped into it, sliding her own hands up his back until they were hooked over his shoulders.

He'd wondered what he would find here. From the moment she stood, clumps of flowers at her feet, and looked at him, he'd wondered. Now he knew there was strength in those long, lovely arms, fire in that soft, full mouth. She opened for him as if he'd touched her hundreds of times, and her taste was gloriously familiar. The press of her body against his, every firm, generous curve, was an erotic homecoming.

He tangled his fingers in her hair, slowly tugging her head back to savor. And as her mouth moved warm on his, he discovered what it was to be savored in turn.

Gradually, thoughtfully, he drew back to study her face. Her eyes were steady, calm. Darker, yes, he mused. He knew by the way her heart had jumped against his that whatever had moved through him had moved through her, as well. But she didn't tremble.

What would it take to make a woman like this tremble?

He knew he would have to discover that secret, and all the others she kept hidden behind those dark, unreadable eyes.

"But," he said, "I can certainly recommend a lawyer for you, if you find you need one."

She lifted a brow. Oh, he was a cool one, she thought, carrying on the conversation as if her insides weren't sizzling. Appreciating it, she smiled. "Why, thank you."

"Excuse me a minute," he said when his phone rang. "Yes, Sissy." His gaze left Savannah's only long enough for a glance at his watch. "So it is," he murmured, noting that it was just after five. "You go ahead, I'll lock up. And, Sissy, the letter I dictated this morning. The first letter? Yes. Don't mail that. I need to make some changes.''

Savannah watched him consideringly. He was sending his secretary off for the day, and they would be alone. She understood what it meant when a man looked at a woman the way Jared was looking at her. She understood what happened between men and women after they'd shared a mutually lusty kiss.

Over the years, she'd learned to be very careful, very…selective. The responsibility of raising a child alone wasn't a small one. Men could come and go, but her son was forever. She wasn't a woman who stepped blindly into affairs, who scratched every itch or accepted every advance.

But she was also realistic. The man currently dismissing his secretary, the man flipping through his daily calendar to coordinate his schedule, was about to become her lover.

''My secretary's got a date,'' Jared commented when he hung up the phone. ''So it looks like we're closing the office on time today.'' Tilting his head, he studied Savannah. ''I'm supposed to ask you, discreetly, where you got your jacket.''

''My jacket?'' Bemused, Savannah glanced down. ''I made it.''

''You're kidding.''

Her bottom lip moved into an expression somewhere between a pout and a sneer, and her chin rose in a gesture he now recognized as an indicator of temper simmering. "What? I don't look like the type who can sew? I don't fit the happy-homemaker image?"

Intrigued, he rested a hip on the edge of his desk, reached out to rub the brilliantly hued lapel of her jacket between his fingers. "Nice work. What else can you do?"

"Whatever I need to do." She didn't bother to protest when he tugged her toward him. Instead, she rested her hands on his shoulders and leaned down into the kiss.

"It's early," he murmured.

"Relatively."

"Where's Bryan?"

"At Cassie's." Mildly surprised he'd bothered to ask, she changed the angle of the kiss and let herself sink in. "I'm going to pick him up about six. I've got about a half an hour."

"It's going to take longer." He shifted, took her by the hips and drew her intimately between his legs. "Why don't you call her and see if he can stay until seven?" His teeth nipped gently over that lovely bottom lip. "Seven-thirty."

She was going to enjoy getting him out of that tie, Savannah thought. "I suppose I could."

"Good. You clear it, then we'll go across the street."

"Across the street?"

"For an early dinner."

She drew back, stared at him. "Dinner?"

"Yes." Almost certain his legs would support him, Jared stood, before he could give in to the urge to tear off her clothes, drag her to the floor and have her. "I'd like to take you to dinner."

"Why?"

"Because I'd enjoy spending an hour or two with you." On top of you, he thought. Inside you. God. With every appearance of calm, he skirted the desk and flipped through his address file. "Here's Cassie's number."

"I know Cassie's number." It was demoralizing to realize she had to take a good, deep breath to steady herself, when he was just standing there, so coolly, so easily. "What's going on here, Jared? We both know dinner isn't necessary."

His stomach twisted into tight slick knots. He could take her. Right here, right now. It was just that simple. And anything too simple was suspect.

"I'd like to have dinner with you, Savannah. And conversation." Picking up the phone, he dialed Cassie's number himself, held out the receiver. "All right?"

Filled with mistrust, she hesitated. With a shrug, she took the phone. "All right."

The restaurant was casual, the menu basic American grill. Savannah toyed with her drink and waited for Jared's next move.

"So, you make clothes."

"Sometimes."

Smiling, he leaned back in the wooden booth. "Sometimes?" he repeated, looking at her expectantly.

He wanted to make conversation, she determined.

She could make conversation. "I learned because homemade is cheaper than store-bought, and I didn't want to be naked. Now I make something now and again because I enjoy it."

"But you make your living as an illustrator, not as a seamstress."

"I like to work with color, and design. I got lucky."

"Lucky?"

Wary of the friendly probing, she moved her shoulders. "You don't want the story of my life, Jared."

"But I do." He smiled at the waitress who set their meals in front of them. "Start anywhere," he said invitingly.

She shook her head, cut into the spicy blackened chicken he'd recommended. "You've lived here all your life, haven't you?"

"That's right."

"Big family, old friends and neighbors. Roots."

"Yeah."

"I'm going to give my son roots. Not just a roof over his head, but roots."

He was silent for a moment. There had been a fierceness in her voice, a fiery determination, that he had to admire, even as he wondered at it. "Why here?"

"Because it's not the West. That's first. I wanted to get away from the dust, the plains, and all those sun-baked little towns. That was for me," she admitted. "I've been moving east for ten years. This seemed far enough."

When he said nothing, she relaxed a little. It was difficult to combat that quiet way he had of listening.

"I didn't want the city for Bryan. But I wanted to give him a sense of belonging, of…"

"Community?"

"Yeah. Small town, kids, people who'd get to know him by name. But I still wanted a little distance. That was for me again. And…"

"And?"

"I was drawn here," she said at length. "Maybe it's the mysticism in my blood and my heritage, but I felt— I knew that this would be home. The land, the hills. The woods. Your woods called to me." Amused at herself, she smiled. "How's that for weird?"

"They've called to me all my life," Jared said, so simply her smile faded. "I could never be happy anywhere else. I moved to the city because it seemed practical. And small towns and long walks through the woods weren't my ex-wife's style."

If he could probe, so could she. "Why did you marry her?"

"Because it seemed practical." Now it was his turn to wince. "Which doesn't say much for either of us. We were reasonably attracted, respected each other, and entered into a very civilized, intelligent and totally passionless contract of marriage. Two years later, we had a very civilized, intelligent and totally passionless divorce."

It was difficult, all but impossible, to visualize the man who had kissed her being passionless about anything. "No blood spilled?"

"Absolutely not. We were both much too reasonable for combat. There were no children." Her choice, he remembered, only slightly bitter. "She'd kept her own name."

"A modern professional marriage."

"You've got it. We split everything down the middle and went our separate ways. No harm, no foul."

Curious, Savannah tilted her head. "It bothered you that she didn't take your name."

He started to correct her, then shrugged. "Yeah, it bothered me. Not very modern or professional of me. Just one of those things that would have made the commitment emotional instead of reasonable. That's just pride."

"Partly," Savannah agreed. "But part of you wanted to give her that piece of you that you were most proud of, that had been passed to you, and that you wanted to pass to your children."

"You're astute," he murmured.

"Lawyers aren't the only ones who can read people. And I understand the importance of names. When Bryan was born, I stared at the form they give you. For names. And I thought, what do I put where it says Father? If I put the name down, then I'm giving that name to my son. My son," she repeated quietly.

"What did you put down?"

She brought herself back from that moment, when she'd been barely seventeen, and alone. Completely alone. "Unknown," she said. "Because he'd stopped being important. My name was enough."

"He's never seen Bryan?"

"No. He packed up his gear and lit out like a rocket the day I told him I was pregnant. Don't say you're sorry,'' she said, anticipating him. "He did me a favor. It's easy for a sixteen-year-old girl to be dreamy-eyed and hot-blooded over a good-looking cowboy, but it isn't easy to live with one.''

"What have you told Bryan?''

"The truth. I always tell him the truth—or as close to it as I can without hurting him. I'm not ashamed that I was once foolish enough to imagine myself in love. And I'm grateful that sometimes foolishness is rewarded by something as spectacular as Bryan.''

"You're a remarkable woman.''

It touched and embarrassed her that he should think so. "No, I'm a lucky one.''

"It couldn't have been easy.''

"I don't need things to be easy.''

He considered that, and thought it was more that she didn't care for things to be easy. That he understood.

"What did you do when you left home?''

"When I got kicked out,'' she said. "You don't have to pretty it up. My father gave me the back of his hand, called me…all sorts of things it's impolite to repeat to a man wearing such a nice suit—and showed me the door. Wasn't much of a door,'' she remembered, surprised to see that Jared had reached out to link his fingers with hers. "We were living in a trailer at the time.''

He was appalled. Probably shouldn't be, he realized. He'd heard stories as bad, and worse, in his own office. But he was appalled at the image of Savannah at sixteen, pregnant and facing the world alone.

"Didn't you have anyone you could go to?''

"No, there was no one. I didn't know my mother's family. He'd have probably changed his mind in a day or two. He was like that. But the things he'd called me had hurt a lot more than the slap, so I put on my backpack, stuck out my thumb, and didn't look back. Got a job waiting tables in Oklahoma City." She picked up her drink. "That's probably why Cassie and I hit it off. We both know what it's like to stand on your feet all day and serve people. But she does a better job of it."

Oh, there was plenty she was skimming over, Jared thought. Miles of road she wasn't taking him over. "How did you get from waiting tables in Oklahoma City to illustrating children's books?"

"By taking a lot of detours." Well fed, she leaned back and smiled at him. "You'd be surprised at some of the things I've done." Her smile widened at his bland look. "Oh, yes, you would."

"Name some."

"Served drinks to drunks in a dive in Wichita."

"You're going to have to do better than that, if you want to shock me."

"Worked a strip joint in Abilene. There." She chuckled and plucked the thin cigar he'd just taken out of his pocket from his fingers. "That's got you thinking."

Determined not to goggle, he struck a match, held it to the tip of the cigar when she leaned over. "You were a stripper."

"Exotic dancer." She blew out smoke and grinned. "You are shocked."

"I'm...intrigued."

"Mm-hmm... To pop the fantasy a bit, I never got down to the bare essentials. You'd see women on the beach wearing about as much as I shook down to—only I got paid for it. Not terribly well." Casually she handed him back the cigar. "I made more money designing and sewing costumes for the other girls than I did peeling out of them. So I retired from the stage."

"You're leaving out chunks, Savannah."

"That's right." They were her business. "Let's say I didn't like the hours. I worked a dog and pony show for a while."

"A dog and pony show."

"A poor man's circus. Took a breather in New Orleans selling paintings of bayous and street scenes, and doing charcoal sketches of tourists. I liked it. Great food, great music."

"But you didn't stay," he pointed out.

"I never stayed long in one place. Habit. Just about the time I was getting restless, I got lucky. One of the tourists who sat for me was a writer. Kids' books. She'd just ditched her illustrator. Creative differences, she said. She liked my work and offered me a deal. I'd read her manuscript and do a few illustrations. If her publisher went for it, I'd have a job. If not, she'd pay me a hundred for my time. How could I lose?"

"You got the job."

"I got a life," she told him. "The kind where I didn't have to leave Bryan with sitters, worry about how I was going to pay the rent that month, or if the social workers were going to come knocking to check me out and decide if I was a fit mother. The kind where cops don't roust you to see if you're selling paintings or yourself. After a while, I had enough put together that I could buy my son a yard, a nice school, Little League games. A community." She tipped back her glass again. "And here we are."

"And here we are," he repeated. "Where do you suppose we're going?"

"That's a question I'll have to ask you. Why are we having dinner and conversation instead of sex?"

To his credit, he didn't choke, but blew out smoke smoothly. "That's blunt."

"Lawyers like to use twenty words when one will do," she countered. "I don't."

"Then let's just say you expected sex. I don't like being predictable." Behind the haze of smoke, his eyes flashed on hers with a power that jarred. "When we get around to sex, Savannah, it won't be predictable. You'll know exactly who you're with, and you'll remember it."

In that moment, she didn't have the slightest doubt. Perhaps that was what worried her. "All your moves, Lawyer MacKade? Your time and place?"

"That's right." His eyes changed, lightened with a humor that was hard to resist. "I'm a traditional kind of guy."

Chapter 5

A traditional kind of guy, Savannah mused. One day after her impromptu dinner with Jared, and she was standing in her kitchen, her hands on her hips, staring at the florist's box.

He'd sent her roses. A dozen long-stemmed red beauties.

Traditional, certainly. Even predictable, in their way, she supposed. Unless you factored in that no one in her life had ever sent her a long, glossy white box filled with red roses.

She was certain he knew it.

Then there was the card.

Until your garden blooms

How did he know flowers were one of her biggest weaknesses, that she had pined for bright, fragrant blooms in those years when she was living in tiny, cramped rooms in noisy, crowded cities? That she'd promised herself that one day she would have a garden of her own, planted and tended by her own hands?

Because he saw too much, she decided, and circled the flowers as warily as a dog circling a stranger. She was so intent on them, she actually jumped when the phone rang. Cursing herself she yanked up the receiver.

"Yes. Hello."

"Bad time?" Jared asked.

She scowled at the flowers lying beautifully against the green protective paper. "I'm busy, if that's what you mean."

"Then I won't keep you. I thought you might like to bring Bryan over to the farm for dinner tonight."

Still frowning, she reached into the box, took out a single rose. It didn't bite. "Why?"

"Why not?"

"For starters, I've already got sauce on for spaghetti." She waited a beat. So did he. "I suppose you expect me to ask you to come here to dinner."

"Yep."

Twirling the rose, she tried to think of a good reason not to. "All right. But Bryan has baseball practice after school. I have to pick him up at six, so—"

"I'll pick him up. It's on my way. See you tonight, then."

Something seemed to be slipping out of her hands. "I told you all of this wasn't necessary," she muttered. "The flowers."

"Do you like them?"

"Sure, they're beautiful."

"Well, then." That seemed to settle the matter. "I'll see you a bit after six."

Befuddled, she hung up. After another long stare at the roses, she decided she'd better dig up a vase.

At six-fifteen she heard the sound of a car coming up her lane. Carefully she finished a detail on the illustration of her wicked queen for a reissue of traditional fairy tales, then turned away from her worktable. Bryan was already clattering up the steps by the time she walked from her small studio into the kitchen.

"...then he popped up, and that klutzoid Tommy couldn't get his glove under it. His mom had two cows when the ball came down and smacked him in the face. Blood was spurting out of his nose. It was so cool. Hi, Mom."

"Bryan." She lifted a brow at the state of his clothes. Red dirt streaked every inch. "Do some sliding today?"

"Yeah." He headed straight to the refrigerator for a jug of juice.

"Tommy Mardson got a bloody nose," Jared put in.

"So I hear."

"His mom was really screaming." Excited by the memory, Bryan nearly forgot to bother with a glass—until he caught his own mother's steely eye. "It wasn't broke. Just smashed real good."

"We're going to work on that grammar tonight, Ace."

Bryan rolled his eyes. "Nobody talks like the books say. Anyway, I got a B on the spelling test."

"Drinks are on the house. Math?"

Bryan swallowed juice in a hurry. "Hey, I gotta clean up," he declared, and dashed for the stairs in a strategic retreat.

Recognizing evasive action, Savannah winced. "We hate long division."

"Who doesn't?" Jared handed her a bottle of wine. "But a B in spelling's not chump change."

Neither, she thought, was the fancy French label on the bottle. "This is going to humble my spaghetti."

Jared took a deep, appreciative sniff of the air. It was all spice and bubbling red sauce. "I don't think so."

"Well, at least take off that tie." She turned to root out a corkscrew. "It's intimidating. You can—"

He turned her by the shoulders, lowered his head slowly and covered her mouth with his. The top of her head lifted gently away.

"Kiss," she finished on a long breath. "You can sure as hell kiss." After picking up the corkscrew that had clattered to the counter, she opened the wine with the quick, competent moves of a veteran bartender. "Fancy wine and fancy flowers, all in one day. You're going to turn my head."

"That's the idea."

She stretched for the wineglasses on the top shelf. "I'd have thought, after the condensed version of *The Life and Times of Savannah Morningstar,* you'd have gotten the picture that I'm not the wine-and-flowers type."

He brushed a finger over the petals of the roses she'd set in the center of the table. "They seem to suit you."

As he folded his tie into his pocket, loosened the collar of his shirt, she poured the wine. "It was rude of me not to thank you for them. So…" She handed him a glass. "Thanks."

"My pleasure."

"Bryan's going to hide out until he thinks I've forgotten about the math. More fool he. If you're hungry, I can call him down."

"No hurry." Sipping wine, he wandered into the front room. He wanted a better look at the paintings.

The colors were bold, often just on the edge of clashing. The brush strokes struck him as the same—bold sweeps, temperamental lines. The subject matter varied, from still lifes of flowers in full riotous bloom, to portraits of vivid, lived-in faces, to landscapes of gnarled trees, rocky hills and stormy skies.

Not quiet parlor material, he mused. And not something it was easy to look away from. Like the artist, he decided, the work made a full-throttle impression.

"No wonder you turned your nose up at what's hanging in my office," he murmured.

"I've never thought art was supposed to be cool." She moved a shoulder. "But that's just my opinion."

"What's it supposed to be? In your opinion?"

"Alive."

"Then you've certainly succeeded." He turned back to her. "Do you still sell?"

"If the price is right."

"I've been thinking about having Regan do something about my office. My sister-in-law," he reminded her. "She's done an incredible job with the inn she and my brother are rehabing. Would you be willing to handle the art?"

She took it slow, watching him, sipping wine. The idea had an old, deeply buried longing battling for air. Painting was just a hobby, she reminded herself. What else could it be, for a woman with no formal training?

"I've already told you I'd sleep with you."

He managed a laugh, though it nearly stuck in his suddenly dry throat. "Yes, you have. But we're talking about your painting. Are you interested in selling some?"

"You want to put my art in your office?"

"I believe I've established that."

One step at a time, Savannah reminded herself. Don't let him see just how much it would mean. "Wouldn't you be more comfortable with some nice pastels?"

"You have a nasty streak, Savannah. I like it."

She laughed, enjoying him. "Let's see what your sister-in-law comes up with first. Then we'll talk." She walked back into the kitchen to put on water for the pasta.

"Fair enough. Why don't you drop by the inn, see what she and Rafe have done there?"

"I'd love to get a look at the place," she admitted.

"I could drive you over after dinner."

"Homework." She shook her head with real regret. "I have a feeling I'm going to be doing long division."

"In that case—" he picked up the wine and topped off both their glasses "—let me offer a little Dutch courage."

She hadn't expected him to stay after the meal was over. Certainly hadn't been prepared for him to wind things around so that he was sitting beside her son at the kitchen table, poring over the problems in an open arithmetic book.

She served him coffee as he translated the problems into baseball statistics. And why, Savannah wondered, as her son leaped at the ploy and ran with it, hadn't she thought of that?

Because, she admitted, figures terrified her. Schooling terrified her. The knowledge that her son would one day soon go beyond what she had learned was both thrilling and shaming.

Not even Bryan knew about the nights she stayed up late, long after he slept, and studied his books, determined that she would be able to give help whenever he asked her for it.

"So, you divide the total score by the number of times at bat," Jared suggested, adjusting his horn-rims in a way that made Savannah's libido hitch.

"Yeah, yeah!" The lights of knowledge were bursting in Bryan's head. "This is cool." With his tongue caught between his teeth, he wrote the numbers carefully, almost reverently. After all, they were ball players now. "Check this out, Mom."

When she did, laboriously going over the steps of the problem, her smile bloomed. "Good job." She brushed a kiss over Bryan's tousled hair. "Both of you."

"How come I didn't get a kiss?" Jared wanted to know.

She obliged him, chastely enough, but Bryan still made gagging noises. "Man, do you have to do that at the dinner table?"

"Close your eyes," Jared suggested, and kissed Savannah again.

"I'm out of here." Bryan shut his book with a snap.

"Out of here, and into the tub," Savannah finished.

"Aw, come on." He looked beseechingly at Jared.

"Actually," Jared began, "I believe my client is entitled to a short recess."

"Oh, really?" But Savannah's dry comment was drowned out by Bryan's whoop of delight.

"Yeah, a recess. Like an hour's TV."

"With the court's indulgence." Jared shot Bryan a warning look, laid a hand on his shoulder. "What my client means is, thirty minutes of recreational television viewing is appropriate after serving his previous sentence and taking steps toward rehabilitation. After which he will, voluntarily and without incident, accept the court's decision."

Savannah hissed a breath through her teeth. "Lights out at nine-thirty," she muttered.

"All right!" Bryan pumped his fist in the air. "You should have gone for the hour," he told Jared.

"This was your best deal. Trust me, I'm your lawyer."

A grin split Bryan's face. "Cool. Thanks, Mr. MacKade. 'Night, Mom."

"Very fast, fancy talking," Savannah said under her breath as her son dashed upstairs to the little portable in her bedroom.

"I couldn't help myself." Feeling a little sheepish, Jared tucked his hands in his pockets. "He reminded me of what it was like to be a nine-year-old boy and desperate for another hour. Are you going to hold me in contempt?"

She sighed, picked up the empty coffee cups, took them to the sink. "No. It was nice of you to stand up for him. Besides, he'd have wrangled the half hour out of me anyway."

"He deserved it." Jared grinned when she glanced over her shoulder. "So do I. After all, we slogged straight through that math assignment."

"You want thirty minutes of—what was it, recreational television viewing?"

"No." He took his glasses off, slipped them into the pocket of his shirt. "I want you to walk in the woods with me." When her brow creased and she glanced toward the stairs, Jared took her hand. "We won't go far. Hey, Bry!" he called out. "Your mom and I are going for a walk."

"Cool," came the absent, obviously uninterested answer. Jared took her denim jacket from a hook by the kitchen door. "It gets chilly after sundown."

"Just to the woods," she insisted as she shrugged

into the jacket. From there, she could hear Bryan if he called her.

"Just to the woods," Jared agreed, and closed his hand over hers. "Do you get lonely out here during the day, by yourself?"

"No. I like being by myself." She walked outside with him, where the air had a faint snap and the sky was so clear the stars almost hurt the eyes. "I like the quiet."

They went down the uneven steps that had been hacked into the bank, then across the narrow lane to where the woods began with shadows.

"I kissed my first girl in here."

The just-greening trees opened to welcome them in. "Did you?"

"Yep. Cousin Joanie."

"Cousin?"

"Third cousin," Jared elaborated. "On my mother's side. She had long golden curls, eyes the color of the sky in June, and my heart. I was eleven."

Comfortable with shadows and starlight, she laughed. "A late bloomer."

"She was twelve."

"So, you liked older women."

"Now that you mention it, that might have been part of the attraction. I lured her into the woods one balmy summer evening, when the sun was going down red behind the mountain and the whippoorwills were starting to call."

"Very romantic."

"It was an epiphany. I drew together all my sweaty

courage and kissed her near the first bend in the creek, when the air was full of summer twilight and the smell of honeysuckle.''

''That's very sweet.''

''It would have been,'' he mused, ''if my brothers hadn't followed us and hidden to watch. They screamed like banshees, Cousin Joanie went tearing back to the farm. Of course, my brothers ragged on me for weeks after, so I had to take on each of them to save my honor. Devin broke my finger, and I lost interest in Cousin Joanie.''

''That's sweet, too. The rites of passage.''

''I've learned a few things since then, about kissing pretty girls in the woods.''

When he turned her into his arms and his mouth moved over hers, she had to admit he was right. He'd learned quite a number of things.

''Where is cousin Joanie now?''

''In a nice split-level in the 'burbs of Virginia, with three kids and a part-time job selling real estate.'' With a sigh, he pressed his curved lips to Savannah's brow. ''She still has those gold curls and summer eyes.''

''One more ghost in the MacKade woods.'' She looked back through the trees. She could see the lights she'd left on in her cabin. Her son was safe there. ''Tell me about the others.''

''The two corporals are the most famous. One wore blue, the other gray. During the Battle of Antietam, they were separated from their companies.''

He slipped an arm over her shoulders so that they walked companionably, their strides matched. ''They came upon each other here, in the woods, two boys barely old enough to shave. In fear, or duty, or maybe both, they attacked each other. Each one was badly wounded, each one crawled off in a different direction. One to the farm.''

''Your farm?''

''Hmmm... A Union soldier, torn open by the enemy's bayonet. My great-grandfather, no friend of the North, found him by the smokehouse. The story is that he saw his own son, who he'd lost at Bull Run, in that dying boy, so he carried him into the house. They did what they could for him, but it was too late. He died the next day and, afraid of reprisals, they buried him in one of the fields, in an unmarked grave.''

''So he's lost,'' Savannah murmured. ''And haunts the woods because he can't find his way home.''

''That would be close enough.''

''And the other corporal?''

''Made it to the Barlow house. A servant took him inside, and the mistress was preparing to tend to him when her husband shot him.''

She didn't shudder. She was well used to cruelties, small and large. ''Because he didn't see a boy, but the wrong color uniform?''

''That's right. So the mistress of the house, Abigail Barlow, turned from her husband and went into seclusion. She died a couple of years later.''

''A sad story. Useless deaths make for uneasy ghosts. Still, it always feels—'' she closed her eyes, let the air dance over her face ''—inviting here. They just don't want to be forgotten. Do you want to know where they fought?''

Something in her tone had him looking down at her. "Why?"

She opened her eyes again. They were darker than the shadows, more mysterious than the night. "To the west, fifty yards, by a clump of rocks and a burled tree."

He felt cool fingers brush the nape of his neck. But her hands were in his. "Yes. I've sat on the rocks there and heard the bayonets clash."

"So have I. But I wondered who. And why."

"Is that usual for you?" His voice had roughened. Perhaps it was what they spoke of in the night wood. Or perhaps it was her eyes, so dark, so depthless, that he knew any man would blissfully drown in them.

"Your great-grandfather was a farmer who saw a young boy dying and tried to save him. Mine was a shaman who saw visions in the fire and tried to understand them. You still try to save people, don't you, Jared? And I still try to understand the visions."

"Are you—?"

"Psychic?" She laughed quickly, richly. "No. I feel things. We all do. The strongest part of my heritage accepts those feelings, respects them, honors them. I followed my feelings when I left Oklahoma. I knew that I'd find where I belonged. And I took one look at that cabin, at those rocks, these woods, and I knew I was home. I watched you walk across the grass that first time, and I knew I'd end up wanting you."

She leaned forward, touched her lips to his. "And

now, I know I have to get back and put my son to bed before he raids the refrigerator.''

''Savannah.'' He caught her hands again before she could turn away. His gaze was intense on her face, almost fierce. ''What do you feel about where we're going?''

She felt the heat, then the cold, then the heat once more, slide up her spine. But she kept her voice easy. ''I find that when you look too far ahead, you end up tripping over the present. Let's just worry about the now, Jared.''

When he lifted her hand to his lips, Savannah realized that now was going to be trouble enough.

She waited until the end of the week before she acted on Jared's suggestion and detoured by the Barlow place. The MacKade place, she corrected, amused at herself for having picked up the town's name for the old stone house on the hill.

The Barlows hadn't lived in it for over fifty years. The last family, a couple from the north of the county, had bought it, lived in it briefly, then abandoned it twenty years ago. It had been up for sale off and on during those decades, but no one had taken the plunge.

Until Rafe MacKade.

Savannah considered that as she turned off the road and up the steep lane. Someone had begun to clear the overgrowth of brush and brambles, but it was going to be heavy going. Someone, she decided, was going to need a lot of vision.

The house itself was three stories of beautiful stone.

Tall windows, arched windows, mullioned windows, gleaming. Most had been boarded up only months before—or so Savannah had been told when she was cornered by Mrs. Metz in the market.

There were double porches. The one that graced the second floor was in the process of being torn down. It needed to be, Savannah mused. It was rotted and sagging and undoubtedly treacherous. But the lower one was obviously new, still unpainted, and straight as a military band on parade day.

Scaffolding ran up the east wing, and piles of material sat under plastic tarps in the overgrown yard. She pulled up beside a pickup that was loaded with debris and shut off her engine.

When she knocked, she heard an answering shout, faintly irritated by the tone of it. She stepped inside and stood, shocked and swamped by the deluge of sensation. Laughter and tears and horror and happiness. The emotions rolled over her, then ebbed, like a breaking wave.

She saw the man at the top of the steps. Smiled, stepped forward. "Jared, I didn't expect to see you. Oh."

She saw her mistake immediately. Not Jared. The eyes were a darker green, the hair slightly longer and definitely less well-groomed. Jared's face was just a bit more narrow, his eyebrows had more of an arch.

But that MacKade grin was identical, as sharp and lethal as an arrow from a master's bow.

"I'm better-looking," Rafe told her as he started down.

"Hard to say. The family resemblance is almost ridiculous." She held out a hand. "You'd be Rafe MacKade."

"Guilty."

"I'm—"

"Savannah Morningstar." He didn't shake her hand, just held it while he gave her a long, practiced once-over. "Regan was dead on," he decided.

"Excuse me?"

"You met my wife last weekend at her shop. She told me to think of Isis. That didn't do me a hell of a lot of good, so she said to think of a woman who'd stop a man's heart at ten paces and have him on his knees at five."

"That's quite an endorsement."

"And dead on," he repeated. "Jared said you might be coming by." He tucked his thumbs in his tool belt.

"I don't want to interrupt your work."

"Please, interrupt my work." He aimed that grin again. "I'm just killing time until Regan gets home from the shop. We're living here temporarily. Want a beer?"

This was the kind of man she understood and was at ease with. "Now that you mention it."

But she hadn't taken two steps behind him when she stopped dead in her tracks and stared at the curve of the staircase.

Intrigued, Rafe watched her. "Problem?"

"There. It was there, on the stairs."

"I take it Jared told you about our ghosts."

She felt weak inside, jittery at the fingertips. "He

told me there had been a young Confederate soldier, that Barlow had shot him after a servant had brought him into the house. But he didn't say—he didn't tell me where.''

Her legs felt heavy as she walked to the stairs, as she followed the compulsion to go up. The cold was like a blade through the heart, through to the bone. Her knuckles went white on the rail.

''Here.'' She could barely get the words out. ''Here on the stairs. He could smell roses, and hope, and then… He only wanted to go home.''

She shook herself, stepped back one step, then two before turning. ''I could use that beer.''

''Yeah.'' Rafe let out a long breath. ''Me too.''

''Do you, ah, do that kind of thing often?'' Rafe asked as he popped the tops on two beers in the kitchen.

''No,'' Savannah told him, very definitely. ''There are some places around this area…this house, the woods out there…'' She let the words trail off as she looked out the window. ''There's a spot on my bank where I planted columbine, and areas of the battlefield that break your heart.'' With an effort, she shook off the mood and took the beer Rafe offered. ''Leftover emotions. The strong ones can last centuries.''

''I've had a dream.'' He'd only told Regan of it, but it seemed appropriate now. ''I'm running through the woods, my battle gray splattered with blood. I only want to go home. I'm ashamed of it, but I'm terrified. Then I see him, the other soldier, the enemy. We stare at each other for a dozen heartbeats, then charge. It's bad, the fight. It's brutal and stupid and useless. After, I come here, crawl here. I think I'm home. When I see her, when she speaks to me and tells me it's going to be all right, I believe her. She's right beside me when someone carries me up the stairs. I can smell her, the roses. Then she shouts, looks at someone coming toward us down the stairs. When I look up, I can see him, and the gun. Then it's over.''

Rafe took a long drink. ''What stays with me the longest, after it's over, is that I just wanted to go home. I haven't had it in a couple of months.''

''Maybe that's because you are home.''

''Looks that way.'' Suddenly he grinned and tapped his bottle against hers. ''A hell of an introduction. Are you up to seeing the place, or do you want to pass?''

''No, I'd like to see it. You've done some work in here.''

''Yeah.'' The kitchen had a long way to go, Rafe mused, but the counters had been built and were topped by a warm slate blue that showed off the creamy ivory of new appliances and gleaming glass-fronted cabinets of yellow pine. ''Regan put her foot down,'' he explained. ''A workable kitchen and a finished bath and she'd handle living in a construction site for a while.''

''Sounds like a practical woman.''

''That she is. Come on, I'll give you the tour.''

He took her arm and started back down the hallway. ''I'd like to start upstairs,'' she told him before he could open the door to the right.

''Sure.'' Most people liked to start with the parlor

or the library, but he was flexible. As they started up, he felt her hesitate, brace. Just as he felt the hard shudder move through her as they continued. "No one feels it anymore," he said. "Not in weeks."

"Lucky for them," Savannah managed, grateful when they reached the top of the landing. She looked beyond the tarps, the buckets and tools and saw sturdy walls that had been built to last.

"We finished—" He broke off as she turned away from the bedroom he and Regan shared. A room that had belonged to the mistress of the house and had been lovingly repaired, redone and furnished. Saying nothing, he followed her to the opposite wing.

The door had been removed from this room, a room with long windows that faced the outskirts of town. The walls had been painted a deep green, the wide, ornately carved trim a bone white to match the marble of the fireplace.

The floors had been recently sanded. She could smell the wood dust. The little room beyond—the valet's room? she wondered—had been roughed in as a bath.

"The master's room," she murmured.

"We thought it was likely." Fascinated, Rafe watched her walk from door to window, from window to hearth.

Oh, it had been his, Master Barlow's, she was sure of it. He would have studied the town from here and thought his thoughts. He would have taken one of the young maids to bed in here, willing or not, then slept the dreamless sleep of the conscienceless.

"He was a bastard," Savannah said mildly. "Well,

he didn't leave much behind.'' With a smile, she turned back to Rafe. ''You're doing a wonderful job.''

Rafe rubbed his chin. ''Thanks. You're a spooky woman, Savannah.''

''Occasionally. I read palms in a carnival for a while. Pretty tedious work, really. This is much more interesting.'' She moved past him, back into the hall, and headed straight for the mistress's room. ''This is beautiful,'' she murmured.

''We're jazzed about it.'' From the doorway, Rafe scanned the room himself. He could smell roses, and he could smell Regan. ''It's going to be our honeymoon suite.''

''It's perfect.''

She meant exactly that. In all her travels, she had never seen anything as lovely. Rosebud wallpaper as delicate as a tea garden was trimmed with rose-toned wood. There were beautiful arched windows framed in lace that had the sunlight streaming in patterns on the highly polished floor.

A four-poster with a lacy canopy dominated the space. There were candles, slim tapers of ivory, and rose burned downed to varying lengths that stood on the mantel in crystal holders. An elegant lady's desk was topped by a globe lamp. Petit-point chairs, curved edged tables. A pale pink vase crowded with sunny daffodils.

No, she'd never seen anything so lovely. How could she have? she reminded herself. Her life had been dingy trailers, cramped rooms and highway motels.

Envy snaked through her so quickly she winced.

"Jared said your wife did the decorating."

"For the most part."

What would it be like, Savannah wondered, to have such exquisite taste. To know exactly what should go where?

"It's beautiful," she said again. "When you're ready to open, you'll have to beat off guests with a stick."

"We're shooting for September. It's a little optimistic, but we might pull it off." His head turned, his eyes changed at the sound of the door opening downstairs. "That's Regan."

Savannah had a firsthand view of what a MacKade looked like when he was very much in love. Another surprising snake of envy curled through her.

"Up here, darling," Rafe called out. "I'm in the bedroom with a gorgeous woman."

"That's supposed to surprise me?" Regan strolled into the room. "Hello, Savannah." It was all she managed to get out before Rafe cupped a hand behind her neck and drew her up for a lengthy welcoming kiss. "Hello, Rafe."

"Hi."

They beamed at each other. Savannah could think of no other word for it. Unless the word was *perfect*. Regan MacKade, with her swing of glossy brown hair, her elegant face with its charming little mole beside the mouth, her lovely blue eyes the color of summer skies, seemed perfect as she slipped an arm around her husband.

Her clothes were beautifully tailored—the teal blazer

and pleated slacks, the smart white shirt with the copper bar pin at the collar. She had a sexy-lady scent about her. Not prim, not overt. Just perfect.

Savannah felt like a grubby Amazon who'd stumbled on a princess.

"I've been giving Savannah the tour," Rafe explained.

"Great." Regan pushed back the right curtain of her hair, and rings glittered on her fingers. "What do you think so far?"

"It's wonderful." Savannah remembered the beer in her hand and lifted to it her lips.

"Let's not stop here." With a friendly smile, Regan led the way out. "Jared called the shop this morning and said he'd like us to work on redoing his offices."

"About damn time," Rafe commented. "The place is as cheerful as a mausoleum. White and gray. Might as well work in a tomb."

"We'll fix that." With boundless confidence and enthusiasm, Regan showed off the house.

Every room, whether it was complete or in progress and filled with nothing more than dust and cobwebs, scraped at Savannah's confidence. She knew nothing of fine antiques, expensive rugs or window treatments.

She didn't want to know.

"Jared's really impressed with your art," Regan went on as they wound their way down to the first floor. "Obviously it inspired him to do something about his work space. I'd love to see some of what you've done."

"It's no big deal. I don't have any training."

Savannah took one long scan of the front parlor, with its curvy settee and elegant side tables, and jammed her hands in the pockets of her jeans. A marble fireplace gleamed like glass, set off with polished brass tools and andirons. And everything, down to the last candlestick, was picture-perfect.

"Nothing of mine would fit in here, that's for sure. Or a lawyer's office, either. Thanks for the tour. And the beer," she added, handing Rafe the empty bottle. "I've got to go pick up my kid."

"Oh." Surprised by the abrupt exit, Regan followed her to the door. "If you've got some time over the weekend, I can fiddle with my schedule. We could work on color schemes and treatments."

"I've got a lot of work." Savannah pulled open the door, suddenly desperate to escape. "You'd better handle it on your own. See you around."

"All right, but—" Regan broke off with a huff when the door closed in her face. She had definitely, and none too subtly, been brushed off. "And what," she asked, turning to Rafe, "was that all about?"

"Don't ask me." Thoughtfully he ran a hand over his wife's glossy hair. "That's a spooky lady, darling. Let's go sit down, and I'll tell you about it."

Chapter 6

When Jared pulled up in front of the cabin, he was puzzled, mildly annoyed, and quite intrigued. It hadn't taken long for word to get to him that Savannah had all but raced out of his brother's house, shrugging off the job Jared had offered her as she fled.

He intended to get an explanation.

Spotting Bryan and Connor in the side yard, he gave a wave. They responded with an answering shout before they went back to the important business of throwing a baseball.

His rap on the door went unanswered, so he walked in without invitation. He doubted he'd have heard one over the screaming rock and roll that shook the cabin. He followed a gut-bursting guitar riff through the kitchen and into an adjoining room.

She was bent over a worktable. The white of the

oversize men's undershirt she wore was streaked with paint. Her hair was twisted back in a braid, her jeans were riddled with holes, and her feet were bare.

His mouth watered.

"Hey."

She didn't look up. A look of fierce concentration remained on her face as she worked delicately with a slim brush dipped in brilliant red.

He glanced around the cluttered room. It had probably been intended as a mudroom, as there was a door leading to the outside. Obviously she didn't need or have time for ambience in her work space, he mused.

The light was full and bright through the windows and showed every speck of dust. The floor was aging linoleum decorated with paint spills. Unframed canvases were propped carelessly against the unfinished log walls, steel utility shelves overflowed with bottles and jars, tubes and cans. He could smell turpentine.

And, with relief, he could see the dented portable stereo that was threatening to split his eardrums. He strode over, switched it off, and almost shuddered at the sudden, exquisite silence.

"Keep your hands off my music," Savannah snapped.

"Obviously you didn't hear me come in."

"Obviously, I'm working." She tossed her brush into a jar of solution, chose another. "Take off."

His eyes lit, but he spoke with measured politeness. "Yes, I believe I will have a beer, thanks. Can I get you one?"

"I'm working," she repeated.

"So I see." Ignoring the curse she hurled at him, he leaned over her worktable.

The wicked queen was nearly finished, and her face was terrible in its beauty. Her body was long, elegant, draped in purple and ermine. Her golden crown was as sharp as blades and glittered with wicked-edged jewels. And in her narrow, regal hand, she held a vivid red apple.

"Gorgeous," Jared murmured. "Evil to the bone. Is this from 'Snow White'?"

"No, it's from the Three Stooges. You're in my light."

"Sorry." He shifted slightly, knowing it wasn't what she wanted.

"I can't work with an audience," she said between her teeth.

"I thought you used to paint on street corners."

"This is different."

"Savannah." Patient, he rubbed a slight red smudge from her cheek. "Did Rafe or Regan say something to upset you?"

"Why should they?"

"That's what I'd like to know."

"They were perfectly polite. Perfectly." When he only cocked a brow, she huffed out a breath. "I like your brother, I loved seeing the house. It was fascinating. And your sister-in-law's just adorable."

It was a woman thing, he realized, and took a cautious step back. "You've got a problem with Regan?"

"Who could have a problem with Regan? We just

wouldn't work well together. And besides, I don't want my art in your office.''

''Oh? Why is that?''

''Because I don't. I had time to think about it, and I decided I'm not interested.'' She aimed a cool, level look at him. ''All the way not interested, Jared. So beat it.''

He moved fast. Lawyer suit notwithstanding, she should have expected him to move fast. He had her up from her stool, his hand clamped on her arm, before she could blink.

That didn't mean she couldn't speak.

''I've told you not to grab me unless I ask you to.''

''Yeah, you've told me. You've told me a lot of things.'' For the hell of it, he took a firm hold on her other arm and watched her eyes flame. ''Now why don't you tell me what's going on here?''

''I don't have to explain myself to you. You think because I let you kiss me a couple of times, I owe you? I've let plenty of men kiss me, Ace. And I don't owe anyone.''

She'd aimed the arrow well. He felt it hit home, stunned by just how sharp the point was. ''You owe me the courtesy of an explanation.''

''Courtesy doesn't interest me.''

''Fine.'' Then he wouldn't let it stop him. He yanked her close and crushed his mouth to hers in an angry, frustrated kiss.

She didn't struggle. Instinct warned her it would be worse if she struggled. Instead, she kept herself stiff and turned her mind off. Cold rejection, she knew, was more effective than heated protest.

But both her body and her mind betrayed her, and she trembled.

It thrilled him—that quick, involuntary shiver, that low, helpless moan. But temper was still sparking through him when he jerked away.

Her face was flushed, her breath fast. He knew by the look in her eyes that she wanted as he wanted. At the moment, that fact only infuriated him.

"I owed you that," he said tightly. "Now you can tell me again how much you're not interested."

She was interested. Interested in having a man look at her, just once, the way she had seen Rafe look at Regan. And, oh, it was demoralizing to realize she had that vulnerable need inside her.

"In a quick tumble, Jared?" In a deliberately insulting gesture, she brushed her fingers over his cheek. "Sure, baby, when I've got the time."

"Damn it, Savannah."

"You see." She sighed, shook her head. "I knew you'd take it personally. You're the type. And like I said, that's not my type. You're terrific to look at, and you've got a lot of heat. But—" she lifted a hand, tugged on his tie "—just too traditional and by-the-book. Now, Lawyer MacKade, you know all about the laws against trespassing, the sanctity of someone's home. I'm going to ask you real nice, since you like things real nice, to leave. You wouldn't want me to have to call your brother, the big bad sheriff, would you?"

"What the hell has gotten into you?"

"A dose of reality. Now go away, Jared, before I stop asking nice."

He'd be damned if he'd beg. Damned if he'd let her see that she'd wounded him where he'd never expected to be wounded. Iron pride chilled his eyes. He turned and left without a word.

When she heard his car start, and the sound of it going down her lane, she sank back onto her stool and shut her eyes.

She gave Bryan permission for his promised sleepover and enjoyed the noise and bother of two active boys lasting late into the night. She was in the bleachers on Saturday, cheering on her son and his team. And if she looked around now and again, scanning for a tall man with dark hair and green eyes, no one else knew.

At Cassie's insistence, she dropped both boys at Connor's late Saturday afternoon. Home alone, she paced the house, fidgeted in the quiet, and finally went back to work.

The queen was finished, but she still had the prince to sketch. No wimpy, soft-eyed dreamer for her Snow White, Savannah mused as she began running the pencil over the thick white pad. Her Snow White deserved some fire, some passion, some promise of a happy-ever-after with heat.

It was hardly a wonder that her first rough sketch resembled a MacKade. Dragonslayers, she thought with a grim smile. Troublemakers. Who said a prince had to be polite? Hadn't most of them won their thrones in battle first?

Yes, she could see Jared as a fairy tale prince. Her kind of fairy tale. The kind of story that had inspired the legends that had been passed down through the ages, before they became softened and misted to lull children rather than frighten them.

Warrior, avenger, adventurer. Yes, that was the prince she wanted to create.

She began to enjoy herself. The familiar process of bringing something to life through her heart and mind and hand was always fascinating, if not always soothing.

If things had been different, she wouldn't have made her living from assignments, but from that heart and mind. Painting what she saw, what she felt, what she wanted—for the joy of it.

She was lucky, she reminded herself, to have this much. There had been no art classes in her life, only stolen moments with a pad and colored pencils. Dreams no one had ever understood.

Yes, she was lucky, because her work and the payment for it allowed her to take time for painting, to justify it as a harmless, not terribly expensive hobby.

Quickly, fueled by instinct, she began to add details to the sketch—the diamond-bright dimple at the corner of that sensual mouth, the arrogant arch of an eyebrow, a hint of muscle beneath the cloak, more than a hint of danger in the eyes she would certainly have to paint a grass green.

Hell, she reflected, if nothing else, her brush with

Jared MacKade had given her the perfect model for her assignment. The illustration would be a good one. She couldn't have asked for more.

She should never had let herself get caught up in the idea of painting for Jared, or selling him work that she had done for herself.

The sound of a car had her bracing and fighting to squash a little flutter of hope.

But when she went to the door, she saw Regan MacKade. The two women studied each other coolly. After a long moment, Savannah opened the door and stepped back.

"I don't know what's between you and Jared," Regan said without preamble. "And if you think it's none of my business, you're wrong. He's family. But I'd like to know why you've decided you can't stand me to the point where you won't even take a potentially lucrative job just because we'd rub elbows occasionally."

"I don't want the job."

"That's a lie."

Savannah's eyes went molten. "Now look, sister—"

"No, you look." Revved, Regan jabbed a finger at Savannah's chest. "We don't have to be friends. I've got friends. Though I'm baffled at how we could both manage to be friends with someone as sweet as Cassie Dolin. She finds you admirable, and it's not my place to tell her you're just plain rude. You were interested in the job when Jared suggested it. Interested enough to come to the house. And according to Rafe, everything was just dandy until I walked in. Now what's your problem? Sister."

Savannah found her temper warring with amusement, and reluctant admiration. Didn't the woman realize Savannah was big enough to break her in half? "I guess you told me."

"So why don't you tell me?" Regan shot back.

"I don't like the way you look."

"You—I beg your pardon?"

"Or the way you talk." Pleased with herself, Savannah smiled. "Let me guess—private education, dances at the country club, debutante ball."

"I was never a debutante." If she hadn't been so baffled, Regan would have been insulted. "And what's that got to do with anything?"

"You look like you just stepped out of one of those classy women's magazines."

Regan threw up her hands. "That's it?"

"Yeah, that's it."

"Well, you look like one of those statues men sacrificed virgins to. I don't hold it against you. Exactly."

They frowned at each other for a minute. Then Savannah sighed, shrugged. "I've got some ice tea."

"I'd love some."

By the time she was sipping her second glass, Regan was up and wandering the front room. She stopped by a landscape, all rocky hills and trees gone violent with autumn.

"This one," she decided. "He needs this one where that horrible white-orchid still life is hanging."

"I'd have thought you'd go for the orchids." When Regan turned, her eyes narrowed blandly, Savannah smiled fully for the first time. "Yeah, I can see I'd have been wrong."

"Greens and mauves," Regan announced. "Deep greens. And those chairs in the outer office have got to go. I've got a couple of library chairs in mind. Deep-cushioned, high-backed. Leather. And I figure hard-wood with area rugs, instead of that gray sea of wall-to-wall."

Yes, of course. Savannah could already see it. Regan MacKade was obviously a woman who knew what she wanted. "Look, I'm not a humble person, but can you actually see my paintings jibing with your taste...or Jared's?"

"Yes. And I think, all things considered, that you and I will work together very well." Regan held out a hand, waited. "Well, are we going to give Jared a break and get him out of that tomb?"

"Yeah." Savannah took the pretty hand, with its glittering rings, in hers. "Why the hell not?"

Later, Savannah walked toward the woods. She had to admit she'd done something she detested in others. She had looked at the surface and made a decision. All she had seen—maybe all she'd wanted to see when she looked at Regan MacKade—was elegance, privilege and class.

But who could have guessed there'd be such grit under all that polish?

She should have, Savannah realized.

And when she saw Jared sitting on a rock smoking

quietly, she realized she had known she'd find him here.

He said nothing when she sat down beside him and took the cigar. The silence was lovely, filled with birdsong and breezes.

"I owe you an apology." It didn't quite stick in her throat, but she handed him back the cigar. "I was… You caught me at a bad time the other day."

"Did I?"

"Don't make it easy, MacKade."

"I won't."

With a quick, bad-tempered shrug, she swung her legs up, crossed them under her. "I wasn't completely truthful with you. There are a lot of things I don't mind doing, but lies don't sit well with me. I wanted the job. I can use it. But I felt…intimidated," she muttered as the word sat distastefully on her tongue.

"Intimidated?" It was the last reason or excuse he'd have expected to hear out of her. "By what?"

"Your sister-in-law, to start."

"Regan?" Sheer astonishment ran up hard against the foul mood he'd been mired in for twenty-four hours. "Give me a break."

It was his quick, dismissive laugh that snapped it. Temper soaring, Savannah bolted up from the rock and whirled on him. "I've got a right to be intimidated by whatever I please. I've got a right to feel exactly how I chose to feel. Don't you laugh at me."

"Sorry." Wisely Jared cleared his throat, then looked up at her. "Why would Regan intimidate you?"

"Because she's…she's classy and lovely and smart

and successful. She's everything I'm not. I'm comfortable with who I am, what I am, but when you come up against someone like that, it's a kick-in-the-butt reminder of what you're never going to be, never going to have. I don't like feeling inadequate or stupid.''

Disgusted with herself, Savannah jammed her hands in her pockets. "And I didn't expect to like her so much. She came by to see me a little while ago.''

"I thought she might. Regan likes to confront things head-on.'' Thoughtful, he studied the tip of his cigar. "Ask her sometime about the night she waltzed into Duff's Tavern in a tight red miniskirt and had Rafe gnawing his pool cue into toothpicks.''

Fascinated by the image, Savannah nearly smiled. "I'll have to do that. I'd like to handle the art for your office, Jared, if you're still interested.''

"I'm interested.'' He turned the cigar around, offering it. When she shook her head, he took a last puff and carefully tamped it out on the rock.

"I wasn't completely truthful about a couple of other things.'' The situation was a first, and she wasn't quite sure how to phrase things, so she decided to keep it simple. "I have feelings for you, Jared. They just sort of popped up. They worried me.''

He was watching her now, his wonderful eyes very focused, very cool. She wondered how many witnesses had broken apart on the stand under that strong gaze.

"Men are a lot easier to deal with when feelings aren't involved,'' she continued. "I could be reading this wrong, but I got the idea you were aiming for a relationship kind of deal, and I've had lousy luck with relationships. So I started thinking about that, and some other things, and figured it was best all around to bail.''

When he said nothing—absolutely nothing—she gave in and kicked at the dirt on the path. ''Are you just going to sit there?''

''I'm listening,'' he said mildly.

''Okay, look, I've got a kid to worry about. I can't afford to get involved with someone who might start to mean something to him that's not realistic. I know how to be careful about that, how to keep things in line.''

He stood now, his eyes never leaving his. ''You're going to keep me in line, Savannah?''

If he touched her, she was very much afraid she'd go off like a rocket. ''I don't think so. That's the thing. I've got these feelings for you.''

''That's interesting.'' He hadn't known she could look so vulnerable. ''Because I have these feelings for you.''

''You do?'' Her hands stayed balled in her pockets. ''Well.''

''Well,'' he repeated, and stepped forward. He put his hand on her cheek, and his mouth on hers.

She wasn't used to being kissed this way. As if that were all—as if she were all—that mattered. It made her weak and woozy. Those tensed fingers went limp. And her heart surrendered.

''Are we straight now?'' he murmured.

She nodded and found that feeling of pleasure could be huge, just having a man's shoulder ready to cradle your head. ''I hate feeling stupid.''

"So you said."

"I don't want to feel stupid about this."

His lips curved as he brushed them over her hair. "Neither do I."

"So we'll make a pact. Whatever happens, neither of us will make the other feel stupid."

"I can agree to that." He lifted her chin for another kiss. "Why don't I walk home with you?"

"All right."

She couldn't help it. She felt stupid and sentimental walking hand in hand with him through the woods, aware of every beam of sunlight, every scent, every sound. She would have sworn that she could hear the leaves growing overhead and the wildflowers struggling toward the sun.

Love, she mused, honed the senses.

"I have to pick up Bryan in a little while." She glanced over. "I can call Cassie and rearrange things."

He knew what she was offering, and could feel the blood humming under his skin. When he brought their joined hands to his lips, he saw the flash of surprised pleasure in her eyes. Not yet, he told himself. Not quite yet.

"We'll both pick him up. What do you say to an early movie, and pizza after?"

She couldn't look at him now, not the way her throat was aching. She knew what he was offering. "I'd say great," she managed. "Thanks."

"Jared's cool." Bryan bounced into the top bunk of his bed, his mind full of scenes from the action flick, his belly stuffed with pepperoni pizza. "I mean, man, he knows everything about baseball, and stuff about the farm and the battlefield. He's even smarter than Connor."

"You're no slouch, Ace." She tousled his hair.

"Jared says everybody's got a special talent."

Interested, Savannah leaned on the edge of the bed so that her face was level with her son's. "He did?"

"Yeah, when we went to get popcorn. He said how everybody's got something inside that makes him different. He knows on account of he has three brothers and they're a lot alike, but they're different, too. He said I'm a natural."

She grinned. "A natural what?"

"Mom." Rolling his eyes, Bryan sat up in bed. "At baseball. And you know what else he said?"

"No. What else did he say?"

"He said how even if I decided not to be a major-leaguer I could use the stuff I know in other things. Of course, I'm going to be a major-leaguer, but maybe I'd be like a lawyer, too."

"A lawyer?" She felt a little flutter of panic. Her son was falling in love as quickly as she was.

"Yeah, 'cause you get to go to court and argue with people and put criminals in jail. But you have to go to school forever, I mean until you're old. Jared went to college and to law school and everything."

"So can you, if that's what you want."

"Well, I'm going to think about it."

He flopped back down, curled into his pillow in a

way that comforted her as much as him. It was the gesture of a child. He was still her little boy.

"Night."

"Good night, Bry." She pressed her lips to his temple and lingered over it a moment or two longer than usual. Long enough to make him squirm sleepily.

She rose, turned off his light, then closed his door, because he liked his privacy.

Her son the lawyer, she thought, and rubbed her hands over her face. With a mother who'd never finished high school.

Then, as the panic gave way to a warm glow of pride for what her son might one day achieve, she smiled.

She walked quietly to her own room and moved to the window to look out at the woods. Through them, she could see the lights of the MacKade farm. And there, she thought, was the man she'd fallen in love with.

She smiled again and laid a hand on the cool glass of the window. All in all, she decided, it had been pretty smart of her to wait to fall until she'd found Jared MacKade.

Chapter 7

He sent her yellow tulips, and she was dreamy-eyed for an hour after she slipped them, stem by stem, into numerous old bottles.

He took her and Bryan to a minor-league ball game in the neighboring county, where the stands were hard as iron and the crowd was rowdy, and won her son's heart absolutely by snagging a foul.

They had pizza at a place with worn wooden booths, a loud jukebox and a pinball machine. The three of them ate sloppily, shouted over the music and competed like fiends over the speeding silver balls.

He took her to dinner at a restaurant where there was candlelight and champagne fizzing in crystal flutes and held her hand on the snowy-white tablecloth.

He brought her a truckload of mulch for her garden, and she was lost.

"You're being courted," Cassie told her over lemonade and paint samples at Savannah's kitchen table.

"What?"

"Courted." Cassie sighed over it. The misery of her years with Joe Dolin hadn't quashed her romantic nature. Not when it concerned someone else. "Isn't she, Regan?"

"Big-time. Yellow tulips," Regan added, glancing up from her samples to the flowers that marched down the center of the table. "It's a dead giveaway."

"We're developing a relationship." Voice casual, Savannah rubbed her suddenly damp palms on her jeans. "That's all."

"He brought you mulch and helped you spread it, didn't he?" Cassie pointed out reasonably.

"Yeah." It made Savannah smile foolishly to remember it. And to remember the way he'd kissed her senseless when the two of them were grimy with dirt and sweat and chipped bark.

"She's got it bad," Regan commented.

"Maybe I do." Damping the smile, Savannah snatched up her lemonade. "So what?"

"So nothing. What do you think of this shade?"

"Too yellow."

Regan blew out a breath. "You're right."

Filled with admiration, Cassie watched the way her two friends chose and discarded colors. She hoped when she had just a little more put aside, Regan would help her pick out new paint for her living room. She'd washed those white walls so often, scrubbed till her shoulders sang, but she couldn't make them bright again.

Then, if Savannah could help her pick the right material, she could make new curtains for Emma's room. Something cheerful, something special for a little girl.

It was hard, harder than she could admit to anyone, to take on these little challenges. To accomplish things that she imagined were just everyday things to some women. How could she explain that for the first time in her life—her entire life—there was no one to tell her yes or no? No one to complain or criticize or humiliate her?

Constantly she had to remind herself that she was in charge, and that if she tried, if she kept at it step by step, she could change the tiny rented house into a home. A real home, where her kids wouldn't remember the shouting and the beatings and the smell of soured beer.

Wistfully she looked around Savannah's cabin. It was no larger than the house where Cassie lived with her children, but it was so much more. Bright colors, carelessly tossed cushions. Dust.

She still attacked dust like a maniac, afraid Joe would walk in the door and pounce on her for forgetting. No matter how often she told herself he wouldn't, couldn't, because he was locked up, she still lay awake at night, shuddering at every creak.

And woke up every morning relieved. And ashamed. Her ears pricked. "The kids are coming back," she announced, and pushed all those old fears aside. "Is it all right if I make more lemonade?"

Savannah merely grunted and studied the colors Regan had selected for Jared's law library.

Then the kids burst in like rockets.

"Only three more weeks," Bryan shouted, and waved both fists in triumph. "The kittens can come in three more weeks."

"Happy days," Savannah murmured, but she smiled when Emma darted over to wrap an arm around Cassie's leg. "Hi, angel face."

"Hello. Bryan let me pet his kittens. They're soft."

"She wants one." Shyness had never been a problem for Bryan. He scooped a hand into the cookie jar and hauled out a fistful. "Can she have one, Mrs. Dolin?"

"What?"

He stuffed a cookie into his mouth and eyed the lemonade Cassie was making. "Can Emma have one of the kittens? Shane's got extra."

"A kitten." Automatically Cassie put a protective hand on Emma's head. "We can't have animals in the house, because—" She broke off, her gaze darting to Connor's, even as her son dropped his head to stare at his feet.

Because Joe doesn't like them. She'd nearly said it, so ingrained was the habit. A habit, she realized, that had prevented her from seeing how longingly Connor spoke of Bryan's expected pets. How much Emma liked to play with the neighbor's little brown dog.

"I don't see why we couldn't."

Her reward was a brilliant and grateful look from her son. "Really?" The disbelief and hope in his voice almost made her weep. "Can we *really?*"

"Sure we can." She scooped Emma into her arms and nuzzled. "You want one of Shane's kittens, Emma?"

"They're soft," Emma said again.

"So are you." It was time she did this, Cassie told herself. Made simple decisions without worrying about what Joe would do. "Tell Shane you'd like one, Connor."

"Cool." Unaware of the drama, Bryan chomped down another cookie. "Then you can bring him over sometimes so he can play with his brothers. Let's go work on your pitching arm, Con."

"Okay." Connor darted after his friend, skidded to a halt. "Thanks, Mama."

"Whoa." At the door, Rafe barely avoided a head-on collision with Connor. He pretended he didn't see the way the boy stiffened and paled, and patted his shoulder, very casually. "You guys are quick. Jared and I lost you in the woods."

"I'm sorry."

"Next year you'll have to try running bases with that speed." He stepped inside, grinned at the ladies. "This was worth a tramp through the woods."

"We're nearly done," Regan told him, and tilted her face up for a kiss.

"No hurry. Hey, gorgeous."

"Hello, handsome." Savannah picked up one of her son's forgotten cookies and offered it.

"Thanks. Cassie—just the woman I want to see."

"Oh? Is something wrong?"

"I've got a problem." To bribe a smile out of Emma, he held out his cookie. "Would you give me a kiss right here for this?" he asked.

Keeping an eye on the cookie, Emma leaned forward and touched her pursed lips to his nose.

"A problem?" Cassie repeated. Nerves humming, she set Emma down and told her to go out and watch the boys play. "What is it?"

"Well, I'll tell you." He leaned back on the counter. "Regan and I found this place a little farther out of town, on the Quarry Road. Needs some work." He grinned at his wife. "We're thinking of moving over in a couple months. Probably around June."

"That's nice."

"Well, the thing is, Cassie, we need somebody at the inn. A—what did you call it, darling?"

"Chatelaine."

"Fancy word for manager, if you ask me. Somebody to look after the place," Rafe explained. "And the guests, once we've got them. Somebody who can cook breakfast, manage the housekeeping. Somebody who wouldn't mind living in and running things."

"Oh." Nerves settled, Cassie smiled. "You want me to ask around. We could put the word out at the diner."

"No, we've already got somebody in mind." Eagle-eyed, Rafe spotted the cookie jar and helped himself.

"We want someone we know, someone we trust." He paused to chug down the full glass of lemonade Cassie handed him. "So how about it?"

"How about it?" she repeated.

"That's not the way you offer someone a position, Rafe," Regan said with a sigh. "Cassie, we'd like you to move in and manage the inn for us. We just can't do it, between my shop and Rafe's work."

"You want me?" If she'd still been holding the glass, it would have been smashed on the floor. "I don't know anything about managing an inn. You'd have to have experience, and—"

"You manage a house and two kids," Rafe pointed out. "You cook almost as well as I do. You know how to handle all the customers at Ed's, run the kitchen there when you have to. And you have a soothing personality. Those are qualifications in my book."

"But—"

"You'll want to think about it." Regan's interruption was smooth as silk. "I know it's a big favor, Cassie, and you've worked at Ed's so long that it would be a big decision to switch jobs. But Rafe's fixing up a nice apartment on the third floor—with its own kitchen—that would be part of the salary. You'd have privacy. Maybe you and the kids could come by and take a look. We'd really appreciate it."

An apartment, privacy. No rent payment. That beautiful house on the hill. A manager. It all whirled in Cassie's head like blurred and colorful dreams.

"I'd like to help, but—"

"Great." Flashing a grin at his wife, Rafe patted Cassie's shoulder. "You just come give the place a once-over, and we'll talk about it some more."

"All right." Dazed, she shifted Emma on her hip. "I'll come by. I have to get along. I promised Connor and Bryan we'd have hot dogs on the grill."

"Go on and round them up," Savannah suggested. "I'll run and get Bryan's backpack."

She waited until Cassie was out the screen door. "You make a very good team," she murmured, looking at Regan and Rafe. "And very good friends."

She was nearly at the steps when she saw Devin on her porch, talking to Cassie. Her back snapped straight. "Something I can do for you, Sheriff?"

Only mildly annoyed at the interruption, he looked through the screen. "No. I just walked over with Jared and Rafe. You've done a nice job on the bank."

"Thanks."

When Emma held out her precious cookie to share, Savannah's brow furrowed. She watched Devin lean forward, take a small bite.

"You taste better," he announced, and made Emma giggle by nuzzling the gentle curve of her neck.

"You can hold me," she told him, tossing out her arms and wrapping them around his neck.

"Thank you, ma'am." He took her, brushing his cheek over her hair before settling her on his hip. As Cassie hurried away to call the boys, Devin looked back through the screen, Emma in his arms. "Some women like me."

Eyes cool, Savannah inclined her head. "So it seems."

"I'm not packing heat, Ms. Morningstar." That lethal MacKade grin flashed, all power and charm. "Just taking in a spring evening with my best girl."

"You're wearing a badge," Savannah pointed out.

"Habit. I've got no problem with you."

"I'm going to keep it that way." She looked across her yard to where Jared was hitting pop-ups for the boys.

"I've got no problem with that," Devin said quietly, and drew her gaze back to his.

"All right." She nodded and headed up to get her son's overnight bag.

Holding Emma, Devin stepped off the porch. He managed to draw Cassie into a brief conversation and charmed one hesitant smile out of her before he had to pass Emma back and watch her and the kids head for their car.

She wasn't quite so thin as she'd been those last months before he was finally able to collar Joe, Devin thought. Though she still looked as though one careless shout would topple her. A man had to be careful with her. The shadows had faded from under her eyes, but the eyes were still haunted.

He worried about her, and wondered. When the car was gone, he tucked his thoughts away and strolled over to Jared. "Your lady doesn't like me."

Jared gave the bat a last swing. "She doesn't like your badge."

"Like I said—she doesn't like me."

Jared looked toward the porch, where Savannah stood watching them, and felt his heart beat off-rhythm. "She's had a rough road."

"I don't doubt it." He'd seen a few miles of it in her eyes. "She what you want, bro?"

"Looks that way."

"Well, then." Devin rubbed his chin in his thoughtful way, still holding Savannah's cool gaze. It would take a hell of a lot more than a shout to topple that one, he mused. "I have to say your taste in women has improved mightily since your timely divorce."

Surprised, Jared leaned on the bat. "I thought you liked Barbara."

Devin snorted out a laugh. "Yeah, right."

"You never said different."

"You never asked me." Devin picked up the ball from the grass, tossed it high, made a one-handed catch that would have had Bryan cheering. "I like this one."

Bemused, Jared shook his head. "You just said you didn't."

"I said *she* didn't like *me*." Devin's grin was sly and slow. "I find that very attractive in a woman."

Jared had him in a headlock in a blink. Experienced in such matters, Devin overbalanced and sent them both tumbling to the ground.

With the faintest of frowns, Savannah watched them wrestle—much as Bryan and Connor were prone to do. Behind her, Rafe and Regan stepped out of the house.

"Well, hell, they got started without me."

"We're going." Regan took a firm grip on Rafe's arm. "You promised to take me to dinner."

"But, darling…"

"You can fight with them tomorrow. Bye, Savannah."

"Mm-hmm…"

At Rafe's shout, Devin rolled aside and rose, narrowly avoiding the hand that snaked out to trip him. After brushing off his jeans, he jogged down to join Rafe and Regan. He sent one quick salute to Savannah and disappeared into the woods.

"What was that?"

A bit winded, Jared climbed onto the porch. He winced a little and rubbed his ribs. "He got me a couple of good ones."

"Were you playing or fighting?"

"What's the difference?"

She had to laugh. "What were you playing and/or fighting about?"

"You. Got anything cold?"

"Me?" She was in the house behind him like a shot. "What do you mean?"

"He said…" Jared let the words trail off, sighed lustily over the icy beer he'd snagged from the refrigerator, popped it open, then drank deeply. "He said he found you attractive, so I had to pound on him a little."

"Your brother, Sheriff MacKade, finds me attractive."

"Yeah." He leaned over the sink to splash cold water on his face. "He likes you."

"He likes me," Savannah repeated, baffled. "Why?"

"Partly because you don't like him. Dev can be perverse. Partly because I do, and he's loyal." He rubbed his dripping face with a dish towel. "And partly because he's got good instincts and a fair mind."

"Are you trying to make me ashamed?"

"No, I'm telling you about my brother. Rafe's cocky and driven. Shane's good-hearted and laid-back. Devin's fair." Thoughtfully, he laid the towel aside. "I guess it bothers me that you can't see that."

"Old habits die hard." But she could see it, had seen it. "He was sweet with Emma."

Satisfied that he'd found a chink, he grinned. "We've all got a way with the ladies."

"So I've noticed." She took the beer from him and helped herself. "Would you like to stay for dinner?"

"I thought you'd like to go out."

"No." She smiled at the yellow tulips on the table beside him. "I'd like to stay in."

Big Mae, who had run the Tilt-a-Wheel in the carnival where Savannah had worked one educational season, had always said if she ever found a man who could cook and who didn't turn her stomach at the breakfast table, she would give up the high life and settle down.

After being treated to Jared MacKade's Cajun chicken and rice, Savannah thought Big Mae had had a very valid point. She sipped the wine Jared had gotten into the habit of tucking into her refrigerator and studied him over the candles on her dining room table.

"Where'd you learn to cook?"

"At my sainted mother's knee." He grinned. "She made us all learn. And, as she had the most accurate and swift wooden spoon in the county, we learned good."

"Close family."

"Yeah. We were lucky that way. My parents made it easy—*natural* I guess is a better word. Growing up on a farm, everybody has to pull their weight, depend on each other." His eyes changed, and looked, Savannah thought, somewhere else. "I still miss them."

A little jab of envy reminded her that she hadn't known either of her parents well enough to miss. "They did a good job with you. With all of you."

"Some people in town would have said differently once. Some still would." The smile was back in his eyes. "We got our reps the old-fashioned way—we earned them."

"Oh, I've been hearing stories about those bad MacKade brothers." Smiling over the thought, she rested her chin on her fist. "'Swaggering around town' is how Mrs. Metz puts it."

"She would." His smile changed, edged toward the arrogant. "She's crazy about us."

"I thought as much. I was getting the car filled the other day at the Gas and Go when she pulled into the station and got Sharilyn out there by the pumps to reminisce." And, Savannah remembered, to try to pump out a little gossip.

"Oh." Jared cleared his throat. "Sharilyn, huh?"

''Who has some very fond memories of you...and a 1964 Dodge.''

To his credit, he didn't wince. ''Hell of a car. How's old Sharilyn doing?''

''Oh, she's fine and dandy. Says, 'Hey.''' Amused, she switched gears. ''So, which one of you bad MacKade brothers was it who stuffed the potato in the tail pipe of the sheriff's cruiser?''

Jared ran his tongue around his teeth. ''Rafe got blamed for it.'' He lifted his wine. ''But I did it. We always figured whatever one of us did, all of us did, so whoever took the heat deserved it.''

''Very democratic.'' She rose to put the dishes in the sink. ''I could have used a few siblings on the rodeo circuit. There was never anyone to pass the blame to.''

''Your father was rough on you.''

''No, not really. He was...'' How could she describe Jim Morningstar? ''Larger than life, and hard as a brick. He liked a good horse and a bottle of cheap whiskey. He could handle the first, but he didn't do quite so well with the second. He didn't know what to do with me, so he did his best. It just wasn't good enough for either of us.''

She leaned back when Jared's hands came to her shoulders as he asked, ''Did you learn to ride?''

''So early I don't even remember learning. Could rope and tie a calf, too. Pulled in a few prizes.'' She laughed and turned to set her hands comfortably on his hips. ''Honey, I learned to do all kinds of wild, wicked

things while you were busy steaming up the windows
of a '64 Dodge and sticking potatoes in tail pipes.''

"Oh, yeah?" He tipped up her chin so they were
eye-to-eye.

"Oh, yeah. I could take a horse that looked like two
miles of bad road and groom him up till he shined. I
liked the ones with temper," she drawled, rubbing her
hands up his sides, over his hips. "The ones with fire
in their eyes and just a little mean in the heart. I'd make
him come to me. Right to me. Then I'd ride him."
Eyes open, she scraped her teeth over his bottom lip.
"I'd ride him hard and long. And when I was done,
he'd be spoiled for anybody else."

His blood went instantly to boil. "Are you trying to
seduce me?"

"Somebody's got to." Taking a good, firm grip, she
fused her mouth to his until the heat burning through
her engulfed him like a flash fire.

His hands gripped like vises on the edge of the sink
behind her, his body pressing against hers. And then
she was moving against him, sliding, rocking, turning
him to iron while her mouth took big, hungry gulps.

"Jared, touch me." Desperate, she yanked his hand
free, closed it over her breast, where her heart was
pounding like steel on an anvil. "Touch me. Touch
me," she repeated, even as his hands streaked under
her shirt and filled with her.

She was like some dark, forbidden dream, warm
limbs straining against him, sliding, tight denim against
tight denim, in painful friction. The flesh in his greedy

hands was firm and full and hot. He pressed his mouth to her throat. He could have sunk his teeth into it, such was his sudden, outrageous hunger.

He knew that if he didn't have her now, tonight, he'd be insane by morning.

When he pulled back, dizzy with appetite, she moaned. "For God's sake, are you trying to make me crazy?"

He stared, fighting for his breath as she fought for hers. Though his hands were at his sides now, he could feel her on his fingertips.

"That was the first part of the plan," he said as he took a deep gulp of air, then added, "I'm finished with the first part."

"Hallelujah."

He could almost have laughed. "Bryan's staying at Connor's?"

"Yes." Impatient, edgy, she grabbed his hands. "Come upstairs."

"No."

Her smile was slow and willing. "All right." But when she lifted her arms, happy to take him where they were, he caught her hands.

"No."

"Jared, don't make me hurt you."

He could laugh. "I'm hoping you will. Get a blanket."

"A blanket?"

"I want you in the woods." He turned her hand over

in his, caught her wrist in his teeth. "I've always wanted you in the woods."

"I'll get a blanket," she managed, and nearly tripped over her own feet in her rush.

She had herself under control again as they walked together under the arching canopy of trees tender with spring, under the dazzle of stars and the glow of a three-quarter moon. She'd meant to seduce him tonight, to draw him slowly, cleverly in. To surprise him.

She hadn't meant to eat him alive.

Then he stopped where the ground was soft and flipped the blanket down. And she was very much afraid she wouldn't be able to stop herself.

"Tell me something, Lawyer MacKade."

He looked over the blanket at her where she stood, hip shot out, chin angled, eyes full of power and sex. He'd have chewed through glass to get to her. "What's that?"

"Is your health insurance up-to-date?"

His teeth flashed white. "You don't scare me."

"Honey, you won't be able to get your tongue around your own name when I'm finished with you."

She lunged, agile as a trick pony, her legs wrapped around his waist, her hands fisted in his hair. He swung her around once, so that his body would cushion hers when they fell laughing to the blanket.

It knocked the breath out of him, and gave her first advantage.

Her hands were everywhere at once, tugging the shirt over his head, running down his chest to yank at the snap of his jeans. And, to his giddy amazement, her mouth was chasing after them.

"Hold it." In self-defense, he rolled on top of her. "Keep that up, and this'll last about twenty seconds." He kept her pinned until his libido could remember it wasn't sixteen anymore. "I've been saving up for you, Savannah." He lowered his head, and the kiss was staggeringly deep.

The sound she made was a feral purr that shuddered into his mouth and out the soles of his feet. While his lips devoured hers, he gave his hands the pleasure of learning that long, lush body.

Firm and smooth, it moved under his touch sinuously, inviting him to linger. She smelled like the woods—dark, mysterious, full of secrets and hidden pleasures. The taste of that mouth feeding avidly on his was full of spice and heat.

Her hands were working on his back, tensing his muscles, nails nipping into his flesh to urge him to press harder, grip tighter. To take, and take, and take. Her breath came in low, throaty moans so erotic he knew he would hear them again in his sleep.

When he reared back, she arched and crossed her arms over her body. With her eyes on his face, she pulled her shirt over her head and tossed it aside.

She saw the fresh, wild desire bolt into his eyes, and reveled in it. In her youth, her body had been a curse—some had said her downfall. But now, watching the man she loved look at her for the first time, it filled her with a sense of soaring pride.

"It should be illegal." His voice was hoarse and thick. "Looking like you."

He didn't touch her, not yet. Fascinated, he unsnapped her jeans, drew them down and away. His oath was reverent. Then his hands skimmed up, from ankle to knee, to thigh and hip, over the muscled stomach that quivered unexpectedly.

"You're the most terrifyingly beautiful woman I've ever seen."

Her smile was slow, confident. She sat up, hooked an arm around his neck and brought his ready mouth to hers. Her murmur was approving as he explored her, inch by slow, delicious inch. She thought he had wonderful hands, firm, and just rough enough. Her eyes fluttered closed, dreamily, when he used his thumb to torment the tip of her breast.

She could wallow in the lovely feel of flesh sliding on flesh, of the light breeze whispering, the hot blanket beneath. There were owls hooting in the trees, ghosts walking in the air.

Never in her life had she known the magic and the generosity of love. She knew only that she would give him anything here. Whatever he asked. Whatever he wanted.

When he twisted her hair around his fist, pulled her head back, she was prepared for anything. But he only pressed his lips to her shoulder, rubbed them gently over the curve.

And she trembled like a startled doe.

"Surprised?" Darkly pleased, he lifted his head and

looked into her confused, clouded eyes. "You have beautiful shoulders." This time he laved his tongue over them. One by one. Her breath caught on two in-drawn gasps. "Sensitive shoulders. They look like they should be carved in marble, but they're soft."

He nipped lightly at her collarbone, and would have sworn it melted. Enthralled with the discovery, he ex-ploited it, lifting her into his lap, so that he cradled her, rather than the ground.

When she was limp. When he knew she was utterly open, he quickly, and with concentrated skill, ripped her ruthlessly to a peak.

She cried out, bucking hard, then pouring into his hand.

Love and pleasure burned through her. Unbearable heat. She turned to him, turned on him, in a wild frenzy of hands and lips. Later, he would think that they had both gone completely mad. But, for the moment, what they did to and for each other was all that made sense.

She made him hiss out her name, and the sound of it sang through her like music. When his heart pounded like thunder under her mouth, she knew it was for her, and only for her. The taste of salty sweat on his skin bewitched her.

He lifted her as though she weighed nothing. She opened, arched, took him deep, so deep that her hands reached out to grip his, from the sheer joy of it. She who cried only when there was no one to see, no one to hear, let the tears fall.

She rocked, matching his rhythm, matching the savage, fearless beat of her own pulse. Endlessly, endlessly, with the stars raining over them and the moonlight slicing through the tender leaves, they took each other.

He was nearly blind from the beauty of her face, electrified from what her body brought to his. He thought he felt something break inside him, around his heart. Then, like some ancient goddess summoning her forces, she lifted her arms high. Gleaming in the stardust, her body went taut, and tightened around him like a velvet fist, and tore him over the edge.

Chapter 8

Savannah awoke with a moan and flung her arm over her eyes to shield them from the blast of sunlight. Her body felt as though she'd ridden a wild bronc over rocky ground.

And then she remembered she'd pretty much done just that.

Her lips curved as the night reeled through her mind. She had thought she knew what it was like to want— a home, a life, a man. She'd been certain she'd experienced every kind of hunger—for food, for shelter, for love. But nothing she had felt before matched what had churned through her for Jared MacKade.

There had been men in her life before—some had passed through, some had stirred her blood. But she had never needed one. And that, she realized, was both the risk and the wonder of this.

There would never be another man. He was the first, and he would be the last, to take her heart.

As both mind and body woke, she heard the song of the birds, the far-off yip of Shane's dogs. She felt the strength of the sun beaming through the spring leaves, and the chill of the early breeze. With her eyes still shielded, she stretched lazily, feeling like a cat waiting to be stroked.

"You have a tattoo."

She made a long, contented sound, flung her arm over her head, and at last opened her eyes.

He was sitting beside her. His hair was tousled from sleep and her hands, his eyes were heavy and focused thoughtfully on an area high on her right thigh. She wondered if there was any other woman in the world lucky enough to wake to such a sight.

"You look good in the morning," she murmured, reaching out to stroke him. "Naked and rumpled."

He wasn't sure how long he'd watched her sleep. But he did know that when he tugged the blanket away from her, to pleasure himself with a long study of her body in the sunlight, he'd discovered the colorful little bird on her thigh.

He simply hadn't been able to get past it.

"You have a tattoo," he repeated.

"I know that." With a little laugh, she rose on her elbows. Those dark-chocolate eyes were heavy and touched with humor. "It's a phoenix," she explained, amused at the way his brows drew together as he focused on it. "You know, rising from the ashes. I got it in New Orleans, when I realized I wasn't going to be poor for the rest of my life.''

''A tattoo.''

''Some men think they're sexy.'' Of course, she hadn't gotten it for a man, but for herself. A brand, to remind her that she could remake herself, rise above what she had been. ''How about you?''

''I'll have to take it under advisement.''

He couldn't say why he was so fascinated by it. So jarred. What other secrets did she have? What other permanent marks from her past? He looked away from it, into her face, and was shaken all over again. The sleepy smile in her eyes, the curve of those lips.

''How're you feeling?''

''Like I spent the night having wild sex in the woods.'' Laughing, she moved to link her arms around his neck. ''I feel wonderful.'' Her lips found his and lingered, soft and warm. ''How about you?''

''Exactly the same.''

She hoped so, she hoped he could. She would have lived her life in bliss if he could feel for her even a fraction of what she felt for him.

He gathered her close and held her as no one else had ever held her. As if it mattered.

''I don't suppose we could stay here forever,'' she murmured.

''No, but we can come back.'' He needed to think, and knew it was impossible as long as he held her. There were responsibilities at the farm that he was neglecting, he reminded himself. ''I have to go.'' But he buried his face in her hair, and his arms stayed around her. "Farms don't take Sundays off."

"I have to pick up Bryan soon." But her head nestled into his shoulder, and her arms stayed around him.

"Why don't you bring him over and...just bring him over?"

"All right."

"Savannah."

"Hmm?"

He caught her hair in his hand, drew her head back. His mouth crushed desperately over hers. "Just once more," he murmured as he lowered her to the blanket.

When he walked back to the farm, his mind was fogged from her. He'd never known a woman who could leave him so dazed, so weak-kneed. He passed the pigsty, where the stock caught the scent of man and grunted hopefully. In the chicken coop, hens clucked and fluttered over their feed. Distracted, Jared nearly tripped over one of the barn cats, who'd come out to stretch in the sun.

Rubbing a hand over his face, he made it to the back door. The smells of breakfast hit him hard, and his stomach realized it was ravenous. He could have eaten the sausages Devin was grilling, and the skillet along with it.

"Coffee." He nearly whimpered the word as he stumbled to the counter.

Devin glanced at him, then over at Shane, who was already gulping down his second cup. A look of pure enjoyment passed between them.

"Your shirt's inside out," Devin said mildly.

Jared scalded his tongue on the coffee, cursed, then collapsed at the kitchen table.

With a grin cracking his face, Shane leaned on the counter near the stove, where Devin was frying up breakfast. "Brother Jared looks a little rough this morning. Looks like he spent the night crawling through the woods."

"I guess I should have sent out that search party." Enjoying himself, Devin cracked eggs into the pan. "It's tough on a man, spending the night in the haunted woods. Alone."

"I feel real bad about it. Let me get you some more coffee, Jare." All solicitude, Shane brought the pot to the table. "Then you can tell us all about it. Don't leave out a thing. We're here for you."

Jared picked up the coffee Shane had just topped off and scalded his tongue again. "I'm in love with a former exotic dancer with a tattoo."

With an expert's finesse, Devin flipped eggs. "She was a stripper?"

"Where's the tattoo?" Shane wanted to know. It earned him a halfhearted jab in the gut. "Okay, just give me the general area."

"I'm in love with her," Jared repeated, weighing each word.

"Well, hell, you've been in love before." Shane strolled over to take biscuits out of the oven. "At least you've picked one that's interesting this time."

"Shut up," Devin muttered. He heaped food on a platter and came to the table. Then he sat and studied

Jared's face. A long moment later, he leaned back and took a considering breath. "All the way in love?"

Experimentally, Jared rubbed the heel of his hand over his breastbone, which ached from the way his heart was swelling. "Feels like it."

With a shake of his head, Shane dumped biscuits into a bowl. "Man, we're dropping like flies. First Rafe, now you." He brought the biscuits to the table, sat, and propped his head on his hands. "It's getting scary."

"Did you tell her?" Devin asked.

"I've got to work it out."

"Next thing you know, we'll have to put on suits again and get married." Grumbling at the thought, Shane started to fill his plate.

"I didn't say anything about *marriage*," Jared said quickly. Panic reared up and kicked him in the throat. "I've been there. I didn't say anything about marriage."

"You weren't married, you were contracted." Cheering up, Shane shoveled in a man-size mouthful of eggs. A good solid breakfast always lifted his mood. "You might as well have cuddled up with a spreadsheet."

"What the hell do you know about it?"

Shane washed down the eggs with coffee. "Because I never saw you look then the way you look now, bro."

Devin ate slowly and nodded in agreement. "Is it the kid that bothers you?"

"No, Bryan's great." Frowning, Jared helped himself to what was left on the platter. He liked the boy, liked spending time with him, talking with him. And the truth was that one of the reasons his marriage had been doomed was that he'd wanted children, and his wife hadn't.

No, the boy didn't bother him. It was the man who had helped create him who stuck in his craw. And, he realized, the other men since.

He just couldn't intellectualize them away. And he didn't like himself for it.

He caught Devin's look, that quiet, knowing look, and jerked his shoulders restlessly. "I just have to get used to it."

Devin dashed some salt on his eggs. "The trouble with lawyers is, they like to gather up all the little facts, every little piece. Then they can argue either side. You were always good at that, Jare. Dad used to say you could twist something simple around from right to wrong and back again. Maybe this is one of those times you should just take it as it is."

Jared wanted to. And he hoped he could.

He didn't move in with her, technically. But he spent most of his nights there, and some of his clothes found their way into her closet, his books onto her shelves.

He got into the habit of swinging by after work to pick up Bryan on practice nights. More often than not, they lingered on the field, tossing the ball.

If a case kept him late at the office, he phoned her. Sometimes he phoned her just to hear her voice.

With casual regularity, he brought her flowers, and baseball cards or some other treasure for Bryan. They were a trio on outings, and they gave the town a great deal to buzz about.

Bryan accepted him without question—a fact that both pleased and distressed Jared. He wanted to believe it was because the boy cared for him, considered them a kind of family. But he wondered if Bryan was simply accustomed to having a man stake a claim.

When that nasty toad of a thought jumped into his head, Jared did what he could to bat it away. It was, after all, the now that mattered. The way she looked at him. The way she laughed when she watched him and Bryan tussle on the lawn. The way, he thought, she arched her back after she'd been bending over the flowers she tended, or how complete her concentration was when she worked in her studio.

It was the way she smelled that mattered, when she walked out of a steaming bath. It was the way she strained against him night after night in bed, as if she could never get enough. And the way she would reach for his hand when they sat together on the porch swing in the evening.

Court had kept him late, and the strain of the day refused to be shaken off. He'd brought work home, and he knew that the headache that was drumming behind his eyes would be violent before it was over.

He stopped off in town to pick up aspirin, searching the shelves in the general store for something that promised to kick big holes in the drums in his head.

"Hi there, Jared." Mrs. Metz, armed with a loaf of

bread and a box of Ring Dings, cornered him. She was an expert at the ebb and flow of gossip.

"Mrs. Metz." The rhythm of small towns was too ingrained for him to hurry on, and he liked her, had fond memories of her feeding him homemade cookies. And chasing him off with a broom. "How's it going?"

"Fair to middling. Need some rain, that's for sure. Spring's been too dry."

"Shane's a little worried about it."

"We're going to get some tonight," she predicted. "A storm's brewing. Heard that Morningstar boy played a good game Saturday."

"Three RBIs, initiated two double plays."

She gave a cackling laugh that sent her trio of chins waggling. "You sound like a proud daddy." Before he could comment, she hurried on. "Seen you and the boy and his mama here and there. She's what my boy Pete would call a stunner."

"Yes, she is." Jared chose a painkiller at random.

"Hard, though," Mrs. Metz continued, shifting her ample weight to block his retreat. "Raising a boy on her own, I mean. Not that lots of women don't find themselves in that kind of fix today. She's from out west, isn't she? I guess the boy's father's still out there."

"I couldn't say." Because it was the literal truth, the pounding in his head increased.

"You'd think the man would want to see his son now and again, wouldn't you? They've been here close on four months now. You'd think he'd want to come around and visit a fine-looking boy like that."

"You'd think," Jared said, careful now.

"'Course, some men just don't give two hoots, much less a holler, about their children. Like Joe Dolin." Her cheerfully homely face puckered up on the name. "I'm happy as I can be you're handling Cassie's divorce and making it smooth for her. Mostly they're not smooth— I know when my sister's second boy got his, the feathers flew. I'd wager Savannah Morningstar's divorce was a rough go."

Oh, no, you don't, he thought. He wasn't going to give her any fuel by saying there'd never been a divorce, since there'd never been a marriage. "She hasn't mentioned it."

"You used to be more curious, Jared." Before he could snarl at her, she beamed a smile at him. "And just look at you now, a lawyer carrying a briefcase. I've come up to watch you in court a time or two."

His anger with her deflated. "Yes, I know." He'd seen her there, in her large flowered dress and sensible shoes. Like his own personal cheering section.

"Better'n watching Perry Mason, that's what I told Mr. Metz. That Jared MacKade's better'n Perry Mason. Your folks would be right proud of you. And here we thought the lot of you would never be on the right side of the law." She found that so funny, she almost doubled over with laughter. "Lord, you were bad, boy. Don't think I don't know who blackened my Pete's eye after the spring dance in high school."

The memory was very sweet. "He tried to muscle in on my girl."

''Sharilyn got around in those days. It was Sharilyn in high school, wasn't it?''

''Briefly.''

''Anyway, she got around, and so did you, as I recall. Girls always fluttering around you and your brothers. Young Bryan's mother must be right pleased to have hooked herself a MacKade, and I got to say, the three of you look real nice together. I got a feeling your mama would've taken to that girl.''

''Yeah.'' Jared felt a clutching in the stomach. What would his mama have said about a woman like Savannah?

He thought about it on the way home, and it added weight to his headache. If his mother were alive, how would he explain Savannah? Unwed mother, exotic dancer, carnival worker, calf roper, street artist.

Pick one, he thought, and rubbed at his temple.

The problem was, he could imagine it all, could see her in each stage of her evolution. And it was too easy to see how each layer was part of the whole that was the woman who was waiting for him.

He was tempted to stop off at Rafe's, or go straight to the farm. Just to prove he could. That Bryan's mama didn't have her hooks in him. But he turned up her lane, because it seemed that anything less would be cowardly.

No MacKade was a coward.

She was playing the music at full volume again. Usually it amused him, the way she would crank up that old stereo and blast rock out over the hills. Now he sat in the car, rubbing his aching head.

He walked to the porch, his heavy briefcase weighing him down. Through the screen door he could see her back in the kitchen, washing dishes, singing along with the stereo in a lusty, throaty voice that would sizzle a man's blood. Her hips were grinding to the beat.

She sure knew how to move, he thought, jealousy and temper slashing through him at the same time the first flash of lightning blazed in the west.

Before he could stop himself, he'd slammed the door behind him. Like a pistol shot, it boomed over the music. She swung around, her loose hair following the flow of her movement.

"You want to turn that damn thing down?" he shouted.

"Sure." Hips still rotating, she sauntered over and flipped it off. "Sorry, didn't hear you drive up."

"You wouldn't have heard a freight train drive up."

She only lifted a brow at the edge in his voice and wiped her damp hands on tight jeans. "Rough day?"

He stalked over, dropped his briefcase on the table where the daisies he'd brought her a few days before still smiled sunnily. "Is that how you danced for money?"

The blow was so quick, so sudden and sharp, she couldn't even gasp. It shivered through her once, viciously, before she gathered herself and rolled over the pain. "No. I wouldn't have made much, if that's all I'd put into it." She walked to the refrigerator for a beer she didn't want, because if there was something in her hands they might not shake. "Want one?"

''No. Didn't it bother you, being stared at, drooled over?''

''Not especially.'' She look a slow, deliberate swallow of beer.

''So you enjoyed it.'' He was prodding, very much as he would prod a witness who'd been sworn in. ''Enjoyed the dancing, the staring, the drooling.''

''It paid the rent. Men liked to look at my body, and I figured they could pay for it.''

''And if they'd pay to look, they'd pay to—'' He broke off, staggered by what had nearly come out of his mouth. He'd had no idea it was in there.

She didn't so much as flinch. This time, it wasn't unexpected. ''Now that you brought it up—'' her shoulders moved in a lazy, careless shrug ''—I thought about it. There was a time that that was all I had to bargain with, so I thought about selling myself.''

The horrified apology that was on the tip of his tongue dried up. ''And did you?''

She stared at him, her eyes cool and blank. ''I'm going up to say good-night to my son.'' Her eyes went from cool to ballistic when Jared snagged her arm. ''Don't mess with me, MacKade. Stay or go, it's up to you, but don't mess with me.''

She jerked free and strode quickly up the stairs.

He wanted to break something. Preferably something sharp that he could stab himself with afterward. Instead, he ripped open the box of aspirin, fought off the lid, then downed three with what was left of her beer.

Upstairs, Savannah settled Bryan in for the night. When she'd closed his door, she locked herself in the bathroom, where she could bathe her hot face over and over again with frigid water.

How stupid she'd been, she thought, berating herself. How blind, not to have seen what he was holding back. How careless, not to have built a defense against what he thought of her, underneath it all.

She would build one now, she promised herself. She would not allow herself to be hurt by the questions he asked, or the ones that were in his eyes. She would not, she swore she would not, allow him to make her feel ashamed of the answers.

She had fought too long and too hard to let anyone make her feel less than what she was.

But, though she tried, she couldn't find that place inside herself, that quiet, untroubled place where she could escape.

It seemed he could follow her there.

Methodically she dried her face and tidied the sink. All the while, she listened for the sound of his car leaving. But there was nothing but the crack of lightning, the mumble of thunder, and the mutters of old ghosts.

He was at the kitchen table when she came back down, his papers spread out. He slipped his glasses off when she hesitated, but she turned her back on him and walked outside to wait for the storm.

It came slowly from the west, and built. Like temper simmering. The wind kicked up and sent the trees waving. The roar of it—rain, wind, thunder—rolled over the hills, screamed through the woods and exploded.

There was a smell of ozone in the air. A magic smell.

A violent smell. Savannah threw her head back and drew it in. When the wind lashed the rain under the shelter of the porch to slap at her face, she stayed where she was. When lightning flashed so close it seemed to singe the trees, she welcomed it.

At length, Jared put his work aside and walked out to her. She was drenched, hair dripping, shirt clinging. The air was cool, but she wasn't shivering. Finally she turned, leaned back against the post and crossed her bare feet at the ankles.

"Something else on your mind?"

He'd taken off his tie and rolled up his sleeves, but he was feeling very much like a lawyer. "The question was crudely put," he began, despising the measured tone of his own voice. "I apologize for that. But not for wanting an answer. I'm asking you if you prostituted."

"That's what's called rephrasing the question. Right, Counselor?"

"I have a right to know."

"Why?"

"Damn it, I'm sleeping with you. I'm all but living with you."

As her stomach clutched and twisted, she angled her head. "Have I charged you anything, Ace?" Her eyes flashed a warning as he stepped toward her. "Don't put your hands on me now. You've got a nerve, MacKade, waltzing in here like it all belonged to you, tossing my past up in my face like you were part of it. Well, it doesn't all belong to you, and you weren't a part of it."

He stepped closer, until he was toe-to-toe with her. The storm flashed and burned in him, around him. ''Yes or no.''

When she started to shove him aside, he pressed her back, grabbed her chin in his hand. She bared her teeth, and her eyes shot daggers at him.

''You think I want to know? I *have* to know, and I'm prepared to deal with whatever the answer is. Because I'm in love with you.'' He jerked her chin higher. ''I'm in love with you, Savannah.''

Her eyes filled, overflowed so quickly his fingers went numb from the shock. She reared back and shoved him with all her strength. ''*This* is how you tell me?'' she shouted. ''Were you a whore, Savannah, I love you? Well, go to hell, Jared. I won't have you cheapening what I feel for you. I hate that you'd make me feel cheap when I hear it, when I tell you what I wasn't sure you wanted to hear from me. I love you so much I'd settle for anything you gave me. Even this.''

''Don't.'' He had to stop himself from springing forward when she reached for the door. He couldn't touch her now, knew he didn't deserve to. ''Please don't walk away. You're right. You're exactly right.''

She stared through the screen at the home she'd fought all of her life to make. She closed her eyes and thought of the man behind her, a man she'd never have believed she could have.

Suddenly she was exhausted, beaten by her own heart. ''I never sold myself,'' she said quietly, in a voice carefully picked free of emotion. ''Not even when I had to go hungry. I could have, there were plenty of opportunities, and plenty of people who assumed I did. But I didn't. I didn't make the choice for myself. I made it for Bryan, because he didn't deserve a mother who would sell herself for food or a night's rent.''

She drew in a deep breath before she turned. ''Does that satisfy you, Jared?''

He would have taken it all back if he could. Yet he knew that if it hadn't come out, it would have festered and poisoned everything they had. Just as he knew that there was still more that had to be said, had to be asked. But not tonight.

''Can you understand that I hate knowing you had to make the choice? That you were alone, and in trouble?''

''I can't change anything about the last ten years, and I wouldn't.''

He stepped toward her slowly, testing. ''Can you understand that I love you? That I've just come to realize I've never loved a woman before, and this terrible need I have for you is making me crazy?'' He lifted a hand, touched just the tips of her wet hair. ''Let me hold you, Savannah. Just hold you.''

He took her gently, closed her in his arms and rocked. Relief coursed through him when her arms finally came up from her sides and circled him.

''I hurt you. I'm sorry. I didn't even know I could.'' Ashamed, he pressed his lips to her hair. ''I thought it was all me. It's gotten so huge I didn't think anybody else could feel like this. Let me plead insanity.''

"It doesn't matter." She thought she would have crawled inside him if she could. "It doesn't matter now."

"Let me tell you again." Gently he tipped her head back, looked into those dark, damp eyes. "I love you, Savannah. I'm so desperately in love with you." He touched his lips to hers, felt the tremor. "So helplessly in love with you. It takes my breath away every time I see you."

She couldn't speak. This was how she had once dreamed he would look at her, with violent love in his eyes. These were words she'd refused to let herself dream of hearing. She threw her arms around his neck and clung for her life.

"You're trembling," he murmured. "You're cold."

"No. No. Oh, I love you. I don't know how else to say it."

"That'll do. Storm's passing." He could hear the thunder rolling away. "We're going to have a good farmer's rain. A soaker. The kind that means something." He hooked an arm under her knees, lifted her. "I want to make love with you and listen to the rain."

He was so gentle, it seared her heart. Kissing her cheek, her throat, as he carried her to the room they shared. When the door was closed, he walked through the shadows and laid her down.

She heard the hiss of a match, then candlelight flickered. He peeled off her damp clothes, stroked his hand over her skin. And suddenly she felt fragile and nervous.

She knelt on the bed to unbutton his shirt, and her

fingers were clumsy. He took them, pressed them one by one to his lips.

There was the smell of rain and wet earth, the whisper of thunder moving off, the give of the mattress beneath her.

Then there was only him. Murmurs and sighs drifted through the sound of pattering rain. He was so tender with her, so gentle, her body seemed to flow through his hands like fragrant heated wax. Each time their lips met, it was deeper and truer. Each time their bodies pressed, it was softer and warmer.

A brush of fingertips, the trail of quiet kisses, and flesh quivered. Dazed with love, they watched each other, listened to the quickening rhythm of hearts.

He slid into her silkily, his sigh merging with hers, his body rising and falling with hers. His lips meeting hers.

He felt her crest sweep through him, a long, slow, undulating wave that carried him off in its wake.

Chapter 9

Bryan loved spending time on the farm. The animals, the men, the open air. He still remembered the confusion and confinement of cities—the places where they had moved and lived in small rooms where the windows always seemed to pulse with noise and the walls were so thin you could hear every laugh or curse from the people next door.

He hadn't minded the city, really. There had always been something to do, somewhere to go. And his mother had taken him to parks and playgrounds—whenever she wasn't working.

He had vague memories of times when she had worked late into the night, or late into the morning. Times when she'd been tired a lot, and sad, too. Though he hadn't really understood why.

He remembered New Orleans, with the pulsing music and the slow-talking people. He remembered his mother had kept a pot of red flowers on the windowsill.

Sometimes he'd sat at his mother's feet, playing cars or reading picture books while she painted things, painted people who'd come by to sit in a little folding chair while she sketched their faces on big sheets of paper with charcoal or colored chalk.

That was when things had changed. Things had gotten better. She'd stopped working at night, and that sad, tired look had left her eyes.

Now, this was best of all. Having a house, the way she'd always promised. Having a yard and friends who could stay your friends because you were staying, too. Friends like Connor. Who was definitely cool, even though some of the kids at school teased him and said rotten things about his old man.

Maybe, Bryan sometimes thought, it was because they didn't know what it was like to have no father at all. The way he did.

But Mom was enough. She always made things work out, always made sure they were a team. As moms went, he figured, she was the coolest.

Like the way she'd asked him if he wanted to live in the cabin in the woods. She hadn't just told him they would live there, the way he knew some parents did things. Then, when they had the cabin—which was in his opinion the best place in the whole world—she'd let him pick out the stuff for his room. The neat bunk beds, the posters for the walls, the big wood chest for his toys.

Now he got to visit the farm whenever he wanted. Mostly.

Shane was great. He never minded if Bryan wanted to hang out and ask questions about things. Devin was okay, too, even if he was the sheriff. He liked Rafe, and the way Rafe would sometimes plunk himself down and wrestle with the dogs.

Jared was kind of scary, because he made Bryan think about how it would be to have him around all the time. Like a father. A guy to play ball with. A man who came home after work every day and listened to what you wanted to say. A man who kissed your mother in the kitchen like it was no big deal.

He wanted Jared most of all, and because he did, Bryan wished for him hard, every night. Somehow, whatever he wished for hard almost always came true.

On the farm, the sun was bright, warming ground that was damp from the night's rain. The early-morning fog had burned off and left the air clear and moist. He was happy sitting on the dirt with the dogs and Connor, with the sound of adult voices never far off. They were going to have Sunday dinner at the MacKades'.

The men were cooking, which Bryan thought was a little weird, but interesting.

''Do you think Fred and Ethel'll have babies?''

Connor continued to stroke the golden fur of the dog nearest him as he considered the question. ''They probably will. That's what happens when people are married. It's the same for dogs, I guess.''

Bryan gave a snort and delivered a punch to Connor's shoulder. "People don't have to be married to have a kid. They just have to be stuck on each other."

If anyone else had made the comment, Connor would have flushed. But because it was Bryan, he only nodded wisely. "Then Fred and Ethel can have pups, because they're stuck on each other."

Bryan looked toward the farmhouse. Through the kitchen window came the sound of mixed laughter. "I think Jared's stuck on my mom."

Connor's pale gray eyes went wide. "Are they having a baby?"

"No." Bryan hooked an arm around Ethel's neck. It was a possibility he'd given some thought to. "It'd be cool if they did. I mean, you like having Emma around, don't you?"

"Sure."

"A brother would be neater, but even a sister would be okay. I think if there was one—you know, a baby—Jared would hang around. Like live with us."

"Sometimes it's bad," Connor said quietly. "Sometimes when a man lives with you, it's bad. They argue and fight, and they get drunk and…things."

The idea of that had Bryan's brow furrowing. "But not all of them."

"I guess not." But Connor was far from sure. "I don't want a man to live with us ever again." Connor's voice was low and fierce. "Not ever again."

Understanding, Bryan shifted his arm from Ethel's neck to Connor's. "If your father tries to come back after he gets out of jail, you'll be ready. We'll be ready,'' he added with a dazzling smile. ''You and me, Con.''

''Yeah.'' Connor almost wished he had a chance to prove it. ''You and me.''

''Looks like they're talking big talk,'' Savannah commented from the kitchen window.

''Connor's never really had a close friend before.'' Hadn't been able to, Cassie thought, with the way Joe hassled everyone who came to the house.

''Neither has Bry. They're good for each other.'' She grinned when the boys started wrestling each other, and the dogs. All four would be filthy, she was sure, by the time dinner was ready.

''That looks familiar.'' Devin stepped up behind the women, tucked his hands in the back pockets of his jeans. Savannah did her best not to stiffen. ''We spent a lot of Sunday afternoons kicking up dirt.''

''We spent a lot of every afternoon kicking up dirt,'' Rafe said.

''Remember that Sunday Mom turned the hose on us?'' With a sigh, Shane popped a radish into his mouth. ''Those were the days. She was so ticked because Gran and Pop were coming to dinner, and we'd gotten into a fight wearing our best clothes.''

''You started it,'' Jared remembered. ''Swiped my baseball and lost it in the cornfield.''

''I borrowed your baseball,'' Shane told him. ''And Devin lost it in the field.''

''Rafe lost it,'' Devin said mildly. ''He was supposed to catch it.''

"You hit it wide. Pulled it," Rafe explained in disgust. "He could never pick his spot."

"Hell I couldn't."

Before Devin could take the argument any further, Regan held up her hands. "Time-out. I believe, with this obvious example of family solidarity, it's an excellent time to make an announcement." She smiled at Rafe. "Don't you think?"

"I think." Rafe took her hand, brought it to his lips before pulling her close. His grin was quick as lightning. "We're having a baby."

There was a moment of utter silence before the explosion. There was a quick whoop from Shane, who took it upon himself to scoop Regan off her feet. She had to be kissed, Rafe had to be punched and pummeled.

"Give me my wife," Rafe demanded.

"In a minute." Shane kissed her again, heartily, then started to pass her to Rafe. Jared intercepted, gave her a quick swing. Regan was still laughing when she found herself in Devin's arms.

"Damn it, give me my woman."

As they tussled and argued over the expectant mother, Savannah leaned back against the counter. "The MacKades—the next generation," she murmured to Cassie. "Scary thought."

"She'll handle it." Cassie blinked back tears. "She can handle anything."

Because everyone else was busy, she scooted over to check on the pot roast herself.

Savannah stepped forward, leaned in to kiss Jared on the cheek. "Congratulations, Uncle Jare."

He couldn't stop grinning. "Rafe's going to be a daddy."

With one brow arched, Savannah glanced over to where Regan was still being passed from brother to brother. "And this, I take it, is the way you guys celebrate—tossing women around."

"We don't have a precedent. It's our first baby."

When he swung an arm around her shoulders, Savannah realized he'd just said it all. It would be a MacKade baby, and would belong to all of them.

It was something she thought about quite a bit as the celebration continued through dinner with constant, and often ridiculous, suggestions for child care, baby names and fatherly duties. It was odd for her to fully realize now, when she was finally settled into a home of her own, finally confident that Bryan had the best she could give him, that neither of them had ever known the fullness of family.

They had each other, and that was important. Vital. He was a happy, well-adjusted child. She could see that as he sat beside her, shoveling in food, giggling at Shane's idea of Lulubelle MacKade if the baby was a girl. There was no doubt in her heart that her son was exactly as he should be.

And yet.

He had never known the joy, or the problems, of having uncles, aunts, grandparents. Siblings. Those were things she couldn't give him. She hoped it was only she who had suddenly come to sense the lack.

"Are you feeling all right, Regan?" Cassie's voice was quiet amid the chaos of male-dominated conversation.

"Wonderful. I don't think I've ever felt better. No queasiness, no fatigue, not any of the things the books warn us about."

"I had them all." Running an absent hand over Emma's curls, Cassie smiled. "Not too bad, really, just enough so that when it came around the second time I knew what to expect. How about you, Savannah?"

"Sick as a dog for three months." Before Bryan could reach over her plate, she passed him the bowl of roast potatoes he'd aimed for. "It was almost worth it, though." She winked at Bryan.

"Three months?" Regan gave a heartfelt shudder. "Every day?"

"Rain or shine," Savannah said cheerfully. "Bry, if you opened your mouth just a little wider, you could probably fit three potatoes in at once."

He managed a sloppy grin with a full mouth. "It's good."

"Just like Mom used to make," Devin put in, and heaped another helping of potatoes on Bryan's plate. "We used to have contests to see who could eat more of them. Jared usually won—right, Jare?"

"Yeah." But he'd stopped eating, and he was looking at Savannah oddly.

"The kid's going to break your record." Shane

tossed a biscuit that Jared was just quick enough to catch.

Intrigued with the maneuver, Bryan snatched one and aimed it at Connor, who nabbed it before it hit the floor.

"Good save," Rafe commented. "Sign him up. You gonna play ball next year, Con?"

"I don't know." Connor broke off an end of the biscuit and shot a look at his mother under his lashes.

"Con's a better pitcher than any of our starters." Bryan cheerfully helped himself to another biscuit and buttered it lavishly. "He can drill it right in the pocket."

"Connor, you never said you wanted to play ball." The moment the words were out of Cassie's mouth, she regretted them. Of course he'd said nothing. There had never been anyone to play ball with him. And his academic achievements had equaled failure as a man, in his father's opinion.

"I can't hit hardly anything," Connor mumbled, reddening. "I can just throw a little since Bryan's been showing me how."

"We'll have to work on your batting." Devin spoke casually. "After dinner, we could start on your stance."

Connor's lips fluttered into a smile, and that was answer enough.

A short time later, the sounds of shouts and arguments rolled in from the barnyard and into the kitchen window. With her hands filled with dishes, Cassie looked out. Devin was crouched behind Connor, and their hands were meshed on a wooden bat as Jared threw underhand pitches.

''It's awfully nice of them to play with the kids like this.''

''And leave us stuck with the dishes,'' Savannah pointed out.

''He who cooks doesn't clean.'' Regan filled the sink with hot water. ''MacKade rules.''

''It's fair enough,'' Savannah allowed. But as she glanced around the cluttered, disordered kitchen, with its piles of pots and mountains of dishes, she wasn't sure who'd come out on top of the deal.

''Do you mind if I ask...'' Regan caught herself, laughed nervously. ''It's stupid.''

Savannah grabbed a dishcloth and prepared to dig in. ''What?''

''Well.'' Brows knit, Regan attacked the first plates. ''I was just wondering, since you've both been through it, what it's like. The big guns, I mean.''

Savannah glanced at Cassie and grinned wickedly. ''Labor and delivery, or a march through the Valley of Death.''

''Oh, it's not that bad. Don't scare her.'' Immediately solicitous, Cassie set down stacked plates to rub Regan's shoulder. ''Really it's not.''

''You want to tell her it's a walk on the beach?'' Savannah asked. ''Then she can curse you and Rafe during transition.''

"It's a natural part of life," Cassie insisted, then struggled with a chuckle. "That hurts like hell."

"Sorry I asked." But Regan blew out a breath when she realized she couldn't let it go. "So, how long did it take?"

"For Connor, just over twelve hours, for Emma less than ten."

"In other words," Savanna put in helpfully, "the rest of your life."

"I'd tell you to shut up, but I want to know how long it took you." Regan wrinkled her nose. "Ten minutes, right?"

Savannah picked up a dish. "Thirty-two fun-filled hours."

"Thirty-two?" Stunned, Regan nearly bobbled a wet plate. "That's inhuman."

"The luck of the draw," Savannah said lightly. "And the maternity ward I was in wasn't exactly first-class. Wouldn't have mattered." She shrugged it off. "Babies come when they come. You'll get through it fine, Regan. Rafe'll be right there. And unless your doctor has a line of pro-football blockers holding them off, the rest of the MacKades will be there, too."

"You were alone," Regan murmured.

"That's the way it shook down." She glanced over when she spotted Jared at the screen door. "Game over?"

"No." His eyes stayed on hers, unreadable and deep. "I lost the draw to fetch beer."

"I'll get it." Cassie was already hurrying to the fridge. "Do the kids want anything?"

"Whatever they can get." He took the six-pack and boxes of juice Cassie handed him, then left without another word.

"No quicker way to get rid of a man than for women to talk about childbirth." Savannah's voice was light, but there was a knot of worry at the back of her neck. Something had been in those eyes, she thought, that he hadn't wanted her to see.

"I mentioned Lamaze classes to Rafe, and he went dead white." Amused, Regan slipped another dish in the drainer. "But then he gritted his teeth."

"He'll do fine." With a last glance at the screen door, Savannah picked up another plate. "He loves you. That's the big one, isn't it?"

"Yeah." With a dreamy little sigh, Regan plunged into the dishwater again. "That's the big one."

On the walk home, Savannah spied her first firefly glinting in the woods. Summer was coming, she thought, watching Bryan dart ahead, charging invisible foes. She wanted it to come. She wanted the heat, the long, hazy days, the close, airless nights.

What she wanted, Savannah realized, was the passing of time. A full year, four full seasons, in this place. In this home. With this man.

"Something's on your mind?" she said quietly.

"I've got a lot on my mind." Jared wished they could stay in the woods for a time. Stay where they could both feel the sorrows and needs of people who had died before either of them were born. "Couple of cases driving me crazy. Painters cluttering up the office. Finalizing Cassie's divorce. Contemplating becoming an uncle."

"You're being a lawyer, MacKade, using words to cloud the basics."

"I am a lawyer."

"Okay, let's start there. Hold on a minute. Bry, hit the tub," she called out.

"Aw, Mom…"

"And hit it hard, Ace. I'm right behind you."

He raced ahead, and from the edge of the woods Savannah watched the lights switch on one by one as Bryan streaked through the house. Through the open window, she could hear him singing, miserably off-key, and was satisfied that he was in his bathtime mode.

"Why are you a lawyer?"

The question stumped him, mainly because his mind was so far removed from it. "Why am I a lawyer?"

"And try to answer in twenty thousand words or less."

"Because I like it." The first answer was the simplest. "I like figuring out the best arguments, wading through and studying both sides until I find the right arguments. I like winning." He moved his shoulders. "And because justice is important. The system of justice, however flawed, is vital. We're nothing without it."

"So, you believe in justice, and you like to argue

and win.'' She tilted her head at him. "Which puts all of that into one sentence. See how easy it is?''

"What's your point?''

"My point is that you also like to complicate things.'' She touched a hand to his cheek. "What are you complicating now, Jared?''

"Nothing.'' Because he needed to, he took her wrist and pressed his lips into her palm. "I'm not complicating a thing. I liked having you at the farm, you and Bryan. Crowded around the kitchen table, with too many people talking at once.''

"And throwing biscuits.''

"And throwing biscuits. I liked hearing you and Regan and Cassie clattering around the kitchen while we were playing ball outside.''

"Typical.'' She smiled a little. "You'd say traditional male-female placement.''

"Sue me.'' He gathered her close. And there, in the quiet, he thought he could hear the struggle. Stranger against stranger, hand to hand, eternally. Right, perhaps, against right. "Feel it?'' he murmured.

"Yes.'' Fear, she thought, closing her eyes. Desperation. And constant bleeding hope. Perhaps she could feel the echoes of it in the woods because she'd known all those emotions so well. "Have you ever asked yourself why they're still here? What they might have left to say or do?''

"The fight's not over. It never is.''

She shook her head. "The *need's* not over. The need

to find home. To find peace, I suppose. It never is. But I'm finding it here.''

When she started to draw back, he tightened his grip. ''I listened outside the door to the three of you talking in the kitchen. It bothered me, Savannah, hearing about you being alone when you had Bryan. It bothered me imagining that, the way it bothered me when you said you'd been sick all that time.''

''Morning sickness is pretty common among pregnant women.''

''Being sixteen, alone, sick and pregnant isn't common. It sure as hell shouldn't be.''

''Feeling sorry for me is a waste of time. It was a long time ago.'' Now she did draw back, and she saw his face. ''But that's not exactly what you're feeling.''

''I don't know what I'm feeling.'' Nothing frustrated him more than not being able to see inside himself for the answers. ''I've got questions I haven't figured out yet how to ask. You make me ask, because you don't tell. And yes, I do feel sorry for you, for the kid who was left to fend for herself, and make choices for herself that no child should have to make.''

''I wasn't a child.'' Her voice was measured, her shoulders were suddenly stiff. ''I was old enough to get pregnant, so I was old enough to face the consequences. And the choice I made was mine alone. No one else could have made it for me. Having Bryan was one of the few right decisions I made.''

''I didn't mean that. I didn't mean Bryan.'' Seeing the heat in her eyes, he gave her a quick shake. ''I meant where to go, what to do, how to live. God, how to eat. And, damn it, Savannah, you *were* a child. You deserved better than what you got.''

''I got Bryan,'' she said simply. ''I got better than I deserved.''

He couldn't make her see what he wanted her to see. For once, he simply didn't have the words. Perhaps they were too simple. ''I wonder what it would be like to create something like that boy, and to love without restriction. Without ego.''

She could smile now. ''Wonderful. Just wonderful. Are you coming home with me?''

''Yeah.'' He took her hand. ''I'm coming home with you.''

He thought about that kind of love, and her kind of life, as she slept beside him. He would never have gone out and searched for a woman like her. It bothered him a great deal to admit it, even to himself.

She wasn't polished, or cultured, had no sheen of the sophistication he usually looked for in a woman.

That he *had* looked for, Jared reminded himself, once. And that had certainly been a pathetic mistake. And yet didn't a man need a woman he understood, a woman he knew? There were huge pockets in Savannah's life he neither understood nor knew. Large pieces of her that were separate from him, tucked away in her memories.

A young girl, pregnant and alone, deserted by everyone she should have been able to count on. He felt pity for that girl, as well as—and it scalded him to realize it—a vague distrust.

Where had she gone, what had she done, who had she been? As much as he wanted to get beyond that, his pride held him fast. She'd borne another man's child, been other men's fantasies.

That thought stuck in the pride, in the ego, and refused to be shaken free.

His problem. He knew it, rationalized it, debated it. As she shifted beside him, turning away rather than towards him, he worried over it.

How many other men had she loved? How many had lain beside her, each wishing he was the only one?

Yet, even as he thought it, he reached out to hold, to possess her. Her body curled warm against his, and he could smell her skin, that earthy, sensual fragrance she carried without the aid of perfumes.

He knew her routine now. In the morning she would wake early, but slowly, as if sleep were something to be eased out of, like a warm bath. She would touch him, long strokes over the shoulders, the back, the arms. And just when he began to tingle and heat, she would rise out of bed. She would arch her back with a lazy, feline movement. Lift that long, thick black hair up, let it fall.

Then, as if there were no difference between a sleepy siren and a sleepy mother, she would slip into a faded blue cotton robe and go out to wake Bryan for school.

And often, very often, Jared would lie in bed for

long, long moments after she padded across the hall. Aching.

He almost wanted to believe she'd woven some sort of spell over him with her gypsy eyes and sultry smile and that go-to-hell-and-back-again attitude. She knew him better than he knew her. Knew his ghosts, recognized them, felt them. She was the first woman who had walked in what he considered his woods and heard the murmurs of the doomed.

It linked her with him in a way that went beyond the physical, even the emotional, attraction. It lifted it into the spiritual. It lifted it beyond what he could fight, even if he wanted to fight.

Whatever it was that bound him to her gave him no choice but to keep moving on the same path toward her.

So he fell asleep with his arm hooked around her waist, holding her close. And dropped weightlessly into dreams.

There was pain in his hip where a mortar blast had sent him flying into the air, and hurled him down again. His head was aching, his eyes were tearing. It was so hard to focus, hard to force himself to set one foot in front of the other.

He didn't remember entering the woods. Had he crawled to the trees or run into them? All he knew was that he was terribly lost, and terribly afraid. His lieutenant was dead. There were so many dead. The boy from Connecticut with whom he'd shared last night's dinner, with whom he'd whispered long after the fires burned out, was in pieces in a shallow ditch where the fighting had been so fierce that hell would have been a relief.

Now he was alone. He knew he had to find somewhere to rest, someplace safe. Just for a while. Just for a little while. His home wasn't so very far away. Just north into Pennsylvania. The Maryland woods weren't so very different from those near his farm.

Maybe he could be safe here until he could find his way home again. Until this war that was supposed to have been an adventure and had become a thousand nightmares was over.

He had turned seventeen the month before, and he had never tasted a woman's lips.

Unbearably weary, he stopped to lean against a tree, drew in ragged breath after ragged breath. How could the woods be so beautiful, so full of color and the smells of autumn? How could that horrible noise keep going? Why wouldn't the guns stop blasting, the men stop screaming?

When were they going to let him go home?

With a shuddering sigh, he pushed off the tree. He skirted a rock and, with a burst of relief, spotted a path. Just as he stepped toward it, he saw the Confederate gray.

He hesitated only a moment, but whole worlds revolved inside him. This was the enemy. This was death. This was the obstacle in the path leading to what he wanted most.

He shouldered his rifle even as the boy facing him mirrored the movement.

They shot poorly, both of them, but he heard the whine of the shell close enough to his ear to stop his heart for a full beat. Then he was charging, even as his mirror image charged.

Their terrified war cries echoed each other. Bayonets clashed.

The enemy's eyes were blue, like the sky. That thought intruded as he felt the first agony of blade in flesh. The enemy's eyes were young and full of fear.

They fought each other like wild dogs. Even in the short time he had left, he would remember little of it. He remembered the smell of his own blood, the feel of it as it poured out of his wounds. He remembered waking alone, alone in those beautiful autumn woods.

And then stumbling down the path. Crawling, crying.

He would remember, for all of the hours he had left, he would remember the sight of the farmhouse just beyond the clearing. The color and glint of the stone, the slope of the roofline, the smell of animals and growing things.

And he wept again, for home.

Someone was with him. The face was older, weathered, set in a frown under a soft-brimmed hat. He thought of his father, tried to speak, but the pain as he was lifted was worse than death.

There were women around him, shouts, then whispers. Soft hands and firelight. Cool cloths, and the pain slipped into numbness.

Every word he spoke was a searing flame in his throat. But he had so much to say. And someone listened. Someone who smelled like lilacs and held his hand.

He needed to tell her he'd been proud to be a soldier, proud to serve and to fight. He was trying to be proud to die, even though the longing for home was fiercer than any of his wounds.

When he died, Jared woke, his heart stuttering. Savannah stirred beside him. And this time, this time, turned to him. In sleep, her arms came around him.

For tonight, it was enough.

Chapter 10

With a stack of three paintings balanced in her arms, Savannah muscled open the door to Jared's offices. Rain dripped from the bill of one of Bryan's baseball caps, which she'd slapped on before making the drive to Hagerstown. Sissy glanced over, then hopped up from her keyboard.

"Let me give you a hand with those."

"Thanks." Grateful, Savannah passed the three wrapped bundles over. "I've got more in the car."

"I'll just put these down and help you bring them in."

"No. No use both of us getting wet." She took a quick scan of the freshly painted teal-colored walls, the deep mauve settee and the leather library chairs. "Coming along."

"You're telling me." Sissy set the paintings down

on the coffee table. "I feel like I've been working in a box and someone just opened the lid and let in air. Let me get you an umbrella, at least."

"I wouldn't be able to hold it. Besides, I'm already wet. Be right back."

Savannah dashed out and sprinted the half block to her car. It was a hard, driving rain, but at least it was warm. No one seemed to be worried about a spring drought anymore—as Mrs. Metz had been happy to inform her when they ran into each other at the post office this morning.

The weather, however inconvenient at the moment, was causing Savannah's flowers to thrive.

By the time she got back in with the last of the paintings, she was soaked to the skin and squishing in her shoes.

"Is the boss in?" She set the paintings down, then took off the cap to run her fingers through her damp hair. "He might want to take a look before I hang these."

"He's with a client." Sissy flashed a smile. "But I'm dying to take a look." She snatched scissors off her desk. "Okay?"

"Sure. You've got to live with them, too."

"I can't believe how fast all this has moved." Quickly she cut the twine on the top bundle. "Once the boss makes up his mind, he moves. No fiddle, no faddle, no— I *love* this!" She ended on a high tone of enthusiasm as she pulled back the heavy paper.

It was a street scene, and the people in it were splashes of vivid color and movement. The buildings were jumbled, giving it a carelessly cheerful theme, and they were awash with lacy balconies, alive with trailing and spreading flowers. On closer inspection, Sissy picked out a toe-tapping fiddler, an enormous black woman in a flowing red caftan, three small boys racing after a yellow dog. She could almost hear the shouts and the music.

"It's wonderful. Tell me this one's going out here."

"That was the idea." Surprised and flattered by the reaction, Savannah dragged a hand through her hair again. "It's New Orleans. The French Quarter. I thought it would liven things up a bit in the waiting area."

"I can't tell you how tired I was of looking at pale pink flowers in a gray vase. I kept hoping I'd come in one morning and they'd have died during the night." Sissy chuckled to herself. "Now this I could look at forever. Did you take art in college?"

The innocent question had Savannah's smile freezing. "No. No, I didn't go to college."

"I had one semester of art," Sissy went on cheerfully, holding up the painting. "And was told I had absolutely no sense of perspective. Squeaked by with a C."

When the phone rang, she huffed a bit, then tilted the painting against the table and went back to her desk to answer it.

Foolish, foolish, Savannah told herself, to feel inadequate. No, she hadn't gone to college, but she knew how to paint. Hadn't Sissy's reaction just proven it?

Odd, Savannah thought, that she should still be nervous after her work had been viewed and appreciated. For most of her life she'd had to convince herself that painting was—could be—nothing more than a hobby. A personal indulgence, those times when she'd had to choose between buying paints and having lunch.

Paints had usually won.

Those days were over. Long over. She'd been incredibly lucky with her illustrations, and enjoyed doing them, intended to continue. But the paintings were her.

Selling bayou scenes and charcoal sketches to tourists was a far cry from selling something that had meant something to her when she saw it, when she painted it.

Smiling and damp-palmed, she dug through the tote she'd brought along for her hammer and measuring tape. She'd already measured the wall on an earlier trip, and now she found the center, marked her spot lightly with a pencil. And waited for Sissy to hang up the phone.

"Should I wait, or can I pound this in there now?" She held up a hanger.

"Now. I'm dying to see it up."

With brisk efficiency, Savannah hammered in the support. The frame was a simple natural cherry—Regan's choice. Savannah had to admit, as she adjusted the painting on the wall, that it had been a good one.

"Bring the left corner up a tad... Yeah, good." Hands on hips, Sissy nodded. "Good. Perfect. It's about time this place started looking more like the boss and less like..."

"His ex-wife?" Savannah finished, with a glance over her shoulder.

Sissy wrinkled her nose. "Let's just say she was very low-key. The kind of woman who never has a hair out of place, never raises her voice, never chips a nail."

"She must have had something to have attracted Jared."

Cautious, Sissy cast a look up the steps. "She was beautiful, in that don't-touch-me-I've-just-been-polished sort of way. Very classic, sort of Grace Kelly without the warmth and humor. And she was brilliant. Really. Not only in her profession, but she spoke perfect French, and played the piano beautifully. She read Kafka."

"Oh." Savannah struggled not to frown. She wasn't entirely sure she knew who or what Kafka was, but she was sure she'd never read it.

"In her way, she was admirable. But about as entertaining as a dead frog in a millpond." Sissy beamed at Savannah. "No one can accuse you of that," she said, and, with a quick laugh, picked up the ringing phone.

No, Savannah mused. No one could accuse her of that. Not of being polished or brilliant, or of reading Kafka. She could speak a little French—if you counted the Cajun variety.

Refusing to be intimidated by the image of the woman Jared had once chosen for his wife, she unwrapped the next painting.

She hung a trio of small still lifes in the entranceway while Sissy went back to work. While the rain pounded outside and Sissy's keyboard clattered, Savannah began to enjoy the simple pleasure of decorating, of choosing a space and bringing it to life. By the time she'd gotten to the second floor, she was humming under her breath.

Unwilling to hammer there while Jared was with a client, she leaned paintings against the walls she'd chosen for them, moving down the hallway and eventually into the office across from Jared's.

The former office, she thought, of the former Mrs. MacKade. No, she remembered. Not Mrs. MacKade. Jared had said she hadn't taken his name.

The walls here were a deep rose, the trim almost a jade, reversing the theme from the lower office. Regan had turned it into a comfortable and efficient sitting room. There was a desk, of course, but there were cozy chairs, tables, books. And, when she poked into a cabinet, a coffeemaker, cups.

Here, Savannah supposed, Jared could entertain or interview clients in a less formal atmosphere. Or perhaps he could use it to relax, unwind. Or maybe he was considering taking on an associate.

It occurred to her then that she knew very little about his work, or his plans, or what his workday was like.

She'd never asked, Savannah reminded herself—and why should he discuss cases with her? She knew nothing about the law except the problems she'd had with it, fighting to stay one step ahead of the system and keep her child.

He would have discussed them with his wife, she thought, then cursed herself for falling into that typical and pathetic mind-set.

Setting her thoughts on the job at hand again, she stepped out into the hall just as Jared's door opened.

"I'll have a draft of the contract sent out to you in a couple of days," Jared was saying. Then stopped, looked, and smiled. "Hello, Savannah."

"Hello. I'm sorry. I was arranging the paintings."

"You going to introduce me to this beautiful young woman, Jared, or do I have to make my own moves?"

"Savannah Morningstar, Howard Beels."

"Savannah Morningstar. That's a name that suits you." The big, barrel chested man of about fifty shot out a hand the size of a small ham and gripped Savannah's. His eyes, a twinkling blue set in pockets and folds of creased skin, were alight with male admiration. "You working for this shyster?"

"In a manner of speaking." Savannah recognized the look, the squeeze. She'd seen and felt it hundreds of times before, and after a quick survey she judged Howard Beels as harmless. She let her smile warm, because she knew he would take it home with him and sigh. "You hire this shyster, Howard?"

He gave a gut-rattling laugh. "A man needs a clever lawyer in this dirty old world," Howard told her. "Jared here's been mine for, what is now? Five years?"

"Just about," Jared murmured, intrigued by the easy way Savannah handled, and entertained, one of his top clients.

"What do you do, Howard?"

"Oh, a little of this, a little of that." He had yet to

let go of her hand. And he winked. "I'm a dabbler. How about you?"

"I'm a dabbler myself," Savannah told him, and made him laugh again.

"Savannah's an artist," Jared put in. "The next time you come in, Howard, you'll see her work on the walls."

"Is that so?" His sharp eyes homed in on the painting leaning against the wall behind her. "That your work there?"

"Yes."

He released her hand to cross to it. Despite his size, he hunkered down easily to study it. "It's right nice," he decided, liking the way the colors flowed and the way the flowers she'd chosen to paint seemed crowded together, more alive than perfect. "How much something like this go for?"

Savannah shifted her weight to one hip. "As much as I think I can get," she said dryly.

Howard slapped his knee appreciatively before he straightened. "I like this girl, Jared. I'm going to give you my card, honey." He reached in his jacket pocket and pulled one out. "You give me a call, hear? I think we could have ourselves a negotiation over a picture or two."

"I'll do that Howard." She glanced at the card, but it gave no clue to his profession. "I'll be sure to do that."

"Don't let any grass grow under your feet, either." He gave her a last wink before turning to Jared. "I'll expect those papers."

Savannah smiled at his retreating back. "Quite a character," she murmured.

"You sure handled him," Jared observed.

"I'm used to handling characters." She tucked the card away. "I've finished downstairs. If I wouldn't be in your way, I could finish up here."

"Sure."

He leaned against the doorway, watching her as she lifted the painting behind her. "A little more to the right," he suggested. "Howard's got an eye for the ladies."

"Yes, I gathered that." Satisfied, Savannah set the painting down and prepared to hammer in the hanger. "And I'd venture to say he's been faithful to his wife for...oh, twenty-five years."

"Twenty-six in May. Three kids, four grandchildren. He has an eye for the ladies," Jared repeated, "but he's one of the shrewdest businessmen I know. Real estate, mostly. Buys and sells. Develops. He owns a couple of small hotels, and the lion's share of a five-star restaurant."

"Really?"

"Hmm... He's on the arts council, works with the Western Maryland Museum."

As the card in her pocket suddenly took on more weight, Savannah nearly bashed her thumb. "That's interesting." Carefully, she set down the hammer. "It looks like I was in the right place at the right time."

"He wouldn't have told you to call him if he didn't mean it. I'm not sure how an artist might feel about having her work in hotels and restaurants and law offices.''

She closed her eyes a moment. ''I'd feel fine about it.'' She hung the painting, stepped back to study it. ''I'd feel just fine.''

''No artistic temperament?''

''I've never been able to afford artistic temperament.''

''And if you could?''

''I'd still feel fine about it.'' She turned then to study his face. ''Why wouldn't I?''

''I suppose I'm wondering why you wouldn't want or ask for more.''

She wasn't sure it was only art that he was speaking of now. But the answer had to remain the same. ''Because I'm happy with what I've got.''

His lips curved slowly as he reached out to touch her face. ''You're a complicated woman, Savannah, and amazingly simple. It's a fascinating mix. Why don't I take you to lunch?''

''That's a nice offer, but I want to get this done. If you're going, I could hang the pieces in your office while you're out.''

''Why don't I stay, and we can order in? I'll watch you hang the pieces in my office.''

''That would work.'' She tucked her restless hands into her pockets, then pulled them out. ''Actually, there's something I'd like you to see. You didn't pick it, but I thought if you liked it, you might want it in your office.''

Curious, he watched the nerves jitter in her eyes. "Let's take a look."

"Okay." She walked down the hallway to where she'd left the painting, still wrapped. "If you don't like it, it's no big deal." She shrugged and shifted past him to carry it into his office herself. "Either way, it's a gift." She set it on his desk, stepped away, jammed her hands into her pockets again. "No charge."

"A present?" He stroked a hand over her shoulder as he went to the desk for scissors to cut the twine.

The idea of a present from her delighted him. But when he folded back the protective paper and saw it, the quick smile faded. And Savannah's heart sank.

The woods were deep and thick, filled with mystery and moonlight. Black trunks, gnarled, burled, rose up into twisted branches that held leaves just unfurled with spring. There were hints of color. Wild azalea and dogwood gleamed in that ghostly light. The rocky ground was carpeted with leaves that had fallen the autumn before, and the autumn before that, a sign of the continuous ebb and flow of life.

He could see the trio of rocks where he often sat, the fallen trunk where he had once sat with her. And in the distance, just a hint through the shadows, was a glow of light that signaled his home.

For a moment, he wasn't sure he could speak. "When did you do this?"

"I just finished it a few days ago." A mistake, she thought, cursing herself. A sentimental, foolish mistake. "It's just something I've worked on in my spare time. Like I said, it's no big deal. If you don't like it—''

Before she could finish, his head came up, and his eyes, swirling with emotion, met hers. "I can't think of anything I've ever been given that could mean more. It's the way it looked the night we made love for the first time. The way it's looked countless times I've been there alone."

Her heart stuttered, then crept up to lodge in her throat. "I was going to paint it the way it would have been in autumn, during the battle. But I wanted to do it this way first. I wasn't sure you'd... I'm glad you like it."

He reached out, cupped her face in his hands. "I love you, Savannah."

Her lips curved under the gentle caress of his, then parted, heated, as he steadily deepened the kiss. His fingers tangled in her hair, still damp from the rain. Her arousal was slow and sweet.

"I should hang it for you."

"Mmm..." Quite suddenly, as her body pressed to his and her mouth began to move, he had a much better idea. He tucked an arm around her to hold her steady and reached over his desk to pick up the phone. "Sissy? Why don't you go to lunch now? Yeah, take your time."

Savannah's gaze followed his hand as he replaced the receiver. Then her eyes shifted blandly to his face. "If you think you're going to seduce me here in your office, have me rolling over your fancy new carpet with you while your secretary's out to lunch..."

Jared walked over, closed the door. Locked it. Arched a brow. "Yes?"

She tossed her hair back, leaned a hip on the desk. "You're absolutely right."

He shrugged off his jacket, hung it on the brass coat hook by the door. His tie followed. Keeping his eyes on hers, he crossed back. One by one, he loosened the buttons of her shirt.

"Your clothes are damp."

"It's raining."

Very slowly, very deliberately, he peeled the bright cotton away. His eyes never left hers as he slipped a finger under the front hook of her bra. Never left hers when he felt the quick quiver of her skin and heard the little catch in her breathing.

"I want you every time I see you. I want you when I don't see you." With a flick of his thumb and forefinger, he unsnapped the hook. "I want you even after I've had you." Lightly he traced his fingertips over the curve of her breast. "You obsess me, Savannah, the way no one and nothing ever has."

She reached out for him, but he shook his head and lowered her arms to her sides again. "No, let me. Just let me."

His thumbs brushed over her nipples, his eyes stayed focused on her face. "I lose my mind when I touch you," he murmured. "This time I want to watch you lose yours."

Fingers, thumbs, palms, cruised over her. Rough, then gentle, tender, then demanding, as if he was refusing to let any one mood rule. Driven, she pulled at him, tried to tug him closer. But each time she did, he stopped, patiently lowered her arms until she had no choice but to grip the edge of the desk and let him have his way.

No one had ever made love to her like this, as if she were essential, as if she were all there was and all there needed to be. As if her pleasure were paramount. Pinpoint sensations percolated along her skin, chased by others, whisper-soft, then still more that seeped slyly through flesh to blood and bone.

She arched back on a keening moan when he closed his teeth over her, shot her to some rugged ground on the border between pleasure and pain.

"Just take me." Her arms whipped around him, her body straining, pulsing.

But he took her hands, locked them to his as he kissed her toward delirium. Her mouth was a feast, full of hot flavor and a hunger that matched his own. But this time he wasn't content to sink into it, or her. He used his teeth to torment, his tongue to tease, until her breath came in tearing gasps.

"Let me touch you," she demanded.

"Not this time. Not yet." He closed her hands over the edge of the desk again, held them there while his mouth raced to her throat, down her neck, over those tensed and beautiful shoulders. "I'm going to take you, Savannah." He eased back, because he wanted her to see his face, and the unshakable purpose there. "I'm going to take you inch by inch. The way no one ever has."

For her pleasure, he told himself. But he knew a part

of it was his own pride. He wanted to show her that no man before, and no man after, could make her feel what he could.

So he showed her, traveling like lightning down her torso, her flesh damp now, not from rain, but from passion.

She gave herself over to him as she had never done with any man. Surrender complete, she braced herself on the desk and let him ravage her, body and mind.

He tugged off her shoes. She let her head fall back, let herself moan deep as he eased her jeans low on her hips, caressed that revealed flesh with his lips. She shuddered, nearly sobbed, as his hands kneaded and his mouth closed over her, fire to fire.

She crested fast and hard. Terrifying. Wonderful. He never stopped, and as the pleasure whipped her ruthlessly higher, she prayed he never would. Naked, stripped of clothes and all defenses, she could do nothing but experience, absorb and give.

He'd never known this kind of desire. To take and to take, knowing as he did that he was filling her with unspeakable pleasure. The blood swam in his head as he felt her peak yet again, heard that breathless cry catch in her throat.

The strong muscles in her legs were quivering. He ran his tongue over them, lingering over the symbol she'd branded herself with, before making his way, purposely, greedily, up that long body.

Her eyes were closed. He used his mouth only to keep her poised and ready for him as he stripped off his shirt. He toed off his shoes, whipped his trousers aside. And dragged her to the floor.

The animal that had been pacing restlessly inside him sprang free. He drove himself into her, mindlessly, shuddering with a dark thrill when she cried out his name, hissing with hot pleasure as her nails scraped his back.

It was all heat and speed and plunging bodies, a rhythmic, tribal beat of flesh against flesh. The blood hammered in his head, his heart, his loins, relentlessly. She arched up to him, straining, straining.

His vision grayed, his world contracted. He emptied himself into her.

Savannah thought, if she really tried, she might be able to crawl to where her clothes were heaped. And she would try, she told herself. In just another minute or two.

Right now, it was so lovely and decadent to lie there on the antique carpet in Jared's quietly elegant office with his body heavy on hers.

She had been, she realized, thoroughly and mind-numbingly ravished. As exciting as making love with him had been before, this was a different level entirely. She certainly hoped they would strive for it now and again in the future.

"I have to get up," she murmured.

"Why?"

"To make certain I'm not paralyzed."

"Did I hurt you?"

She kept her eyes closed, let her lips curve. "An-

other few minutes of that, and you'd have killed me.''
Making the effort, she found the energy to stroke a
hand through his hair. "Thank you."

"Anytime." He let out a long, heartfelt sigh before
he pressed a kiss to her throat. "Of course, I don't
know how I'm ever going to work in here again."
Moaning a little, he rolled off her. "I'll have a client
sitting in the chair while I go over the details of his
case, and I'll get a flash of you leaning naked against
the desk."

She laughed, then discovered she really did have to
crawl. Her legs might never support her again. "He'll
get suspicious when you get a stupid grin on your
face."

"And start drooling." Spent, Jared reached for his
shirt. He angled his head to get a glimpse of her tattoo.
"Hell of a way to kick off the new color scheme."

"Didn't you ever kick off the old one?"

He had to concentrate on remembering how to button his shirt, so it took him a minute. The snort of
laughter came first. "You mean me and Barbara? I'm
not sure she ever unbuttoned her double-breasted blazer
in here. Not her style."

In her underwear, Savannah turned to study him.
"You *were* married to her, right?"

"That's what it said on the license."

"Why?"

"It has to say that. It's the law."

"Why were you married to her?"

"We had a lot in common. I thought." He shrugged
it off. "We both wanted to establish ourselves in our

respective professions, knew a lot of the same people, attended a lot of the same functions.''

It disturbed him still how empty it sounded when he pulled things apart and looked at all the pieces. ''She was a sensible, reasonable and sophisticated woman. That's what I wanted—or thought I did. A kind of contrast to the hotheaded-troublemaker image I'd carved out for myself when I was younger.''

''You wanted dignity.'' Still sitting on the floor, Savannah buttoned her shirt.

''That's accurate enough. It seemed important then.''

''It's still important. It always is.'' Though she realized it would sound a bit foolish while she tugged herself into her jeans, she said it anyway. ''I always wanted it, too. Not in the double-breasted-suit sort of way. Not *my* style. Just in the way people look at you, what they see when they do.''

She pulled on a shoe. ''That's why I like living here. I can start fresh.''

''We all look back.'' He walked over to the coatrack for his tie. ''It's human nature.''

''I don't.'' She said it almost fiercely as she pulled on the second shoe. ''Not anymore.''

He gave his full attention to the tying of his tie. ''There's no one? Of all the people you've known, the people who've touched you?''

She started to answer lightly, but then it struck her. He didn't mean people. He meant men. And she remembered what he had said as he made love to her, made her churn and shiver.

The way no one ever has.

And so, she thought, hurt, that was the crux of it. "You mean lovers."

"You said lovers. I said people."

"I know what you said, Jared. No, there's no one who was important enough to look back to."

Bryan's father. He nearly said it, nearly asked, but it stuck in his throat. In his pride. "You're angry," he stated, noting the glint in her eye.

"It just crossed my mind that what happened here was a kind of demonstration. A chest-beating male sort of thing, to illustrate that you're better than anyone I might have had before."

Now his own eyes glinted. "That's a remarkably stupid observation."

"Don't tell me I'm stupid." She snapped it out, then managed to pull herself back under control. Don't let it matter, she reminded herself. Don't let it sting. "You can relax, Jared, you proved your point. You're an extraordinary lover. Right over the top." She sauntered over to brush a hand over his tensed jaw. "I enjoyed every minute of it. But now I don't have time to hang your paintings. I've got some errands to run before I head back home."

He put a hand on her arm. He understood her well enough now to know that careless arrogance was one of her ways of covering anger. "I think we have something to talk about."

"It'll have to wait." Reaching behind him, she flipped open the lock. "We've eaten up your lunch hour, and I imagine Sissy'll be breezing back any minute.'' She gave him a light, careless kiss before shaking her arm free.

"We have something to talk about," he repeated.

"Fine. You get it all worked out in your head, and we'll talk about it tonight." Knowing she was goading him, she curved her lips in a cocky smile. "Thanks for the demonstration, MacKade. It was memorable."

She wouldn't have gotten two feet if Sissy hadn't rushed in below. "Hey, Savannah," she called up cheerfully. "The way it's coming down out there, you're going to want to trade your car in for an ark."

"Then I'd better get moving," Savannah said, and walked down the stairs without looking back.

Chapter 11

He bought flowers. Jared wasn't sure whether he was apologizing or he'd simply gotten into the habit of picking them up once or twice a week because Savannah always looked so surprised and pleased when he walked in with a bouquet.

He didn't like to think the clutch of late-spring blooms was an apology, because he didn't think he'd been completely wrong. Technically, he hadn't asked, he'd only intimated a question. And why the hell shouldn't he ask?

He wanted to know more about her, the who and what and why of her past. Not just the pieces she let drop from time to time, but the whole picture.

Of course, his timing and delivery had been poor. He could admit that. He could even admit that it had nipped at his temper that she'd seen through him so easily. But the bottom line was, he had a right to know. They were going to have a calm, reasonable talk about just that.

Perhaps because he was so primed, so ready, he found himself simmering when he drove up the lane and saw that her car was gone.

Where the hell was she? It was after six. He stood by his car, frowning, looking over the land. The rain had left the tumbling flowers on the bank vivid and wet. The azaleas she'd planted had lost most of their blossoms, but their leaves were a rich and glossy green.

He remembered the first day he'd seen her, digging in the earth, with pots of flowers surrounding her and the rocky, neglected bank waiting.

She'd done something here, he thought. Those roots she'd talked about were still shallow, but she'd dug them in. He needed to believe that she had made that commitment, and found comfort in the green of the grass she preferred to mow herself, in the mixed colors of the blooms she tended religiously, in the woods beyond that they both seemed to share on such a deep, personal level.

He saw Bryan's bike standing beside the walkway, a bright orange Frisbee™ that had ended its flight in the middle of the sloping lawn, a wheelbarrow full of mulch parked beside the porch.

Details, he mused, little details that made a home.

And it hit him suddenly and forcefully that he wanted, needed, it to be his home. Not just a place where he left a few of his things so that it was convenient to spend the night. Home.

He didn't want Savannah to be just the woman he loved and made love with. He'd failed at marriage once, and had been sure, so sure, that he would never put himself in the position where he could fail at something so personal and public again. Hadn't he told himself he would be content to drift along in this relationship?

But he'd been lying to himself almost from the beginning, because he hadn't been content and didn't want to drift. So he poked at her, prodded, subtly and not so subtly, for those answers to who she was, where she'd been. While part of him, the part that was pride and heart, was wounded every time she didn't simply volunteer the answers.

He wanted her to confide in him, to share with him every part of her that had been, that was, that would be. He needed her to turn to him when she was troubled or sad, or when she was happy.

He wanted, Jared realized, drawing a slow, steady breath. He wanted her to marry him, have children with him, grow old with him.

He started up the walkway, pausing to lay a hand on Bryan's bike. He wanted the boy. That, too, was fresh and revealing news. He didn't want Bryan to be Savannah's son, but their son. Helping Bryan with his homework, boning up on baseball, cheering from the bleachers at a game. Jared realized he'd gotten used to those things, looked forward to them. Looked forward to that quick grin, the shouted greeting.

But it wasn't enough. It didn't make them family.

Love would. He'd grown to love the boy in a very

short time, without even realizing it. Marriage would. Not just the legal contract, Jared reflected. The promise.

He and Barbara had broken that promise, and had proceeded to negate the legal contract without flinching with another. All very clean, very tidy, very civilized.

Wasn't that the core of it? There was nothing very civilized about the way he felt about Savannah or Bryan. He felt protective, proprietary, possessive. They were difficult emotions. Untidy emotions.

Wonderful.

Calmer now that he'd sorted through the problem, and its solution, he went into the house.

There were shoes where there shouldn't be, books and glasses and toys scattered instead of in their proper place. A pair of earrings tossed on a table, a trail of mud that hadn't been quite scraped off on the mat.

It was home.

But where the hell were they?

He'd grown accustomed to finding them there. Bryan in the yard, or poring over his baseball-card collection in his room. The radio should have been blaring, or the TV turned up too loud. She should have been in the kitchen, or in her little studio in the back, or taking one of her cat naps on the sofa.

He went into the kitchen, laid the flowers down on the table. No note. No hastily scrawled explanation tacked to the refrigerator. Frowning, he laid his brief-case beside the flowers. The least she could have done was leave him a note.

They'd agreed to talk, hadn't they? He had reams to

talk about, and she wasn't even here. He looked in her studio. A half glass of watered-down lemonade stood on her worktable near a clever, sly sketch of a flying frog.

Under other circumstances, it would have made him smile.

His mood darkening by the minute, he headed upstairs. Dragging off his tie, he walked into her bedroom. *Her* bedroom, he thought, sizzling. By God, that was going to change. He tossed the tie on the bed, followed it with his suit jacket.

They were going to have a long, serious discussion, he and Savannah. And she was going to listen.

He grumbled to himself as he changed into jeans and hung his suit in the closet amid her clothes. His teeth were set. One of the first things they were going to do was add another closet. A man deserved his own damn closet.

In fact, they were going to add on another bedroom, one big enough for his things, as well as hers. And another bathroom, while they were at it, because they were going to have more children.

And an office. She wasn't the only one who needed work space.

Then he was going to build Bryan a tree house. The kid should have a tree house.

They needed a garden shed for her tools, and the lane needed work. Well, he would see to those things. He'd see to them because... He was going insane, Jared admitted, and sat down on the edge of the bed.

He hadn't even told her they were getting married, and he already he was adding on to the house.

What was he getting so worked up about? Why was he so angry with her, with himself? Panic, he wondered. Little licks of fear. Worry that when he mentioned marriage, she would laugh and tell him that wasn't the kind of thing that interested her.

Dragging his hands through his hair, he rose. She was going to have to get interested, he decided. And fast.

He might have calmed again, might have gone reasonably downstairs and started dinner for the three of them. He might have done that. It was in his mind when he noticed the box on her dresser.

He caught the glint of belt buckles. Big, showy buckles. Rodeo. He lifted one and studied the embossed horse and rider. Her father's things. She'd received her father's assets. And she hadn't told him.

There wasn't much. The prizes Jim Morningstar had won years before, bits and pieces of a man who had obviously traveled light and without too much sentiment. There was a larger box beside the dresser. Old, worn boots, a battered hat, a few articles of clothing that were still folded, as if she hadn't touched them.

He saw the letter from his colleague in Oklahoma, the standard cover for the dispensation of effects, the itemized list, the offer to assist if there were any questions.

Jared shifted it aside. And found the photographs.

Most were crinkled, as if they'd been carelessly shoved in drawers, badly packed in a move. He saw

Jim Morningstar for the first time. An impressive candid shot of a man, face hard and set, eyes narrowed as he sat a horse in a high, narrow stall.

The dark coloring, the high cheekbones Savannah had inherited. But there was little else in this tough, leathery face that had been passed to her, unless it was the set of that chin, he mused. The set that warned that if life aimed a fist, this one would meet it straight on.

He found another, poorly framed, of the same man standing beside a young Savannah. Jared's lips curved as he studied her. She was maybe thirteen, fourteen, he thought. Tall, her body, tucked into jeans and a plaid shirt, already curving, her hair raining out of a cowboy hat.

She looked straight at the camera, her lips hinting at that knowing woman's smile she'd have in later life. She stood hip-shot, a certain arrogance in the stance. One of her hands rested lightly on her father's shoulder. Jim Morningstar had his arms folded over his chest. He didn't touch his daughter.

There was another of Savannah, a still younger Savannah, astride a horse. It was a classic pose, the buckskin-colored horse rearing up, the rider with her hat swept off her head and lifted high in one hand.

She looked, Jared thought, as if she would dare anything.

There were more of Morningstar with other men—grinning, leather-faced men in hats and boots and denim. Backgrounds of corrals, stables, horses. Always horses.

It played through his mind that they might clear

space for a paddock, use the barn at the farm and get a horse or two. Savannah obviously loved them, and Bryan might—

Every thought leaked out of his head as he stared at the last photo.

Yes, she would have been about sixteen, though her body was fully a woman's, clad in a snug T-shirt tucked into tight jeans. Yet the face had a softness, a slight fullness that announced that the girl hadn't quite finished becoming a woman yet. She was laughing. The camera had frozen her in that full-throated moment. He could almost hear it.

She was wrapped around a man. And the man was wrapped around her. Their arms were entwined, their faces were laughing at the camera. The man's hat was pushed back on his head, revealing curls of shaggy blond hair. He was tanned, lean, tall. His eyes would have been blue, or perhaps green. It was hard to tell from the snapshot. But they were light, the corners crinkled with the smile.

The mouth that was cocked crookedly in that smile had been passed on to Bryan.

This was Bryan's father.

Jared felt his anger begin to pulse. This was the man. A man, he repeated in his head, not a boy. The face was undeniably handsome, even striking, but it didn't belong to a teenager. This man had seduced a sixteen-year-old girl, then abandoned her. And nothing had been done.

Morningstar had kept the photo. Because, Jared thought with a tight-lipped snarl, he'd known.

And nothing had been done.

Savannah watched him from the doorway. Her emotions had been on a roller coaster all day. This looked like one more dip.

She'd wanted to forget the edginess, the anger she'd felt when she left Jared's office. She'd hoped to come home, find him here and share with him her small triumph in selling Howard Beels three paintings.

With a very good possibility of more.

She and Bryan had cackled about it all the way home. Over Howard himself and the way he'd hemmed and hawed over what she considered a highly inflated asking price, and settled on an amount that had been considerably more than she'd anticipated.

She'd even stopped off and bought a bottle of champagne so that she and Jared could celebrate. So that she could celebrate with him the fact that her long-buried wish of painting for a living was working its way to the surface.

But she could see there would be no celebration now. Not with that look on Jared's face as he studied what her father had left her. She didn't know where his anger came from. But she had a feeling she was going to find out.

The hell with it, she thought, and pushed away from the door jamb. Let's get it over with.

"Not much of an estate, huh?" She waited until his head came up, until his gaze shifted to hers. The fury in them almost buckled her knees. "I imagine most of your clients have a bit more to deal with."

He knew how to take things one step at a time, to

start at one point and work his way to the heart. "When did you get the shipment?"

"A week or two ago." She shrugged, then walked over to the window to look down. "Bry's down in the yard. We picked up the kittens. He's in heaven."

Jared MacKade also knew how to stay on a point. "A week or two. You didn't mention it."

"What was to mention? I took out the check and gave it to that broker you recommended. I didn't feel like dealing with the rest, so I put it aside until this morning. I guess I'll put the buckles away for Bryan. He might want them one day. The clothes'll go to charity, I suppose."

"Why didn't you tell me?"

"Why should I have?" She turned back, vaguely annoyed, vaguely curious. "It's not a big deal. No long-lost lottery tickets or pouch of gold dust. Just some old clothes, older boots, and papers."

"And photographs."

"Yeah, a few. He wasn't big on souvenirs. There's one of him in the chute I like. It shows who he was, always gearing up for the next ride. I figured Bryan might like to have that, too."

"And this one?" Jared held up the snapshot of Savannah and the cockily smiling cowboy.

She lifted a brow, shook her head. "I don't know how I got into those jeans. Look, I'm going to throw some burgers on the grill."

When Jared shifted into her path, she was genuinely surprised. She tilted her head, studied him. And waited. "Have you shown this to Bryan?"

"No."

"Do you intend to?"

"No. I don't think he cares what his mother looked like at sixteen."

"He would care what his father looked like."

She could almost feel her blood slow, go sluggish. "He doesn't have a father."

"Damn it, Savannah, are you going to tell me this isn't Bryan's father?"

"I'm going to tell you that isn't Bryan's father. A couple of rolls in the hay doesn't make a man a father."

"Don't slice words with me."

"It's a very important distinction in my book, Lawyer MacKade. And since this seems to be a cross-examination, I'll make it clear and easy. I had sex with the man in the picture you're holding. I got pregnant. End of story."

"The hell it is." Furious, he slapped the picture down on the dresser. "Your father knew. He wouldn't have kept this, otherwise."

"Yeah. That occurred to me when I found it." And the hurt had come with it, but it had been slight and easily dispatched. "So what?"

"So why wasn't anything done? This isn't a kid we're talking about. He had to be over twenty-one."

"I think he was twenty-four. Maybe twenty-five. It's hard to remember."

"And you were a minor. He should have been prosecuted—after your father broke his neck."

Savannah took a deep breath. "In the first place, my

father knew me. He knew that if I'd slept with some-one, it was my choice. I was a minor, technically, but I knew exactly what I was doing. It wasn't a mistake or an accident. I wasn't forced. And I don't appreciate you casting blame.''

''Of course there's blame,'' Jared shot back. ''That son of a bitch had no right touching a girl your age, then taking off when there were consequences.''

Her eyes lit. ''Bryan is not a consequence.''

''You know damn well that's not what I meant.'' Pulling both hands through his hair, he paced away. ''There's no going back and righting wrongs at this point. I want to know what you intend to do now.''

''I intend to cook hamburgers. You're welcome to stay, or you're welcome to go.''

''Don't take that attitude with me.''

''It's the attitude I've got.'' Then she sighed. ''Jared, why are you gnawing at this thing? I slept with a man ten years ago. I forgot him. He forgot me.'' To illus-trate, she picked up the photo and dropped it carelessly in the wastebasket beside the dresser. ''That's that.''

''Just that simple?'' It was that, Jared realized. Ex-actly that that gnawed at him. ''He didn't mean any-thing to you?''

''That's right.''

''You conceived a child with him, Savannah. That boy who's down in the yard, playing with his kittens. How can you just dismiss that?''

Temper streaked through her. ''You'd prefer a dif-ferent story, wouldn't you, Jared? A different story you could live with. One about the poor, innocent, neglected girl looking for love, seduced by an older man, betrayed, abandoned.''

''Isn't that what happened?''

''You don't know who I was, what I was, or what I wanted. You don't want to know, not really. Because when you do, when you hear it, it'll stick in your craw. How many men has she been with? Can I believe her when she tells me she didn't sell herself? Even her own father didn't stand by her, so what does that tell me? Now that I look back, I remember she was ready to hit the sheets with me from the get-go. What kind of a woman have I got myself tangled up with? Isn't that what you're wondering, Jared?''

''I'm wondering why there are so many things you don't tell me. Why you shrug off ten years of your life and how they affected you. And, yes, I'm wondering what kind of woman you are.''

She threw her head back. ''Figure it out.'' She started to storm out, then came up hard, toe-to-toe with him. ''Keep out of my way.''

''I'm in your way, and you're in mine. And it's long past time to settle this. You say you love me, but you pull back every time I touch a nerve, every time I want a clear picture of what brought you to this point in your life.''

''I brought me here. That's all you need to know.''

''It's not all I need to know. You can't build a future without drawing on the past.''

''I can. I have. If you can't, Jared, it's your problem. You know what you're doing?'' She tossed the question at him. "You're harping on a face in a photograph. You're insulted by it, threatened by it."

"That's ridiculous."

"Is it? It's all right for you to have been married before, to have had other women in your life. I haven't asked you how many or who or why, have I? It's all right for you to have been wild and reckless, to have sauntered around town with your brothers, looking for trouble or making it. That's just dandy. Boys will be boys. But with me, it's different. The problem is, you got tangled up with me before you thought it through. Now you want to shift the pieces around, see if you can make me into more of what seems suitable to the man you are now."

"You're putting words in my mouth. And you're wrong."

"I say I'm right. And I say the hell with you, MacKade. The hell with you. You want a victim, or you want a flower, or someone who looks just right at some fund-raiser or professional event. You've come to the wrong place. I don't read Kafka."

"What in the sweet hell are you talking about?"

"I'm talking about reality. The reality is, I don't need this kind of grief from you."

His eyes narrowed. "It's not just about what you need. Not anymore. That's reality, Savannah. I don't have to justify wanting to know how you could toss out that photograph, or dismiss your father's things and not even tell me you had them. I don't have to justify asking you what you want from yourself, from me. From us. Or telling you what I want, what I expect and intend to have. That's everything. Everything or nothing.''

''Down to ultimatums, are we?''

''Looks that way. Think about it,'' he suggested, and strode furiously out.

Steaming, she stood where she was. She listened to the door slam below. It took every ounce of willpower she had not to race to the window, to watch him. Maybe to call him back. Minutes later, she heard the sound of his car.

So, that was that, Savannah thought. All or nothing. He had a nerve, demanding she give him all, leave herself nothing to fall back on. Nothing to cushion a fall. She'd been there once, and the bruises had plagued her for years. By God, she wasn't going back.

Steadying herself, she went downstairs. She ignored the flowers on the table, the champagne chilling in the refrigerator. Maybe she'd drink it herself later, she mused as she took out some hamburger. Maybe she'd drink the whole damn bottle and get herself a nice fizzy buzz. It would be better than thinking, better than hurting. Better even than this simmering anger that was still hot in her blood.

But when the door slammed and she looked around she hated herself for the stab of disappointment when she realized it was her son.

''Is Jared mad at you?''

''Why?''

''I could tell.'' Uneasy, Bryan sat down, propped his elbows on the table. ''He stopped to look at the kittens and stuff, but he wasn't paying attention. And he said he couldn't stay.''

''I guess he's mad at me.''

''Are you mad at him, too?''

''Yeah.'' Slapping patties together was a fine way to release a little violence. ''Pretty mad.''

''Does that mean you're not stuck on him anymore?''

She looked over, and her own temper cleared enough that she could see the worry in Bryan's eyes. ''What are you getting at, Bry?''

He moved his shoulders, kicked his feet. ''Well, you've never been stuck on anybody before. He's mostly always here, and he brings you flowers and hangs around with me. You kiss each other and stuff.''

''That's true.''

''Well, Con and I thought maybe you were going to get, like, married.''

A quick arrow shot straight into her heart. ''Oh.''

''I thought it would be kind of cool, you know, because Jared's cool.''

She put the patties aside. To give herself time, she ran water, washed her hands and dried them thoroughly. All the while, all she could think was, what had she done to her little boy?

''Bry, you know that people kiss each other all the time without getting married. You're smart enough to know that adults have relationships, close relationships, without getting married, either.''

''Yeah, but if they're really stuck on each other, they do, right?''

"Sometimes." She skirted the table to lay a hand on his shoulder. "But it's not always enough to love someone."

"How come?"

"Because…" Where was the answer? "Because people are complicated. Anyway, Jared's mad at me, not at you. You can still be pals."

"I guess."

"You'd better go out and make sure those kittens keep out of trouble. I'm going to fire up the grill."

"Okay." He dragged his feet a little as he started toward the door. "I was thinking if you got married, he'd be sort of like…"

"Sort of like what?" she asked.

"Sort of like my father." Bryan moved his shoulders again, in a gesture so very much like her own when she blocked off hurt, another shaft of pain shot through her. "I just thought it would be cool."

Chapter 12

Bryan's wistful statement dragged at her mind and spirits all through the evening. To make it up to him for a disappointment she felt unable to control, she made the casual meal into their own private celebration.

All the soda he could drink, french fries made from scratch, wild, involved and ridiculous plans on how they would spend the fortune they would amass from selling her paintings.

Trips to Disney World weren't enough, they decided. They would *own* Disney World. Box seats at ball games? For pikers. They would purchase the Baltimore Orioles—and Bryan would, naturally, play at short.

Savannah kept up the game until she was reasonably sure both of them had forgotten that what Bryan really wanted was Jared.

Then she spent the night staring at the ceiling, thinking of all the wonderful, hideous ways to pay Jared MacKade back for putting a dent in her boy's heart.

Hers wasn't all that important. She knew how to hammer it out. Time and work and the home she'd continue to make would all help. She didn't need a man to make her whole. Never had. She would see to it that her son never felt the lack of a father. But she would punish Jared for raising Bryan's hopes.

The bastard had made himself part of their lives. Flowers, damn him. Playing catch in the yard, taking Bryan over to the farm, awakening her in bed the way no one, damn him again, no one ever had.

Then looking down at her from his lofty lawyer's height. Questioning her morals and her actions and her motives. Making her feel more, then making her feel less, than she'd ever been. Making her question herself.

He wasn't going to get away with it. Without realizing it, she shifted to the center of the bed, so that it wouldn't feel so empty. He couldn't worm his way into their lives, then start making demands. Who was she, where had she been, what did she want? She didn't owe him any answers, and she was going to prove it.

He'd wormed his way in, all right, she thought, scowling at the ceiling. He'd made her feel foolish and inadequate and, for the first time in ten very long years, vulnerable. Now he thought he could worm his way out again because she wasn't just exactly what he preferred in a...

She sneered at the word. In a *wife*.

She hated him for that, really hated him for making

her start to think, start to hope and even plan along those lines, without her even being aware of it. Until Bryan brought it up, she hadn't realized she was dreaming, just a little, about happy-ever-after.

Like the fairy tales she illustrated, with their strong and passionate princes.

It was embarrassing. It was humiliating. A woman like her, a woman who had managed through sheer will and grit to shrug off the bruises life handed out, to be brought this low by a man.

She'd survived alone. She'd gone hungry, worked until she was dizzy with fatigue, had taken jobs that scraped at her pride. She'd been turned out by her own father when she needed him most.

And none of that, not one of the painful or difficult experiences in her life, had ever left her as low as this.

And none of that, she had made certain, had ever brought Bryan one moment's sadness.

She took a deep breath, then another. She would show Jared MacKade just what kind of woman she was. The kind of woman who didn't need him.

Jared decided brooding on the front porch with a beer on a Saturday afternoon wasn't such a bad thing. He was almost enjoying it. It was a beautiful day, and he was pleasantly fatigued from the morning's work.

His brothers were with him, and it was a good feeling, to have all of them there. Just passing an hour, he mused, at home. Watching the grass grow and the dogs race over it.

Maybe, just maybe, in a little while, he'd stroll on

over to the cabin. He figured he'd given her time enough to stew, to calm down and see reason.

He'd given himself almost enough time, as well. He was almost ready, not quite but almost ready, to admit he'd been somewhat heavy-handed. Maybe just the slightest bit unreasonable.

Still, she'd been ridiculous. Accusing him of being threatened by a photograph, of wanting a different kind of woman. Of not being satisfied with her because she didn't read Kafka.

God knew where she'd come up with that.

He didn't appreciate the comparison of her life with his, either. Made him sound like a narrow-minded sexist. Which he certainly was not.

It was different, that was all.

"Talking to himself," Devin commented as he whittled a piece of wood.

"Been doing it since he got here yesterday." Shane yawned and kicked back in his chair. "You ask me, Savannah kicked his butt out."

That, and Rafe's snorting laugh, snagged Jared's attention. "She did not. I left to make a point."

"Yeah." Rafe winked at Devin. "What point was that?"

Eyes narrowed, Jared tipped back his beer. "That she'd better start seeing things the way they are."

This statement was greeted by hoots.

"His way," Rafe pointed out. "It always has to be his way or no way."

"Bull." Unoffended, Jared crossed his ankles. "It just has to be the right way."

From his perch on the top step, Devin shifted, leaned his back against the post. "So, what was she doing wrong?"

"She holds back. I get a call from Howard Beels this morning, thanking me for introducing them. Seems she went over there yesterday and he bought three of her paintings." Just thinking of it had him simmering again. "Does she tell me? No. What kind of relationship is that? I don't get anything out of her without a direct question, and then she only answers half the time."

Amused, Shane stretched his arms. "And I just bet you've been full of questions, too. What happened then? What did you do? What chain of events led to that? And where were you on the night in question?"

Jared's punch would have been stronger if Shane hadn't been a full arm's length away. "I don't interrogate her. I ask. I want to know about her. A man has a right to know the woman he's going to marry."

Rafe choked on a gulp of beer. "When did that happen?"

"I knew it." With a heavy sigh, Shane flipped the top of the cooler and got out a beer for himself. "I just knew it."

Eyes bland, Devin studied Jared. "You asked Savannah to marry you?"

"No. I didn't get a chance to tell her—"

"Tell her." Now Devin grinned. "Typical."

"You might try to see my side of it," Jared grumbled. "I realized that's what I want. I was thinking about it, going over it, and then I see she's gotten the effects from her father. She hadn't told me it had come. There was a photograph of her with Bryan's father.''

''Hmm...'' Rafe's comment went for all of them.

''When I asked her about it, she got defensive.''

''Hostile witness,'' Shane murmured, and earned a glare.

''She tossed it out,'' Jared continued. ''Like it meant nothing.''

''Maybe that's just what it meant,'' Devin put in.

''Look, the bastard got her pregnant, then abandoned her. Her father kicks her out. She's sixteen, for God's sake. It means something. But she won't come out with it. She won't tell me. What she does is start accusing me of idiotic things. Then she says, get this, she says that I figure it was all right for me to sow wild oats or whatever, to get in trouble and kick some butt. But I expect her to be untouched or a victim, or words to that effect. It's insulting.''

Rafe regarded the lip of his beer bottle. ''It's true.''

''The hell it is.''

''Sorry, bro. You pass the bar, buy yourself a couple of lawyer suits—''

''Do you want me to break your nose again?''

''In a minute. Anyway, after a while you decide it's time to get married, so you pick out an ice queen, one with no baggage, no secrets, no noticeable flaws. You know why?''

Temper percolating, Jared eyed him. ''Why don't you tell me?''

''Because the image worked for you. It didn't take you long to realize the woman didn't, because you're pretty sharp most of the time. Now, Savannah, there's a woman with baggage, some secrets, a few flaws. The image is a little hard to tuck into a box, but the woman works.''

He wanted to argue, to debate, to tear the hypothesis to shreds. And discovered he couldn't. So he swore instead.

''Kafka,'' he muttered as a light dawned. ''Barbara read Kafka.''

''Doesn't surprise me,'' Rafe said cheerfully.

Trying it all from a new angle, Jared took out a cigar. ''The argument is still valid that if two people want to build a future together, they have to trust each other enough to share the past. I want the boy, too,'' he said, blowing out a stream of smoke.

''Are you going to let a photograph stop you?'' Devin asked quietly.

''No. I'm not going to let anything stop me.''

''Two down,'' Shane complained. ''You know, women start getting ideas when your brothers get married.''

''Live with it,'' Jared told him.

All of them glanced over at the sound of a car coming up the lane, fast.

So she'd come to her senses, he decided, proud of the fact that he'd given her the night to think it over. Now she was here, sorry she'd lost her temper, he imagined. Ready to sit down and discuss it all reasonably.

He rose, moved over to lean on the post opposite Devin. He'd be big enough to apologize, as well, he thought. And to explain himself more coherently. He was sure that years from now they'd laugh over the whole foolish mess.

He lifted the cigar to his lips, ready to welcome her, when she squealed to a halt at the end of the lane.

The woman who unfolded herself from the car didn't look conciliatory. She looked wild, glowing and stunning.

"Oh-oh" was all Shane said, but he rolled his eyes merrily at Rafe.

She didn't speak, but stood with her hands on her hips, scanning the four men. An audience, she thought. Even better. Didn't they all look smug and pleased with themselves just for being men?

She swaggered around to the trunk, unlocked it. The box came first. The dogs jumped and circled around her in excited greeting as she carried it to the side of the car. With a wide smile she overturned it. Several articles of clothing tumbled out. Suits, ties, shirts, socks. Still smiling, she gave the heap a couple of good solid kicks to spread things out.

Delighted, the dogs trampled over the clothes, sniffing and barking. Fred proved his recognition of Jared's scent by lifting his leg.

On the porch, four men watched in silence, with varying degrees of emotion.

Ah, Jared's favorite tie was snagged on her foot, she discovered. Eyes on his, she ground her heel into it.

Rafe grinned like a loon. Shane let out one full belly laugh. Devin watched in rapt admiration.

Jared just watched.

She wasn't finished. Not by a long shot. Back to the trunk she pulled out a leather-bound address book he'd left on the nightstand. Her smile cool, she held it open as if to demonstrate. Then tore the pages out and let them flutter onto the heap of the now dirty, dog-haired clothes.

She took out his shoes. The good Italian leather first. Holding them down for Ethel to sniff, Savannah let the first one fly, then the second, and the dogs gave grateful chase. Tennis shoes went next. Two pairs, one of which, she was delighted to note, was only two weeks old.

She hoped the dogs chewed them to shreds.

There was shaving gear to deal with. She pitched a piece here, a piece there, drawing out the event until Shane simply rolled out of his chair onto the deck of the porch, helpless with laughter.

But she'd saved the coup de grace. The wine.

There had only been one bottle open, but she'd tossed that before she left. She uncorked all three, all fine vintages, expensively French. Chin up, eyes challenging, she walked back to what was left of his clothes. She tilted her head first, darkly pleased when his eyes went to green slits. With a veteran waitress's skill, Savannah poured them out, all at once over his best suit.

Done, she let the bottles fall with a clink on the grass. Still without having uttered a word, she strolled back to the car, slid behind the wheel. With a final smile, an arrogant salute, she backed up, swung around and drove down the lane.

Other than Shane's helpless laughter, there wasn't a sound until Devin finally cleared his throat. He studied the mess on the lawn carefully, even patted Fred's head when the dog devotedly brought him one of Jared's mauled shoes.

"Well," he said at length. "I'd say she made her point, too."

"She's a spooky woman," Shane managed, mopping his streaming eyes. "I think I'm in love with her."

Because he knew what it was like to be at the mercy of his own heart, Rafe rose and slapped a hand on Jared's shoulder. "You know, Jare, you got two choices."

He was all but quivering with fury. "Which are?"

"Run like hell, or go get her. I know which one I'd choose."

Jared didn't do anything for a couple of hours. He knew himself well enough to understand that his temper could be dangerous. He worked off some steam, and worked up a sweat in the barn before washing up.

When he finally headed out, his anger was still there, but strapped in. She figured she was dumping him, he thought, like she'd dumped his things.

But she was going to figure again.

"Hey, Jare." From the side yard where he was playing tug-of-war with the dogs over one of Jared's shoes, Shane sent up a shout. "Tell Savannah we really enjoyed the show, okay?"

"Remind me to kick your butt later."

She'd humiliated him, he fumed. In front of his

brothers. Seeking control, he jammed his hands into his pockets and veered toward the woods. Not to mention that she'd ruined a good portion of his wardrobe.

Thought she was damn clever, he was sure. He imagined she'd sat up half the night planning it all out. If he hadn't been the brunt of it, he'd have admired her finesse. The sheer nerve of it.

But he had been the one who took the brunt of it.

The woods closed around him, but he didn't experience the usual sense of peace and companionship. His mind was on the other side of them, on Savannah. And, he thought with relish, on revenge. Let's see how she liked it when he went into her closet and—

He stopped himself, took another deep breath. Look what the woman had brought him to. He was actually considering vandalizing her belongings in some sort of juvenile one-upmanship.

Wasn't going to happen. He would gain revenge by showing her that, despite her outrageous behavior, he was a reasonable man. To make certain he would be, Jared detoured off the path and sat down on the rocks.

He couldn't feel them—the ghosts that haunted this place with their sorrows and hopes and fears. Perhaps, he thought, because for the first time in a long time he was plagued with too many of his own.

He'd known loss. The jarring, devastating loss of his parents. He'd lived with that, because he didn't have a choice, and because, he thought, there were so many good, solid, important memories to draw on for comfort.

And, of course, he'd always had his brothers.

He'd known sorrow. He had been struck with it when he finally admitted his marriage had been a mistake. Not a disaster. Somehow that would have been better, less pale, than a simple, easily rectifiable mistake.

Hope, of course. His life had been full of it, a gift from his parents, from his roots. Wherever there was hope there was fear, the price to be paid for the sweetness.

He'd known all those emotions, used them or overcome them. But until Savannah, he'd never known anything so sharp, so vital. So frightening.

The wind changed as he sat there, picked up, where it had been calm before. It fluttered the trees, whispered through the leaves that filtered sunlight. And chilled.

They came here. He sat very still as he thought of it. The two boys, wearing different colors, came here. Each of them wanted only to find home again. To escape from the madness into the recognizable. The familiar. To find the sense of it all again, the meaning of it. The continuity of family, of people who knew and loved them. Accepted them.

Maybe, in some odd way, that was what they'd fought for.

For home.

What an idiot he'd been, Jared realized, and closed his eyes as the wind scooped up dead leaves and swirled them around him. The two boys had never had a chance once they chose their path. But he had a chance. The same fate that had doomed those two soldiers so long ago had placed Savannah and Bryan right in front of him.

Instead of accepting, he'd questioned. Instead of rejoicing, he'd doubted.

Because what frightened him most was this blinding love. A love that demanded he protect, defend, treasure. And he couldn't protect the girl she had been, defend that girl against the cruel and thoughtless blows of life when no one else would help. She'd had to face it alone, without him. And, if necessary, she still could.

That left him feeling impotent, and scorched his pride.

So, he was an idiot. But she wasn't going to get rid of him easily.

He heard a rustling, and when he opened his eyes he wouldn't have been surprised to see a young Confederate soldier, bayonet ready, fear bright as the sun in his eyes, step off the path.

Instead, he saw Bryan, head down, feet scuffling leaves. He would have laughed at his overactive imagination if the boy's pose hadn't been one of such abject dejection.

"Hey, Ace, how's it going?"

Bryan's head came up. The smile, a bit more cautious than Jared was used to, fluttered around his mouth. "Hi. Just out walking. Mom's in a mood."

"I know." In an unspoken invitation, Jared patted the rock beside him. "She's pretty steamed at me."

"She said you were steamed at her, too."

"I guess I was." Instinctively Jared draped an arm

over Bryan's shoulders when the boy settled beside him. "I'm over it. Mostly."

"She's not." Ready for male bonding, Bryan rolled his eyes. "She kicked me out."

"No, kidding? Me too."

The idea of that had Bryan chuckling. He didn't think his mother had told Jared to go play outside, for God's sake. "We can go live at the farm, till she cools off."

"We could," Jared said consideringly. "Or I could go on over and try to smooth things out."

"Can you?"

Jared looked down, and for the first time saw the worry in the boy's eyes. "She's not really mad at you, Bry. She's mad at me."

"Yeah, I know. Can you make her not mad at you anymore?"

"I hope so. When you tick her off, does she stay that way long?"

"Nah. She can't, 'cause..." There was no way to explain it. "She just can't. But she's never let a guy hang around like you, so maybe she can stay mad at you."

"She's never..." He stopped himself. It was wrong to ask the child. "Maybe you should give me some pointers."

"Well." Bryan pursed his lips as he thought about it. "She really digs the flowers you bring her. No one ever did that before, except once I brought her some little ones for her birthday. She got all mushy about it."

"No one ever brought her flowers," Jared murmured. He wasn't just an idiot. He was a champion idiot.

"Nuh-uh," Bryan continued, warming up. "No one ever took us out to ball games or for pizza, and she likes that, too."

This time he could ask, because it was for the boy. "No one ever took you to ball games or for pizza?"

"Nah. I mean, Mom and me went, sure, but not with a guy who like set it up and stuff." Bryan was thinking that over, how much he liked it, when inspiration struck. "Oh, yeah. And when you're going to take her out, like on a date, she sings in the shower. She went out on dates before and all, but she never sang when she was getting ready. So maybe you should take her on a date. Girls like that stuff."

Jared determined there were going to be lots of ball games, lots of pizza, lots of dates and lots of flowers in Savannah and Bryan's future. "Yeah, they do."

"Have you got any love words?"

"Excuse me?"

"Like in the movies," Bryan explained. "You know how the woman gets all moon-eyed when the guy says love words. Only the guy has to be kind of moon-eyed, too, to make it work. She might like that."

"She might."

Bryan sighed at the thought. "It's probably embarrassing."

"Not if you mean them. Here's the thing, Bryan." Jared scooted away just enough that he could face the boy fully. "I figure I ought to run this by you, since you've been the man of the house for so long. I'm in love with your mother.''

As his stomach clutched and jittered, Bryan lowered his gaze. "I kind of figured you were stuck on her."

"No, I'm in love with her. Moon-eyed. I'm going to ask her to marry me."

Bryan's gaze whipped back up, and this time it held steady and searching. "For real?"

"For very real. How does that fly with you?"

He wasn't ready to commit. Though he liked the strong weight of the arm on his shoulders, his stomach was still jumping. "Would you, like, live with us?"

"Not like. I would live with you, and you'd live with me. But there's a catch."

That was what he'd been afraid of. He braced himself, kept his eyes level. "Yeah? What?"

"I'm going to ask you to take my name, Bryan. And to take me on, as your father. I don't just want your mother, you see. I want both of you, so you both have to want me."

There was an odd pressure on his chest, as if someone had just sat on him. "You want to be my father?"

"Yes, very much. I know you've gotten along just fine without one up till now, and maybe I need you more than you need me, but I think I'd be good at it."

Bryan's eyes goggled. "You need to be my father?"

"I do," Jared murmured, realized he'd rarely spoken truer words. "I really do."

"I'd be Bryan MacKade?"

"That's the deal."

While he hesitated, Jared's universe simply ground

to a halt. If the boy rejected him, he knew, it would cut straight to his heart.

But Bryan didn't know for sure how things were done between men. He knew what to do when his mother offered him something wonderful, something he'd hardly dared to dream of but had wished for hard, really hard, at night. So, in the end, that was what he did.

Jared found his arms full of boy.

The breath Jared had been holding whistled out in almost painful relief. Have a cigar, he thought giddily, you've got yourself a son.

"This is so cool," Bryan said, his voice muffled against Jared's chest. "I thought maybe you didn't want somebody else's kid."

Gently, for he suddenly felt very gentle, Jared cupped the boy's chin and lifted it. "You won't be somebody else's. We'd make it legal, but that's just a paper. What really counts is what's between you and me."

"I'll be Bryan MacKade. You'll make her go for it, won't you? You'll talk her into it?"

"Talk is my business."

Furious at herself for snapping at Bryan, Savannah ruined two illustrations before admitting that work was hopeless. She'd been so pleased with herself when she drove away from the MacKade farm. Drunk with the power of causing fury to run hot and cold over Jared's face.

Now she was miserable. Miserably angry, miserably

frustrated. Miserable. She wanted to kick something, but wasn't so far gone she'd take it out on the two kittens napping in the corner of the kitchen.

She wanted to break something, but after a frustrated search through the living room she discovered she didn't have anything valuable enough to be satisfying.

She wanted to scream. But there was no one to scream at.

Until Jared strode through the door.

"You don't have so much as a cuff link left here, MacKade. Everything's in your front yard."

"I noticed. That was quite a show, Savannah."

"I enjoyed it." She crossed her arms, angled her chin. "Sue me."

"I might yet. Why don't we sit down?"

"Why don't you go to hell?" she drawled. "And be sure the door kicks you on your way out."

"Sit down," he repeated, in a tone just firm enough, just reasonable enough, to light a very short fuse.

"Don't you tell me what to do in my own house!" she shouted at him. "Don't you tell me what to do, period. I'm sick to death of you making me feel like some slow-witted backwater bimbo. I don't have a fancy degree—hell, I don't have a high school diploma—but I'm not stupid. I muddled through with my life just fine before you came along. And I'll do just fine after you've gone."

"I know." He acknowledged that with a slight inclination of his head. "That's what's been worrying me. And I don't think you're stupid, Savannah. On the contrary. I don't think I've ever met a smarter woman.''

"Don't play that tune with me. I know what you think of me, and I can live up to most of it."

"I think you can," he said quietly. "I think you can live up to everything I think of you. If you'd sit down, I'll tell you what that is."

"I'll say what I have to say," she tossed back. "You want to know about me, Jared. I'll tell you about me. A parting gift, for all the good times. You sit down," she demanded, and stabbed a finger at a chair.

"All right. But this isn't why I'm here. I don't need to know—"

"You asked for it," she said, interrupting him smartly. "By God, you'll get it. My mother died young, but she left my father and me first. She didn't go far, just across the corral, so to speak. Another smooth-talking cowboy. My father never got over it, never forgave, never gave an inch. Certainly not to me. He never loved me the way I wanted him to. He couldn't. Even if he'd tried, he couldn't. I wasn't a nice polite little girl. I grew up hard, and I liked it. Getting the picture?"

"Savannah, please sit down. You don't have to do this."

Enraged, she stalked over to him. "Listen. I haven't even gotten started, so you just shut up and listen. We didn't have much money. But then, a lot of people don't, and they get by. So did we. He liked to take risks, and he broke a lot of bones. There's more than manure on the rodeo circuit, more than sweat. There's desperation, too. But we got by. Things got a little interesting when I grew breasts. Men liked to stare at them, or sneak a feel. Most of the guys on the circuit had known me since I was a kid, so there wasn't much trouble. I knew when to smile and when to use my elbow. I was never innocent. The way I lived, you'd better grow up knowing.''

He didn't interrupt now, but sat quietly, his eyes unreadable. And her hands were cold.

''I was sixteen when I took that tumble into the hay. I wasn't innocent, but I was a virgin. I knew, but I let myself forget, because... Because he was good-looking, exciting, charming, and, of course, he told me he'd take care of everything. No one had—''

''No one had ever taken care of you before,'' Jared murmured.

''That's right, and I was just young and stupid enough to believe him. But I knew what I was doing, knew the chance I was taking. So I got pregnant. He didn't want me or the baby. Neither did my father. I was just like my mother, cheap, easy. He told me to get out. He might have thought differently the next day. He had a quick temper. But I wasn't cheap, and I wasn't easy, and I wanted the baby. Nobody was going to take that baby away from me. Nobody was going to tell me to be ashamed. They tried. Social services, sheriffs, state cops. Whenever they could catch me, they tried. They wanted me in the system so they could tell me how to act, how to raise my child or, better for everyone, to give him away. But that wasn't better for me, and it wasn't better for Bryan.''

"No. The system's flawed, Savannah. Overburdened. But it tries."

"I didn't need it." She lashed back at him. "I got work, and I worked hard. I waited tables, I served drinks, I cleaned up slop. It didn't matter what kind of work, as long as it paid. He never went hungry. My son never went hungry, and he always had a roof over his head. He always had me. He always knew I loved him and that he came first."

"The way you never did."

"The way I never did. Whatever it took, I was going to give him a decent life. If that meant taking off most of my clothes and dancing for a bunch of howling idiots, what difference did it make? I didn't have an education, I didn't have any skills. If I'd been able to go to art school—" She bit off the thought with a furious shake of her head.

"Is that what you wanted?" He kept his voice neutral, as he would have with a fragile or high-strung witness. "To go to art school."

"It doesn't matter."

"It does matter, Savannah."

"I wanted Bryan. Everything else was secondary. You wanted to know about men. There were a few. Scores less than you've imagined, I'm sure. I wasn't dead, just driven. I never took money from them, but I took food a couple of times, and there's not much difference. And, damn you, I'm not ashamed of it. The only reason I didn't steal was because if I'd been caught, they might have taken Bryan. But I would have stolen if I'd been sure I'd have gotten away with it. I didn't know I could peddle my paintings until one of the girls at the club asked me if I'd do one of her for her boyfriend and offered me a twenty. That's when I got the idea to take Bry to New Orleans.''

She was pacing the room as she spoke, her words rushed and hurried in her effort to get them out and over. But now she stopped, slowed herself. ''That's all there is. At least any other, finer details escape me at the moment.'' She turned to him again, her face calm now, and cold. ''Cross-examine, Counselor?''

''You could have taken other routes.''

''Sure.''

''Safer ones,'' he added. ''Easier ones, for you.''

''Maybe. I didn't want safer ones. I didn't want easier.''

''What did you want, Savannah? What do you want?''

''It doesn't matter.''

''It matters.'' He rose, but didn't go to her. ''It very much matters to me.''

''I want a home. I want a place where people don't look at me like I'm dirt. Where the people who think they're decent don't whisper behind their hands.''

''You have that here.''

''And I'm keeping it.''

He had to sacrifice his pride to ask, but he discovered it wasn't so very difficult. ''Do you want me?''

Taken by surprise, she only stared for a moment. ''That's not the issue.''

''Then maybe I should put it another way.'' He reached into his pocket, drew out the small box he'd tucked in it before he left the farm. After lifting the lid, he held it out. "I came here to give this to you."

The ring was a simple, traditional diamond in an outdated and lovely gold setting. Mesmerized, Savannah gaped at it before slowly stepping back.

"It was my mother's," Jared said, in a voice that betrayed none of the raw nerves inside him. "It went to me, as I'm the oldest. I'm asking you to marry me, Savannah."

She couldn't breathe. Bryan would have recognized the weight that had dropped down on her chest. "Didn't you hear anything I've just told you?"

"Yes, everything, and I'm grateful you told me, even under the circumstances. This way I can tell you I love what you were, what you are and what you will be. You're the only woman I've ever loved, and it's so amazing to find you admire someone as much as you love her."

She stepped back again, as if he were holding a gun instead of a promise. "I don't understand you. I don't understand you at all. Is this some sort of vicious payback because I ruined your clothes?"

"Savannah." His voice was patient now. "Look at me."

She did, and the weight on her chest doubled and pushed tears into her eyes. "Oh, God. You mean it."

"You're going to cry." He almost shuddered with relief. "Thank the Lord. I thought you were going to toss it in my face."

"I thought...you didn't think I was good enough for you."

The smile that had beamed onto his face froze. "Do I deserve that?" he murmured. "Sweet God, I hope not. I'm supposed to be good at making my case, but I've sure as hell screwed this one. I was afraid. It's hard for me to admit that. I'm a MacKade, and we're not supposed to be afraid of anything. I'm the oldest MacKade, and I'm supposed to be able to handle anything. But I couldn't handle how I feel for you. I was afraid of what was behind you, of what you wouldn't say to me. I thought it might explode in my face and ruin what I wanted to build with you and Bryan. And part of me was afraid—terrified, really—that you'd be able to toss me aside the way you did that photograph."

"Bryan." The weight on her chest dissolved like water. "You want Bryan?"

"Am I going to have to get down on my knees here?"

"No, don't." She wiped impatiently at the tears. "I couldn't handle it. I was worried that— It seemed that—"

"I wouldn't want him, because it wasn't me who rolled in the hay with you ten years ago? That wasn't it. Maybe it was part of it for a while. Pride gets in the way. What bothered me most is thinking of you being hurt, of the two of you scraping by. I can't help wanting to go back and save you, to protect you and Bryan. I can't help feeling, well, a little unmanned, really, because I can't go back. And because I know you don't need me to. And maybe it bothered me some that you'd managed to turn it all around into something admirable.

You see, I wanted to take care of you, both of you, but you've done just fine without me.''

''We'd do better with you.''

Emotions trembled through him. Stepping forward, he laid a hand on her wet cheek. ''That's the best thing you've ever said to me. That's the second incredible thing that's happened to me today.''

She managed a smile. ''There was another?''

''When I talked to Bryan in the woods. We were sitting on the rocks, where two lost boys met, trying to find their way home.''

''It's a strong place.''

''Yes. Not as sad after today as it once was. Bryan was giving me advice on how to coax you out of being mad at me. I was supposed to bring you flowers, which I will, and take you on a date, so that you could sing in the shower while you get ready.''

She gave a watery, embarrassed chuckle. ''He's got a big mouth.''

''Then I'm supposed to come up with some love words, like in the movies. Girls like that stuff, I'm told.''

''I guess I'm going to have to start keeping an eye on those girls. I'm glad you talked to him, Jared.''

''That wasn't the best part. I told him I was going to ask you to marry me and that I wanted to be his father. He hugged me,'' Jared murmured, struck by it all over again. ''It was just that easy. He had a lot of faith that I'd be able to talk you into it. I hope I'm not going to disappoint him.''

She did the simple thing and leaned into him, resting

her head on his shoulder. "Before I answer the question, I'd better warn you. I don't believe in quiet, civilized divorces. If you try to worm out of this, I'll just have to kill you."

"Sounds fair, as long as it holds true for both sides." He turned his face into her hair, and knew he was home. "Ah, morning sickness and thirty-two hours of labor might put you off from trying again."

She squeezed her eyes tight, squeezed him tighter. He was offering her more children. He was offering her a future.

"Don't be an ass, MacKade. I'm tougher than that. And this time around I'd have someone to swear at in the delivery room."

"I want to be there for you, through everything. You're going to have to learn how to need me."

"Too late," she murmured. "I already know all about that."

"Take my name, Savannah. Take me."

"Savannah MacKade." Closing her eyes again, she held on tight. "I think it suits me just fine."

* * * * *

From No. 1 *New York Times* bestselling author Nora Roberts

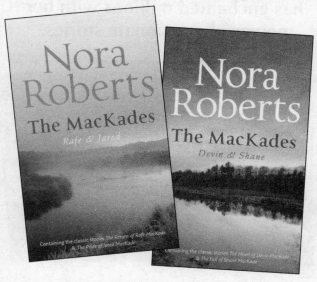

The irresistible MacKade brothers are back and once again stirring the heart of every female that crosses their path.

Rafe and Jared
Featuring *The Return of Rafe MacKade* and *The Pride of Jared MacKade*

Devin and Shane
Featuring *The Heart of Devin MacKade* and *The Fall of Shane MacKade*

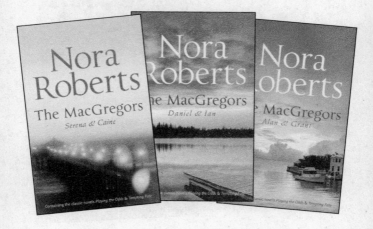

From No. 1 *New York Times* bestselling author Nora Roberts

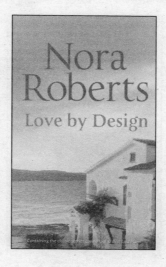

Two classic novels about the walls people build around their hearts and how to break them down...

Features

Loving Jack

and

Best Laid Plans

From No. 1 *New York Times* bestselling author Nora Roberts

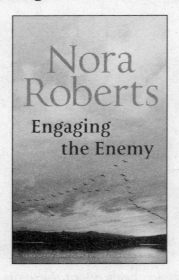

Sometimes the last man on earth you'd ever want is the very one your heart secretly yearns for…

Features

A Will and a Way

and

Boundary Lines

From No. 1 *New York Times* bestselling author Nora Roberts

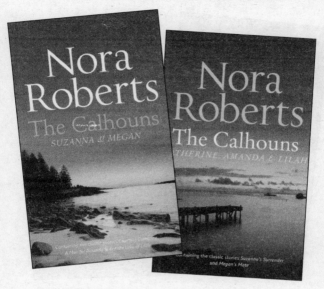

Atop the rocky coast of Maine sits the Towers, a magnificent family mansion that is home to a legend of long-lost love, hidden emeralds – and four determined sisters.

Catherine, Amanda & Lilah
Featuring *Courting Catherine*, *A Man for Amanda* and *For the Love of Lilah*

Suzanna & Megan
Featuring *Suzanna's Surrender* and *Megan's Mate*

From No. 1 *New York Times* bestselling author Nora Roberts

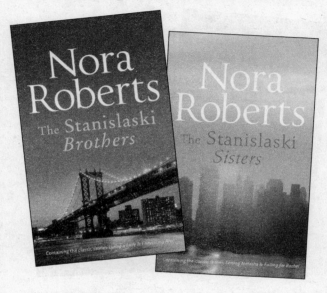

A collection of four passionate stories featuring the strong, irresistible brothers and the spirited, sexy sisters of the Stanislaski family

The Stanislaski Brothers
Containing *Luring a Lady* and
Convincing Alex

The Stanislaski Sisters
Containing *Taming Natasha*
and *Falling for Rachel*

BL/111/T&A

From No. 1 *New York Times* bestselling author Nora Roberts

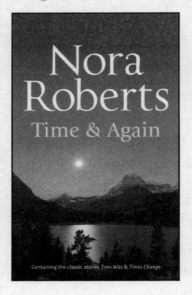

Two enchanting tales about a passion so powerful it transcends time itself

Features

Time Was

and

Times Change